BLOODY SUN

Errick A. Nunnally

SPENCE
CITY

Spence City, an imprint of Spencer Hill Press

Please visit our website at www.spencecity.com

First Edition: June 2014
Errick A. Nunnally
Blood For The Sun: a novel / by Errick A. Nunnally – 1st ed.
p. cm.

Summary:
A werewolf must find the murderer of a child in Boston while
coping with frightening memory loss and the rest of the
supernatural community.

The author acknowledges the copyrighted or trademarked status
and trademark owners of the following wordmarks mentioned in
this fiction:
Acura NSX, Harlequin, Jeep Grand Cherokee, Kool, Maglite,
Moleskine, Woodford Reserve, Yellow Pages, Ziploc

The World of the Ancient Maya (second edition), by John S.
Henderson. Published December 1997 by Cornell University
Press ISBN 978-0801431838

Cover design by Lisa Amowitz
Interior layout by Marie Romero

978-1-939392 84-8 (paperback)
978-1-939392-88-6 (e-book)

Printed in the United States of America

For my mother, Betty P. Nunnally (1944–2009),
without whom this story might never have existed.
(Comic books are apparently the right mix of
nighttime reading for your kids.)

ONE

Damn the world, I'm hungry. My mouth was watering and I was only somewhat ashamed to admit that the thought *wasted meat* kept crossing my mind. Children are a guilty pleasure—even an addiction.

I swore them off a lifetime ago.

Standing outside, I could smell the death of her. The number 1329, stenciled on the façade, identified the building from its indistinguishable brothers and sisters. It was near dawn in the Peter O'Neil projects, and a dead black girl lay upstairs in a building that looked as if the bricks had been molded with clotted blood.

Two City of Boston detectives met me here. These were the right people to care, but there were never enough of them. The forensics team hadn't arrived yet. Delayed, I presumed, by the unusually high rate of murder this year or some clever words from one of the detectives.

The cops were concerned because, over time, they've developed two necessary survival skills: one, the ability to detect a predator, and two, the wherewithal not to ignore that information. My attendance was always a problem or, more precisely, an indication of a bizarre problem, a discussion no one wants to have— even with themselves.

Roberts gave me a cop-look that drinks suspects up in one glance: height, weight, facial hair, distinguishing marks, and hair color. He'd worked these neighborhoods long enough to consider everyone a suspect. Intentionally or not, all the young black men from the inner city try to look the same. I kept my hands out of my pockets because cops liked that; it keeps them calm. I wondered if he was trying to file me away into some kind of category, a place where the psychic buzz I give some people makes sense.

When someone looks at me, they see a very tall, very dark African-American. The curly gloss of my short black hair, however, makes me easier to pick out amongst other blacks. I'd only recently begun wearing it shorter; the length had become far too conspicuous and accentuated the aboriginal cut of my face.

My observation of Roberts in return was more than a look. Since my second birth, I assessed people in a crazy-quilt manner that included more than their appearance. The detective was a black man of average height. Only somewhat lighter than me, he had smooth, shiny skin like wet molasses and a flared nose as wide as his mouth. He was wearing his hair close-cropped and faded on the sides and back. Clean-shaven, he had a stony look of pride frozen onto his face above his upturned chin and ice in his eyes. Beyond that, the intangibles were what keyed him into what was left of my memory. His scent was an oily burst of pheromones betraying his ethnicity. People with strong ethnic backgrounds—near purity of genealogy—sometimes have particular flavors to their scents. Roberts was as African as one can be in America. I can forget a person, but their scent would always be a reminder.

His partner, on the other hand, was white, ignorant, and smelling of cheap aftershave—all but one of which were curable characteristics. He was the kind of man who didn't mind foregoing a shower but managed to project the appearance of cleanliness by shaving closely and combing his hair neatly. He probably went through bottles of cologne the way he did packs of cigarettes. A microscopic byproduct of smoking preceded him as a warm front spearheads a nasty storm.

The fresh new detective stuck his hand out with a grin in the predawn hours and said, "Detective Pepperman. So, Mister No-Name, you're gonna help us out?"

I stared at his hand. My nose caught the traces of glycoprotein, salt, and water. Pepperman had picked his nose recently. The young man's palm hung in the air, limp, pale, and useless.

I turned away and answered over my shoulder: "You can call me 'Alexander.'"

I just wanted to be escorted to the body, eager to possibly get started on something new. Tracking lost children was only a means to an end, keeping me engaged in reality just enough to stave off the looming insanity. All Roberts had honestly been able to tell me on the phone was that the victim's blood appeared to be missing. I was curious to get a good look. It was clear to me just about where the corpse lay by the scent spilling out of the housing fortress and into the chill air, but it pays not to seem utterly inhuman when out and about. Roberts believed that I was just an odd character with a macabre background, and I intended to keep it that way. No one can save me anyway.

"Okay, seriously? *That* high and mighty? This wasn't a good idea to begin with and now I know it ain't gonna work."

"Pep, hold on—"

"Bullshit. This is unacceptable." Then to me he said, "I wanna see some ID. Now."

I glanced at Roberts. He only clenched his jaw, eyes on Pepperman. The young detective had a right to be indignant; it was his career that might be jeopardized by my unauthorized presence. Fine, we could do it the hard way; I didn't mind.

"Save that cop shit for someone you've got authority over." I squared on Pepperman, hands loose at my sides, my eyes looking through to the back of his head. "I'm not here for you; I'm here for the dead kid upstairs. You want to get to the bottom of her murder faster? I'm here for that. You want to try to get me under your thumb? You better try something more than that old shit you pull on these young punks around here."

Pepperman started to sputter, but Roberts stepped in. "This is my call, Detective; let it go. I'll take the heat for this, if needed."

The junior partner shook his head and threw his hands up. "Yeah, okay, fuck it."

Roberts knit his brow and led the way. At the same time, Pepperman sniffed his fingers and looked away. I followed Roberts into the building while Pepperman took up the rear. Was it a mistake to snub him like that? Probably. Did I care? Not at all. There were more important matters at hand and not much time. I didn't need any more acquaintances anyway.

It is a fact that the first twelve hours of a murder investigation are the most crucial. If the situation is a missing person, you've got on average twenty-four to forty-eight hours to find that person dead or alive. Over time, the immediate organic evidence that I could access would fade from the reach of my senses as well as forensic science's abilities to detect with true accuracy. We had gotten lucky with this one—Terrell, a friend of Roberts's and a Boston Housing Authority officer, had found the body and reported it directly to his friend. I shouldn't put any emphasis on Roberts's luck because it had been fortunate for me to be in town when he'd called. This thought made me wonder, *why am I in Boston anyway?* I couldn't recall.

It was also a fact that, if we didn't get going soon, I would most likely forget why I was here, where I was, and who I was speaking with.

Not being able to remember things in short order is typical of my life, and I washed the frustration away. Best to focus on what I've been able to train myself to remember. Whatever was eating my memories away didn't have as much luck when I worked at it. It's a blessing and a curse to have a long life; the human body wasn't designed to live much longer than a hundred years or so, and I'd already doubled that.

Preserving my memory is a steady battle. I was more frequently reminding myself of an Alzheimer's sufferer nowadays: a forgotten cup of coffee gone cold in front of me, occasional confusion as to where I was or how I got there, familiar people and things suddenly seeming foreign and less than benign. The mundane operations of living day to day were fast becoming an alien landscape. It'd be thrilling—a new experience—if I could remember why the fuck it was supposed to be thrilling. "Autopilot" had become the operative word in my life. Getting involved in cases like this had been what kept me alive scores of years ago, but now it seemed as if I were just going through the motions. There should be more satisfaction in doing such a thing, but a veil of grey was slowly being drawn across my life.

Roberts was taking a hell of a chance by inviting me to this crime scene, but the choices we had to make were going to be hard and fast. The small fortune of advance notice wouldn't last long. I expected other dubious steps would be taken as we moved forward.

The stairwell we'd entered was slim and dull; it ascended into the murky light delivered by the building's cheap light bulbs.

"Damn, it hasn't been long enough since I've been back in these buildings; too many memories—not a lot of 'em that good." Roberts was speaking to no one in particular, and I got the impression that he wasn't looking forward to viewing the little girl's body—a perfectly human reaction.

At the top of the first set of stairs, a bulky black man sat waiting. Thick hair puffed out from under his Housing Authority cap, broad shoulders stiffly hunched up to his ears. Every line in his face pointed down; he had "sullen" permanently etched into his face. Roberts shook hands with Terrell, made some brief introductions, and gave us the rest of the story about the scene of the crime as we ascended together.

The stairwell only had apartment access on the first four floors. According to the warning tape and plastic sheeting, the fifth and sixth were in the process of being fumigated for pests. While the top two floors had been flooded with poison, the bottom four remained occupied. I held that thought, rolling it around in my mind, tasting the bitterness, and working hard to justify it as part of the lousy framework I expected from life on the North American continent. Culturally embedded bad habits are hard to shake. Especially when I kept finding evidence to support them. It never helps that I've always had the poor habit of looking for the policies and behaviors that do nothing but exacerbate the problem.

Weak yellow lights struggled behind thick plastic and tiny bars, kept captive under lock and key. I wondered under what conditions would the light bulbs need to be protected from a threat, or to have their escape prevented. Viscous spots, miscellaneous bits of paper trash, and a few empty drink bottles lay strewn along the stairwell. The smell of beer and old grease became more insistent as we moved deeper into the building and away from what passes for fresh air in the city.

It occurred to me that the hallways and stairs were constructed narrowly to add more apartments to the complex. Projects weren't designed for comfort; they were designed to warehouse people. This wasn't how people should live.

Incomprehensible graffiti decorated the walls, and every landing featured a thick, glass-brick window set deep in the outer concrete wall. I wondered what archeologists might make of these box-like structures a millennium from now—if they were still standing.

These dwellings were scheduled to come down, and half of them already had. A more colorful set of projects, shaped like tiny, civilized homes, were planned to go up. An identical situation, but at least everyone would have their own front door.

We crossed the second landing, heading for the third, when the wet scent of bloody flesh fully coalesced and twirled up my nose with a jab. Salty, wet iron and copper, sticky and cloying. I licked my lips and swallowed, still salivating, and felt a broad and gauzy sense of shame again. When my thoughts cleared, I remembered exactly why I was doing this. A raw mixture of guilt and need tugged at my stomach; the slippery surface of morality and logic is an unhappy place.

Idly, to distract myself, I searched the layered scents of the hallway: bubble gum, chicken, bacon, pizza, paint—shit and piss from the body—and the mixed, sweeter aroma of long-burnt tobacco versus the acrid residue of crack cocaine. The crack was the most distinct despite the bodily fluids, like the difference between burnt toast and fresh-baked bread.

The blood-scent continued to become stronger. The scent riding the thermal updraft grew as it hit the top of the well, filling it. The flies buzzed louder the closer we got.

These project buildings, like most I'd seen, were overexposed on the outside. A lack of trees or other natural sun barriers allowed the buildings to act as brick ovens, capturing the heat and holding it despite the cooling night. So it was hot in the stairwells, the most poorly ventilated part of the structures, since the windows were cemented bricks of thick glass. No one kept their steel-lined doors open for very long to help ventilate the space.

On the third landing, Roberts and Pepperman had no choice but to acknowledge the smell. Neither one commented, but—not surprising to me—Pepperman pressed a handkerchief to his nose. Rounding the last corner, we finally saw the body. Roberts removed a small white vial from his coat and offered it to Pepperman. The rookie glanced at it and shook his head. He didn't want the mentholated cream usually rubbed on children as a cold remedy.

"Aaaahh, shit," Pepperman swore, recoiling at the sight of the little girl.

Roberts shook his head sadly, clenching and unclenching his jaw. "Do your thing, man; let's get this done."

A skinny blond boy stood naked in the dead girl's thin, congealing blood pool. Still seven years old, he always reminded me of the awful things I'd seen and done; he wouldn't let me forget. He was always silent, staring, an incorporeal soul, an ethereal corpse. Guilt clogged the back of my throat again and I mumbled an apology to the child in my native tongue, using my real name, pledging my soul, if I still have one, and whatever else I had to give. There was no response from the boy, his features melting from anger to sorrow and back again repeatedly. He is the ghostly embodiment of a memory I cannot seem to lose. *Curious, that*, I noted briefly before letting the thought dissipate.

He never speaks; he only accuses. With time, he vanishes because he died a long time ago. I've never been able to determine what he's seeking when he comes, but I know why he comes, and I'm relieved when he goes. Whether he's a ghost or simply a hallucination is another aspect I've never been able to determine either. What I am sure of, however, is that no one else can see him but me. *Appropriate*, I posited, *since I was the one who ended his life.*

I surveyed the landing, remembering that my eyes, like a child's, are unnaturally clear, devoid of the terminal oxidation which plagues the aged. It was the first significant change I noticed when I became what I am today.

Any fool could tell this was a murder—the girl's throat was missing, and that doesn't normally happen during anyone's day. Her head, still attached to her body by a hand's-width of flesh and bone, was resting on its chin. The unnatural angle of repose was a potent reminder that she had been killed by a cold hand. Her feet and legs were pointing up the stairs, while her chest lay flat against the concrete floor. One of her dirty yellow sneakers was missing. I looked around and spotted the missing footwear in the shadows of a far corner.

Wading through the scents in the air around her, I tried to sort out the killer—or killers—by scent. I regarded her body more closely—she was approximately eight years old, yellow bloodstained T-shirt, unkempt braided hair with yellow clips, blue jeans, worn and tattered sneakers. No socks.

Socks. *Two pair, always there, Netty and Claire.* My sisters, gone so very long ago. The mnemonic and its memory passed. I needed to focus on the present.

She'd been round in the face, like most kids, but now her flesh sagged slightly, stiffening into a death-grimace—black skin going gray. Her eyes were open; she'd likely seen her attacker. A fat, pearlescent black fly crawled across her drying eye, a surreal and inarguable display of evidence that she was dead. Had she fought him? I looked closely at her hands, careful not to disturb the body, nor to step in the small pool of blood. I didn't need to touch her, but forensics would.

Despite the wan yellow light, the details were clear and sharp—another benefit of my condition. She had dirt under her nails, as well as some torn skin. Good girl. The forensics team would do what they could with that evidence. I stooped in closer to her hands. Her fingers were curled in intense rigor. I couldn't detect any heat radiating from her; she'd been dead long enough to lose her warmth. Since most of her blood had been taken, I could only guess that she had probably died within the last six to eight hours.

Pepperman leaned close to Roberts and whispered, "What the fuck's he doing?"

Roberts whispered back, "Shut up and wait."

Their voices carried clearly to my ears despite their hushed tones.

There was a scent of stale sweat, definitely not hers. *His*. The man who'd killed her. The spoor had the usual flavor of a human male, but the stale quality was overwhelming and confusing. Like a stink from the grave, it reminded me of barren water. Precious, life-giving liquid that had been excessively purified, removed of everything that made it worthwhile, set apart from the replenishing, life-giving cycle. Something that has lost its identity. It still had the familiar textural quality, but it was unremarkable, a hollow structure. Besides that, the pheromone's flavors were indeed male. I've hunted vampires and revenants before, but never anything like this.

I looked around the body more closely and a shape caught my eye. The thin blood pool under the body turned at an unnatural angle, counter to the grade of the floor. It stopped and curled slightly inward, leaving a warped, crescent moon shape. On further inspection, it occurred to me that the edge of something has been there when the blood had gotten to this point. The edge of a bucket? Perhaps a two-gallon bucket. That's what it looked like to me—round on the bottom and ample for carrying the nearly three liters that would come from a young, human body.

Vampires don't need buckets or weapons, so why was her blood taken in such a crude manner? Her throat wound was wide, but not jagged. Two deep cuts had left a shape like a slice of watermelon in her throat. The general etiquette of deception amongst the vamps is to slash the throat after feeding to mutilate the bite and to leave enough blood so that no one will easily suspect. However, blood let into the air would soon become distasteful to a vampire. The most efficient—albeit time-consuming—method would be to bind the victim, apply an intravenous catheter with a stopcock, and drain them at one's leisure. No vampiric evidence left, just a bizarre assault. Murder with no biological trace evidence. I couldn't begin to imagine how many humans might've had to suffer the trick.

"It was a man, she fought, and some of his skin is under her fingernails. He used a blade to cut her throat twice—precise, but not skilled—and a bucket to catch the blood. There's a partial footprint on the edge of the stairs, and a shape left in the blood from the bucket; he must've caught her going up—or chased her, but here's where he got her." I stepped onto the stairs. "I can't tell you where the missing part of her throat is—possibly in the bucket. Obviously he did it quickly, but he spilled enough blood to leave spatter on the walls. So, he doesn't seem too practiced, or she fought, but he was precise nonetheless. Her other sneaker is in the corner over there. This eight-year-old girl sank her nails into him as he held her bleeding out over a bucket."

"How do you know it's one guy, how do you know he used a bucket, and—hello—there's dozens of sticky footprints in here?" Pepperman sneered.

Enjoying his discomfort, I said, "The footprint is a bare one, no shoes. Who the hell else would walk through here without shoes on, other than the killer, and leave a fresh print?" Ignoring him, I went on. "Her trousers are loose; she may have been molested." I didn't bother adding that I'd know the killer when I got near him. Mentally, I catalogued his scent, taking slow deep breaths and sifting his particulars from the rest. I wasn't supposed to be there, and I wasn't going to stay much longer. It was at that moment that I noticed the wall behind the detectives. There was some kind of symbol drawn on it in dark brown. It was barely visible in the gloom of the stairway, on warm grey walls spattered with graffiti. As I stared at it, the drawing stood out from the rest.

Pepperman's voice cut the awkward silence. "Oh, please, you got some DNA analysis too?"

Roberts just stared at Pepperman. The new guy was getting nervous, and rightly so, but he wasn't keeping his discipline. I was certain that Roberts would have a talk with him later about that.

Against all better judgment, I wanted to make him more skittish, really get his hackles up. There was an echo of encouragement from somewhere deep inside of me, a nagging chatter that wanted to take any uncovered opportunity to generate fear and maximize it.

I walked over to Pepperman and got uncomfortably close before speaking again. "There's a symbol drawn on the wall in her feces."

"Aw, gross, look out, man," Pepperman said and moved to get his back away from the wall so he could turn and look.

I plucked a notebook from his shirt pocket as he passed. He moved to put his hand on the weapon at his hip, but Roberts caught his arm. I ignored them both. When I scribbled the shape and variations of it down on a single page, a tremor of some sort passed through the room. A current like electricity tingled up my spine, causing me to grimace.

"Did you feel that?" I asked quietly.

The detectives looked at each other and shrugged.

Still feeling the ripples of power prickling my bones, I said to Roberts through gritted teeth, "Never mind. I'll be in touch if I find out anything about this symbol." I scratched out the variations that had not caused the tremor of power and tore the page out of the notebook, tossing it back to Pepperman. That shock gave me concern. What I'd felt was magic. The pure force of magic is everywhere, but dormant. Active magic makes monsters like me physically uncomfortable; I never stick around to gauge the intensity, just like I'd never been dumb enough to stick my finger in an electrical socket. I can't stand the stuff, and I respect it by avoiding it.

For a moment, I considered abandoning this puzzle, but the idea of learning something entirely new kept me from dropping the challenge. I'd avoided magic long enough, I decided. Immediate relief came with that decision. My brain felt alive again, memory losses held at bay. Whatever was eating my thoughts could be kept in check by being active and engaged. That much I knew. *Hoped*, I corrected myself.

Turning back to the next flight of stairs above the girl, I imagined again what had happened. I couldn't wrap my head around the blood theft—nothing I'd personally experienced gave me any answers. There was also the possibility that I simply didn't remember any potential explanations. There have been plenty of killers who enjoyed going barefoot—even stark naked—to kill. No one, however, in my experience, smelled like what I'd scented. So far, I could always trust my nose. Smell is among the most powerful anchors for human memories—doubly so for shapeshifters like me.

The cuts were not practiced, but precise. That had to mean something. I looked at the girl again, leaning over to see as much of her that was pressed against the concrete floor as I could. There was a purple bruise on her dark skin—right arm, bicep. The scratch she'd dealt was done with her left hand. He'd pinned her with one hand. He was strong, probably, and I bet he didn't flinch when she dug in. As I examined, I relayed all of this to Roberts.

"Do what you will." I let him know that I would be in touch. I headed downstairs to the exit. They talked the entire time I moved down the stairwell.

Pepperman started running his mouth first in what I'd come to identify as his usual abrasive tone. "Who the fuck is that again?"

"Someone who seems to know something about this kind of sick shit." Roberts answered.

"And you trust him?"

A pause before Roberts answered again. "My boss trusted him." He was being careful of his answers, clearly thinking his words through.

"Trusted? Oh, my God, is that how—working with this guy?"

The silence was uncomfortable and the only thing that saved Pepperman from Roberts, I think, was Pepperman's tone. He wasn't trying to be disrespectful. I didn't wait for Roberts's explanation. Whatever story was a part of the official record, I already knew the truth.

The stars had disappeared from the sky as the sun brightened the cloud-free expanse. Exiting the building, I passed Roberts's friend, Terrell, the Housing cop. He was smoking a cigarette and, if a man that dark-skinned could be described as such, he was ashen. The smell of the tobacco raked up the inside of my nostrils and tap-danced on the membranes in front of my brain, dragging the brand of smoke he was inhaling into focus. I looked at him and he seemed unnaturally old as he pressed the Kool between wide lips under his thick mustache and took long drags. I've found that the deeply shaken don't want comfort; they want answers, and I had none. I moved to pass him without comment, but he spoke.

"You gonna be able to do anything to help find this motherfucker, man?"

"I'll try."

"Who does this kind of shit to a little girl, man?" He took a very long drag on his cigarette, as if the fumes would do him better than air.

As the wind changed direction, I was grateful for the light, spring breeze carrying the smoke away from me. "Too many people."

Terrell shook his head. "I have seen some shit here, man. Some. Shit. Kids—and I mean *kids*, not teenagers— pullin' the trigger, slingin' the drugs. Boys *and* girls! All kinds of shit too, man—smack, crack, straight coke, weed, even some pills. Little motherfuckers too dumb to mix up their own meth, though—thank God for that small favor. As many of those clowns we've run out of here, none of the shit they were usin' blew up on us or created a fuckin' meltdown. Shit.

"One time, I had a kid point a shotgun at me—right at my chest, not a foot away! I walked right into that shit. Fucker pulled the trigger too, but it was a modern piece, automatic. He didn't know *what* he was doing with that thing, hammer couldn't fall, damn gun wasn't cocked. Turns out it wasn't even loaded." He took another drag from the cigarette.

"Did you kill him?"

"What?"

"The boy, did you kill him? He had a weapon on you, pulled the trigger; what'd you do?"

"Aw, shit, man, I couldn't kill him—couldn't do it. He wasn't but eleven years old."

"But he could've killed you—would have if he'd known what he was doing."

"Yeah, he could've, but that's the point—*he didn't know what he was doing*. None of them do. I did smack the shit out of him, though." Terrell laughed mirthlessly. "He dead now anyway, tried to pull the trigger on a bigger fool than him. Where the fuck is this all going?"

An idea occurred to me and I showed him the notepaper I'd written on. "Have you ever seen this on any walls here?"

His hand shook as he took the page and studied it for a moment. "No, nah—uhn, wait. Yeah. Yeah, farthest north building. Number 1331, I think. In the sub-basement, maintenance access tunnels, the dirty little veins that feed this cesspool.

"Sometimes the drunks or crack-heads or bangers or all three get comfy down there and we gotta run 'em out. It's pretty nasty down there. And creepy." He shivered and handed the paper back. "Some o' them tags is written on the pipes and whatnot."

"How can I get down there?" I could hear sirens in the distance and the sky had brightened to a deep purple. Dawn was coming with a full police complement, and I was using as much body language as I could to persuade this fellow to show me the way.

He hesitated, then took a halting a step. I stopped him. "You don't have to come, if you don't want to."

The Housing cop swallowed hard before tossing the butt of the cigarette away. "Nah, these my projects, an' I know 'em better 'n you—better 'n Rob, too. Lemme give him a call, let him know where we're going, and I'll show you."

A short conversation later, he pulled a flashlight out of the back of his pants and led the way.

TWO

The underbelly of Peter O'Neil wasn't nearly as pleasant as the stark topside. Long, wet corridors stretched beneath the heavy, brick scar of a project. Not enough space for men of my height to walk better than stooped. Long pipelines hissed and gurgled. Every other bulb on the line of weak, caged lights was out, adding an uncertain edge to the pipes' shadows. There was a sliver of concrete just wide enough for a man to walk on, the sides dropping away to channels for the overflow of rainwater from the drains and sewers. Sporadic bits of paper and plastic trash carried in living muck from the project's occupants bobbed here and there. Smells became intense suddenly and then were gone as quickly as they came, replaced by the dead odor of eternally moist concrete and iron.

I have learned through hard experience that some people react severely in the presence of one of us. There seems to be some kind of psychic static field emitted from the supernatural batteries that keep us going. The more psychically sensitive the human, perhaps, the more uncomfortable they can be. Terrell was handling it well—more so than Roberts and Pepperman. These reactions could give me a leg up in some situations, but in others, it was an incalculable risk. Some notice, some don't; the ones who do develop a neurotic edge when they do. A deep-water fear where you have no idea what's below, what might be waiting to pull you down.

"Where are we going?" I asked.

"What?" Terrell sounded exasperated.

"I said, where are we going?"

"Man, you asked me where some o' that shit is written; why you askin' me this now?"

Damn it. I'd forgotten. The loss crept up on me and stole a bit of my past again. Time for one of the bad habits that come with memory loss. My number one tactic was to feign ignorance. "Huh?" My grunt echoed.

"What?" Terrell said again.

"Yeah, no, sorry." My discordant apology echoed as hollowly in the tunnel as my sentiment. Terrell, for his part, ignored the ridiculous exchange, just like everyone else. *Hooray.*

We came to a cross-tunnel and Terrell hesitated. I waited patiently, listening to the muffled sounds from above and those that emanated from the tunnels. Rat claws clicked on distant pipes, and hard-soled shoes sounded faintly on steel steps. I cocked my head for a better listen, then turned to Terrell. "Lost?"

He answered absentmindedly, "Naw, naw. Jus' tryin' to remember where…" Terrell grunted and I could practically see the memory pass over him. He turned and I followed him down the concrete tube to the left.

As we walked, I listened for the footsteps I'd heard earlier. Dress shoes on concrete. I picked the rhythmic sound out and focused on it—step, scuff, step, step, step, scuff, step. It sounded like Detective Roberts. He had a walking pattern where he scuffed the heel of his right shoe every other step or so.

"Detective Roberts is down here with us," I said to Terrell. He stopped abruptly, then took a halting step, not realizing how closely I'd been following him.

"What? How the hell do you know that?"

"I can hear him. The point is, do we wait, or does he know his way around down here?"

"I can wait. The marks you showed me are 'round here somewhere. Take a look; I'll go back to the cross and pick up Rob."

He shuffled off and I thought back to our underground travel. I reckoned we'd gone about a block as the crow flies, but the right-angle turns made it seem farther. We had to be right on the edge of P.O. I didn't bother to pull the small Maglite I carry but began to scan the darkness for the symbols. I only carry the thing for effect; it unnerves people when you can see in the dark and they can't. My eyes adjust in seconds to light changes; it can take up to twenty minutes for a human being's eyes to adjust.

As I probed the murkiness, I searched my feelings, did an honest accounting, and tested my tolerances. What happened was ugly, disturbing, abnormal, and otherwise depraved—no doubts there. My feelings, as numbed as they might be, I was glad to note, were still present on this matter. I was bothered by the girl's murder. I chose to do this for selfish reasons; my motivations were poor, but at least I could do something to square the circle. This pleased me. I was going to need to work on that if I could remember to do so. *Little black girl, your head a-twirl, something something something.* I'd get there; I needed to remember this one. Every time I've uncovered "occult" involvement, it has been false practitioners, pretenders. This was my first real one.

With age comes a gnawing uncertainty, if I'm not careful. For humans, age can bring arrogance and feelings of superiority, curt intelligence and biting wisdom. The mind, however, is the most fragile part of our bodies for both pre- and post-human. When we don't take care of the mind, it betrays us and a growing insanity takes over. The memory loss is a bitch, too. I didn't know how much longer I had. Still don't. Until I can ultimately figure it out, it's not worth worrying about.

I spied the glyph. On top of what looked like a crude map of the projects aboveground, the glyph was in the center of the drawing. It was an off-white color, mixed with rust from the pipe. Chalk? Baked bone, maybe; something nasty, I was sure. The remnants of the dead applied to a decaying cold-water pipe. I studied the drawing and oriented myself to the configuration of the map—north at the top, south at the bottom. Using this, I could conceivably find my way to any cluster of buildings above. Our murderer's escape route had likely been through these tunnels.

What did the glyph mean? I double-checked the scrap of paper that I had scribbled on against the scrawl on the pipe. My age already guaranteed long and garbled memories. After all, it's difficult for someone of a *normal* life-span to dredge up memories in any comprehensive manner. It can get rather confusing in my head.

I hesitate to involve any human being in my affairs for any significant amount of time. It's not always for fear of what might happen to them, it's for fear of what I might have to do to them. There are plenty of scenarios where a human being would need to be eliminated to keep the peace between the natural and the preternatural.

How I'd become involved with Lieutenant Brown and, subsequently, Detective Roberts was a unique occurrence among monsters, as far as I know. In legend as in life, we are not known for saving people— especially children. Lieutenant Brown and I had been acquaintances since he was ten years old. *How now, Brown cop?* Brown was a bulldog of an officer, sank his teeth into a case and gnawed until he'd gutted it and knew it from the inside out. It's why I gave him a way to contact me if needed. He knew what I was but had never contacted me for a job until he bit into an odd case of murder or mayhem that followed no pattern.

Revenants are psychotic vampires, tough as anything, and they bite. Brown managed to track one down and corner it. I wasn't able to save him a second time. Roberts does not know my nature, but Brown trusted him with my information so that I could continue to account for situations like this. Someday soon, I'm sure, with the pace of technology, our existence will be public knowledge.

I could hear two pairs of footsteps approaching. Terrell had found Roberts and they were on their way. I thought it over and decided to leave. I'd call Roberts later with any evidence relevant to his side of the case and tell him to thank Terrell for me.

Moving quickly, I traveled about half a block, where I found an access hatch that screeched with disuse when I opened it. I was sure Roberts and his friend had heard that. I'd be gone before they even came close.

Above ground, the sun was making its full presentation; the warmth drew tendrils of condensation from the ground as I vaguely made my way downtown.

Public Internet access had definitely revolutionized the gathering of information. The invention of the Internet has led to an even more fascinating resource—collective intelligence. A group of people can be smarter and faster than any one person, more often than not. At any given time, the Web tied together hundreds or thousands of people posting new information or working on similar problems.

There are a number of sites that speculate about us. Some of them get particularly close—I check sometimes; why not? On occasion, some of the sites disappear entirely, the owners, perhaps, having gotten too close to the subject matter. Apparently, someone else checks on occasion, too.

Books, Boston, Boylston. Books, 5 letters; Boston, 6 letters; Boylston, 8 letters. A seven-letter word is missing? No. I remembered that seven is the final piece of this mnemonic. The Boston Public Library is at 700 Boylston Street. It's the central location for the city.

A cool, clear day under steel skies made the four-mile walk more pleasant. The main branch had multiple stations for Internet access and a measure of privacy for each. The stations are wiped every night and it's exceedingly difficult for anyone to trace or establish an electronic trail. I'm a resident of several states, and my library cards are keys to the larger world. Fortunately, I always have a solid research repository in public libraries. Pick one, any one, in a generally well-off part of town, and it's the source of all knowledge in the Americas. Usually orderly and well-kept, and there are plenty of people to help find things, too. Some of the kids whose lives I've saved have grown up to be useful in this regard. Others are somewhat more complicated.

Because of the effect that I have on people, it is simplest to "persuade" others to stay away while I work. One of the guilty pleasures I cling to is that I enjoy doing this. I can frighten nearly any human being if I put my mind to it—even those who are otherwise intimidating. Unnerving someone who's capable of great violence, however, can tend to backfire. Humans who dabble in the dark arts, attempting to divine things that non-humans have created, are beyond dangerous, in my opinion. On the rare occasions that I have come across magicians, they have been immune to my charms.

First, I took a look at all the computer stations. There was one at the far wall, away from the sunlight and cornered so that the bookshelves and adjoining cubicles made it nearly invisible. When I'd come onto the floor, I could smell a distinct, heady mix of urine, alcohol, and human fungus. The scent led to the computer stall I wanted to use. I knew because the cube had an inhabitant even a normal human could smell.

"Whazzat," the homeless man slurred, head bobbing uneasily above his sagging shoulders.

The force that is the monster inside of me most easily affects the souls of the broken or weak. A sense of shadows crept from me and over him. At times like this, I feared the echo of the voice encouraging me to take matters a bit further. The homeless are wonderful prey for sadists. I'm not interested in practicing sadism on society's discards.

The man's eyes opened fully and cleared in an instant. He glanced nervously around and collected himself. Sidestepping me widely, he disappeared down the stacks without looking back. Poor normal man. His particular scent faded with him, but the cloud of unwashed smells lingered on, his oils smeared here and there. I sat down at the station and started my search for sites that catalog various glyphs and their meanings.

The energy that magic taps into caused the hair on my body to rise up and brought my own power closer to the surface. Let others dabble with altering the preternatural force; I have enough internalized power to preoccupy me already.

I sat in front of the blank screen, having logged in absentmindedly, with no idea what I was doing. I didn't have an email address, so what was I searching for and what the hell was I doing here? Feeling uncomfortable, I clenched and unclenched my fists, looking around for clues. There was nothing but the computer in front of me and no one nearby. *Typical*, I thought, *I slip in and out so often, who would know what I was doing?* Swallowing any self-pity, I just started checking my pockets for some kind of hint. Bits of lint in most pockets, Maglite, a pen, battered Moleskine, nearly a thousand dollars in bills, some coins—one truly odd-shaped coin, almost a square, with a hole in the center—and a couple of crumpled pages from someone else's pocket notebook.

I returned the other items to my pockets and flattened out the papers, recognizing my handwriting and, thank the powers that be, all but one drawing of a glyph scratched out. I was searching for information on glyphs such as these. *Little black girl, your head a-twirl, where did your blood go?*

So far, the only clues on this job were related to magic and crude blood theft. Those involved were real craftspeople. I'd never had to deal directly with a witch or a coven and I didn't want to. A real witch—warlock, sorcerer, wizard, what have you—would probably be nasty enough, but a crowd of them was another matter entirely, and there was nothing in my experience to help me deal with it. I was starting to regret ignoring magic-users so vehemently all these years. Taking all of my information secondhand was no substitute.

Either way, they were using a glyph that had power enough for me to notice when simply copying it onto a piece of paper. A question suddenly occurred to me about the little girl—where were her parents? Surely, someone in the building must have heard something or known the girl. How had the killer been able to slip in and out of the building, chase a girl down, and slaughter her without being seen or making a sound—inside a project building of limited space? The night didn't offer that much cover. The police would uncover who the little girl belonged to; the other questions, however, were most likely to go unanswered.

These were the kinds of questions that get me involved in situations like this—serial killers, rapists, or otherwise. It has become a self-sustaining cycle now that a number of the kids I've saved have gone on to adulthood in justice or counseling roles, feeding me the bizarre situations they come across. Usually serial killers fascinated by the occult, and the occasional monster like me. None of those cases, however, had ever panned out to involve real witchcraft.

I caught myself not only considering how I might have committed the murder, knowing I had done it before, but whether I could do it again. I wanted to; I had to admit there was something that I was purposely keeping the lid on. You can't take a murder back, and I was more than the average murderer. No do-overs.

She may have been running around on her own or visiting a relative in the building. Roberts would find out some of the why and how. I might have to disappoint him, though. I probably wouldn't be able to give him enough information without getting him deeper into a situation that might get him killed in a way that no cop would ever consider.

I found some of what I was looking for rather quickly after a search for "glyphs" yielded results for "Mayan" as well. Using the search nailed down specific terms that I could use to find more information, among them, "Ancient Mesoamerican Civilizations." Far too many results came from typing that in, but one of the first few sites that I visited from the list featured markings similar to those of my sketch.

Eventually, a graduate school's website returned something very useful—a full key of Mayan glyphs. I wrote down the information I found, left the computer station, and wandered into the stacks for some books on Mayan history and civilization. The Web, though good for quick facts and searches, still didn't compare to a carefully compiled reference book.

The mark I'd seen, drawn in the victim's feces, didn't seem to have a direct definition on the Web and, on further inspection, didn't appear to be similar to the others I'd seen in the tunnel. I would need a specialist. I *could* find people with a more intimate knowledge of iconographic magic more quickly than the human authorities could. It would mean going to places that I hadn't visited in over fifty years. Another shot of excitement ran through my brain, countered by uncertainty. Exploring this wouldn't be as clear as ballroom dancing or scrimshaw.

What I had been able to gather from the Web indicated that one of the drawings was truly a layering of glyphs and not a single character. Comparing this info to the books' tables determined that it was very much of pre-Mexican origin—most likely Mayan—and it could be arranged a number of ways. The Mayan writing system had been pictorial in nature and reflective of various things in ancient Mexico and the Gulf. The accompanying collection of glyphs, however, could only have one meaning—they were numbers. The numbers corresponding to this set consisted of 12, 19, 19, 5, and 5. Their composition indicated a date. When this combination was translated and compared to the Gregorian calendar system, it was April 12, 2012. What was the date for, a beginning or an ending? It was currently a week before that day, and if memory served, there'd be a full moon that night. I copied everything down that I thought relevant.

The cycle of the moon, the amount of blood in a human body, the location of the library in a city I hadn't visited in years. Of what vital use were these things in my life today, and why could I remember them and not *why* I'd come to Boston?

I'd been sitting in the library for over three hours. Many years of practice let me track the passage of time accurately without looking at a timepiece. Some things are so clear, but others, quite literally, are not.

I needed a jump on this puzzle. There were places that my kind and others could congregate safely. Places that I'd avoided for some time now. I'd be able to find my occult iconographer there.

Before leaving the library, I picked up the Yellow Pages and thumbed through them. Under "bars" I found what I was looking for. A business card-sized ad for one place in particular that had a small mark in the lower left-hand corner—a six-pointed star with the upper- and lowermost points longer than the other four. The top point is crossed perpendicularly by a short line and the bottom one barbed as an arrow. One end of the symbol points to Heaven and the other to Hell or some equivalent; I wasn't sure—I hadn't made it to either realm when I'd died the first time.

Just to be safe, I copied the information and kept it in the palm of my hand. Pinning it to my chest with a phone number to call might've been a better options in case I were to be found wandering around aimlessly.

By the address, the place was deeper into downtown on the borders of Chinatown. It was late morning, but I knew the venue would be attended at all hours. I decided to walk, ignoring my growling stomach, and simply think. Well, maybe I wouldn't ignore my stomach.

During the uneventful stroll, Ana crossed my mind. I hadn't seen my daughter for several months. She had a decidedly unusual and sometimes disturbing habit of showing up when I least expected her to. One would think that it would drive me crazier. Truth be told, she's the only part of my life that keeps me sane. Being attached to her, loving her as I do, has made these times easier. Despite our sporadic meetings, she's been a consistent thread in my life. She was the first one I'd ever tried to save, the child of neighboring friends. I was too late to stop the revenant who'd taken her. I could have spared her this existence, but it was the first time in years I'd allowed myself to be near a child and feel something other than hunger. I half-expected her to melt out of nowhere and touch my elbow, but it was closing in on midday and even a vampire of her abilities would be hard-pressed to be out strolling in the sun.

I had no idea what she'd be into at that moment and I didn't worry about it. I'd taught her as much as I could about how to survive as an immortal—*potential* immortal. We most certainly can be killed. She was topping one hundred years of age and it would probably be another decade or two before she felt the itch of memory loss and insanity that eventually comes to us once-human creatures. An atypical consequence of becoming a vampire so soon after birth—she has no recollection of the sun, her parents, or her humanity. She has always been a vampire.

Beings like us exist in the gutter between magic-bred creatures—the completely supernatural or entities existing outside of this plane—and the humans that would experiment with sorcery.

Walking amongst the midday crowds of humanity is sometimes difficult, to say the least. What I am—what I've become—is a kind of super-predator. When I walk around a city, I walk amongst prey. It's good, though, doing this and controlling the angry, steady buzz that makes some people nervous around me, reminding myself to be more human than monster. So I tell myself. When I closed my eyes and listened in a crowd, I could feel the power whispering to me, urging me to let it loose and sate its hunger. Words or hallucination? Like the little blond boy, I can't tell.

My path cut a swath through the pedestrians; they kept their distance. It's not normal for me to be casually bumped while walking down a sidewalk. It pays to keep cool and project as little threat as possible. Otherwise, I'm sure there could be an electric current of indiscriminate panic around me right now. Still, the whispers continued. I pressed on. Really, what other choice did I have?

The thoughts unwound a peel of familiar ire that I'd been living with since…since I can't recall. This line of thinking only riled me more, and I prayed to whatever would listen that I could stop trying to consider the reasons that keep me going day to day.

I turned left onto the street the club was on and stopped. Ahead of me, I could sense power, smell the ozone of static electricity. An acute chilling in my bones provided a potent reminder that I was walking into a place that welcomed magic. I glanced up at the surrounding buildings before moving forward, steeling myself for whatever might be waiting inside, strolling through a tickling net of energy strung around the place like cobwebs.

The small hairs on my back stood up and my skin prickled with tension. I had a natural distaste for magic use that I didn't understand, and I'd have to work harder to quell it if I was going to get anything done today.

It'd been some time since I'd last set foot inside one of these places, and that bleed of power hadn't been present before. I'd not frequently come across magical things on other jobs, and although this was exciting and new, I didn't particularly want to start now. I'll never learn enough about anything; all I can hope is to learn enough to survive. Virtually everything I knew about magic was secondhand or hearsay, and that needed to change now if I was going to continue.

The last time I'd been in one of these haunts, jazz was the popular music in the country and everyone knew their place in society—even the purely magical beings. They rarely made an appearance in these locales, and when they did, it was through a summoning or other arrangement. They needed the help of someone on this side of reality. Around the time I'd stopped frequenting these establishments, other beings became more prevalent, turning up often among us middle-breeds, elbow to elbow at the bar, for reasons unknown.

Looking around, I spotted a nearby café with a brightly painted sign highlighting its sandwich specials. I decided to postpone my field trip for a full stomach.

Outside of the café was a podium with an attractive hostess keeping it company. She pretended not to see me when I walked up.

"Excuse me."

"Oh! You surprised me. How can I help you?" She smiled nervously, my very presence fraying her confidence.

"Not a problem; table for one." A sudden urge to tease caught my groin; I needed to get away from her before she started squirming, before I started plotting how to make her scream for me. Already, panic danced around the corners of her eyes. I attempted a smile and she cringed.

"This way, please." She hurried off, heading for the farthest and loneliest corner of the restaurant. Perfect.

"Is this—?"

"Just fine, thank you." I cut her off; she mumbled something about a "nice meal" and strode away. A very small part of me was grateful as the rest of me watched her sashay in heels back to the front of the café.

From the sign out front, I remembered which three sandwiches I wanted to eat. At least, I thought I did. Ignoring the menu, I scanned the specials card to jog my memory.

The waiter sauntered over and introduced himself. I asked for water and put in my order. He scooped up the menus and hurried off, only to be replaced by another waiter pouring water. Ice rattled into my glass and I thanked the young man. I took one long pull on the drink, placed it on the table, and wondered where the menu was. I had water; I'd just been seated, so the hostess should have put it down in front of me.

Remembering her, I casually considered waiting until her shift ended to taste her panic on my tongue as I licked the sweat off her neck. I spotted her across the room, seating a couple. Even though she tried to avoid looking in my direction, I had her eye when she incidentally scanned the room. I waved, and her jaw clenched. She straightened herself and headed to my table.

"Yes, sir, what can I help you with?"

"Can I have a menu, please?"

She faked a smile and dropped one into my hands, avoiding contact, then hurried off. It all seemed familiar, but I dismissed the feeling, distracted by the counter-sway of her long hair and trim ass. Not long after the hostess left my sight, I was perusing the menu, looking for the specials, when the waiter arrived with three plates on his arm and an appreciative grin on his face.

"I certainly hope you have time to enjoy each one of these, sir. Let me know if you'd like me to wrap anything up. Enjoy your meal." Then he was gone.

I slowly put the menu down on the seat nearest me and gritted my teeth. Hot anger found its way to my scalp and sizzled there. Feeling as if someone else had been wearing my skin for the last fifteen minutes, I could hear an undercurrent of commentary below the sparse crowd in the café. Scratching and tapping echoed in my ears as I looked around to pinpoint the source. Nothing. I swallowed hard to ease my frustration, but I had no success until I heard a yelp and the tinkle of broken glass. I looked over to see the hostess shaking her head and trying to compose herself as waiters and patrons alike looked on. I wrapped my ire and frustration around myself like a cloak of chain mail and tucked into the meal so that I could get the hell out of there.

Hunger sated, I returned to the club's street, vowing not to let myself get hungry like that again. I plowed into the magical bleed, ignoring any chills and sparking minute flashes of heat on my skin as the energy pinged off me.

The door of *The Sweaty Magus* was painted red and stood out in an empty expanse of brick wall. Not the expected blood red, but a primary hue, and coarsely done as if painted with a rag. Brass studs, evenly placed along the trim of the burly door, were set in a solid frame. Of the wood, it was the oak I recognized—couldn't mistake its scent. The door itself, however, came across scrambled, an unstable mix of scents. More magic. There were two steps leading up to the barrier and no knob or attendant. Another course of frustration burbled through my blood.

Conditions had changed; I recalled when we could trust each other for no other reason than to honor our collective secret existence. Not that the planet is filthy with monsters, but if we didn't police ourselves, nowhere would be safe. I let the anger pass and moved on. At the merest touch, the door swung open for me. I swallowed my confusion and frustration; things were getting interesting again.

It was dark inside. That there were no windows was a clear indication that vampires were welcome here. My eyes adjusted immediately in the short hallway. I noted four steps downward. The ceiling dipped just low enough to obscure an immediate view of the place. Blue light swam at the end of the short hallway, swirling on the wall as reflected ocean does on a jetty. At the base of the stairs, I had to duck to enter through a blood-red beaded curtain.

Muted sounds of dance music thumped further inside, but the lounge I'd entered wasn't intended for dancing, and the music played at a reduced volume here. The light in the hallway pulsated softly from the bar. It was a sizable affair—blue on top and full of water in a large glass tank that formed the bar's face. A number of enormous white worms undulated back and forth while a gentle current from a hidden source kept the water surging gently against the glass. Stools ran along the curving bar, and patrons sat two or three to a group, always leaving one empty stool between groups. It was a clientele that was polite as well as discreet.

Along the opposite wall, more customers huddled in low-lit booths, nursing drinks and speaking in muted tones. A short distance after that, just before the hallway at the back of the room, a row of four doors with brass knobs gave the appearance of dressing rooms. Everything in the space had a tint of blue painted across its surface.

Marble tile encased the floor around the bar and a blue-patterned carpet covered the rest of the room beneath our feet. Azure fabrics hung along the ceiling, giving a soft and cool feeling along with the concave walls. The club was built in a serpentine layout, with more length than width.

Some of the patrons had less-than-human demeanors and I made it a point not to notice. I could taste the diversity of species in the room.

I approached the bartender, who seemed to be blue himself, but his pale skin was simply catching the reflected light from the bar. He was as tall as me, with long, straight black hair and clothes as dark as his mane. A touch of Mongolian showed along the contours of his face. He had been watching me since I'd entered. When I got closer, I noticed an intricate pattern of tattoos disappearing into his hairline. He spoke first.

"What can I get you?"

I did have one long-standing habit that I brought with me from the past that I seemed to consistently be allowed to remember. I answered honestly, "Whatever you have in a bourbon, preferably over ten. Neat."

The barkeep smiled and rummaged around in a floor cabinet behind him to produce the brand Woodford Reserve in a simplified container wax-stamped with the Roman numeral XIII. I knew the brand, but I didn't recognize this bottle at all. He presented the bottle ceremoniously, with one hand, then poured and served.

I took the smooth drink down in one long, slow pull. The alcohol rushed up my nose and burned pleasantly down my throat. Hints of burnt caramel, vanilla, and a sure hit of charred oak in the finish—just enough. Whiskey was the only thing I could count on to take the flavor of blood out of my mouth—when I tired of it. *Which isn't too often,* an errant thought countered.

I pursed my lips in appreciation. "Good. Why haven't I seen this year around?"

He winked and said, "It's a special edition, secret society stuff, just for us."

Appropriate for this place, I reckoned. "I'll have another," I told him, "and I promise to sip."

To that he replied, "If you don't mind, you'll need to check any weapons you have on you." He placed a rectangular container on the bar.

I've carried guns long enough that I know I'm not showing. I looked at him more closely and saw that the tattoo wound its way in a wispy line to the corners of his eyes. He was wearing some kind of spell, I guessed. No telling what he could see with it. I removed the two guns, cleared the chambers, and popped the magazines out. Then I placed the guns in the container and the magazines in my pocket. He didn't ask for the bullets. The barkeep pushed the container into a drawer under the bar and handed me a tag with a number on it.

The Browning Hi Power pistols have been a familiar presence at the small of my back for a long time now. Similar in appearance to the American service .45, these particular 9mm pistols were manufactured for Canadian military use. I learned how to customize them and did the work myself using plating techniques and etching pearl grips by hand with a fine-tooth finish. Then I forgot how to do it.

"If I had minded?"

"All actions have consequences."

If anything were to happen in here, it wasn't likely to happen with guns anyway. I dropped some cash on the counter and sat down.

"I might have to try to get drunk," I remarked dryly. He merely cocked the eyebrow again in response. Maybe he didn't know exactly what I was, but there was one thing I couldn't seem to do properly anymore, and that was get drunk. I healed so quickly that my system metabolized alcohol before I got more than a mild buzz. Maybe he *did* know what I was.

The hint of a smile passed my lips and I told him, "My name's Alexander. I need to speak to the owner. Is he in?"

He looked uncomfortable with the thought but replied quickly enough.

"Benjamin." He hooked a thumb at himself, then said, "Social call?"

"Business. If he's not available, do you happen to know if anyone here is good with pictorial writing, iconography, hieroglyphics?"

"Okay." He held his hands up briefly. "There's two people that I know of—Ms. Ducat, and the owner, Mr. Majispin, is an expert, I believe. I don't see Ms. Ducat at the moment, but I know she's here somewhere. I *can't* tell you how to find Mr. Majispin."

There was something odd about his inflection, the pause and emphasis on the word "can't." He had, on the other hand, told me the owner's name, at least.

"Understood. What's Ms. Ducat look like? Maybe I'll see her."

"She's about your height, always in heels, thin, very pale, crystal blue eyes, long straight nose. She favors high-collared clothing and her hair is dark brown. Done up, usually."

I nodded, turned my eyes away from him and shrugged. Fine. If you never expect too much help, it's tough to be disappointed. It occurred to me that he'd used his full first name, not some sawed-off variant. We were probably alike in that respect and disliked having our names compressed into some sobriquet by those too lazy to pronounce a few extra syllables.

"Is the owner here today?" I asked.

Long pause. Benjamin's brow knit before he replied carefully, "As I mentioned, I can't—"

I held up my hands for him to stop. I knew the look and the tone; I'd just asked the same question twice. I used another time-honored evasion— switch the subject. "What does he look like?"

"He's about five foot two, straight black hair, close-cropped and parted on the left, and always wears a white suit with black tie and patent-leather shoes. East Asian, clean-shaven. Good luck."

Benjamin walked away, a quizzical look on his face, to serve other customers. So, Mr. Majispin didn't like being sought out, and the barkeep followed orders well. It was probably a standing rule here. These safe houses were built on trust, as there was no real rule of law governing us. I couldn't possibly see the harm in looking for the two people. So far, this place was interesting enough, anyway. I'd been in safe houses before, but things had changed more than I'd imagined with the years. The caliber of the so-called music verified that.

I nodded to Benjamin and rose from the bar, then froze. That familiar weight wasn't pulling at the small of my back. I patted the empty space, a churning little pit of worry spreading in my stomach. Where the hell had I left my pistols? Benjamin watched me, eyebrows raised, and then I remembered. I decided not to be worried about the nines, remembering where they were; I knew I could find them if needed. Still. *At home under the sea.* I imagined the box and the guns beneath an alien ocean, doing my best to cement the memory, repeating the phrase to myself as I walked, with one hand at the small of my back fingering the empty holsters and twirling the numbered tag with the other hand. *At home under the sea.*

Down a cushioned and largely unadorned hallway obviously lay the dance floor. Soft, upholstered décor went from blue to red abruptly in the hallway. At the end, a heavy curtain muffled the music pounding from the other side. As I listened to the rhythm, it occurred to me that this kind of music was called "trance," a relentless beat mixed with various sweeping, electronic, pulsing sounds. Any vocals were generally full of echo and reverb. It was a nonstop style of music the DJ could string from one track to the next.

Of course, Ana had informed me of this after treating me to one long, tortured weekend of listening to homogenous rhythms. She interpreted them as more an emotional driver of physicality—the act of dancing. The music reminded me of why I had started to avoid these places as they had become more modern. I found the music as distasteful as the increasingly magic-sourced clientele. Over the years, be-bop gave way to free jazz and that gave way to less-orchestrated, noisy attempts at entertainment.

Next to the heavy covering, a set of stanchions with a thick velvet rope was pushed into the corner, along with a dark, circular end table whose only purpose appeared to be to hold a clipboard with a sheaf of papers on it. To my right, a simple door with a small brass plate on it, the word "Detour" etched into it.

When I pushed through the curtain, I was completely unprepared for the scene.

The dance floor was crowded, not packed, but this was because a majority of the dancers were above the crowd on platforms and railings, swings, poles—whatever would hold them. Many of them looked human upon brief inspection, but a closer look revealed antennae, fine ridges, iridescent wings, scales, and claws. More worldly adornments like scarring, tattoos, and piercings were scattered among them. Catwalks and other protuberances allowed dancing on nearly every surface, and the poles supporting them provided risqué dancing opportunities. They were one pulsating mass from top to bottom and had already reached a fugue state, moving as one, writhing to the flashing lights and the beat in the circular room. Heat boiled in the conical space, washing aggressively around and amongst the dancers.

I looked back from where I'd apparently come. What was down there? I couldn't remember. I swam in a little puddle of panic before deciding, as always, my best course of action was to keep moving forward. I turned back to the dance floor, determined to stay present and in control of my mind.

As far as I was concerned, all of these strange people meant only one thing. I'd heard rumors of human and demon progeny, but had never seen any in person. Meaningless, since they probably used some kind of charm to alter their appearance and move about freely in public. As I understood it, humans rarely survived any kind of entanglements with demons. I didn't understand how any normal human could survive successful copulation with a being that isn't even supposed to be able to exist on this plane.

At the apex of the dance floor, there was a ridged cone of a ceiling with one lonely fan at its center. I was reminded of the gravity-defying properties of bubbles in a scene from that movie about a boy and a candy factory. The dance hall itself looked like the inside of a corrugated jug.

A heady wave of the dancers' mixed odors rode the rising heat. Aromas flitted by, at once familiar and not. A light film of sweat immediately broke out on my skin; the color red was a main theme on every surface, reinforcing and reflecting the heat. The DJ was ensconced in a glass cage set to the left side of the dance floor. His teeth were bright red, eyes hidden behind reflective lenses—seemingly affixed to his face with no discernible rims or stems. I'd seen human clubs like this, but hadn't yet had reason to experience this particularly modern and otherworldly spectacle.

This was definitely the younger set of the supernatural world. They reveled in their natural power, taking the steady burn of this music to a new level. I could feel the heat of social friction pouring off of the dancers, diving deep into my skin. The energy washed around my legs, threatening a flood. My stomach convulsed and began to burn with need. I felt a sudden presence next to me, and she spoke as if in answer to my thoughts.

"Yes, flooding. That's the idea. An orgy of shared, carefree energy; a natural high." She trilled the vowels in her final word, drawing out the soft ending.

I looked directly at the figure standing beside me, but I couldn't make her out. My senses failed me; I became even more agitated. She flitted in and out of my range of perception. All I could discern was that she was smiling and moving her hands in a way that I couldn't follow. Her speech was akin to the grinding *purr* from an obscenely large cat, and whenever she pronounced vowels in the high-octave range, her voice skipped as if it were a flawed recording.

"Ah," she said, dragging the soft "h" out in a long breath, "you're a predator. All-Eater."

Her diction had an archaic, distant phrasing—the kind that still found its home in remote pockets of Europe. She was able to move into my peripheral vision without my seeing it, both disturbing and very fast. My agitation boiled.

"Oh, don't be angry at what I am, shapeshifter."

What was she? I took a guess. "Faerie?"

She smiled and curtseyed once in the corner of my eye, facing me all the while. Then she was in front of me. I'd never met one of the Fae before, and her surreality was particularly agitating. Thinking on it, no one I'd known had ever met one. They were legendary among even us monsters who roamed the Earth.

"Very good, *regno,* you of long-lived wisdom and knowledge within another. Pretty nesting dolls."

"What?" It'd sounded like she'd used one of the Latin words for "king," but the rest of her statement was simply puzzling. She just giggled in response. I was having difficulty hearing; the music…

"I didn't think you could exist here."

"Oh, but we can,"—she smiled large, inhuman, and popped in and out of existence—"when the…mood is right. Mmmm, the two of you are such good company."

Two? Was she drunk and seeing double? All I could make out was that her head was large and disproportionate to her body. She wasn't touching the ground. Then I also realized—she *was* tipsy, somehow drunk, barely making sense. She was here for this overflow of—what? Tribal magic? She gasped and began to flicker like an old movie. I could feel it too; the sundry, whipped-up power had risen to a point over my waist, above her ghostly breasts.

An old and familiar presence started to pour out of my skin to join the rising tide, and I could barely hang on to the power. A deep, throaty rumble bubbled from the back of my throat, drawing the attention of the magical being. I had an urge and not the self-control to stop myself. I reached out to touch her.

My hand moved in above the swell of her breasts. When I made contact, it was like touching a balloon full of electricity. She laughed suddenly, prodding my volcanic anger. The hot power of the dancers had swelled above my head and I was drowning in it, a counterpoint to her revelry. I was damnably hungry again.

All of my senses were firing at once. I stumbled forward, trying in vain to escape, moving against a syrupy undertow. A haze fell in at the edges of my eyes—too much input and too little control, the flow of power in the room sweeping my inhibitions away. My mouth watered as I locked eyes with possible prey.

I knew that what I was about to do was wrong. It was as if I were observing the events of my life unfolding before me, an obtuse voyeur wallowing in the spectacle of my predicament. I watched myself turn and pick a target. He was a young man, soft in the jaw, shoulders hunched and standing by the wall, no doubt looking to be victimized—the weakest, indeed. The predator in me cycled to the surface, casting aside the ballast of my humanity. Negative energy flowed from me into the room, but the swirling current of the dancers' magic swept it away from the crowd, keeping the power at bay, allowing them to remain unaware. I took another step, then two, and struggled to control myself.

I felt, rather than heard, the faerie squeal like a tickled child.

An agitated male voice cut through the cacophony. "Damned faeries."

It wasn't important; my attention was still focused on the young man. He didn't know what was coming, didn't realize. No one understood. I struggled with the urge to spring forward and drag my victim down. Just as I mounted a final effort, a small hand seized my arm. Difficult-to-ignore power burned in that palm. I turned and faced a dusky man in a glowing white suit.

"Come with me. There will be an accounting."

He tugged on my arm with a jolt of distracting energy, and I welcomed it. I used the moment to will the all-consuming horror deep down into myself, pushing with everything I had, mentally working the mercurial mass as deftly as I could back into its cage. Sweat drenched my back and neck.

Majispin barked a question at me. "What is your name?"

I got the impression that it was the second time he'd asked.

"Alexander," I managed to choke out.

Allowing him to lead me, I followed as he pulled me around the dance floor to a doorway opposite the one I'd entered. I caught a glimpse of someone who matched Ms. Ducat's description moving in the opposite direction. She was in a state of multifarious, eighteenth-century undress with pleats and numerous buttons. She watched everything keenly, the wisps of a smile tickling the corners of her mouth. As we passed her, the heady scent of flowers filled my nose.

We were moving down another padded passageway—this one was purple—up to a heavy drape. My escort pushed me through. On the other side, a powerful blow to my ribs knocked me aside, and I doubled over from the shock of the punch.

THREE

My ribs ached, but nothing was broken. The second punch rattled my head in a wink of flashing white. Disoriented, I instinctively tucked my chin and bent my knees, bringing my hands up, bobbing to my left. The follow-up punch whizzed across the top of my head, skimming hair. I drove my right fist up into my assailant's midsection and followed up with a left hook to the side of his head for good measure. Both were solid shots and he staggered back, arms flailing for balance. I didn't continue. Instead, I took stock of my surroundings. This was all a mistake.

Majispin had remained back by the doorway. The room wasn't full, but small groups of gawkers shuffled backwards and stood by the walls.

My opponent was a hair over six feet, as tall as I am but more muscularly built; he had blond hair and a sculpted nose bisecting a pair of perfectly balanced dark-brown eyes. The ugly red mark on his bruised cheek must've matched mine.

Those brown eyes narrowed at me. Where he was light in complexion, I was dark. He wore a tight, black, long-sleeved T-shirt and a leather vest; jeans and heavy boots complemented the leather. He'd hit me faster and harder than a normal human of his size. Combined with a complexion that had seen plenty of the outdoors, this told me he was a shapeshifter. I was sure he could sense the same about me as we took stock of each other.

Judging by his wild follow-up, he was an untrained fighter and accustomed to using his size and speed as an advantage. That's a method that doesn't work easily with me. He still had his fists up, standing in an ineffective boxing crouch, when Majispin spoke.

"That's enough. Have you come to your senses?"

I slowly turned my head towards him but left my eyes on the big man.

"Yes, thank you."

"Don't thank me, damn it; what cause have you?" he snapped.

The blond, his muscle I presumed, continued to eye me.

"Tell him to back off."

"I'll tell Mark to do no such thing. You were getting ready to attack one of my customers! What the hell were you doing in that room? It's a *private* gathering; the entrance was secured."

That it had been an exclusive gathering was patently obvious in hindsight, but the room hadn't been secure. These houses had changed more than I expected. Direct intervention or punishment by the owner was a rare occurrence; expulsion had been the preferred method in my day. That dance-floor ritual was something that had never been permitted; the clubs used to be smaller and tended to frown on large gatherings of any kind. The truth was that I had no idea what I'd walked into, despite my long experience in the world.

The crowd in the room thinned as some left the area altogether and others retreated to a safe distance to wait. Akin to a pack of schoolchildren, they acted as if they knew or suspected what might happen next. I couldn't explain myself, since I hadn't known what had been going on in that room. The entrance had not been secure, and I'd never been overwhelmed like that—not involuntarily, anyway. I was still shaking off the effects of the magic; I could feel it oozing away from my skin to rejoin the melee back on the dance floor, prickles of electricity passing through my veins. A trickle of sweat tickled my temple and I clenched my jaw against the chill it caused. I almost didn't have a chance to learn the lesson.

"The passage was not secure" was all I could muster.

"Nonsense," Majispin hissed, "you couldn't just walk past Barros. We're done talking, by the way." He jerked his head in a small motion, giving his man the go-ahead to attack.

Mark lunged at me, feinting with his left and swinging hard with a looping right at my head. Stepping forward and thrusting the long bone of my left forearm into the soft part of his right forearm, I brought my fist down into the side of his neck like a hammer. Mark's head jerked and his eyes swam with the impact. I slid my arm forward on the right side of his neck so that when I sidestepped his mass, my bicep popped the side of his head and momentum flung him to the ground over my hip. His legs looped over awkwardly and I dropped a knee into his ribs. He grunted and gasped at the impact. My hands controlling his arm and neck kept him further immobilized. I could see the dumbfounded look in his eyes, wondering how he'd tipped over onto the floor.

I addressed Majispin carefully. "There's no need for this."

I was talking at Mark's face, but I knew Majispin was listening. The crowd stayed back, thankfully, or I'd probably have had to start injuring people to make some space. There was a moment of dead air between us; only the thump of music from the adjoining room could be heard.

"Well, shall I stop him, Mark? Do I have to do that for you? Do I have to do your job?"

I was beginning to think I'd have to kill Mark *and* Majispin if the owner kept being stubborn like this.

The owner was an unknown quantity. There was a sense of something about him that was elusive. His scent and appearance were human, but the sum of those parts added up to a mystery for me. I had the impression that penetrating whatever invisible shroud he held over himself would take time—time I didn't have.

Mark grunted way back in his throat; I continued to hold him tightly. He managed to growl one word around my fingers:

"No."

I think that bought me some time. I didn't really want to confront Majispin; this was his domain. If I let Mark go without killing him, he'd be compelled to come at me again. That would hamper my escape and I wanted nothing more than to bolt at that moment.

Mark tried to apply leverage, kicking with his legs to unbalance me and scrabbling at my fingers on his throat. He wasn't weak, and he was recovering just as quickly as I had.

A steadily darkening field edged by a haze of roiling purple light had begun to manifest behind Majispin. He was summoning…something. My only choice was using Mark as a shield and breaking for the back. I punched Mark in the side of his head—which bounced squarely off the floor. Then I heaved him to his feet, twisting an arm, and put him between me and Majispin.

Tightening my grip, I could see the blood under the skin around Mark's neck and forehead pumping desperately as he tried to regain control of the situation. Out of the corner of my eye, I could see Majispin winding his hands around each other. I was planning on not being where I was in the next moment, when someone in the crowd cleared their throat and spoke loudly enough to be heard over all.

"Ahem. Alivara, would you do me a favor?"

Majispin was stunned. I didn't think he could quite believe that someone had interrupted. I'd been surprised as well, but I didn't let up on Mark. I knew who it was—knew her well.

Ana melted from the crowd and smiled at me.

"Please, let Mark go."

I released Mark's arm and gave him a little shove in Majispin's direction to create some distance. He stared from me to Ana, alternately massaging his wounds and not quite believing that this small, young girl had politely asked me to do something and I had done it.

Majispin embarrassedly clasped his hands behind his back, whatever he'd been working on forgotten.

"Ana, dear, would you mind?" Majispin had asked through clenched teeth.

"First, the favor." She raised an index finger and the corners of her mouth upturned.

Did she have Majispin bewitched somehow? I hadn't seen any bite marks on him, but they could be easily hidden. It was unlikely; Ana is a bit more discerning about who she feeds from, and Majispin simply didn't fit anything resembling that profile. I wasn't sure that she'd be able to control someone like him in any case. Besides, I'd never known her to play with her food.

She remained beautiful and would remain forever so as long as she could stay alive. Her biological mother had been a first-generation Chinese immigrant to America—for whatever foolish reasons immigrants come here. She'd eventually married the man she worked for, a man I had known and respected despite the color of his skin.

Ana's eyes were a strong reminder of her Asian lineage. Her nose was straight and puckish; her face ended in full lips on a petite, ovular head. Shockingly pale, alabaster skin, never touched by the sun, provided a marked contrast to her shimmering black hair. It

Errick A. Nunnally

was short—in that instance—moussed and spiked on top, buzzed on the sides and back. She wore a dark-red blouse tied below her small breasts with precious few buttons keeping it closed, and a line of glitter from neck to belly. Tight black pants came up to just below her hips, and a very slim chain of gold wound its way around her waist. Her belly button was pierced, as was an eyebrow—twice—and both ears multiple times. At least three earrings adorn each ear whenever I see her. Her lips were glossed, but she wore no other makeup that I could tell from this distance. Does a hundred-year-old teenager really need any? I can't help but wonder—for the love of blood, with our healing prowess, why spend the time re-piercing your skin like that? I never approved…and it never mattered.

Majispin chewed the inside of his lip, glanced from me to Ana, and smiled. He raised his hands in defeat.

"I would assume that you do not wish me to harm your…" He paused, searching for the appropriate word. "…friend, here?"

Ana continued to smile at Majispin as if to a five-year-old, then suddenly bounded up and threw her arms around me. I responded in kind and whispered in our shared dialect, Kainai, into her ear: *"What are you doing here, Little Crow?"*

She responded in the same language, *"I could ask you the same question, Walks Too Far."* Her occasional use of the nickname my mother had given me was always a sarcastic touch, and as always I regretted telling her about it when she was still a child. I gave up complaining about it decades ago, realizing that I simply shouldn't have told her.

"Indeed." I smiled. Despite the rashness of my actions in the last few minutes, I felt a hundred miles better. As always, she showed up when I least expected her and when I most needed her.

The crowd relaxed around us, and Majispin shooed everyone about their business. Two men had since entered the room and one of them, a big Mexican, suffered a stern talking-to from Mark. Barros, I assumed, the one who was supposed to have secured the doorway. Both of the new men were notably large and most likely formed a small pack of shapeshifters. How were they involved here? In Majispin's employ? Or his control?

The owner addressed Ana. "That sounded like a Native tongue. Curiouser and curiouser, Ana. You continue to fascinate me. For how long, do you think?"

Ana extricated herself from me and turned to the wickedly smiling Majispin. She shrugged, cocked her head, and asked, "Do I get that favor now?"

"Oh, my dear, I haven't hurt this man, have I?"

"That wasn't the favor I asked for. I haven't asked for anything yet."

A wave of anger crossed Majispin's face that was only apparent in his posture and a single, long blink. His smile hadn't cracked for a moment. How he could bear to deal with Ana long enough to learn anything about her was a mystery to me. Despite her age, she has a talent for behaving as if she truly were an awful teenage girl.

"As you wish, my dear, within bounds."

"Of course," she said lightly. "I believe he has a question; your answering it is my favor." She waved a hand casually in my direction. Sharp as usual, she had immediately understood that I was there looking for some kind of information.

"Very well, I'll answer one question—if I can, and not of a personal nature."

"I wouldn't purposely be that rude, Mr. Majispin," I said, attempting politeness.

He turned his gaze from my daughter to me and his features hardened. I don't think he believed me.

The woman I had assumed was Ms. Ducat glided by, her dress so long you couldn't see her feet. An invisible parade of flowers and makeup floated in the redolence of her wake. She nodded sagely to Majispin, who gave a slight bow in her direction. She was gone as quickly as she'd arrived.

"A friend of yours?" I asked him.

"An associate," he replied flatly.

I produced the two slips of paper containing the glyphs and handed them to Majispin. He didn't look at them but indicated for us to have a seat at a nearby table. He curtly told Mark to go clean himself up. I'd cut the man's head on the floor, and blood smeared the side of his face.

When the three of us sat down, a waiter appeared at Majispin's side. Quietly, and without asking, the magician placed an order for the three of us—another neat single-malt for me, a "Faithful" for Ana, and a dram of La Fin d'Artemisia for himself. He whispered the order, but I was sure he knew I could hear him. I knew Artemisia had once been an outlawed brand of the distilled liquor absinthe, but I was unaware of this variant. The only drink I didn't have a clue about was the "Faithful."

Majispin still hadn't looked at the paper I'd given him. He watched Ana and me quietly as we waited. Neither Ana nor I are ever eager to have just anyone know or understand our relationship. So we sat, two predators, waiting. I breathed deep and slow, while she didn't bother to breathe at all. Only needing air to speak, she adopted the eerie stillness that only vampires can effect. Abruptly, one leg began to bounce impetuously over her knee, eyebrows raised, one fang peeking over her lip, breaking the spell.

Our drinks came—or rather, two drinks came; Ana's small goblet was empty. Majispin downed his in one quick pull, and I sipped mine, content to taste it.

The young man who'd brought our drinks was unremarkable except for the tiny flesh-colored ring at his neck. The adornment was barely perceptible, and he was clothed in a nondescript manner, wearing black pants and white shirt. He smiled cordially at Ana as he fished in his pocket and produced a small metal box. From within, he unwrapped a tiny device that I couldn't make out. He carefully pushed the small item to the ring at his neck. Holding it with one hand, he raised Ana's goblet to his neck and twisted the device. A tiny tattoo on the back of his hand—three wavy lines, a symbol for water—undulated beneath the tendons there. Almost immediately, blood poured into the cup. It ebbed and flowed with his heartbeat.

I watched him intently, fascinated that a creature would so easily and willingly spill its blood for a predator. Once finished, he handed the glass to Ana. She took it elegantly, swirled it under her nose, and swallowed it in one graceful motion, ensuring that the blood was still hot and fresh. All the while, she stared at the young man. He had a dreamy look to his eyes as her mouth and neck worked. Each tiny gulp seemed to bring a wave of pleasure to him. How powerful *was* Ana? I couldn't feel anything, but that didn't mean she hadn't cast herself over him somehow.

They seemed to have been sharing a luscious and quiet moment, lovers exchanging a private look, partaking in something that no one else could possibly know about. I was curious about that, but I kept my mouth shut. I could ask her later.

Most of the personal details regarding vampirism I'd inadvertently learned from Ana as she'd grown up. It had been difficult enough constantly explaining that she had a sun allergy of some sort. Ana's unusual "birth" sometimes made for some less-than-practical observations regarding vampires, so I constantly wondered about the validity of what I'd learned over the years.

She finished the drink and handed the glass back to the young man. He bowed deeply, thanked her, and with watery eyes took his leave.

Ana looked at me, re-crossed her legs, smacked her lips, and said, "What?"

"Nothing," I replied. "I just found that interesting."

She smiled and bit her lip, the tip of one fang showing again. I hate it when I amuse her. She's the only person I know who can make me *feel* old.

Majispin had been studying us and chimed in. "They're fetishists, Alexander. It's really as simple as that. Good business for an establishment where vampires are welcome. I only hire the best; they take care of themselves and their blood. Don't tell me you're prudish on these matters? I think you could try to be a little more expansive when it comes to these sub-cultures."

Majispin had a British-tainted accent that made his every utterance sound superior and condescending. Not to mention he was *being* superior and condescending. And damn irritating.

"What I do with my time is my business." The words came out of my mouth cold. Few men enjoy an unsolicited opinion. I've never been one of the few.

Majispin cocked an eyebrow and replied with equal warmth. "No offense intended. To business, then."

He finally looked at the paper on the table for a moment, glanced at us, then dug in his front coat pocket to produce a pair of gold-wire spectacles that had been out of fashion for a hundred years. He wiped them ceremoniously and placed them on the bridge of his nose. The frames, I could see, had been etched in a twirling pattern that was too delicate to make out from across the table, and I noticed an odd texture to his fingernails. Were there spells carved into his very person, or was it simply a style? He blinked once, slowly. Then again. Ana and I waited patiently. She surveyed the room, occasionally catching an eye and smiling or waving. I watched Majispin for several minutes; he seemed lost.

Ana looked back at Majispin and frowned. "Alivara."

"Hm? Yes?" Majispin looked up and blinked rapidly, "Ah, sorry. Yes." He removed his spectacles and deposited them back in his coat pocket. Without preamble, he began tossing questions at me, and I lobbed answers back.

"Where did you get this?"

"Very near the murder of a child."

"How was it drawn, with what?"

I sat back, wondering where this was all going, and answered, "With feces."

"Gathered from the child?"

"Yes, I assume so."

"Hm. And for whom?"

The last question baffled me. It took me a moment to answer. "I have no idea."

"Were there others like this around the same area?"

"I didn't search the entire area, as it was within a project development. There are quite a few buildings there. What I did find, below the complex, was a stylized map of the same area and other symbols."

"I think it's safe to assume that the map gives the locations for other potential inscriptions or ceremonies."

I nodded, having deduced something similar, but I only wanted to stop the murderer, not the drawings.

"I also assume that your question has something to do with this symbol?"

Ah, that's right, I hadn't yet asked my question.

"I need to know what that symbol is used for, what it is. I already know it's of South American origin, or style, at least."

"Umm-hmm." Majispin nodded. "It's a symbol of some power, of course." He grinned and went on. "I've seen some form of it before, but never in practical use. You say you saw it inside the projects near the sacrifice?"

Little black girl, your head a-twirl, where did your blood go? "Yes."

"It's essentially one part of a containment spell. It's most typically used, if I'm remembering correctly, to seal off territory."

"To keep others out or to keep something in?"

"Yes."

Ana suddenly announced, "Boring. I'm going to dance." She kissed me on the cheek and said, "I'll see you later." She'd heard enough and faded away.

Her hand brushed Majispin's shoulder as she rounded his chair to leave, and she smiled warmly. I found myself back to wondering what *their* relationship was.

"Will I see you later?" Majispin asked.

"Maybe." She smiled and disappeared down the red corridor towards the pile-driving music. I did not approve, and again, it did not matter.

Majispin turned back to me, the same question probably on his mind as well—*what is his relationship to Ana?*

"I'll verify the symbol's use with my associate, Ms. Ducat, and you'll stay in touch, yes?"

The sorcerer's curiosity had apparently been piqued. I rose and picked up the paper from the table. As I did this, I met his eyes cruelly, holding them, willing him to fear. The effort wasn't wasted on Majispin.

He stood from the table, smiled, extended his hand, and said, "Yes, I think you will." All of his scent markers clicked in and out of existence, throbbing uncertainly; some kind of spell, I assumed. It made me wary.

I took his hand, neither smiling nor showing animosity, neutral. A dull thread of electricity crept up my arm and tingled through my head and toes.

Majispin spoke in a level, menacing tone. "I hope we understand each other."

I was seriously tempted to remove his head right then, but instead growled back, "You'd better hope we do. It's been a pleasure measuring cocks; my apologies to your staff."

Majispin sneered disapprovingly at my crude witticism. Which was fine with me, because there was plenty more where that came from.

I couldn't stand wondering why my daughter was involved with this man, and it was time to go.

After picking up my weapons at the forward bar, I was glad to be outside of the club or safe-house or whatever they might be called nowadays. The sky had crumbled, a clear encroachment of darkness bleeding into the failing light giving way to a crepuscular hue; I'd spent hours inside. Surely I'd avoid the dance floor the next time I had to be there. I decided to call Detective Roberts and share what little I could and hear what he'd learned on his own. I found an ideal pay phone several blocks away, at the edge of a brick plaza near the library, and dug his number out of my battered Moleskine. I could hear Ana berating me to get a smart phone.

"Roberts."

"Hello, Detective, it's Alexander."

There was a notable pause before Roberts spoke. "Have you learned anything since this morning? Hold that thought, I'm switching phones."

Bland music filled the line for a few seconds. When he answered again, all background noise had disappeared.

"Okay. What'd you find out?"

Roberts was showing extra care. How much did he know or sense? Or was he keeping his discourse with me from his partner? I'd likely find out soon enough. We were both in dangerous territory. I wasn't officially a part of his investigation; Roberts could get into hot water for sharing information with a civilian. Also, he, or someone else, might get killed trying to deal with a situation that the normal are incapable of dealing with.

"The symbol from the wall at the murder scene is used in a ritual that's supposed to create some kind of enclosure. The child was the trigger for that particular location."

Roberts sighed sadly. "So there could be more. Do you know how many?"

"Not yet."

"Any idea where another might turn up?"

"Possibly at the locations indicated on a stylized map I found in the maintenance tunnels."

"Shit." He cursed sharply, and I realized that this meant more to him than I'd imagined.

"Or not; I don't know yet. There's also a date—April twelfth, this year."

"Wait a minute; what map? What the hell could that mean—a due date? When do you think you'll find out more?"

A great number of questions, of course. The biggest problem was that this was absolutely the real thing, not some poseur trying to communicate with Satan. I needed to tread lightly with Roberts. If it was a due date, there wasn't much more than a week to find the killer. Who knew how many more victims were in the crosshairs? "The map was written on a pipe where Terrell last saw me. He can take you to it. Look carefully; you'll be able to orient yourself and determine the other locations. And, of course, I'll be in touch. Did the coroner find anything?"

Roberts paused for two breaths and quickly made up his mind whether to answer me. "The girl was killed with something sharp, which we already knew; it's impossible to tell what kind of knife it was, other than it was curved, very well-tooled, and highly illegal, with at least a fourteen-inch edge. We got enough DNA from the vic's fingernails but no one to compare it to. The girl's name is—was—Rhonda Lloyd. She lived with her mother and two younger sisters in the adjacent building. The mom's like some picture-perfect statistic, so the kids are mostly raising themselves."

"And no one saw anything, correct?"

"Yeah, nothing. Unfortunately, I'm counting on you far too much. We're not getting the department commitment necessary to lock down that area and dig something up. No one gives a real shit. Yet. They'll jump if another kid gets murdered." That last bit had an edge of sarcasm that nearly drew blood through the phone line.

"I'll run down what you've given me. Try to tie it to any known believers in this kind of crap, maybe come up with some suspects."

There had been a hesitation before Roberts answered me; it nagged at my brain. I remembered the sealed-off apartments above the murder scene.

"Detective, did you check out the apartments above the murder scene, the ones marked for fumigation?"

"Yes. We did."

Again the hesitation. I wondered what exactly Brown had told him about me.

"You found something."

He sighed then, sounding much older in one quick breath. "We found a lot of something. We think the killer had been waiting up there, using the apartments as a kind of hideout."

"And the tenants?"

"Look, I'm not supposed to be telling you this stuff."

"What did Lieutenant Brown explain to you?"

Roberts sucked his teeth and thought about it for a heartbeat. "He said to give you the weird shit."

I waited, letting him come to the right conclusion on his own.

"All the tenants were long dead. Scattered around their apartments. We're still waiting on conclusive lab results for how long and, officially, how they died."

"Their blood?"

"Present, but no way to account for the total amount. It was everywhere; there were more flies and shit upstairs than I ever dreamed I'd see in one place."

"There will likely be more deaths."

"Fuck that," he snapped quietly. "Give me something other than voodoo."

"I'll be in touch."

I hung up thoughtfully. There was a more immediate matter at hand that I had to deal with. I was being watched.

FOUR

I took a slow look around the plaza. There were the usual couples, people getting off of work, the early crowd for dinner, and the flotsam of humanity flowing through the plaza. Which one of these people didn't belong? The woman idling, the one person who didn't appear to have a destination in mind and was obviously not homeless or looking out for a friend.

She was standing about thirty feet away from me, actively avoiding my gaze. I hadn't thought it mattered if she knew I'd spotted her or not. If she wanted to play it like I hadn't, then that would be fine.

She had copper-tinted, curly red hair that fell across the back of a long, supple leather coat of dull black. She wore nearly all black—boots, pants, choker—but her blouse was shimmering white and hovered just above her navel. The color of her eyes was still a mystery at this distance. What I could easily tell from here was that she was attractive.

The herd of humanity around us prevented me from picking up her scent, but that wasn't going to matter until much too late. I turned in the opposite direction and headed down Dartmouth Street and kept walking. I knew that, the closer I got to Storrow Drive and the last line of buildings, the more isolated the surroundings would become. A series of alleys along the way could offer the perfect opportunity.

I waited until the wind shifted so that I could be downwind. The buildings in the area acted as channels for stiff breezes. I turned off the street and down an alley, toward the winding river way.

A gust of wind blew up the back of my jacket and I paused, trying to remember where I'd been and what I had been doing. As always, forward seemed to be my best option, so I kept moving down the street.

The streets had quickly become empty as I walked, with fewer windows facing the narrow roads and even fewer pedestrians. The sidewalks in this area are composed of cobblestone or gone altogether, leaving broken asphalt and pebble-laden dirt. I knew I was in the Back Bay neighborhood by the ruined cobblestone and parkway, but the *why* was elusive. A female scent blossomed around me for the briefest of moments and I turned to look back. An attractive woman paused in mid-step, startled that I'd turned around.

Oh, yes, that's what I was up to.

With supernatural speed, she moved, but I was a half-second behind her. We leapt fences and scaled the fire escapes. I can only imagine what we might've looked like if anyone saw the two of us; we were practically running up the wall, finding hand- and footholds that no normal person could manage. In and out of the ancient wrought-iron fire escapes we went, our powerful fingers finding purchase in the old bricks as our weight rattled the rusted metal when we passed.

As we moved, I drank up the scents coming from her—lilacs, a powdery deodorant, and a flowery undercurrent that must have been a body lotion of some sort. The mixture of scents struck me as… pleasant. All of it mingled with the leather of the long jacket and her distinct, female scents.

She reached the rooftop before I did, her long coat billowing out and her hair swinging wildly. She glanced back, and I saw a flash of golden-brown eyes as I grabbed her and we both cleared the edge of the roof. She was off-balance and I used that surprise and leverage to push her ahead of me and towards the brick kiosk surrounding the roof access door. At the last moment I spun her, controlling one arm by pinching her at the elbow and pushing my forearm under her chin. She slammed hard against the brick wall. Mortar came loose and settled in our hair; the bricks sagged inward with the impact.

She was definitely Latina and no doubt a shapeshifter. As she looked at me through her curls, I could see that she was grinning, a sensual curve of her thick, wide lips.

"Well, you *are* as *irritable* as advertised," she purred.

Increasing the pressure with my forearm, I asked her why she was following me.

The first obvious flash of anger on her face creased the area between her eyes, and she snap-kicked upward into my crotch, forcing me to let her go and allowing a right hook to connect with my temple, spreading stars across my eyes.

It was a stupid, careless mistake on my part; I'd left myself wide open. I kept my eyes on her, ready for the next blow, and willed myself to breathe. I caught another familiar scent mingled with hers, but couldn't pin it down.

"No need to be so *rough*, jeez," she said with a slight Spanish accent and waved her hands for emphasis. "Majispin just asked me to keep an eye on you, *God*." She brushed mortar out of her hair and off of her shoulders. "It was kinda fun until you went full psycho."

I wasn't sure what to do at this point. She hadn't been the aggressor. The game was up. So I apologized as concisely as I could in Spanish.

She replied in the same language, "Your accent is just *too* clean. Where'd you learn?"

I couldn't recall where I had learned, so I concocted a plausible answer. "Spain. A long time ago."

Her eyes gave me the impression they were used to anger. She pursed her full lips and said, "Okay, fine, we're cool."

I grunted and tried to relax; a queasy pain still traveled down my legs and up into my stomach.

"I'm sorry I kicked you in the balls. I'm sure they could be put to some better use than as kicking bags." She chuckled at the last.

"Yeah," I grunted, "I can think of a couple of things."

I didn't know what to think. Majispin must've known I'd spot her. Or had he? Maybe he didn't have a complete idea of what I was capable of doing, either. I thought of the future and what that might mean for me if I navigated this successfully—if I survived. Nothing was certain; stay on the job, stay busy.

She shrugged and wandered over to the ledge to sit down and speak. "My name's Maria. What now?"

"Now you tell me what Majispin wants you to find out by watching me."

She arched an eyebrow and leaned back over the ledge. I knew that she was muscular and supple, but knowing and seeing are two different matters. Her outfit accentuated what little flesh was showing. I didn't want to be attracted to her, but she displayed many of the qualities to which I was attracted—tough, wore little makeup, and kept her nails trimmed. She was a woman of action and enough years to be comfortable the way she was.

That she was in good shape meant nothing too serious. As a shapeshifter, frozen in time until her death, she'd naturally exhibit the best tendencies of her human form at the time she was turned—peak physical appearance. Even if she were obese and crippled when she was turned, her physical ideal would be tapped from somewhere deep within her DNA. Only your age didn't change. An infected seventy-year-old man would be an exceptionally fit septuagenarian as long as he could stay alive.

I kept thinking while Maria continued to chew over my question. My inspection of her must've been obvious, because she continued projecting a coquettish demeanor, chewing her lower lip lightly, arching her back. I hated it; I loved it. I wanted her, and either she was trying to play me or she was honestly interested. Everything about her rattled things low on my body; I had the distinctly male thought that I had at least a fifty percent chance. So I gritted my teeth and held my tongue.

Passing the infection is largely a way to end one's existence, as only one person of any given bloodline can carry the affliction. Once it was passed, the current carrier instinctively kills and eats the former. Since I hadn't kept track of my bloodline, the chances that I'd lose myself in a completely insane and berserk moment or die at someone else's hands were disproportionately high. The limitations of transmission apparently meant that there were a limited number of shapeshifters in existence. I had no idea what happened when one of us was killed without passing the curse on. The rest of the bloodline appeared to be safe, but who knew for sure?

Vampires are similar, but their parasitic nature means needing to go through a great deal of victims to find others that they could turn. I was certain they didn't mind.

I hadn't always avoided packs of shapeshifters, but my emotions had become dull and tumultuous over the last century. It made me wonder what I was becoming. I was certainly not more human—maybe something less—definitely something less. We all were.

Rising up from the ledge, Maria crunched over to me and stood uncomfortably close, looking straight into my eyes. Then she finally answered my question, smiling. "No. If Majispin wants you to know what he thinks, he'll tell you."

A jolt of anger creased the back of my skull. I was mostly angry with myself for handling this woman the way I had *and* for being attracted to her. The fact that I was losing my mind inch by inch, though clearly not her fault, pissed me off as well. It must've showed, because her body language became warier, and I knew my aura was bleeding out a prickling energy. Both of us could sense strong moods in the other.

Sucking air through her teeth, she swayed slightly, determined to resist the flood. She couldn't do much outwardly other than stay on her feet and keep a cautious posture. And I liked it. Liked that she dug in and prepared to resist. I liked that she seemed to enjoy the challenge.

I suddenly realized why I'd become so itchy—I hadn't allowed the change in days. A growl crawled from the back of my throat, and I took a step towards Maria. She matched the distance by moving one step sideways and backwards. She was ready for me when I sprang, and that's what I'd wanted. I wanted her to see me coming, wanted her to be ready. Because there was little she could do to stop me.

For a split second, the world around us blurred as she jabbed with her left and let loose with an overhand right. I swayed backwards, dodging the jab, and countered the real punch, swatting her right elbow, redirecting the force, while I drove inward and slightly to her right. My fist connected with her ribs and drew a grunt of pain. She was off-balance when I hooked my arm under hers and splayed my left hand across her face, fingers looped around her nose. When I twisted to my left, taking her head and shoulders with me, she let out an involuntary squeak of surprise and pain, feet leaving the ground as she went down on her side, her left arm trapped with me and my right knee in her ribs.

She kicked one way and then the other, trying to shift my weight off of her; I increased the twist on her arm across my leg and settled my knee further into her ribs. She managed to keep the pain from showing on her face, but I felt her heart rate increase under my hand, and her aura spiked with heat. She didn't take well to being dominated, didn't panic or flail—another check mark for her in the "like" column.

Maria let out a sharp breath and snarled, "You know this'll only work once, right? Better do whatever it is you're gonna do right now, motherfucker."

At that moment, I could've broken her arm, pummeled her face, and collapsed her rib cage. She had no defense in this position.

Tell her what you'd like to do to her, a whispering thought encouraged, *maybe she'll like it; you know you will. I know what you like. Take it.*

Sweat prickled across my brow, and a feeling like a cannonball dropped into my stomach. I had heard a clear, independent voice ripple between my ears. Struggling to settle myself, I took a deep breath, swallowing her scent, wallowing in it, and said, "Don't follow me anymore." I said it slowly to be sure she understood every word. To be sure she understood all the implications. I let her go gently, our hands brushing lightly as we disconnected. Her eyes held a questioning look on me, betraying that she knew my mood had suddenly shifted for no discernible reason.

She left as quickly as she could, glancing at her forearm where I'd held her. I hoped I'd rattled her as badly as I'd wanted. (I hoped I'd see her again.) For a moment, I hated myself for hurting her. (I hated not being able to approach her normally.) Any bruises on her ribs or arm would heal in a matter of hours, if not sooner. I could have done much more, but I hadn't.

Yes, you could've done many things, rasped the words across the back of my skull.

I sat down hard in the roof's gravel, slamming my hands to the sides of my head, grinding my teeth. This was wrong. It was new and different and wrong.

"My mind is my own." I repeated the mantra under my breath and imagined a chest of my making with all of my things inside. *It is mine.*

I'm not certain how long I sat there, but before I took my leave, I noted that Maria had scratched the back of my hand with her short fingernails. The wounds were closing already. I licked the four scratches, once each, and tasted her. Against all rational thought, I hoped she tried to follow me again—I was in lust and I knew it down to my dark core.

It was then that I recognized the other scent embedded in her skin. It belonged to Mark, the blond muscle from the club.

FIVE

A series of "green" tracts named the Emerald Necklace encircles a chunk of Boston. The largest swath of greenery in the city is Franklin Park, nestled among the run-down neighborhoods of Dorchester, Roxbury, and Roslindale. The interior of the park is over five hundred acres, a good portion of which is fairly dense forest and hiking trails. After dark, people wisely stick to the well-lit concrete trails bordering the lone thoroughfare that cuts from one end of the park, near the zoo, to the other end, in Forest Hills. Street lamps are sparse along the asphalt paths, which makes it a prime place, in this city, for me to run and hunt unseen.

I left my clothing in a bundle, next to a large rock. The moon peeked in and out of a slow-moving mass of white clouds. Still within city limits, it was difficult to see the stars due to the glare of civilization. The moon was only half-full and meaningless to me.

I gave up my humanity in a single, relief-filled burst of energy—the luxurious feeling of putting your feet up after a long day or the venting tingle of much-needed urination. The depictions of painful transformations in the movies are ridiculous. It's a sudden pleasure, a sharp, deep breath of fresh air, the satisfaction of relaxing a muscle after a strenuous period. Mentally, it's disorienting. I can feel a sick slide, as if to nowhere, a sudden drop where I need to have faith there's somewhere to land in the darkness. Transforming is more like transposing. The monster is a difficult horse to break and as addictive as the nastiest drug.

The form we assume is only reminiscent of a *Canis lupus*. It'd be more accurate to describe us as furry, muscular primates with lupine heads, larger than any human.

My coat of fur is charcoal-black from my head to my short curved tail. My hands become ape-like, with long palms and sharp nails. Spiked ears that can swivel a full one hundred and eighty degrees protrude from the topmost sides of my head. Despite how I perceive my form, children can mistake me for an extremely large dog if I whine and pant enough.

After the change, sounds are richer and easier to discern. My scent abilities increase with the moisture on the tip of my snout—the entire world of sensory perception becomes sharper and addictive. Some of us become lost in the form and never revert, wandering into deep forests and mountains bordering civilization, mistaken for other monsters.

Within my mouth exist two successive rows—on both top and bottom—of pointed canines and jagged molars facing slightly inward. It is nearly impossible for prey that I've bitten to escape—unless a chunk is torn out. Once the eating has begun, there is no end in sight except the belly. In this form, my first line of defense is my ability to eat and digest just about anything. Not everything *tastes* good, though. Vampires taste horrible. Like chewing wet lumps of coal.

My eyes remain in the binocular position but are set deeper in a wide, heavy skull. A crest of bone runs from the area just above and between my eyes to the back of my head, hidden by thick hair. The shapeshifter's face is akin to extruding the head of a gorilla into a canine-like snout. If I have to, I can dislocate my jaw and still bite down. It's not the preferred vise without the counter of the jaw-hinge, but it's still strong enough to remove most body parts in one snap. Crunching through flesh and bone is a distinct and horrifying pleasure.

Dropping to all fours, I circumnavigated the densest parts of the park, only sensing a human being once or twice near the paths. More of the homeless lived on the Common downtown than stayed in that park. I let the pleasure of roaming without purpose drive me long enough to rouse my appetite, which wasn't long at all. It had been a good night for hunting—low light, cool air, and only a very slight breeze. I stayed close to the tree trunks and out of the bundles of dry branches that had fallen, minimizing noise.

I tracked the scent of a groundhog, staying downwind to avoid alarming it. It was large, judging by the amount of spoor the creature had laid down, and had crossed and re-crossed its own trail several times. There was without doubt an established run through here to some food source. I was patient and waited for it to come to me. I remained crouched, silently waiting; I didn't have to wait long.

The pest cautiously broke through the undergrowth with a large chunk of rotting vegetable in its mouth. Easily two feet long from nose to tail-tip, the mammal weighed enough to trample a trail from the nearby hospital and halfway house. The wind shifted and the groundhog's body tensed. It scented me and bolted frantically. I captured it in two bounds; the soft, furry thing continued to scramble as I clamped down on it. One vicious shake of my head and its spine snapped; the struggling stopped. I swallowed it in two wet bites, savoring the explosion of blood and juices in my mouth. Contented, I licked my chops and smelled the air. A now-familiar scent hovered there. Maria.

I couldn't remember forging any kind of a real relationship with anyone since I'd adopted Ana. Maria stirred something mischievous and sexual in me, and on some level, I resented that perceptible loss of control. If I let go, there might not be a return.

The smell of her in the air reminded me of the taste she'd left on the back of my hand earlier, as I rolled her aroma over my tongue. I sat back on my haunches, facing the direction she was coming from. It only took a few minutes for her to slowly emerge from the underbrush.

Her coat's coloring was a dark grey with silvery accents. Our coat colors didn't mean anything; the fur doesn't normally match the hair color in human form. Maria was no exception. In this state, it would never occur to me what her ethnic origins were or what cultural baggage she might carry.

She watched me with golden-rimmed eyes that sparkled eerily in the moonlight filtering sporadically through the overgrowth. Slowly, she approached, keeping her body low and eyes on mine. Before she got too close, I growled and snapped at the air in front of her and licked my chops. She stopped mid-step but resumed moving forward in short order. I snapped at her again, and she darted back and forth.

We played at this, running through the forest, darting around trees and rocks. It had been an interminably long time since I'd done anything resembling play. For the better part of an hour we plunged through the underbrush, spooking late-night jogging addicts—they should reconsider their after-hours pastime, anyway. Several times Maria nipped or scratched me, a natural in this form, besting me in her way, showing me up. Payback for earlier. It was a vulnerability I was wary of showing, but allowed for reasons I was only willing to interpret as lust.

When we reached the edge of the park, where I'd stashed my clothing, I steadied myself to return. This was when the transformation became painful as the extra mass was shunted back in, folded upon itself.

Bones crackled and ached as I shifted back to human form and stood breathing for several beats, soaking up the cold night air as condensation rose off of my sweaty brow and back. Barely human and mostly monster, I have been forced to grudgingly accept this thing I harbor. Every shape twist is another taste, one step closer to full addiction.

Maria sat and watched me as I dressed. With her head cocked to one side, she looked like a gigantic, evil puppy.

When I walked away, I knew she was still watching me. I felt the thrill of something that I'd missed since my teenage years. I'd spent most of my adult life working to support my ailing mother and our land. I was turned at forty, five years after my mother's death, by a several-times-over great-grandfather. My fingers absentmindedly brushed the back of my hand. I could feel two of the forty scars I'd counted on my body. *Forty scars, for forty years.*

For nearly sixty years I ran with packs and other individuals regularly. After that period in my life, I avoided regular contact with shapeshifters and humans alike for so long that I seemed to have numbed my instinctive ability to make an emotional connection. *You used to be better then, more like me.* The errant thought reverberated weakly through my mind, causing me barely a shiver. I had never been fully invested in relationships. I would always have one shoe on my foot, ready to move on. This thrill, though, was something new again. The last few hours had left me invigorated, feeling more like what might pass for normal. Allowing the transformation, hunting…playing, it had all helped to reorganize my mind.

When I looked over my shoulder, she stood in human form, enveloped in leafy shadows. I caught a glimpse of her brown, supple flesh as she disappeared into the brush. I knew that, if she wanted to, she could track me to the apartment I kept in Dorchester. That gave me pause, but I recklessly tossed the thought aside and allowed the possible misjudgment to lie unresolved.

Leisurely, I headed up to my third-floor apartment, not at all interested in cleaning up the mess I'd left. A scent, potent to me, hung in the stairwell and I knew it wafted from my apartment. The sparse one-bedroom has only a few items of furniture in it and hordes of missing-person bulletins in short piles around the rooms. The most common among the bulletins come in the mail, addressed to "current resident," every few days, with a cheap advertisement on the reverse side. They always started the same way: "Have You Seen Me?"

All the furniture I possessed in Boston was in the living room. Two couches, a green wooden chair, and a cheap card table sagging under the weight of an ancient steel office lamp and a wired telephone.

The wooden chair stank of everything but blood. It was an acute reminder of nearly losing myself before Roberts had called, clear evidence of the brink I'd been teetering on. I owed him something of a debt for his timeliness.

I had forgotten who I was, sitting in that chair, staring blankly at the window, hands clutching the sides of the seat in stark fear. I couldn't feel my fingers at the time, but I could now see the marks my nails had made digging into the old pine. My memories and feelings had been sliding away from me with the same uncontrollable urge that had caused my bladder to release and given me a sweat-soaked, salty sheen.

What had passed for my life had been slipping away from me, inch by gruesome inch. Some memories I could let go willingly, but others were precious; I had scrabbled at those memories with the impatience of a drowning victim. The entire time, the voice nagged, that inner voice whose raspy whisper urged immoral, unbound freedom: *Let go and live. Let me live.*

Before I settled down to sporadic sleep, I threw the chair out, collected a mop and bucket from the superintendent's closet, and washed the floor. Since the bedroom proper was occupied with a growing mass of missing-persons media, I bunked on the couch closest to the window in the small living room. My thoughts raced ten different directions between short naps.

Just before dawn, Ana crept in through the window I'd left open for such an occasion. She squeezed her way between sash and sill, as inhuman as I yet so very different. I'm sure she knew I was awake, but she tiptoed about anyway, grabbing a blanket from the other couch, farther from the window and the inexorably rising sun. After a few minutes of this, I spoke first.

"Good morning, Little Crow."

She paused, and I heard the smile in her voice when she said softly, "Morning, Da."

"What has the princess of the underworld been up to this evening?"

"I could ask the same of you," she said dryly.

"I'm no princess."

As usual, when we met each other like this, she was as clean as a spring wind. Her scents gave no hints as to where she might have been, other than to an herbal bath. Unless she explicitly told me, I wouldn't know if she'd bled someone to death or simply had tea with a friend. I hoped the former, because I'd taught my little girl who amongst teeming humanity needed culling.

Judging by her tone, she had some idea that I'd been around someone else, but how would she know exactly who that was? It then occurred to me that she already had some relationship with Majispin and his club.

Without warning she lobbed a conversational grenade in the guise of a personal question. "How's your…memory?" It was how she operated; I didn't begrudge her.

At least she hadn't referred to it as my "condition" this time. She was smart, knowing that it would just make me angry. I must've thought too long, because she spoke again.

"Da? I asked—"

"I heard you; I remember the question." It came out a little harsh, not as I intended. I followed up quickly. "I'm fine, no worse than usual. I think."

She puttered about a bit and asked, "What are you going to do?"

"What I always have, Little Crow—keep walking."

A soft, amused snort was her only response from the gloom. She was the strongest reason I continued to meander through this life, hoping to stumble on the cause of the memory loss and possibly fix it. As long as she existed, I would. I'd promised.

I took a stab in the dark to change the subject. "Do you know Maria?"

"And her little pack."

As I awoke fully, she became more sluggish. "What can you tell me about Majispin?"

"Right now," she said very sincerely, "I'll tell you a bit about Maria. And Mark and Barros. Seth, too, I guess. Do you want to know about him, too?"

I sighed. "Yes, *all* of them—what's that supposed to—all right, okay, what about them?"

"Right. Well, you need to be cautious with that girl, Dad."

I mulled this over for a moment. Ana wasn't prone to light warnings, especially with me. I wasn't sure what she meant exactly, so I prodded.

"She doesn't exactly fit the description of 'girl' any more than you do anymore."

"That's not what I meant; you're not…entirely accessible and she's unavailable, she's—"

"Taken?" I finished.

"Well, something like that," her voice slurred with the haze of sleep dripping off of her last words.

Was Maria with Mark, or just a member of the pack? Ana might not know, but she always seemed to have some insight on information that I never considered.

"Wait a minute; what do you mean, I'm not 'accessible'?"

Reflected sunlight was starting to seep into the room, mixing with the dust in the air. Motes danced as morning filled the apartment. In the dim light, Ana curled up on the couch. She'd twisted herself into a heap on the cushions, her eyes closed, but she wasn't asleep yet. She was old enough and had enough power running through her veins to stay awake after sunrise, but a few consecutive days of that behavior would eventually put her out cold.

"You don't need my help to answer that question, Da."

I changed the subject, hoping to get more concrete information out of her. "Thank you for what you did yesterday. Lucky you showed up."

A smile passed her lips and she giggled once, softly, in the back of her throat. "You have no idea. Majispin can be dangerous when he wants to be. He could've killed you, I think. Or not, I guess—I can't be sure with you."

"Tell me about him, Ana; I need to know something about him."

She sighed and offered a deal. "I'll tell you about him if you tell me about your family."

Ana knew that my parents were a precious memory for me. This was her way of helping me to retain the memory. So, of course, I agreed. The only love I still knew was curled up on the couch opposite me; how could I have not agreed?

"I've known Alivara since I first passed through Boston seven years ago. One of his interests is the bloodlines of vampires and shapeshifters. Where they come from—or more precisely, where their *power* comes from. He can practically smell it on us—or the potential—and has been tolerant and interested in me ever since. Not romantic at all"—she yawned—"not really physical in any way. Just…interested. He's odd, in a scientific, nerdy way, but loyal to the safe-house coalition."

It figured that he'd be here in Boston. I'd probably meet more scholarly types soon enough, offshoots of the centuries-old education system here.

I didn't get the impression she was going to say any more on that subject, so I added, "Mark and his little pack can't really hurt me. I'm not worried about them."

"I know, Da."

The way she said it gave me the impression that she thought I was being stubborn. I was, but that wasn't the most important subject on the table right now. I had no idea how long I could keep the storm of insanity at bay. Despite the last few incidents, I counted myself lucky, and I had no options other than to forge ahead. The case at hand was intriguing enough to help, fortunately. The memory problems were constant, but the trouble I'd been in before today had been far too much. I had no interest in spending any amount of time as a schizophrenic amnesiac. I'd spent enough time fooling around.

Keeping my promise, I told my daughter about my family, keeping the words and cadence exactly as I'd honed them when she was much younger, mimicking the fables of the time:

"My father's back had been carved with the hard experience of slavery and a life on the run, for months, into the northwest wilderness trails that led to Canada. It was a hard-won freedom. He was tall, with shoulders that cut across the vertical plane of his body like a cross of oak; skin the color of the coal he mined; close-cropped hair, tight curls hugging his oval head; a broad flat nose atop which balanced deep-set, almond-shaped eyes; corded muscle spanning the length of arms that ended in hands that could crush a brick. My father feared no man.

"My mother's forehead had been broad and punctuated only by delicately curved eyes; thick, silken black hair indicative of her lineage with the Kainai of Saskatchewan; a stout torso which rightly reflected the raw strength she could bring to bear when chopping wood or handling horses; small, roughly hewn hands, calloused across palms where many a rope had been woven or leather cured; round, undefined thighs and soft knees that belied the speed with which she could run; all wrapped in sun-kissed skin and a warm smile."

I recalled my sisters up to the day they'd married back into the tribe. The tribe my mother had never really left, despite marrying my father. Memories: the small home built of wood that my parents had chopped out of the surrounding wilderness for themselves, the rifle with which my father taught me to shoot during one long summer, and the gift of a hunting knife whose sheath my mother had fashioned with her own hands. I'd broken that blade off in a white man who'd shot at me and missed. Local law had been clear in my case, the error resting solidly in the dead man's poor judgment and not mine.

The fragments of my life were spread across my mind as a tattered old blanket full of holes, frayed along the edges and pulled tight at the corners. New tears were threatening to open up every day.

The vague notion that someone had left the room tickled my senses, and I knew that Ana's consciousness had gone wherever vamps go at sunrise. Neither of our species dreamed—that we can recall. She'd be still until the sun had set. For me, now that the sun was up, it was time to do additional investigation at the P.O. projects. It'd been a little over twenty-four hours since the start of this mess.

Before leaving, I tacked a blanket over the window, ensuring that sunlight came nowhere near my little girl. Showered and changed, I called a cab and waited out front. I was determined to make a conscious effort not to rush. Rushing discovery, even with a tight deadline, is a good way to make deadly mistakes. In the meantime, I observed my surroundings, trying to learn, trying to stay whole.

This part of Dorchester has more teenagers—generally more children—per square mile than any other part of the city. With the overcrowding and addition of automobiles, weekday mornings could be a nightmare of humanity. As I sat on the stoop, dozens of kids passed in both directions on the busy street. School buses and other forms of transportation came and went, leaving horrific plumes of exhaust. All the kids looked like African-Americans, but came from a diverse ethnic diaspora—Cape Verdean, Haitian, Jamaican, Puerto Rican, Dominican, and some true continental Africans. The list of dark peoples that had managed to cram themselves into a few neighborhoods of the largest part of Boston went on and on.

The tiny crowds bent around my little spot on the stoop. These kids hadn't developed a real sense of danger yet. Sometimes that made my job easier—a fragile adult might become hysterical around me, but a resilient child was much easier to manage, if I found them alive. Whatever horrible thing plucked at my memory, it allowed most of the worst to remain. It was how I managed to remember so many of the dead or damaged kids. The dead ones were better off, I knew. Their suffering began and ended. The ones that lived—most of the ones I remained in contact with—were irreparably damaged. Still, they were stronger than they knew. Some, like my Lieutenant Brown, grew up to help others, but too many ran headlong into a second chance at a horrifying death.

Observing all these children, my thoughts returned to the unusual murder. Rhonda's death might have been one of many, the first of many, or the last. It was definitely not an aberration or an individual event, in either case. I hoped a trip back to the P.O. projects would sort it out. Unusually optimistic of me. She'd been drained of blood, and a symbol of power had been drawn on the wall using her waste. A symbol normally used in multiples to cast magic across areas much larger than P.O. So, the questions remained— Why these projects? Why a child? That last question was easy enough. Almost everything about children was enticing or useful—usually both—to predators, human and otherwise. The blood, though—why take it? I could only hypothesize that it would be used elsewhere— maybe to bind a spell. I didn't know enough about magic to come up with a solid possibility. All I knew was that the blood of children was especially attractive and powerful. I reckoned I would have to ask Majispin sooner rather than later.

Ana herself had been turned and her parents slaughtered when she was only a few months old. The vampire that'd done it was the freakish offspring of the vampire I politely referred to as her grandfather. I'd killed the monster that bit her and raised Ana myself. She'd stopped maturing at roughly sixteen. At the time of her…birth, I'd been incapable of killing her when I saw that she'd turned rather than died. I hadn't always been that kind with children.

The blond boy's face flashed in the corner of my eye. I swore that I'd just seen him, but there was nothing there. I was certain he'd appear again. He'd died by my hand for all the wrong reasons at a time when men easily committed crimes based solely on the color of skin. I had been no different.

Ana was just a baby when I met her and hadn't the opportunity to chart her own course. She'd barely had time to be human before any possibility of innocence was stripped from her. Her creation had been an accident, theoretically impossible, but she'd survived. This girl-woman was an aberrant fact, an anomaly among vampires. I'd never been able to find another like her or any reference to such a being. Yet, inexplicably, she existed. Thrived, even. I suspected that only through her grandsire would any answers be found.

The cab arrived and I slipped into the back. The driver operated with more manic haste than the usual hack. He was probably suffering from having me in his cab, despite the bulletproof glass between us. He was right; I could go through a barrier like that if I had to, but I wouldn't without good cause. I still couldn't deduce what it was in the human condition that determined how an individual reacted to me—genetics, visual cues, psychic aura, pheromones? The driver, I'm sure, was accustomed to having off-color characters in his cab, but I was something different. He masked it well, but I could tell by his scent—and his driving—that he just wanted to move on to the next fare. I had him drop me off on the edge of the property so that I could walk in.

P.O. buzzed with activity, since all the children were on their way to school or just on the way to nowhere without responsible adults in their lives. I didn't see many older kids. I assumed the teens were still in bed, debating whether to get up and take control of their lives. Sleep is a safe haven for the congenitally demotivated.

I cut straight to the heart of the projects and took a look at my copy of the unusual map that I'd been introduced to yesterday. Orienting myself with the drawing, I determined where two additional locations had been indicated with tiny marks reminiscent of the symbol I'd found in the stairwell.

I meandered off toward the closest location. It was late morning and the sun had nearly reached its apex when I saw her.

"Hello, Maria." I walked past her as I spoke. She was still following me, but getting better at it.

She smirked and fell into step next to me. The two of us together must've looked odd and out of place in the projects. Neither of us adhered to the current fashion trends in the area.

"So, tell me, Alex—"

I stopped walking and she took a step further in the direction we were headed. When she looked back curiously, I told her, "Don't shorten my name." I started walking again; she fell back in next to me.

"Okay, Alexander." She drew the second half of my name out slowly in a mocking tone.

I looked at her from the corners of my eyes. She was wearing the same long coat as yesterday, but with jeans and a black knit top. Her belly was covered and her cleavage showed this time. Her hair looked even more shiny and metallic in the sunlight, and the smells coming off of her were just as pleasant as the sights. She simply wasn't intimidated by me, and I couldn't keep my eyes off of her. I checked my reflex to be a bastard and instead gave control back to her.

"What were you going to ask me?"

She chewed her plump lower lip for a second before answering. "How did you get into this?"

"What do you mean?"

"Well, this,"—she waved her hands around—"this situation, this life, I guess. What brought you here?"

I drew an embarrassing blank. I still couldn't remember why I was in Boston or what I'd been doing before I got here. Maybe I needed to keep some kind of diary or journal. Maybe I already did and couldn't remember where it was. Her question was broad, from my perspective, and I wasn't sure how to answer. To buy time, I checked my pockets and found an old Moleskine. Mine, of course. It bore names and other information about some of the kids I'd saved. Or avenged.

I must've brooded for too long, because she sucked her teeth and said, "Forget it."

"No, no. I—it's just—I can't...explain. It's not something I can explain."

Maria smirked and scrunched up her eyes. Then she grimaced and snorted dismissively. "Boy, you need some help."

"You offering?"

"No, I'm following."

"Why are you doing that, anyway? Majispin pay that well?"

She flashed a smile, showing her canines, and said, "Doesn't matter. I can see that you're busy."

We rounded a corner, leaving the more public area in front of the buildings, and I impulsively pressed myself into her. She accepted my abrupt advance, kissing me back and pressing the palms of her hands into my ribcage. I held her muscular arms at the triceps and drank her up with every sense I could: smell, taste, touch—even hearing. I can only assume—or hope— she was doing the same to me.

Her fingers slowly clawed around towards my back as my hands drifted into the hollow between her spine and her buttocks. It was a lovely, smooth spot, and I could feel the tingle of her power against my skin. I played at the bare fuzz of hair there and she metaphysically swelled at my touch. I began to swell in ways more physical. Her fingers curled as she grabbed two fistfuls of my shirt and pushed with a gasp.

"What—what was *that*?" Tension pulled at the outer corners of her eyes, she'd closed up, become wary.

I chose honesty; it was the best I could do under the circumstances. "I don't know."

"You—how old *are* you?" She touched her mouth and licked her lips, drawing a shiver as we both realized that, when we had disengaged, there had been a smudge of blood on our lips. "A little early for blood, don't you think?" She spoke quietly.

Who had nipped first?

SIX

Maria gently pulled away from me, never taking her eyes from mine, and disappeared with a thoughtful look on her face. I'm sure she didn't go very far, but some distance was probably going to do some good. I forged on to the first location alone.

I circled the brick building once before entering, barely displacing Maria from my thoughts with more immediate matters. The building's structure was the same as all the others—four or six stories tall, two broken steel doors at ground level, a single steel staircase ending at the roof access, and glass-brick windows on each flight. There were apartments on either side of the staircase, putting eight on each floor. The roof access was intact but had been broken and recently repaired. No familiar signs—or scents—were apparent. The usual smells, obvious to anybody with a nose on his face, floated in the hallway—dirt, sweat, cigarette smoke, and grease.

The next location was the same.

As I meandered, I didn't see many adults. Since the children's exodus earlier, there didn't seem to be many people wandering about at all. I noticed, odder still, that most of the younger kids I had seen were unescorted. It's a lie that only blond kids from the suburbs disappear or are missed.

In the emotionally tumultuous event of a child's disappearance, the more upscale the area, the higher the alert status. Mothers and fathers or older brothers and sisters escort their children or siblings everywhere. Kids aren't allowed to be out on their own. Here, it seemed to be different—or indifferent. In the poorer parts of cities, there is always a stunning disconnect from whatever is happening in the rest of the country. Come war or recession, very little changes below the poverty line.

Typically, in black neighborhoods, there is a small outcry that involves a few would-be community leaders, residents, and the local media. They all condemn the current administration for ignoring the needs of inner-city residents, then meet with some "concerned" business interests in the area to secure money for... what, exactly? No one ever follows up. The civil rights era produced far superior leaders, but the circumstances had been very different; there had been a clear goal for all ethnic minorities.

Anything that hollowly echoes the civil rights era is *de rigueur*. Then nothing. A child murdered here might get a buzz on the blood-hungry news for a night or two, but there is no closure to the story, no change made. It is sad and, like other unsavory thoughts and memories, tends to stick in my head, if not my craw. Luck, for Rhonda, would come as a media blitz. Her murder *was* grisly enough.

As if in response to my bitter thoughts, the sounds of bolts and latches being opened came to me from four doors down the hallway, nearest the dull window. In the weak yellow lighting, the figure would normally have appeared as merely a silhouette, but to my eyes he was clear as a glass of water.

In his late thirties to early forties, he wore the current fashion trends of the area—oversized jeans hitched above his thighs, dark hooded sweatshirt, large loose-laced sneakers, and a baggy leather jacket emblazoned with yet another fashion designer sucking at the neck of hip-hop trends. To set the entire outfit off, he wore what looked to be a new and stiff baseball cap, brim flat as a plate, pulled down below his ears.

"Hey-yo," he immediately called out, "who you?" Blocky diamonds glinted at his earlobes.

I didn't respond. Keeping my eyes on him for a second or two more, I turned and headed for the stairwell.

"Hey, bitch, I'm talkin' to you!" He began to bluster down the hallway, doing his best impression of a hyper-aggressive teenager.

I was on the second landing when I heard the soft *thunks* of his sneakers on the stairs. In a moment of confusion, I couldn't recall what I'd just been doing on the floor before. A man rushed down the stairs behind me, swearing to himself. Out of some vague sense of courtesy, I stepped onto the next floor to let him pass, but he collided with my back, pushing me forward into the hallway.

With one hand bunched up at the back of my collar, I felt him press the cold barrel of a weapon into my right ear as he growled at the back of my head, "Said I was talkin' to you, bitch-nigga. What the fuck you doin' in my block?"

I didn't think about it; I simply reacted. With my right hand I grabbed the center of the gun, wrapping my fingers around the slide and his fingers, pulling it away, and simultaneously snapped my head back into his face. We stumbled backwards for a moment as I pitched my weight into him. He kept moving as I spun to my right, still holding the weapon, cracking his trigger finger and keeping the barrel pointed away from me. My fist smashed into his cheek just as he gasped in pain at his broken finger.

As I twisted his wrist, he sank to one knee, and I pointed the weapon at his head, keeping his finger in the trigger guard. One pull and he'd be dead, head spattered on the greasy wall behind him. He screamed at a pitch I'm certain his vocal cords weren't used to producing.

"Fuck you, mothafuckah, I'm Nine-Six! Yo' ass be dead tomorrow! Go 'head, pull that trigger! Fuck you, bitch!"

I looked down at the anger- and fear-filled sound of a man's voice, a little taken aback that I had an adult male under my control, reacting to me. I sorted my recent memory and found a patchwork experience, gaps in the timeline leading up to this moment. The punk locked in my hands continued to yell threats. What the hell had happened to bring me here to this? I drove my knee into the side of his head, bouncing his temple off the concrete wall, and he crumpled unconscious at my feet. Pocketing the magazine and ejecting a round from the chamber, I disassembled the gun and dropped the firing pin assembly into my pocket, letting all the other pieces clatter to the floor.

A whisper forced me to turn, but I was alone in the hallway. A diaphanous chuckle echoed deeply down the stairwell, and an electric flood of fear lit across my back as I rushed down the stairs and outside to the welcoming warmth of sunlight.

A tiny, precious moment had been stolen from me. A piece of time that I could've used to make some other judgment and perhaps avoid the situation. Now my problems were compounded. The unconscious thug upstairs would undoubtedly spread the word when he awoke, and any freedom I'd enjoyed so far, traveling around these projects, would be over. If I wanted more answers, I'd have to do something about him. *Kill him.*

Yes, I could kill him. Everything about that choice felt right. What else was there to do? I got myself back together and hurried back upstairs. My assailant still lay in the same place, awkwardly crumpled against the wall. A small pool of blood had formed on the floor beneath his face. Head wounds like to bleed.

I scooped up the pieces of the pistol and grabbed him by the collar, dragging him up the stairs. His sneakers popped off and tumbled down a few steps, and his pants were now at the thick of his thighs, struggling to fall farther. Down the hall and back to his door; a quick search turned up his keys, and we were inside, still unseen. The apartment was poorly appointed—cheap dining room set, ratty old couch, and one rickety lamp. From the living room, I could see two identical bedrooms, each with a mattress on the floor and tattered covers. I found wire clothes hangers in the bedroom closet, grabbed a sheet, pulled two wooden chairs away from the kitchenette, and went to work on the lamp. This distraction was going to cost me time, but the action brought a kind of clarity to my mind I hadn't felt in years, as if a veil of static had been drawn back. I felt a strong sense of purpose and self-congratulation. A kind of black joy bubbled in my chest, feeling like a foreign substance invading my heart, sticking like fresh-spilled crude.

Stripping the man clean, I used the wire hangers to bind him to the chair and attached the loose wires of the lamp, stripped of their protective rubber, around the tip of his penis. I then cut the rest of the cord in half, stripping the cut ends of rubber as well. After I dropped the pieces of the gun into his lap, I sat down opposite his chair. Then I casually slapped him across the side of his head.

My captive moaned, rolling his head to the side. He winced and opened his eyes and started mumbling, but his incoherent voice began to rise, punctuated by invective as he realized his situation. When his volume got too loud for my taste, I stuffed torn strips of sheets into his mouth, shutting him up, forcing him to breathe entirely through his nose. Then I sat and stared quietly at him, waiting for his muffled curses and struggles to subside. Soon enough, he began to mimic my silence; only his eyes betrayed panic, too wide at the edges. When he started to make noise again, I could make out a screeching "what?" over and over, trying to talk around the cotton stuffed in his mouth. When he tired of this, I answered him.

"I don't know what to do with you."

He stared for a few moments, then tried to speak again. I slowly reached forward and pulled the gag out of his mouth. His leg hammered up and down, flexing at the ankle, nervous energy.

"Whatchu want wif me, man? Wha's…? You a freak, you into some shit? I know people can do all kinds of shit for you, man, all kinds. I got some money in the bottom drawer, bedroom on the left, take that and go—just go and leave me. You want some white? Next t' th' money, take a hit. Just—just leave me alone."

I'd been idly going through the contents of his pockets, discarding bits while he talked. His license gave me his name. "David." From me, the name was a statement, a matter of fact for the record, but David perked up immediately.

"What is it, man? Whatchu want? What do you want from me!?"

I pushed the rags back into his mouth and left the room to find the money and drugs. I pocketed the cash and dumped the drugs into the toilet. When I came back and sat down, I told him what I'd done. I didn't think it would have been possible, but a more acute fear blossomed around his eyes, and he started squeaking from the back of his throat again.

In response, I plugged the cut cord in and held up the two open ends of the wires. When I touched them together, the current jumped from the socket to David's

Errick A. Nunnally

crotch. He jerked in the chair, straining against his coat-hanger bonds, eyes rolled to the back of his head. When I separated the wires—less than one second later—sweat was pouring down from his hairline and he had pissed himself. He was struggling for air when I pulled the gag out again.

"David." He looked up at the mention of his name. "What am I doing here?"

He shook his head weakly and I touched the wires together again. Just for a moment. I wanted him alive and conscious.

"I need to know, David—who am I, what am I doing here? Can you help me?"

His breath came ragged, his chest jumped with every heartbeat and he said, "I don't... I don't know how... I don't..."

Another quick jolt and he started crying, ragged sobs. Finally, we got to the emotional state he should have been in when he first met me.

"I need to know, David. Tell me."

Again, my hands moved to close the circuit. I hesitated. David moaned in the background, protesting any movement from me. What the hell was I doing? *This wasn't—I'm not—I choose to do what I do, it's my decision. David can't help me; no one can.*

Embrace it came unbidden from the depths of my mind.

No! I will not. I thought of the chest again, carefully organizing the contents, every detail of the container from the iron hinges to the roughly hewn planks it is constructed from.

David's stink of fear and hopelessness bathed the room. My skin tingled with the need to coax more out of him. A crumpling sound like cellophane being crushed burned in the background of my hearing as I leaned over David.

"Who am I, David?"

"I don't—I dunno what you—please. Please don' kill me—please."

"Just so we understand each other, David, who am I?"

"No one, man, you're no one, you're a fuckin' ghost." Tears and snot bubbled on his upper lip.

"I am not a *fucking ghost,* David. I am the end of everything you have ever known."

"Yes, yes, okay, please don't, please…" He pleaded, sobbing into his chest.

I put one hand on the back of his head. *That's right, you know how.*

"No, no, please…" The human thing sobbed.

I put my other hand on his jaw. *One quick twist will do it.*

"I don't—I'm sorry, please…" My plaything gibbered, pliant and small in my hands.

Lifting his head, I looked into his eyes, I needed to see them.

"No, no, no…"

I left the apartment, my heart hammering in my chest, David's sobs and the echo of the slammed steel door subsiding with distance.

Outside, my breathing came fast and shallow; a cool spot of sweat formed at the small of my back. I felt something clutching at me and pulling on threads deep inside my head.

I raged at nothing, wishing I could claw at the back of my eyes. "Leave me!" I shouted at the top of my lungs, hard enough to hurt. A slithering, then the sound of sand swirling down a pipe. The static in my ears subsided and I was calmed.

When I opened my eyes, two old women stood staring, clutching each other and their purses. They hurried inside the building.

I needed focus; I had to redouble my efforts and stay in the present. *This is my body to control,* I told myself, not sure if I believed it or not. Swallowing hard, I cleared my mind and walked, keen to get back on track. Keen to forget David and what I'd done to him. I wouldn't forget David, but I could ignore the incident like I had ignored others. Hyperactive ignorance. So many people practice it daily, but I'd been perfecting the art for decades. It wouldn't be long before I could stop pretending that David hadn't happened. I'd believe it soon enough, but I wouldn't forget, and I wouldn't feel remorse. David was a worthless thug, but if he were going to die by my hands, it'd be *me* in control when it happened.

The second location I visited resulted in more of the same. I was hitting dead ends. As I began circumnavigating the entire property P.O. occupied, I rolled over what little information I had in my head one more time, distracting myself, creating distance from my recent…indiscretion—murdered little girl, the major volume of her blood missing, a symbol drawn on the wall in her excrement. The killer had been male but left no traces other than what the victim had managed to scrape under her fingernails. The weapon was a sharp, curved knife of some sort. *A man tied to a chair, wired to an electrical socket.*

Symbols similar to the one near the body had been used to indicate two other points on a stylized map etched in the subbasement. Next to the map was a series of Mayan glyphs that, when translated, gave the date as April 12, 2012. My thoughts dropped off beyond this, so I wrote on a scrap of paper, committing each thought, purposely excluding David. *He doesn't matter,* I tell myself again. *None of them mattered.* Organizing my thoughts like that usually helped to bind the random chaos in my head. I needed another hiding place for the memories of the man I'd just tortured.

Next to "April 12th, 2012" I wrote that it was the day of the new moon. And next to that I wrote

"Significance?" Majispin either couldn't or wouldn't tell me enough regarding the symbols. I knew they were used geographically to enchant large spaces, but the P.O. projects had been ruled out as too small for the spell to work. So a couple of square miles were too small. Think bigger—hundreds of miles, and for what purpose? I wrote these thoughts down and shoved the scrap into my pocket, hunching my shoulders against another guilty act.

The project's property was a massive, ugly scar of brick and concrete that nearly bisected the neighborhood. With its total size, the construction was so large that the people who lived at one end had no experience with those on the other. Their one commonality was the complex interplay of environment and psychology that kept them poor. The change was especially abrupt when I passed in front of the first of the colorful, cookie-cutter townhouses intended to replace the repetitive brick buildings. Everything appeared normal, but moving the people from point A to point B didn't make them any different.

I found a battered pay phone in front of a run-down convenience store on the edge of P.O. and called Detective Roberts. A full day's wandering around the projects and I hadn't learned much more than I'd initially picked up yesterday morning. Night was falling and it would soon be nearly two days since the first murder.

"Detective, it's Alexander."

"Hold on."

There was a shuffling followed by a click and bland music. I could confess what I'd done, tell Roberts everything, let him handle it—try to handle it. I was starting to wonder how many people I could loop into an electrical circuit and terrorize when Roberts's voice came back on the line, devoid of background noise.

"Okay, what do you want to confuse me with this evening?"

Kidnapping, torture, attempted murder.

"If you don't want to know…"

"No, no. Sorry, go 'head."

I asked him if anything had been reported at the locations I scouted. He told me no. I outlined my general thoughts on this. Explaining the map again and the marked locations, I thought it simply made sense that there'd be another killing soon. Murder synced with the lunar cycle, maps of locations, the symbols— ritual. Why else do these things? The locations had to be significant. Roberts was less than enthusiastic but took it seriously.

"Me and Pepperman planned on checking it out. I'll get in touch with Terrell; he can help, too. You've saved us some investigative time; give me the exact locations."

I read off the building numbers to him, and he promised to stake them out after dark. So would I, but I didn't let him know that. The air was cooling quickly. I had some time to get a bite to eat and then come back. Damn it all, I'm always hungry.

After dark and a pair of rotisserie chickens, I staked out a rooftop that had a viewing angle of both buildings. It wasn't perfect, but it would let me see who came in and out, to a degree. I watched Roberts and Pepperman arrive and meet with Terrell. They were arguing, and the heat of their breath showed in the cool, humid air. Roberts headed to the farthest building, Terrell to the other, and Pepperman got back in the car. The white man stood out in these projects like a horse on fire. Terrell and Roberts would have to stake out the positions inside the building. Pepperman fumed and waited closest to the structure that Terrell was in.

I tried to summon patience, but my thoughts kept clicking from one random fact to the next. First, the call from Roberts, then the blur of a trip to Rhonda Lloyd's murder scene. Sequential memories kept popping into my mind without the binding, mundane memories in between. One moment bled into the next. Roberts, Rhonda, P.O., Pepperman, and so on.

My thoughts drifted inevitably to David. Briefly, I considered visiting his apartment and seeing if he'd been found yet, but I couldn't foresee any good outcomes from that. For me or Rhonda Lloyd. He was fortunate to still be alive, and it was fortunate for me that he was unlikely to call the police.

Just as well, since I'd been more disturbed by my loss of control than the man-boy I'd tuned up—*tortured*. A grim smile ticked at the corners of my mouth as I mused that it might be better if I simply remained around the discarded bits of humanity. That way, whenever the urge came, I could—*no*. Too much, let that foolish thought go, as enticing as it may be. For once, I was getting a sense of when the coaxing may start, delicate gibberish that planted deeper and deadlier ideas. I couldn't afford to diminish my behavior: I'd tortured David and nearly murdered him, not "tuned up" or other distancing language. That kind of thinking, I sensed, would tip the scales against my favor, so I tried again to put the whole thing in my warped perspective.

Thinking back across the last couple of days, I couldn't recall going to Majispin's. In my mind I just appeared at the bar, speaking to Benjamin. Then I was suddenly at Franklin Park with Maria. What had I eaten there? Had I killed someone? There was no reason for me to have killed anyone—of that I was certain. Fairly certain. I meditatively focused on the facts of the case, going over them one after the other, trying to cement them in my brain. I strove to remember the mundane bits between each of the facts, but all I found were a hot rush of darkness and the chitter of something gnawing at my mind, the very essence of who I am. My reverie broke when Maria climbed onto the roof. Upwind, in the chilly air, her scents drifted enticingly around me.

I couldn't afford to take my eyes off the buildings, so I didn't look at her when I spoke. "You shouldn't be here."

I could feel the heat of her body near me when she answered in Spanish, "Just checking in. Anything new?"

"That's what I'm trying to find out. Can't do that talking to you." That's just how it was.

She took a deep breath and sighed. "I don't have much of a choice here, Alexander. Besides, I think we need to figure out what happened between us earlier. I've never felt anything like that, and I sure as hell know I didn't want your blood in my mouth at the time."

She was beginning to distract me; I started to wonder what it was that bound her and the others to Majispin enough that she'd feel she had no choices. As well as what it was that had flared up between us.

"Maria, please."

A light crunch of gravel behind us caused Maria to spin. I didn't flinch because I knew exactly who it was. Ana.

"Yeah, Maria, please, tell us what you *did* want in your mouth," she said coarsely, disappointing me.

I prayed to any god who would listen for the pair of them to leave. My attention was being divided. I had the feeling that, if I took my eyes off of the building, something would happen.

"Please *this*, you fuckin' nibblehead."

I got the distinct impression that Maria flipped Ana the bird, which I knew was a bad idea. On the other hand, my little girl's a professional antagonist. Maria was swimming in deep water if she wanted to engage Ana.

"Still Alivara's lapdog, Maria? That's why you're here, isn't it, or is it something else? Mmmm, you're

Mark's lapdog, too. Busy, busy. Following *him* around isn't going to solve any of your problems with Mark."

Behind me, the sharp sound of gravel crunching again. I knew Maria had charged Ana. I spun around to stop her, and my fingers brushed the hem of her coat, but all I was left with was the hope that Maria wouldn't get hurt too badly.

What I saw was a remarkable display of power and restraint. Maria had nearly reached Ana when she bounced backwards as if she'd struck a rubber wall. There was no sound other than Maria's grunt. My daughter hadn't given ground, but Maria tumbled ass over teakettle in the gravel on the roof, an incredulous look on her face.

Telekinesis is a rare and precious trait among vampires; Ana's line was gifted. She touched her hand to her forehead and winced. Rebuffing Maria hadn't been easy, although she wanted it to look that way. The raw telekinesis that Ana could do always took a toll.

I snapped at them both, "Put a cork in it and go away—both of you!"

A new scent caressed the air; Maria picked it up a beat later. Mark. Mark, whose scent was quickly becoming far too familiar. I turned on her.

"Go, keep your boyfriend out of here, and you,"—I spun on Ana—"practice your button-pushing powers somewhere else and some other time."

Maria moved first; she cleared the edge of the building, leaping to the asphalt below. Ana frowned and moved in the opposite direction. The moment they took their leave, I heard a scream fade into a gurgle and three pistol reports. It came from the building Terrell had chosen.

I was at the door and through before I heard Pepperman outside, shouting into his radio. The smell of blood and gunpowder had cut across the stairway. I cleared two flights in an instant and saw Terrell lying back on the stairs, clutching his bloody chest, a male child pinned underneath him and not moving, his gun lying nearby. One of the apartment doors was ajar. Rhonda Lloyd's killer had been here; I could smell him. When I put two fingers to the boy's carotid artery, I could feel a strong pulse. He was still alive; Terrell had managed to save him.

At the top of the stairs, the nude wraith of my long-past evil stood. His right hand was missing, left, presumably, wherever I'd torn it away. His left hand twitched. I winced and begged forgiveness under my breath, begging the boy's father this time. Abruptly, the apparition pointed to its left, at the open door. I didn't have time for any ghosts or insane hallucinations right now. I blinked and looked down at Terrell. Without thinking, I had placed both of my hands over his wound, trying to hold the blood back. This was my fault; if I'd been paying closer attention…

I knelt over him as his eyes started to cloud over; he stared at a space somewhere between me and oblivion. He'd been stabbed in the heart and didn't have a chance in hell of surviving. It was a clean blow, driven straight up under his sternum. He tried to say something. Stuttering, wet sounds came from his mouth as he tried to form words.

Pepperman pounded up the stairs and paused on each flight, making sure the landings were secure, muttering "clear" under his breath each time.

Terrell stammered several times before he managed to squeeze the words out.

"…was crying…muthafuckuh stabbed me…shot 'im…" And then he was gone.

A hairsbreadth away from dashing through the apartment's door, Pepperman shouted at me, "Freeze, goddammit; don't you move, you sunnuvabitch! Lemme see your hands!"

I looked down at my bloody palms and up at the barrel of his weapon, looking past it and into his eyes, trying in vain to project calm for once instead of fear and unease. "Terrell's dead, there's a child pinned underneath him, the boy's alive, make sure—"

"Shut! The fuck! Up! Hands!" He brought the radio to his mouth. "Roberts, I've got Alexander here, there's a lot of blood, it looks like Terrell's bleeding out and there's a kid, no one's moving. Call a bus!"

A garbled reply came over the radio; Roberts was no doubt on his way. The blond boy, obviously invisible to Pepperman, still stood at the top of the stairs, pointing insistently at the open door. The stump of his right arm had begun to drip blood, and a tiny waterfall dribbled over the edge of the top stair, mingling ethereally with Terrell's blood.

I could make out Pepperman's pounding heartbeat between his ragged breaths in the quiet stairwell. He was sweating and quivering with adrenaline.

"Fuck, man, Roberts trusted you!"

I didn't have any more time to waste. Pepperman was blinking rapidly, betraying his nervousness. I watched his eyes and snatched the gun out of his hands between blinks, popped the slide's pin out, and split the weapon neatly in two. A look of ripe fear passed across his face as he completed the blink and realized he'd been disarmed.

I pointed. "The killer ran into this apartment!" Then I was gone, charging through the apartment to follow the trail of the murderer, the irony of my statement to Pepperman not lost on me. He thought I'd killed Terrell, after all.

SEVEN

The apartment had had two occupants, from what I could glean passing through. There was the typical accompaniment of archaic and worn furniture along with the elderly couple. They appeared to have been slain in what were likely their favorite chairs. The scent of the murderer had been clear in the room. He'd been waiting right here. Waiting for the right time to kill a child and perform his ritual. The smell of carbon and hot metal hung in the air; something had been masking the presence of the two corpses. A glance confirmed my suspicion—a small metal plate cradled a pile of grey powder in the center of the floor. The man's scent was pungent. Whatever spell had been wrought had been broken.

I tracked him through the apartment to the third-floor window in the back. It was a long drop for a human but not unheard of. I leapt out and landed easily. The trail picked up again and led to one of the access points for the utility tunnels. The lock on the door was clean and functioning, the man's stink all over the jamb. I twisted the lever on the door until the bolt snapped.

As I plunged through the doorway, my eyes adjusted immediately to the darkness and my ears told me there wasn't anyone nearby. It was wet down there; the walls were moist where a weak current of runoff water sluiced down the center of the shaft. Water—especially filthy water—carries an enormous amount of smells with it, making tracking harder but not impossible.

The trail ended at a square grate in the concrete floor, leading deeper into the sewer. Kneeling, I placed one hand on the grate and listened intently. The uneven splashes of my quarry running through water floated back to me. I lifted the grate and dropped in. The water level was instantly up to my ankles and soaking into my shoes. The murderer's scent was lost in a monstrous stench. I cocked my head and listened again. The splashing footsteps had stopped, but after a few beats, the faint sounds resumed. I waited long enough to be sure of the direction, and moved after him.

As one passage intersected with the others, the water level rose. When it had risen to a point just below my shins, I could hear sobbing. The killer was crying, just as Terrell had tried to tell me, crying in heaving, muffled sobs. A sad rhythm issued, warbling from the back of his throat as if he were afraid to open his mouth and release the sorrow.

We were definitely under the main streets now. Light from the concrete lampposts shone through unevenly spaced grates above. The air was rank, and the slimy water made it difficult for me to move as gracefully as I wanted. I saw him stumbling ahead and quickened my pace. He was still crying and occasionally glancing over his shoulder. I could make out a thick, curved blade in his right hand. Just as I sprang at him, he turned and tried to slash me with the knife. Stepping into the attack, I caught his knife arm with both hands and pulled him off his feet. He was strong, but I was stronger by far. That close, I could smell Terrell's blood on the blade, but it was the clear view of the murderer that gave me pause.

He wore average clothing—jeans and a dirty white T-shirt, no shoes. The shirt had three blackened bullet holes in the chest. No blood. Held at arm's length, he continued to sob in the back of his throat. He was a white male, but beyond that his description defied my experience. Of his visible flesh, his head and arms were completely hairless—even his fingernails were gone. His mouth and eyes were sewn shut. Despite the tight stitching job, tears still streamed down that tortured face, and his sobs leaked between dry, cracked lips. His right ear was missing—the hole sewn shut—and his legs shuddered with his sobs as I held him kneeling in the water.

What had I captured?

I didn't have time to think about it as the water behind me exploded, and I was knocked sideways by the subsequent impact. I dropped the killer and turned to meet my new and obviously more powerful assailant. It was a vampire. He'd been hiding under the shallow water, likely compressing his pliable body, a trick I'd never seen before and obviously hadn't anticipated. I didn't get but a moment to make him out when he snarled and pounced anew. I was prepared to meet him when a sharp pain shot through my leg. Another had come from beneath the water. They had moved through the sewer like reptiles, flattened to the bottom, avoiding detection. There was no telling how many more might be nearby.

Venom, pumped through the fangs of a vampire, can paralyze, anesthetize, or cause hallucinations in prey. Depending on the amount, and the skill of the vamp delivering the venom, it can kill by asphyxiation or blood loss, as the bites have a nasty tendency to stay open. In short, large doses could kill me. I smacked the second vampire off my leg as the first slammed into me again. I managed to turn and not fall, rolling with the blow, guiding the flying vamp over my left side. I had a clear view of the two when a third vampire rose up and sank its fangs into my shoulder. I went completely berserk. I didn't have much time before the bites would slow me down enough for them to kill me using purely conventional means.

The fight was lacking in any finesse or real skill. I began to shapeshift in mid-swing when the venom hit me full-on. I gasped with the impact as my lungs spasmed, and I struggled to keep taking in air. I'd hoped to fight them off in my more dangerous form, but the vampire's drug held back the full transformation. So far, I'd managed to avoid getting bitten a third time, but the clawing and punching wore me down faster. Simply hitting a vampire isn't always the best option. They're pliable, obviously, and able to squeeze through tight openings like mice.

That's probably what has driven some of the myths about them, I thought, absurdly, as the poison ran its full course in earnest.

I threw every bit of discipline I had into focusing on guiding the action instead of reacting to it. One of my assailants feinted and another dove in. I ignored the feint and grabbed the attacker. Instead of punching him, I spun him around. With my hands planted firmly around his throat, under his jaw, I put my foot into his back and pulled his head off in a gush of viscous fluids. The head made a decent projectile as I threw it at the nearest vampire. The headless body immediately began to dissolve into a pungent, floating black puddle of ichor. The other charged me and took me off my feet. I plunged my clawed hand into his chest and held the fanged head back with the other. The last vampire was closing in as my immediate opponent dug his nails into my face and neck.

Out of the corner of my eye, I saw a figure sweep the third vampire away from me. I kept pushing my hand further into the monster on top of me until I reached its spine. Vampires have no real heart to speak of; they are largely an animated nervous system. Other than burning, removing the head is the best way to kill them. A stake through the heart, regardless what it was made of, would be laughable. I pulled as hard as I could, and his head began to sink into his body. I savored the incredulous look in his eyes as his spine snapped and the bastard dissolved on top of me.

The damage to my face and neck combined with the venom had been too much; I couldn't feel my limbs. Succumbing to the numbness, I began to sink into unconsciousness. I'd be trapped here, perpetually drowning if my head went below the water, comatose until the sewer drained or someone moved my body long enough for me to recover. I heard footsteps splashing away down the tunnel. Struggling to move to higher ground as I drifted off, I saw my savior for the first time through a purple haze of failing consciousness.

Maria was still following me.

EIGHT

I don't dream. Not that I can recall, anyway. One minute I'm asleep or, more precisely I think, dormant, and the next I'm fully awake. Whatever internal clock I have tells me the time. It is, more often than not, a light sleep, easily disturbed. Under conditions where healing was necessary, it was deep. Deep like the harrowing month I'd been drowned in a raging river, stirring only to drown again until I'd been washed into a shallow eddy where I could recover. The sleep I'd fallen into this time was far more comfortable. I was grateful that I didn't have to wake up face-down in a sewer.

When I opened my eyes, I was looking at a century-old ceiling covered in layers of thick paint that made the detailing look like a softened butter sculpture.

It was decidedly warm, and I found that I was covered with an intricately knit, off-white coverlet with little baubles on the edges. A cat would have loved it. I lay on an overstuffed couch with a high back and a floral pattern. A plethora of pinks, greens, and black. And I was naked. My shoes sat nearby on the floor, dry and filthy, but my pants, shirt, and jacket were out of sight. Judging by the smell of soap and the feeling of my dry skin, I had been cleaned up.

I turned on my side to see the space. Maria sat across the room, watching me. She wore a fluffy bathrobe with no hint of clothing beneath. A single line of water trailed from her wet hair between her breasts. The smells of shampoo, conditioner, and female scents floated in the air. A light-purple bruise had blossomed on her cheek, and two shallow scratches trailed from her neck into the robe as well. Her toes, I admiringly noted, were clean and unadorned. Her brows were knit tight when she reverently said, "Damn, you heal fast."

I touched my hands to my face, where the vampire had sunk its nails in deep. Only stiff, shallow depressions under my fingers indicated that the wounds had ever been there. I was incredibly hungry and irritated as a result. The loss of energy from the fight and subsequent healing had shut me down like a toy whose batteries had been yanked. I'd slept through the remainder of the night. It was late morning now, I could tell. Time to get moving again.

"Mmm, at a steep cost. Where are we?"

Maria sat back and crossed her legs with her hands folded in her lap, an enticing length of caramel-colored thigh disappearing into the darkness under her robe. I regretted my words immediately. She grimaced and said, "That's it? No 'thanks for saving my ass, Maria'? 'If you hadn't been there, I'd've been toast, Maria'?"

I sat up and shook my head slowly. She was right. Without a hint of sarcasm or contempt, I looked into her eyes and thanked her.

She brightened considerably. (And that thigh slid back out.) "Now, that's more like it. You hungry?"

I couldn't remember the last time I'd had to sleep for more than four hours. "Where are we; what happened?"

She rolled her eyes and sucked her teeth. "My apartment. I chased off the last vampire; I couldn't take you to Majispin's, and we were closer to my place, anyway."

"Why not Majispin's?" I asked more out of curiosity than any desire to have awoken there.

"He's…" She paused, trying to find the right words. "…a real curious scientist, you know? He's real interested in you and your girlfriend."

In the very short time I'd known Majispin, here was the second warning I'd received about his curious nature. Still, I was confused—what girlfriend? Then it hit me. Ana.

"She's not my girlfriend. Where are my clothes?"

"In the dryer; I washed 'em. What was going on down there? Did you find out who done it?"

"I'll tell you if you give me my clothes."

She sneered. "Too proud to get 'em yourself? The dryer's in the kitchen."

I didn't think she intended to embarrass me, and I was fairly certain she wasn't trying to arouse me— which was unfortunate, because I was firmly interested, to put it mildly. I got up to head for the kitchen with the blanket wrapped around my middle, bunched in front of my crotch and trailing behind me. She snorted.

The narrow apartment was a departure from what I knew of Maria. I got the distinct impression that she either didn't spend much time here, or her public persona was very different from her private one.

Everything that had been in my pockets was piled on top of the dryer. My old Moleskine was still cinched shut and damp. I didn't think Maria had looked at it. Assorted scraps of paper had been flattened and air-dried. Everything else appeared unmolested. I dressed in front of the dryer, keeping the solid evidence of my arousal hidden, and stuffed everything back into my pockets.

I could hear her coming down the hallway, bare feet slapping lightly on the hardwood floors. This was an apartment in one of the older buildings of Boston. It meant we were in an aged part of town, probably a brownstone of the South End, very similar to a triple-decker in either Roxbury or Jamaica Plain. The awkward size of the apartment had the distinct features of a century-old brownstone that had been desecrated, carved into six or more smaller apartments.

I mused for a moment on how clear my memory seemed at the moment. What had tipped the scales back to my favor? Perhaps my near-death experience had informed some part of me that we were better off living in a state of contention than dead.

"Thanks for washing my clothes. And my ass. Did you see the man I'd chased into the sewers?"

She leaned against the counter and watched me for a moment, then said, "No, just a couple of vampires. And you're welcome; ass-washing is one of my specialties. I clean ass well."

I laughed, trying to remember the last time someone had caught me with humor like that. "There were three vampires and one…" I was at a loss to describe the creature I'd captured for a moment. "…I need to talk to Majispin." My stomach growled in disagreement.

Maria chuckled and opened the refrigerator to pull out a baked ham, bone-in. She used a huge carving knife to slice off comically thick chunks. She worked with her back to me, and her tone was serious when she spoke.

"Alexander, listen: Mark was…upset that your scent was on me like it was yesterday. He's, um, nervous, I think, that you're going to supplant him as the 'big dog' in our pack. He might be…" She waved the knife, searching for the word. "…plotting to get rid of you."

I pushed through the distraction of her shapely bottom jiggling enticingly as she cut the meat. "Isn't it your responsibility to comply with the pack leader's decisions? Especially if you're bonded to him?" Purposely avoiding comment on the small size of the pack, I added, "That bruise doesn't look like the kind of wound these vamps would have left."

She took a deep breath and sighed while she collected the meat she'd sliced. A couple of pieces of crusty bread and spicy mustard finished two simple sandwiches. She handed them to me and said, "Yeah, I suppose not."

It didn't necessarily bother me that Mark might have hit her. What bugged me was that Maria let him get away with it. As a full member of a pack, if Maria disobeyed his directives, within reason, any member understood they might get smacked around to keep everything in line. That was the deal—follow or be dealt with. It was up to the pack leader to determine how that was interpreted. On the other hand, those rules were also open to interpretation by the 'shifter being dealt with, as well. As Mark's subordinate, girlfriend, or even bonded partner, she was choosing to accept the abuse. She certainly could defend herself—all shapeshifters are tough, regardless. Mark likely had the edge in sheer power, but I doubted he was as skilled as Maria, so why take it?

I'd run with two packs in my second life. I could only recall one clearly, but the experience had been enough. As far as I was concerned, all pack politics were bullshit, made-up rules that I didn't cotton to, so to hell with the whole thing. As insane and chaotic as our lives became as we aged, there was no possible way for any kind of real traditions to be created.

Her voice, serious and even, broke my reverie. "He hasn't made a decision yet, and I don't know where Majispin stands on this. You just being here could be a problem, Alexander. I don't see how this is avoidable if you continue to stick around."

"I have a job I choose to do; no one controls me. I don't play these pack games and I don't have to, Maria." We were standing closer than either of us should have been comfortable with. "Neither do you, really. It's ultimately your choice. I think you know that."

My hand hesitated halfway, then touched her arm. My other hand slid around her waist and I pulled her in close to kiss her gently on the lips like a normal human lover, as if the real me weren't there. Right then, I was just a man crossing the flirting line with a spoken-for woman, and I was observing myself kissing her, engaging in behavior older than either of us, testing boundaries and allegiances.

She leaned back against the counter and pulled me closer. Her hands wandered from my belly down to my waist and undid the top button of my jeans. I cupped her buttocks and pulled her tighter, picking her up off the floor. Her ass slid onto the counter, and she wrapped her legs around me. I was desperately aware that the bathrobe was no longer masking her heat.

Our kiss broke, but our faces remained touching. She nibbled around the side of my face and licked up the side of my neck. A moan of desire escaped my lips and, in that moment, I had never wanted another woman more. She undid the next button on my jeans and froze.

My power surged to the forefront and raked through her body to seize her aura. She gasped as our energy twisted together and began to drown us. Her eyes were desperate, but she clung to me even harder than before, grinding her hips in an unmistakably passionate and vigorous pulsing. It was right and wrong all over.

I felt like a cold dish going into a hot oven—one of us was going to break. Desperately, I mentally lunged at the current, imagining it as a tangible thing and drawing it back. The heat pulled away like a big dog on a leash. I yanked hard, being careful not to pull Maria off the counter, and instead, I lowered her feet to the floor. We panted and sweated in rhythm. With a final effort, I pulled the last vestiges of my power from her as a veil from a cage, allowing her to be herself again.

Coming back from the foolish moment was more difficult than I could have ever imagined. I shook my head at her as she raised her hands to cup my face.

I needed to get out of there; we needed to be in public, doing something other than testing each other's boundaries.

Scooping the sandwich off the counter, I kissed it before taking a huge bite. As I walked down the hall chewing on a mouthful of ham, I told her, "Do what you think is right, Maria; I don't judge. Mark and his crew aren't a concern of mine."

"So, I'm not a concern of yours?"

It was a careless choice of words on my part, but I needed to escape what was happening between us—whatever might have been happening between us. I opened the door but stopped before exiting and turned. Maria had one hand on the loop holding her robe closed and trailed the other across her collar. I stared directly into her eyes as she nervously tugged on the belt, the barest of movements. Any more and the robe wouldn't cover any of the devilish parts. I took a deep breath and backed out of the apartment before anything more happened. I couldn't let my desires supersede my current goals, and I certainly couldn't trust my power when I was alone with her.

I wasn't sure if Maria were genuinely interested and simply wanted a way out of her connection with Mark and company, or if she were being compelled by something within me, beyond my control. Either way, my behavior with her—at the park, in the projects, and here—had been—was—impetuous. *And it felt good*, I added mentally. *Take what you want*, echoed somewhere inside, *take what you need, do what you want. Do it.*

Back down the hall, I could feel the light prickle of Maria's aura on my back. I stopped at the stairs and clenched my teeth, trying to push the feeling away. I hadn't been with a woman in… I couldn't remember.

Intimate moments had been few and far between for me—especially women that would look me in the eye and turn my bullshit back at me. I tried to relax but only succeeded in reaching out to Maria with my own energy. She was pressed against her closed door, listening the same way I was. We were in sync—our breathing, heart rates, and desires, ebbing and flowing together.

A jolt of weary sadness swam through my stomach, and I hurried downstairs, breaking the connection with a snap. I certainly wasn't falling in love, but I had definitely fallen into a lust of some sort. The strange new behavior of my personal energy was only making matters worse. Or was it the cause of *my* behavior? I began to wonder how much I could even trust myself anymore.

Outside, I noted that I was indeed in the South End, closest to Roxbury, near Washington Street. I found a pay phone in front of a corner store—pay-to-talk land lines were scarce with the rise of the mobile phone, and only the poorest of shops still had them outside.

The staccato sounds of Latin percussion drifted on the morning air. The day was warming up nicely, which meant it would probably rain soon enough. Boston didn't usually go long in the spring without rain. Or snow. I wanted to call Detectives Roberts and Pepperman, but considering my little incident with Pepperman, Terrell's murder, the confirmed involvement of vampires, the murderer himself—they'd have more questions than I could safely answer. This case had too quickly become stickier than I'd thought.

Abruptly, I couldn't remember what I wanted to say to Detective Roberts, anyway. Instead, I called Majispin. If anyone currently involved might know what I'd chased into the sewers, it'd be him.

The phone rang six times before a male voice answered.

"Yeah, The Magus."

"Mark, I need to speak with Majispin." I could virtually hear him stiffen over the phone.

"Whatever; come down."

"I don't need to come down there for this; just let me talk to him."

"That's not how it works, man; *come down*." With a hard *snap*, the connection broke.

I had no idea why it couldn't work over the phone, but I wasn't going to let Mark get to me. I had to go to the club, and I knew nothing would happen there if I didn't provoke it. Technically. My best bet would be to keep to myself during this visit. I tried in vain to remember how I'd last stumbled into the conical room, in order to avoid repeating the error. All I could recall were the fairy and my prey.

As I headed out to the main street and started walking, Maria appeared at my side. She'd most likely heard, at the least, my side of the conversation. She was definitely getting better at tailing me, since she'd managed to stay upwind and out of sight this time.

"Heading to Majispin's?"

I looked at her. She made no attempt to cover up her injuries. *I like that, too*, I thought.

She held up a set of keys and pushed the button on the small black remote. A nearby Acura NSX beeped and flashed once. Exasperated that I could remember the make and model of this particular car—at this particular moment—I mentally ran down the other models, wondering what it was that determined what I could and could not remember. Useless information always seemed to be at hand. I was more concerned with cherished memories and critical moments that got snatched away. Like back in the projects. Creating problems like David. I gritted my teeth, wondering if anyone had released him yet. At least he was alive when I left him. Hooray for small gifts. I'd send him a card when I had a chance.

Errick A. Nunnally

She smiled and said, "You didn't think I carried you all the way here, did you?"

I shrugged, knowing that she was strong enough to pick me up and carry me if she wanted to. We made our way over to the sportster. She hopped in easily, but I had to fold myself into the passenger seat. I had no idea how she'd jammed me in here last night.

"It was a bitch cleaning that nasty water out of my car, man; you owe me big-time."

I wasn't sure how serious she was, but I could see that it would be a pain to have to clean the leather. I didn't detect much more than a trace of the sewer on the red interior. Red leather. There seemed to be a color scheme that came with Maria. As we pulled out, I noticed that she had on red shoes, red lipstick and a small ruby in her nose. All of her other clothing was black. It occurred to me that she might not have slept at all last night. That would have hampered her healing time and would explain why her wounds, though closed, still looked pink and fresh. If she were trying to get on my good side, it was working. *Staying* on my good side was a whole other matter. I still hadn't decided for myself if a relationship with Maria was as dangerous a proposition as Ana had suggested.

My daughter could be infuriating at times, but I was proud of her independence. Besides, she listened to me when she needed to. Sometimes, she was right—too often, actually.

After her initial comment, Maria drove us to the club in relative silence. I winced when she tuned the radio to a local top-forty station. I think she was enjoying my sour reaction to the noise coming out of the dashboard. How did some of us manage to stay so young in mind and manner? How old *was* Maria, anyway? I had no real measure to hold her to, just a feeling. Like Ana, she could be holding on to her youthfulness—though Maria had obviously been turned much older than Ana.

I simply couldn't tell definitively without asking, but unlike Ana, she wasn't manifesting any power that I could detect, just the usual supernatural buzz here and there. I tried to discount the pull when I relaxed around her.

Navigating to the edge of Chinatown like a lifelong Boston driver, Maria found parking in reserved spaces around the back of the building just as the sunny sky released a misty spray.

Inside, the club was bustling, but not packed. These places always had a near-constant buzz of activity around the clock. It was good to know that something in my experience had remained the same.

Late morning meant nothing to the patrons of the establishment. The first person we saw was Mark. The two men with him had to be Seth and Barros—I recognized them from my fight with Mark. They'd entered behind Majispin then. Seth was tall, slim, and lithe, but it'd be a mistake to assume he was weak. He wore a formfitting grey mock-turtleneck with a black suit jacket and pants. There was cunning in his sharp, black eyes, and a cool demeanor on his fair skin. Not a dark brown hair on his head was out of place, and his features were almost unnaturally straight. Barros was just the opposite—dark and hulking. He appeared to be Mexican by his dusky skin, broad lips, and thick eyebrows. If he weren't, then he was seriously trying to be. He wore a black bandanna down to his brow and time-honored leather and denim from neck to ankle. Black, curly hair spilled out of the back of the head wrap and onto his shoulders. If his image said anything, it was *cholo*.

Both men held their hands loosely at their sides. I took it as an indication that they were there to back up Mark and not necessarily to start trouble. My eyes lingered on Seth for a moment longer than they should. He was relaxed, but his gaze carried more heat than I'd initially thought. He was watching me as if I'd stolen something from him.

The pheromones washing out in waves from Mark, on the other hand, were pure hate. He hadn't yet developed the talent of masking his emotions so as not to betray them chemically, or he just didn't give a shit. I assumed the latter. All of them seemed relatively young, but again there was no way for me to confirm my hunches other than to ask.

If Maria was right and they were plotting to eliminate me if I stuck around, the three of them didn't *seem* unified. There were no indications that Seth and Barros shared Mark's anxiety or were doing much more than what he told them to do. Something still nagged at me about Seth, something just out of my perception. Regardless, he remained forcibly relaxed but vigilant. Maria slowly took her place next to Mark. He didn't look at her as he growled a question in her direction.

"I called you. Were you home?"

She almost waited too long to answer, but piped up before Mark's dander got up any further. "Yes."

He glanced at her. "We'll *talk* later." Turning his attention back to me, Mark started in. "As for you, I don't think you should get too comfortable around here."

I already knew I could take Mark. The three of them together would be another matter entirely, but Seth and Barros weren't assuming any kind of a threatening posture. How tight was this little pack?

I didn't even remotely want to get into that question now and simply asked, "Where's Majispin?"

"Don't worry about that; you'll see him when you see him. Who do you think you are anyway, man? You waltz in one day, and the next you're playing in someone else's sandbox."

Seth gave a barely perceptible snort, and Barros looked sideways at him with one eyebrow cocked. I still couldn't discern what it was, but Seth seemed to be looking at me with an eye to the personal. The main problem, however, was still standing right in front of me. Mark was starting to get on my nerves. He was the leader of this pack, but it seemed to be more of a business arrangement than anything else. Still, I didn't need or want this.

"Fine. I'll wait at the bar." I moved to go around Mark, and he put his hand on my arm. I turned, looked him in the eyes, and put as much heat and gravity as I could into my voice. "I will own that arm, Mark, and more, if you ever touch me again." I pulled away and, putting some distance between us, turned my back on him.

Mark started to sputter, but Seth spoke softly to him, counseling caution and patience. All of it seemed very familiar to me—*too* familiar. In a freezing realization, I became aware that I knew Seth from somewhere— some*when*—else. It was now painfully obvious that he remembered me clearly.

I sat down and hunched my shoulders bitterly. I was getting upset; none of this was working the way I wanted, and now this new wrinkle. I *knew* Seth, and I couldn't remember from where. The chair next to me scraped across the floor, and the monster in question gracefully maneuvered himself into the space. He didn't look at me, at first, just stared at his reflection behind the bar. Neither one of us spoke.

Finally, he licked his lips and snarled, "You can't remember me, can you?"

I let the silence between us answer for me. He plunged on.

"Is this what it's going to come to for us? Swiss cheese for brains, or is that just you?"

Now he was trying to pique some insecurity in me. He had, however, confirmed my suspicion that I'd done something to him or someone close to him—more likely the latter, I was willing to bet. I was too caught up in searching my head to pay any more attention to Seth when he said something else that didn't even register with me. When he repeated himself, I tried to listen.

"Hair parted in the middle, mustache and beard?" He waved his hands in front of his face; the 'shifter's entire demeanor was understated. He was ideally suited for a number two or three position in any organization, I noted. Again, it felt like I was having the same thoughts and feelings—as if I were living a moment one more time, to maybe get it right.

I could sense Mark just out of range, preparing to speak again, when Majispin entered the lounge. The sorcerer looked disheveled. He needed a shave and, I could smell, a shower. His suit was wrinkled, as if he'd been sleeping in it. The corners of his eyes twitched, and he'd broken into a light sweat coming into the spacious room.

Mark shut up altogether and Seth slid away from the bar as Majispin entered. The club's owner looked from Seth to Mark, then me, and back. His voice quivered when he finally addressed us.

"Seth, Barros, Maria—leave now. Mark, have a seat at the bar. Alexander." Majispin painted my name with honey and indicated, in a shaky, halfhearted wave, a table in the corner. As he melted into a chair, relief washed over his face, and he motioned to Benjamin at the bar. A pitcher of water and two glasses appeared at the table.

"Water. Do you mind?"

I shook my head. I didn't mind, and I needed the respite from trying to recall Seth. I was still a bit drained and, consequently, thirsty. Majispin seemed to be in some kind of withdrawal. Time was wasting, so I ignored it and plunged right in.

"Last night, I met the killer. He got away when three vampires ambushed me in the sewers." I went on to describe the killer and the smoldering plate in the empty apartment.

Majispin knit his eyebrows and rubbed the stubble on his face before speaking. "No doubt the apartment was warded to prevent detection. As for the killer"—he paused and drained the rest of his glass—"that"—he coughed once—"was a Thrall."

I'd never heard of such a thing, to the best of my recollection. Before I could ask about it, Majispin began speaking again.

"I've done some more research regarding your glyphs. I'm certain that, once laid, the symbols will unite a larger spell, combine two magical constructs, as it were. However, it makes no sense to cast them in the area you discovered them; it's too small. The power would dissipate before becoming effective. There's no way for me to tell what the second spell—the one being bound to the container—is."

"Another dead end, but what about this 'Thrall'?"

"The creature you chased is—was—a living human being who has been completely subverted to someone else's will. Basically, it's done like so—all the hair must be shorn from the body, as well as the finger- and toenails. Remove one ear; sew the cavity shut. The eyes, sewn shut; the mouth, stuffed with the severed ear and sewn shut. Once this is all done—the poor soul is still awake and alive at this point—a six-inch iron nail that has been inscribed with multiple incantations is driven through the sternum, symbolically into the heart. Stripped of all free will, subject only to its creator's commands. The person it is done to remains within, unable to do anything but experience its own actions. They are usually full of great pain and sorrow. It is an incredibly difficult operation and morally reprehensible."

"That's an understatement."

"Oddly enough"—Majispin yawned and went on—"the only person who cannot be turned into a Thrall is one who can fully submit themselves to the will of another, a person of great faith and devotion already."

"Sounds submissive to me."

"Certainly, certainly logical. Why not?"

I was fast revising my list of torturous things that could be done to a person. This was the most severe personal invasion that I'd yet heard of. The question that came to my lips was obvious. "Who around here can make these things?"

Majispin took a deep breath and leaned back. He closed his eyes and swallowed twice. A look of nausea crossed his features. When he opened his eyes, he didn't look at me, and said, "I can."

Mark hadn't moved during this entire episode. He sat deathly still and barely blinked. I got the impression he was seriously avoiding Majispin's attention. This was probably a good tactic, as it allowed him to stay in the room and overhear the entire conversation.

"Anyone else that you're aware of?"

Majispin looked up at me and then slowly around the room. His gaze stopped on Mark, who still hadn't moved.

The order came sharp and fast. "Mark! My planner." His employee moved quickly. No one could pay me enough to step and fetch.

Mark disappeared through a side door and returned with an antique pen and a leather-bound day planner. The book was inscribed with three gold-embossed roman characters: AMM. I idly wondered what Majispin's middle name could be.

He slipped his glasses on, opened the planner, and smiled briefly. He then held the book up so I could see its contents. Flipping pages from A to Z, he said, "What do you see?"

I squinted, felt a barely perceived crackling pain behind my eyes, and replied, "Nothing." The pages appeared blank.

He smiled again and started flipping to particular sections of the enchanted book and scribbling on a loose scrap on the notepad.

He held the page up and said, "There are three others that I know of. I will contact them first, then perhaps you can visit them."

"Perhaps?"

Majispin frowned and said with conviction, "This is a delicate matter, Alexander. I don't have this information because I hand it out recklessly. If I am even suspected of something like that, the coalition will turn against *me*."

I understood. The safe houses were a loose network with a few rules that had to be followed in order for it to work. It guaranteed at least one of two things—threadbare support or crushing retribution.

"In many ways, I'm more concerned about the vampires," he said.

I had my own concerns on that front; vampires weren't usually as coordinated as that. They might congregate or even hunt in small groups, but they didn't normally have the need for action like I'd seen.

"Why?" I asked him, curious about his opinion.

"Can you imagine the kind of damage a gang of vampires would do? Shapeshifters don't usually make up a pack of much more than eight or nine—something about the dynamics, racial memory, something, I don't know, but something always destabilizes a larger group. The same goes for vampires, only their groups are even smaller—three or four, no more than five. If there are more than that, involved *and* well coordinated, not destabilized, and working with a witch?"

Majispin's voice trailed off. I got the picture, had even experienced it. Then again, we could all be wrong; things change. I already knew he was wrong about pack dynamics.

He suddenly paled and swallowed painfully. He looked like he'd downed a hook. Without another word, he rose from the table and made his exit by way of the side door that Mark had so recently passed in and out of. I assumed it led to his office.

When Majispin's footsteps had finally receded, Mark rose from his seat and strode towards me. Before he could say anything, I commented, "Your boss seems to be suffering withdrawal symptoms."

Mark chewed this over quietly and muttered, "Wormwood. This time."

So, Majispin was addicted to wormwood…or something? Odd. And now he was trying to kick it?

"He's always experimenting with poisons. I don't know why he does it."

I waved my hand dismissively. "What do you want from me, Mark?"

I don't think, of anything that might have happened, he expected me to simply ask as I did. There was no malice in my voice, no derision, just a simple question.

"I want you gone. I want you to stay away from Maria. I want you to stay away from my pack."

Three things. Okay, in the interests of not forcing his head into his chest cavity, I decided I'd answer to the best of my ability. "I'll be gone soon enough. Maria won't stay away from *me*. I don't give a holy shit about your pack." I put more heat into the last part of the response than I intended—and it came naturally, as if I'd done it a million times before.

I got up and left Mark with the color rising from his neck to his scalp. I didn't care; it was already enough of a pain to deal with Majispin and his way of only telling me less than I needed to know. Mark would just have to handle his business without involving me, or I'd kill him. I hoped I'd made that clear enough. Besides, something else was tickling at the edges of my awareness, an errant memory just out of reach.

I couldn't just sit still and wait for Majispin, so I decided to attempt to learn more about this particular brand of sorcery that I'd so recently become embroiled in. It was a serious mental effort not to keep kicking myself for being so adamant about avoiding the purely metaphysical. It'd be beneficial if I had some idea of where else to find help. I did have an idea how to find out, so I stopped at the bar to speak with Benjamin. He grinned through his long hair as he looked up from cutting lemons and limes. Bartenders, next to libraries, are the nexus of all information.

"How long have you worked here, Benjamin?"

The corners of his mouth turned down as he thought about it and absentmindedly continued slicing. "About four years now. Why?"

"Just curious. All the employees here seem to have their own particular flavor of loyalty to Majispin."

"What flavor is that? Is mine citrus or minty?" He spotted a customer and strode off before I could answer. He returned shortly.

"Whatever the flavor is, it isn't pleasant. No offense; I think you're just a good employee."

He smiled again. When he did, the barbed edges of the tattoo nearest his eyes curved. The familiar, muted *click* of a shot glass hitting the bar sounded in front of me, and Benjamin poured. I cupped the drink on the bar in both hands, surrounding the small container with my fingers, but didn't drink. I thanked Benjamin and kept my eyes on him.

"Your tattoo—how far does it go?" I asked.

"You are inquisitive today." It was a simple statement with no hint of emotion. He subsequently answered, "It goes all the way, of course." As he spoke, he turned and lifted his wiry, straight hair from the back of his neck and shoulders. The tattoo, noticeably thicker, wound a beautiful pattern down the back of his neck and under his shirt. It did, as I suspected, crisscross his scalp as well.

"Nice," I said, and swallowed my drink. "It must've taken some time to complete. How'd you like being bald?"

"A temporary problem. The potential benefits outweighed the discomfort. It's kept me healthy and employed." He let his hair drop and faced me. "So," he began, "I gather this 'flavor of loyalty' is causing some friction?"

A grimace crossed my face for an instant.

He chuckled and said, "I think I know of someone who might help you understand a few things."

He wrote down an address but wouldn't give me a name or directions. It hadn't taken the barkeep long at all to figure out that I wanted a second opinion.

With that transaction concluded, I abruptly remembered something of where I knew Seth from: I had killed someone over forty years ago that he was close to. Well, *shit*.

NINE

The address that Benjamin gave me was deep in Chinatown. He'd been awfully cryptic about the whole deal. Either that or he really didn't know if this was a worthy source or not. I was going with the latter; I didn't have much of a choice. Having no real contact with the world of sorcery was costing me. I'd need to remember to check in with some of my more broken kids and see if any of them were dabbling or knew of someone. I hoped not. Regardless, I needed to get out and do something, even if it was only the illusion of progress. I wasn't terribly interested in trying to remember more about Seth than I already had—or anybody else I might have screwed over, for that matter.

Chinatown is one of the most culturally infused, chaotic, and gloomy places in Boston. The whole area was built on a landfill, if my bitch of a memory serves, and is a mishmash of businesses and residential properties. Despite the oversimplified name—used in over twenty-five states—it's not just the Chinese that are represented here, but they are the majority population in this town.

"Over twenty-five states?" Where the fuck did that thought originate? I hated those random bits; they were more of a distraction than of any practical use. I clutched the address in my palm like a child sent on his first errand to the grocery store. It would be peachy if

I didn't occasionally forget where I was going during idle travel.

The architecture in the area is virtually all brick and iron. What sets it off from most other neighborhoods in Boston is just how tightly packed and built-up the area is. Even on the sunniest of days, the place remains gloomy. There are dark alleys placed randomly between buildings, and the erratic streets are only for the experienced. The smells coming out of the area have more depth and layers than most people I've met; every organic scent mingles and collides. From the backs of boxy, refrigerated trucks to run-down station wagons doubling as cargo carriers for quasi-legal businesses, products from the oceans and farms of America and beyond lived in Chinatown.

Upon initial inspection, the neighborhood seems to be overrun with restaurants or markets. When you take a closer look, it becomes obvious that a savvy citizen would never have to leave the confines of this neighborhood. Everything is available in Chinatown if you know where to look. If you don't know where to look, don't bother being surprised when you realize you can rent a video from a gift shop or buy a bus ticket from a fish market.

Despite the gathering clouds, the sun was at its peak, and light shone from directly above. Still, the further in I went, the faster the sun seemed to be setting. Shadows were lengthening perceptibly, and the air around me cooled. My sense of space and the passage of time were being affected; I could feel what was becoming a familiar and uncomfortable tingle along my spine. A resurgence of the feelings that drove me to ignore this counterculture world of magic came thundering back.

My destination was close. Not unlike Majispin's club, this address was a single doorway in a vast brick wall. Every surface was moist on the side street I'd turned onto, as if it'd rained recently. The smell of mortar hung low in the air. It had *not* been raining recently. The streets had dried since the smattering of rain earlier.

A small gentleman stood in front of the heavy wooden door at my destination. He held a large umbrella by his side. The door was inlaid with complex, swirling gold loops that crisscrossed and formed what could be mistaken for a mat of hair, but on closer inspection was an intricate interpretation of waves and air. Not exactly Chinese characters, more like Japanese painting patterns set in metal. As I moved, reflected light slid across the patterns. The fellow stood squarely in front of the door. He grinned broadly and had the most magnificent set of teeth I'd ever seen on a human being. His smile seemed to be painfully glued to his face. He nodded his head once and bowed deeply as he stepped aside. A grand gesture from him encouraged me to enter. The umbrella remained perfectly perpendicular to the ground as he moved.

As the door swung open, a glance revealed that it didn't seem to have hinges of any sort. I looked back at the small man, hearing a sharp *whip* of a sound. He gave a tight wave and disappeared as the door shut with a dull *thud* and the first spatters of rain peppered his now-open umbrella. A sudden, unfamiliar feeling washed over me. Unsure, I froze in place. My eyes refused to adjust properly to the gloom. I was at a distinct disadvantage and all too conscious of it.

I could make out a draped litter at the end of what seemed to be a cavernous hall. A figure reclined inside the translucent platform, but no attendants waited at its sides to bear it. I took one hesitant step and then another. Before I'd gone ten paces, a cacophony of ragged noise thundered in the hallway at a deafening volume. Startled, I crouched and felt, more than saw, the first blow go whizzing by my head. The second slammed into my back, and a third and fourth hit the sides of my head. It appeared that I had four opponents.

Spinning and swinging wildly, I didn't connect with anything, but the intent was to drive them back, and it worked for the moment. They all wore matte-black clothing, appearing as *bunraku* puppeteers. I could barely perceive the humanoid figures in the gloom. They darted in and out, striking as one eight-armed entity. A pair of hands yanked my jacket up awkwardly onto the back of my shoulders and head. Another two hands simultaneously removed my guns from their holsters The strange scraping noise of metal colliding with metal pressing in from all sides was loud enough to rattle my teeth.

I was being beaten to a pulp. I felt my nose compact and its cartilage separate from my skull. My own thick blood clung to the front of my shirt, sending a chill down my spine until a solid kick to my kidney sent a searing white shock through my body. Going wild, I still missed every one of them. My larynx was crushed and, by the sound of the impact, my cheekbone had been fractured; air drew raggedly through my mouth as I struggled to breathe through the cascade of blood down my throat and the indented cartilage nearly blocking my airway. The sound of an oil tanker being ground to death against an unyielding reef continued to screech—an absurd counterpoint to my beating, destroying my sense of equilibrium. At least two ribs had been snapped. Nothing made sense, and the only light I could follow lay in the litter ahead. The bright flashes behind my eyes as blows rained down weren't helpful at all.

I was trying to release the monster inside me, near hysterical that I couldn't see or hear. One orgasmic burst of energy, and I'd probably begin destroying this building and everyone in it with my bare hands and teeth, but something held the transformation in check. I could hear the muffled hum of the monster in the dark center of my body. I had to maintain some semblance of control if I was to get out of this. The strikes were coming faster and harder, but I refused to drop, still struggling to fight back.

The figure shrouded within the litter ahead sat stock-still, not paying my situation much mind at all. The inside of the archaic contraption seemed to glow of its own power. I still couldn't understand what I was missing. Then a thought hit me. Simultaneously, a foot to my forehead sent a white flash of light between my eyes, and I realized I still couldn't see properly. Against all of my natural instincts, scrambling on my back and elbows, dragging a crushed knee, I yanked out my mini Maglite and turned it on. The four figures immediately disappeared like smoke in a high wind; the beam penetrated their forms and they vanished. I clumsily turned in a circle. There was no sign of them.

As steadily as I could, I held the light on the litter. The figure inside clapped slowly. Silence hung raw in the air but for the clipped *pop* of handclaps. I touched my hand to my face and found nothing out of the ordinary. Not one shred of evidence supported the damage I'd taken. No blood, no pain. Only my adrenaline-charged body, shivering a bit, gave any indication that anything had happened.

I rushed forward and snatched the litter's glittering veils open. "Who are you?" I demanded roughly. "Tell me why I shouldn't kill you now."

"Nothing from this world can kill me," she breathed, amused.

"I don't think *all* of me *is* from this world," I snarled.

She arched an eyebrow and tilted her head. "That would be perceptive, if you knew at all what you were talking about."

I could feel my ill temper slipping away, being dulled by curiosity. "Why all this, the attack, that noise?"

She winked and said, "You chose it."

I growled in response. I hated incessant industry and purposeless violence. I wanted her dead. My power poked and prodded, desperate for release, trying to influence my every thought. I struggled to maintain my own equilibrium, and images of David bound to a chair, quivering, begging for mercy, slid through my thoughts. I couldn't make sense of the urges that racked me, a kind of dichotomy of thought and emotion. The energy spinning soundlessly at my core seemed to have a mind of its own.

"Manners," the disturbingly beautiful woman said, and my center of power quieted momentarily, a remorseful feeling brushing through me like an alien reaction. I had merely hesitated, but the sensation emanated disturbingly from elsewhere. Looking around, I had the distinct feeling that I wasn't in my own world anymore.

She wore what appeared to be the single longest piece of silk wrapping that I'd ever seen. Opaque, white fabric wound over her left shoulder and tucked inside the endless, skintight wrapping spreading across the litter's floor that started just above her breasts and ended beyond her feet, which were bundled somewhere in the cushions,. An intricate pattern shimmered on the surface in white stitching. It was impossible to see exactly what the texture was, but it looked to me like the luminescent patterns of pearlescent shell.

I slowly pulled myself backward, switched off the Maglite, and settled back on my knees. I took deep breaths to continue to calm myself while I watched the sultry woman. Presumably, I would find answers here, and rampant anger wasn't going to help.

Her dark hair looked to be interwoven with thin strands of gold and copper, her shimmering brown skin speckled with tiny, reflective silver flecks. It wasn't makeup, or I would've smelled the telltale signs of plant oils, oxides, and other minerals. There were no scents around her that I could place, other than the bamboo and silk that surrounded her person and her litter. Her own personal odor was elusive. I didn't have any reference for it in my experience, which again suggested otherworldliness to me. And there was something else, a feeling I couldn't put my finger on, a tingle at the base of my skull and a gentle vibration across my back and shoulders, finishing in my groin. The only thing I could tell for sure what that she was here and that she was smiling coolly.

What I could feel, though, suggested something else. Her very presence both tugged at the core of my power and quelled it, the energy desperately wanting to be free to interact with this woman—all the more reason to shut it down, pack it into the tightest ball imaginable, and sit on it. Still, it ebbed and flowed, a powerful tide in a tiny bowl.

"You," she paused, "have a need to know."

Her voice was carried on a warm breeze in the air. It was like feeling her speech pass over me. Her lips didn't match the sounds I was hearing, as if she were dubbed.

I licked my lips and said, "I do." I tried not to sound too demanding when I asked, "Why was I attacked?"

"Every test is different, self-determined. You set the extents and, if you pass, your need to know is satisfied. *Your* path is led by opposing natures."

"Wha—what do you get out of this?"

She smiled, showing her teeth. Sharp, curved canines flashed, and she leaned back, putting her lips back together. The shape of her eyes was almond-sliver thin, and when she smiled, they disappeared entirely into slits. It wasn't exactly obvious that she wasn't a vampire, but I could tell that she wasn't. The sharp teeth I'd seen were more feline or reptilian, whereas vampires sported extended human canines. I didn't know what she was.

"A promise," she said, "on the authority of your inheritance that you'll perform one task for me when needed."

I didn't understand. What "inheritance" was she referring to?

Pursing her lips, she stated more to herself than me, "Unaware of your legacy; I always forget." She leaned forward on one hand and continued to me, "Well, it's a good thing you've visited, hm? No matter, your word in body is all I ask for now; all else will fall into place after that."

I took a deep breath and sighed. I didn't think there'd be any good that could come out of this except the answers to what I was looking for. This meeting opened up so many new questions that the promise of learning more, of unraveling something new, piqued my survival instincts. The more I could learn, the more stable I could keep my mind.

"I won't swear to anything that would be harmful to my family or my world," I said. It was the best I could come up with for reassurance.

"Done."

"Very well," I answered, raising my arm to my mouth. A quick nip with my canine drew blood. Several drops fled my arm to spatter on the floor in front of the litter. Blood oaths were proof of many things.

She moved faster than I could follow, grabbing my wrist with one hand and cupping the falling blood with the other. The silken slip whirled around her, drawing itself away.

"More than blood, Alexander."

Her eyes flashed, and a terrible grin spread beneath her nose. She smeared my blood across that grin and pressed her mouth to mine as the silk swirled away, leaving her hairless, sparkling skin exposed. She hooked one hand into my belt and broke the leather in one sharp pull. With irresistible strength, she forced me back and stripped me to the thighs in one motion. I'd never met a woman capable of this kind of might or singular ferocity.

I struggled to keep up, egged on by her beauty, passion, and power, but she certainly led. Her mouth bore into mine, and she cupped my groin roughly. I found her firm breasts and squeezed, pinching the nipples hard and wondering if I'd have glittering bits all over my hands as I let them slide down her back to cup her ass. She stroked me where it mattered and lurched upward to lower herself over my hardness, enveloping the whole of my body, it seemed, in liquid warmth. There was an explosion of pleasure, and my back bowed uncontrollably as she rode me, drawing power from me and thrusting it back, commingling my energy with hers. I was a fool to have even tried to match what was happening. Riding this was out of the question. She was in full control.

There was such viscous heat, as if I'd been dropped into a vat of bubbling honey. I was drowning in her energy; it clung to my every pore and drove its way into my skin. The orgasm I experienced was more powerful, pleasurable, and painful than any other as it was drawn from deep within my core and into her through my cock. I opened my mouth to scream full-throated, and her golden-nailed hand clamped down on my face, muffling my scream, then she plunged down and sucked the air out of me, smothering my mouth with hers. I dug my nails into her back as hard as I could, and she grunted, amused, deep in the back of her throat, and came into me with a glittering shiver as her hair cascaded softly around my shoulders.

She was on her feet with the living silk busily wrapping itself around her when I came to my senses, drenched in what I hoped was simply a puddle of sweat, gasping for air.

"Now, learn what you must."

Raggedly, I drew my pants up and struggled to move. When I pulled my battered drawing of the symbol from a pocket and offered it to her, her movements, so precise and fluid, indicated that she did not require the scribble. She gestured to the floor; I rolled over to look, and a trill of pleasure skittered across my skin.

All around me, duplicate symbols were drawing themselves the size of manhole covers in glowing embers. I shakily stood up to get a better look. There were fifteen of them scattered about. No, not scattered; there was a pattern. They lay in groups of three. The groups themselves—what was their meaning? Three. Symbolically, three is one of the strongest configurations. It made sense for an enclosure; you'd need no less than three barriers. Besides, we exist in three dimensions on this plane. Occasionally, a line of flame darted from one group to the next in a grand arc. Lines of glowing embers appeared in between all the flaming symbols. The pattern they formed looked like the veins of a living organism.

I turned back to the woman, finding my voice hoarse. "How does this help?"

"Look closer," she breathed. The room was getting warmer.

I looked again. She continued to probe while I stared at the glowing shapes.

"What do you know of the symbols?"

"That they're used to create a larger spell, an enclosure." I just didn't have the personal experience or training to put two and two together with magic. I had naïvely hoped that whatever happened here would simply regurgitate some useful information.

"Do you know how large?"

"No one seems to know." I added sarcastically, "Or wants to tell me."

She chuckled deep and throaty. "Think bigger than what you see before you, Alexander. We don't have much time left."

The fiery show started to fade. I tried to look more closely, but I couldn't see the significance. It struck me that I should copy down the placement of the groups, and I hurriedly scribbled it on the back of the original scrap of paper. Then I traced dotted lines and arrows in the patterns and directions that the arcs of fire were moving. The more intricate veins would have to go unrecorded.

Just before the groups of drawings disappeared, they burst into pillars of flame. I spun to face the woman, but she was gone. A wall of golden shingles— no, that was incorrect, they were scales—flashed before my eyes with a gust of hot wind, and the room went dark.

My eyes quickly adjusted to the gloom this time. I easily made my way down the large space to the door. Outside, there was no one to see me off. Slightly disgusted with myself for not being in some kind of control of that situation, I slammed the door and stomped across the street. From the other side, I glanced over my shoulder, did a double take, and found a vast, empty wall of bricks.

My hands clenched involuntarily when a wave of need rushed through me, followed by a tingle that reminded me of naked power and delicious, metal-flecked skin.

Was I addicted to her as well as indebted? And what had she meant by my "legacy?"

Damn it all.

TEN

The sky was hazy just about an hour before dawn as I made my way out of Chinatown. I'd lost time, I noted uncomfortably, while dealing with…her. Had I been in her realm or she in mine? There were roughly three days before the date that I'd deciphered from the Mayan writing. What now? Five groups of three, all placed randomly. Perhaps not? A frustrated anger clenched my jaw, struck hotly between my eyes.

Another wave of tingling need washed over me as I passed a billboard advertising airfares from Boston to New York and Washington, D.C. To the right of the headline, a map of the East Coast with exaggerated illustrations of dotted red lines crisscrossing it reinforced the message. I was struck with an idea. "Think bigger," indeed. I'd need a map to test my theory. It might be time to call Detective Roberts again. I hadn't spoken with him for a solid day and then some. If my theory panned out, he could prove its validity.

I found myself heading to the library, but I veered off towards Majispin's club. The main branch at Copley wouldn't be open for another few hours anyway, and I was sure that someone at the club would be able to rustle up a map. The place was a constant hub of activity. This would also give me an opportunity to find out more about who else might be able to make a Thrall—and to clean up a bit. It'd been three days since this mess started, and if Majispin wanted answers, he was going to have to start giving me unfiltered information in return.

As I stepped inside, Benjamin motioned me over to the bar. I held up one finger asking him to wait and made a beeline for the bathroom to see a man about a horse. As I stared at my reflection above the sinks, something was different. I couldn't easily identify the shift, but my demeanor had changed somehow. The outlines of my visage were definitely a bit blurry. Looking closer, I could see movement in my eyes, a vibratory effect, one of the strangest things I'd ever seen and all the more disturbing because it was *my* eyes that were doing it. I closed them and rubbed the back of my hand across my eyelids, scooped some cold water onto my face, and made a stop at the urinal before leaving the bathroom.

When I returned to the bar and sat down, Benjamin slid a tiny envelope towards me. Opening it, I found a note card with a short message on it: "Wait for me at the bar, I'll be down soon as I can. –A. Majispin." I turned the note over once and decided it couldn't hurt to wait. I needed to take a break, anyway. The paper suddenly burst into blue flames. Benjamin put a rocks glass on the bar and I dropped the flaming paper in. We watched the blue fire completely consume the note. I looked at Benjamin and rubbed my singed fingers together.

"Sorcerers don't relish leaving personal objects lying about."

Fair enough. Benjamin placed an empty shot glass in front of me and raised his eyebrows as well as a bottle of whiskey. Morning, noon, or night, there was no need to decline a kindly offered drink. I nodded and Benjamin poured. I sipped the drink slowly.

"Why do you have glitter all over you?"

I looked at my arms. In the odd light at the bar, I could see there was a mixture of silver and gold flecks all over my skin. As I watched, the flecks disappeared, sinking away. The burning feeling of tiny shards of power dripping into me sent a shiver all over my body.

"Oh, man, you *actually* saw her, didn't you?"

I just stared at Benjamin. There was no need to answer.

"Wow. I mean, wow. I've never tried, because, well… I came into this information and once you know, you'll never find her. I told you, and you had no idea who you were going to see. Did you get what you wanted?"

Taking a deep breath, I tried to decide whether to be angry or not. I was responsible for my own behavior, not Benjamin. I'd asked him for another source and he'd given it to me, simple as that. At least, I hoped that was the case. "Do you have any idea what it's like?"

"No. As far as I know, she's a big player and usually cuts to the chase if she's going to help. Like I said, I came into the information and couldn't use it, you seemed like you could, and that's it." Benjamin had stepped back and raised his hands in a non-threatening gesture.

I checked myself—there was a power bleed, I was angry, and it was leaking off me. I might not be able to control all of my emotions, but my actions were for me to decide. So, with effort, I pulled it back.

Instead of recriminations or angry words, I sighed and asked, "Got a map handy?"

"National, New England, Boston?" he replied, as if I'd asked him the most mundane question in the world, everything smoothed over.

An aside occurred to me. "Do you ever sleep?" His only response was to wink and slide a couple of maps at me. Either Majispin paid him very well or he never left the bar. I started to wonder if he had legs or if he were a suspended automaton on an articulated robotic arm back there. Stupid thought. Whimsical thought. What the hell was wrong with me? As if in response, a peal of anger raked up the back of my head. *Not mine.* I spun in the chair and peered around the room. No one was paying any attention to me. The anger had surprised me, practically cut a hole in my head. The feeling passed as quickly as it had come.

I took a deep breath and listened to myself, feeling as much of my being as I could. Every cell seemed to be abuzz with positive energy. Maybe wild sex with otherworldly beings wasn't such a bad thing. Fat chance of that turning out true; I had been stripped of any inhibitions when she took me—or so I told myself. What had happened back there? Taking a few deep breaths to calm myself, I looked deeper, through the layers of slowly fading gratification, to understand where that anger came from. I found nothing but the boiling core of my own power. A rippling pit of mad energy underneath what was starting to seem like a faulty cap I'd made for it years ago.

I cursed harshly at myself and wondered if the Dragon carried some kind of pan-dimensional STD. Then a shot of pure pleasure rode my groin to discomfort. I decided it was best to stop thinking about her in any regard before something worse happened.

With the national map spread out in front of me, I pulled out my pen and began to mark off East Coast cities—Boston, New York, Philadelphia, Trenton and Washington, D.C. I held up the quick sketch of the placement of flaming glyphs from last night. They matched closely enough. The five groups of three were geographic indicators of the cities I'd marked. That's how much landmass the spell would encompass. Perhaps the dotted lines were the route that had been traveled, indicating the order of the sacrifices.

Occasionally, couples or groups appeared from behind the thick curtain at the end of the room and made their way to the exit. The sun was fast on the rise, so most of the folks leaving were vampires. I began to idly consider what Ana had been up to for the last several hours. My last words with her had not been entirely peaceful. Our relationship was too strong and old for a simple disagreement to tear us apart, but she might have concluded whatever business she had in Boston and left town by now.

The heady scent of wildflowers enveloped me, and I knew Ms. Ducat was heading my way. She wore another high-collared affair with her hair pushed up in anachronistic curls.

"Good morning—Alexander Smith, yes? We've never been properly introduced, no." She extended a slender, gloved hand.

"No, we haven't." Or at least I didn't think we had. It probably didn't matter. "Ms. Ducat, correct?" I took her hand, impossibly soft underneath the thin leather, as if the glove were filled with air and packing foam.

"Pleased to meet you. Alivara has shared some of the details regarding the pictograph you've been investigating. Very interesting, yes. I confirmed that it is of Mayan origin, but I disagree as to its usage, I do." She smiled and held her face like stone while she eased onto the barstool next to me.

Her teeth were somewhat large for her jaw; it made her smile grotesque. "Really," I said neutrally, folding up the map.

"What are you working on there?"

"Planning a trip," I replied dryly, and placed the map in my jacket, along with any scribbling I'd done. "You were saying that you disagree with Majispin's assessment of the symbol?"

She rocked back on her stool. "Oh! Yes, absolutely. I've found that symbol to be used in rituals of protection, not necessarily to enclose, as he's surmised, no. I've found that with all of their industry, the Mayans had a leg up on everyone at the time, oh, yes. Partly due to large-scale spells such as those required by the symbols in question. In fact…"

I could barely make out what she was saying; something about her manner had piqued my senses. A gesture? The teeth? What? The more I thought about it, the more flowery her perfume seemed to become. My eyes began to water as the scent slammed against the upper membranes of my nose. I'd never met this woman before—I was sure of it now—but I might have met an acquaintance or come across an object she was intimate with. I could be getting some residual pheromone or other scent-based artifact that was tickling my memories.

She was still talking, and I tried to focus on what she was saying rather than what she was inadvertently doing. "…so it'd be helpful if you told me what you've learned so far on your own, it would. I could help you connect the dots, yes, I could. Perhaps there's some threat that's caused this behavior, or it could be a response to some other outward stimuli."

"They're murdering children. Is that ever a reasonable response to anything?"

"Oh, that's not what I meant at all; you've taken me out of context, certainly! You must understand; can you blame the caged tiger for biting the hand that feeds it? Hm? I think not. When we—any of us—are threatened, we respond using whatever means we have at hand. That's all, just a more clinical review, not a dismissal of the moral context."

It was an unusually long and desperate explanation of her position. "Well, I haven't learned much really. Hasn't Majispin given you the facts so far?"

She rocked back again and said, "Oh! No, he's quite close to the vest with his information. It's a trait that makes him suited to run one of these places, yes, indeed." She indicated the club around us. "Now, if you want my help, you have to help me understand what you've discovered, yes."

I turned in my seat so that I faced her. Truth is best delivered straight, without preamble. "I never said I *wanted* your help, miss."

She stiffened slightly. I could swear I saw some kind of shift in tension under her skin. This close, I couldn't help but try to penetrate that overpowering scent of flowers surrounding her. I didn't give a damn what her feelings were at this point; I just wanted to get a handle on who or what she really was. Dogs have the same problem sometimes; they start investigating a smell or sound and are distracted to no end by it. Thankfully, I wasn't a dog. I could control myself, but the urge was still strong.

I smelled him before I saw him. I knew he'd cleaned himself up recently. Despite his own elusive personal scent, additives such as dry-cleaning chemicals, cologne, shampoo, and soap complicated the mix. There was some kind of herbal lotion on top and a substance I couldn't put my nose on.

The most beguiling thing about Majispin, for me, was that all of his scent markers would quickly become jumbled, like I only had a half-second to decipher the message before it became scrambled again. I was getting used to it. He could spell away his scent markers, but the very absence of them was enough for me. I supposed he had never considered that, or he was solely concerned with being tracked. Perhaps Ms. Ducat used a similar method of illusion? If she did, the next obvious question was why.

"Alexander, Ms. Ducat." Majispin took her hand.

"Mr. Majispin." She bowed her head.

I nodded as he took the seat on my left; Ms. Ducat remained on my right.

Ms. Ducat abruptly chimed in. "I'll be taking my leave now. Good day, Alivara. Thank you for the conversation, Mr. Smith. Yes, conversation."

Majispin came to his feet as she slid off of her stool. I looked at her and said, "Call me Alexander."

She stumbled as she made her exit, catching her heel on the barstool. I reached out in the split-second between her stumble and recovery to balance her. The arm I got hold of was pliant, almost boneless for a moment, as if I'd grabbed a thick tentacle that'd suddenly sprouted a bone structure. She regained her footing quickly and pulled away from me at the same time. Ducat walked speedily into the rooms at the rear of the building.

Again, I wondered where Ana was. She was the only one I felt I could trust to speak to about this sort of thing. I didn't know what Majispin's relationship with Ducat was really like, and I couldn't risk speaking with him about my reservations. Perhaps I'd ask Benjamin later. I was sure he was used to that kind of chatter. On the other hand, he worked for Majispin.

I turned my attention back to Majispin, who shrugged. "You're looking better," I said to him.

"Ah." He drew the vowel out, ending with a soft hiss. "The wormwood. A little experiment of mine. No concerns, no concerns. I understand you saw the Dragon last night?" He finished the statement a bit too eagerly.

Benjamin passed by, and I looked from him to Majispin. The barkeep shrugged and said, "He asked." Then he moved down to the end of the bar and began fiddling with something under the counter.

I wasn't crazy about the fact that Majispin knew where I'd been, but more intriguing was his intonation when he'd said "the Dragon." A reverent tone, as if speaking of acknowledged authority.

"What exactly do you mean by '*the* Dragon?'"

"Benjamin told me you'd gone to see the Queen last night—what?" Majispin put his hands up and understanding bloomed across his face. "That's right, you couldn't know! Ha! Priceless."

"Couldn't know what, exactly?"

"In order to find and actually see The Dragon, certain conditions must be met." Majispin leaned in and explained, ticking the points off on his fingers. "One, you can't know you're going to see her, and two, you have to pass whatever test gets tossed at you to have your need to know satisfied. How'd it go? What'd you learn about her?"

Majispin was like a little boy turned loose in a candy shop. It seemed to me that he'd perhaps tried to see the Dragon once or twice and failed because he *knew* he was going to see her. Knowing definitively what she was explained the heat and hints of gold everywhere. Dragons were supposed to be one of the most powerful and reclusive interdimensional races. I'd gotten to meet and be fucked by one—and not just any one, apparently, but one known as the Queen. It made me wonder if there was a King. It also made wonder as to the depth of the fucking because I was now absolutely certain that I was the fuckee. I struggled unsuccessfully to control my shiver of pleasure. *Damn it.*

"How do you even know that much detail? What's your angle?"

"Oh"—Majispin leaned back and affected a casual disposition—"just curious, you know, as many interdimensional beings that pass through here, they can't be here very long and they're not normally here for conversation—if you take my meaning. They need help to be here, some kind of cooperation or, perhaps, someone from here travels to their side—*hmph*, but that's not healthy. The Dragon, however, seems to make regular appearances; it's only natural to wonder why or perhaps to be curious about who might be helping her—don't you think?"

I didn't see anything wrong with that line of thinking. Another method of dealing with Majispin occurred to me, coupled with Ana's observation that he was essentially a mad scientist, an information junkie whose need to know overpowered his better judgment on occasion.

I told him what I wanted him to hear, what I thought would torture him a little bit and make him squirm for more information. "We're dating." I was tired of not getting a straight answer for questions, of important memories dissolving when I wasn't looking.

Majispin leaned back and narrowed his eyes at me. Anger had crept into his face. He swallowed it, adjusted his cuffs, and moved on. "Why are you here this time?"

"For the containment spell, using the glyphs, how many living sacrifices have to be made at each anchor point, and why take their blood?"

Majispin twitched and answered, "For a conjuring as powerful as this, at least two. The blood, according to my research, will be used, most likely, to 'seal the deal.' In the end, it's a potent reminder of what's been sacrificed. You see, an imprint of sorts, remnants of the child's soul, remains in the blood."

The idea of someone callously using what is so essential sent a chill between my shoulder blades. A glimmer of empathy tightened my jaw, and I plunged on in my thoughts. Humans wasted time with empathy when problems needed to be solved. Sure, I was a problem solver. That's certainly why I'd tied David to that chair. Right?

So, why three glyphs, three locations? The extra one was likely a backup. The three locations here in Boston were all in the same area. That made sense. If this were all true, the spell could be only one sacrifice away from being complete. The moving lines in the Dragon's fiery

Errick A. Nunnally

diagram might have ended here. I wasn't sure I even wanted to know what the spell would or could contain.

Majispin had been watching me mull over his answer. Before he could ask me any questions, I gave him an order. "Give me the names and addresses of the others you know of who could create a Thrall."

Majispin responded coolly, "Your turn to give me something, Alexander." Then he asked what I knew had been burning a hole in the back of his addictive little skull. "What is your relationship with Ana?"

I briefly considered a lie or deflection, but I simply didn't have the wherewithal to come up with anything at this point. Irritated, I said exactly what I wanted. "None of your damn business. Got any other stupid questions?"

"No. No questions, just an order—get the fuck out of my club. Now."

He meant it. I could see it, smell it, and feel it; he wanted me gone. That wouldn't change anything, however; he knew the stakes had gotten too high, and he knew we needed to work together to protect what precious little order we had amongst monsters.

"Grow up, sorcerer; put your petty interests aside and focus on the problem at hand. There's more at stake than your fetishistic little needs."

Majispin ground his teeth so hard I could hear it. He put both hands flat on the table and leaned forward. No doubt he wanted to tell me what he thought, but instead he swallowed the words and leaned back.

"*Fine.* What is it that you think you've figured out?"

I took a deep breath and told him what I suspected, glad to have again avoided a confrontation with him. It wasn't going to compromise anything I was doing to share what I suspected about a plot.

He licked his lips and let his eyes wander around the lounge. He blinked once, then again, and said, "So, the culprits have visited these other cities, and you believe that Boston is the last stop for the spell to work? I can't imagine where the information to construct something like this is coming from. The details of pulling this off have been lost to time, possibly forever."

I'd need Detective Roberts's help to easily verify that Boston was the last stop. Majispin owed me some info. It was my turn again. "The names and addresses, Majispin."

"That's not information I hand out lightly."

"It's the next logical step."

"I'll contact them personally."

"They know you. If any one of them is involved, they'll hide it. I'm sure they'd be aware if you were trying to divine something magically. My talents don't involve spellcasting at all. You can let them know I'm coming."

It took him the space of ten heartbeats before he produced his day planner from nowhere, accompanied by a tiny sucking *thump*, and scribbled on a scrap of paper with his ornate pen. The magical stunt had driven a brief and dull pain through my skull. In good health and spirits, it seemed that he was able to do more for himself. Previously, Mark had been ordered to fetch. Majispin had inadvertently demonstrated a weakness, and I made note of it.

Tearing the page out, he passed his hand over it twice, muttering under his breath. Then he handed it to me. The paper felt charged with static electricity or some other unspent energy.

"The names will disappear for each location that you visit or contact, so move wisely. Only you and one or two others will be able to read this. Do not attempt to copy down the information; it will not work and it might be disastrous. This sheet of paper is your only source, and it is delicate information, Alexander. Keep it close."

I nodded and answered his last question. "I do believe that Boston is the end of the loop for the spell, but I have to confirm it."

"Boston being the last stop does make sense. Chronologically, anyway." Majispin spoke mostly to himself and nodded. Then he looked up at me and smiled. "But we already knew that, Alexander. Tell me something—do you hear voices in your mind at unguarded moments? A little whisper, perhaps? Maybe you've chalked it up to conscience or tension?"

I was startled by the question, unsure that I'd heard him correctly. What the hell did Majispin know? Worse yet, I didn't like the implication that he knew more about me than I knew about myself. "No."

"Hmm. Not a single voice, just one, once in a while? Maybe you thought it was your imagination, an errant thought?"

Narrowing my eyes at Majispin, I did what I could that didn't involve killing him; I changed the subject. "Maybe it'd be best if we stayed on task. What, if anything, do these cities have in common, and what do the Mayans have to do with any of this?"

Thinking along the same track, smoothly shifting gears, Majispin said, "The Mayan culture is practically dead, absorbed into the larger Central American civilization. We need to know more about the significance of April 12, 2012. I'll look into that and I'll contact the safe houses in the suspected cities. Those ancient peoples were masters of time and such calculations."

I shrugged, downed my drink, and waved the list of names at Majispin. "I'm sure we'll talk later. By the way, do you know what flowered scent it is that Ms. Ducat wears?"

He looked confused but answered, "I've never smelled anything on the woman."

That much perfume and Majispin couldn't smell it? Interesting. Maybe the wizard had burned his nasal passages out with some idiotic experiment.

I left to find a pay phone. It was past time to contact Detective Roberts. I didn't have any idea how to explain Terrell's death. What could I say? A killer zombie stabbed him with a knife while trying to get at a child? I didn't want to even try to explain that; it'd only be endangering him and his partner. The more they knew, the more they'd meddle in things they had no defense against. I needed to know, however, what he could learn about the other locations, information only he would be privy to. After a brief moment of mental static, staring into the distance, I went ahead and made the call.

My call bounced into his voice mail. He could have been out trying to track me down through the phone number I'd given him years ago. More likely, his shift had ended and he was gone. If he were going to try to locate me physically, I'd disappear from his life forever. The only rule between us was that I didn't officially exist. His former lieutenant had informed him of that before meeting an untimely death. Lieutenant Brown had held the secret, right to his dying breath at the hands of a maniacal vampire.

Only sparse crowds swirled around me on the plaza. All of these people were the early risers of Boston, ridiculously intent on getting to work and starting their days. I couldn't remember the last time that I had "worked" for pay. A long life and simple needs made it easier to stockpile wealth and set up the life that I had. I don't know if I'm even capable of working for someone else anymore.

No one paid any attention to me and no one hung about. A light mist rose off of the small plot of grass nearby as the sun warmed it. It was safe to speak as I pleased, so I left a precise message—I had not killed

Terrell; I hadn't gotten a good look at the assailant; there was clear evidence that the killer had lain in wait inside the nearest apartment; see if there was any truth to my theory regarding any of the other locations in New York, Philadelphia, Trenton, and Washington D.C. This, I hoped, would give him some information that he could use. I believed that all the cities on the list had two things in common—extensive housing developments and plenty of poor people in them. The structures were low-rise, low-rent, and full of the "unimportant" population. They contained a lot of children too, a lot of kids ripe for the picking.

I didn't want to jeopardize one of the few law enforcement contacts I had, but I would abandon Roberts if I had to. Would I kill him if it came to that, to preserve the stability between Earth's humanity and other worlds? I wasn't sure, but that's what I told myself, anyway. It was a burden we all theoretically carried; the majority of the planet's inhabitants couldn't know what was going on right under their noses.

Someday, soon probably, one of us would slip up—purposely or not—and the truth would be out. The magic of Humankind, technology—used for communication, observation, and the analysis thereof—was growing dramatically. It really was only a matter of time before the whole truth was in the hands of human authorities. I wondered if I'd be around to see it. Given the nature of Man and the legendary angst between the natural and supernatural, it'd mean war, and I was certain our limited population couldn't win. It didn't matter. Humanity didn't need us and I was comfortable with that.

I'd forgotten where I was going. Shoving my hands petulantly into my pockets, I turned in a stupid circle, pissed at my own mind. My hand found folded papers in my pocket and I pulled them out. Mostly my own handwriting, random notes, memory ticklers. Sure, I recalled what I was doing, but not where I was going *now*. Then I came to the list of names that tingled in my fingers, and I remembered what I'd wanted to do first.

I decided to go to the library, but before I could take a step, he turned up at my elbow.

"Seth." The one word from my lips made him tense for a microsecond. I started down the sidewalk, and he fell into step on my right. The little blond boy, whisper-quiet as still air—his usual silence—walked on my left. The boy stared alternately from me to Seth as we walked and his one remaining hand tried to grasp mine, the boy's ghostly fingers leaving a tingle at my fingertips with every attempt. I truly wanted to remember his name, but that bit of information had permanently left my head.

"Anything yet?" He snarled through clenched teeth.

I told him what I remembered. "I killed someone you were close to." Seth merely pinched his face, skeptical, waiting for me to go on. I remembered Seth's face when he'd worn a beard and parted his hair in the middle. All trimmed and neat; most whites in that area wore beards, but not as cleanly as Seth had—where had this memory originated? The name of the 'shifter I'd killed—who'd nearly killed me—popped into my head. *Curry*. The way the name came to me felt like a note had been slipped secretly into my hand, purposely released into my memory. I tried to shake it, but the feeling wouldn't go away; the notion I was being watched flowed over me.

The memory continued to flow. I recalled that everyone called him "Curry" because of his fondness for spicy food, Mexican-style chow with plenty of hot peppers. I'd always thought it odd that a man nicknamed "Curry" would live where curry wasn't terribly common: Nevada. I ran with his pack on the edge of the desert in Nevada—that's where it happened.

The membership of the pack was well over the number that Majispin had described as the critical mass for a group of shapeshifters. It felt good knowing that the magician was wrong. Curry overflowed with charisma, charm, and enough supernatural power to hold the group together. It seemed that Majispin hadn't been considering all the variables, but I hadn't run with every pack in the world, just the two that I could recall.

Curry had tenuous connections with the Las Vegas mob at the time. He wasn't above enforcing or moving drugs for them, and he could readily disappear any malcontents as needed. It was a lucrative and dangerous business. He had dabbled in legal prostitution on the side, earning legitimate money as well as laundering it, and he'd owned a remote bar with a lonely, seemingly dried-up gas pump out front. During "business hours" he could usually be found in the back room. Eating. His appetite, like mine was now becoming, had been voracious.

Curry was on the cusp of pure, supernatural insanity when I'd joined them. At the time, I didn't know what I was looking to get out of my second life, and joining his pack seemed natural. I also didn't know what to expect—or the warning signs—when an older shapeshifter was going to lose it.

I stopped walking, lost in thought, and the little boy continued down the sidewalk, leaving small, bloody footprints. I watched him until he disappeared into a crowd across the next street.

Seth grabbed my arm and shook it.

I smacked his hand away and squared up on him. Our noses were nearly touching.

Seth scowled and said, "Going to finish what you started?"

I met his gaze with steel of my own. Regardless of whatever else I might be feeling, fear wasn't one of the emotions. He tensed, suddenly realizing that forty years ago, I could've killed him with some effort, but now the scales were a bit different. Pushing the thought from my head, I stepped back.

"I'm sorry about Curry; I did what I thought was right. That's no apology and it sure as Hell isn't a request for forgiveness —"

"Curry? You think this is about Curry? Shit, man, how screwed up are you that you'd forget her?"

Oh, gods, I *had* forgotten, like every damn thing else. He was talking about Tina.

ELEVEN

Seth spoke fiercely in low tones. "Curry had it coming—anyone with a brain could see that—but Tina didn't deserve your shit!"

Staring into Seth's dark eyes, I waited. I waited for something useful to say or think or do to come to me. For once, a useful insight popped into my head long before I was in danger of being killed—Seth had loved her. She was Curry's girl, and Seth was his closest advisor; he'd loved her from afar. Crossing that line would've brought Curry down on him harder than a mine collapse. I'd stupidly crossed that line myself, so I had some idea of what it was like. By the time I'd come fully on the scene, Curry's abuse of Tina had begun to graduate from mental to physical.

Embarrassed, I snapped at Seth, "I don't need you to tell me the mistakes I've made!" With that heat, I leaked psychic energy. Seth was enveloped in a wave of tangible anger. He blanched and his breath caught. I put my hand up, not to push him away, but to pull that power off of him. I clenched my fist and pulled. The wash of energy resisted like a wet blanket. This sort of thing never used to happen, and I needed to control it.

A faint line of gibberish echoed in my ears, pleading for action, to impose discipline, to kill as needed, to *lead*. I took a step back and hushed everything inside me, listening intently, trying to find the source. This time I was absolutely sure this was coming from somewhere deep inside me. I felt a soft snap and the empty feeling that I'd lost something, but the loss itself wasn't clear.

Walking away, shoulders hunched, I left Seth standing there. He wore a completely dumbfounded look and muttered something about comeuppance and Mark being right to be paranoid. I had business to attend to, and the dead weren't as patient as people liked to think. I found the little blond boy in front of the library, a terrible smile sliced across his bloody face. He watched as I shuffled through the revolving door. He'd disappeared by the time I glanced back. Better to concentrate on other things right now. Not Seth, my long-dead young victim, or my most recent one. Certainly not the Dragon.

I could try not to, at least.

My thoughts kept revolving around the events over forty years ago that had brought me into Seth's universe the first time. I'd gotten my hands on one of the last Indian Chief motorcycles made in the 1950s, restored it, and rode it south from Canada, through the U.S. into Nevada. The damn machine, at thirty years of age, as beautiful as it was, broke down every two or three hundred miles. My saddle sores were tremendous, but when you have a preternatural healing ability, it's the least of your worries. I still don't know what answers I had been looking for, but it gave me plenty of opportunities to learn the intricacies of a seventy-nine-cubic-inch engine.

An insistent tug on the thought brought me fully alert. The memory came up short. I could feel it being twined around something, spinning away. I seized on it, projecting as much of my imagination as I could into the idea of pulling it back, struggling with the effort.

Soon, I recalled that it was early in the spring when I'd hit the road with little in my possession beyond the bike and some necessities. I pulled harder and unraveled the rest of the memory. When I opened my eyes, one of the librarians at the front desk was staring at me. I must've looked like I was going to collapse. When I touched my forehead, my hand came away moist. I smiled at the woman and moved on, unspooling my thoughts, happy to have learned that whatever was eating my memory couldn't do it when I was in the midst of recalling them.

I had traveled many open roads where I could see America as it had once been and where I could indulge myself and 'shift freely. By the time I'd reached Nevada, alone and lonely, still unsure of where I was going, I'd met some of Curry's boys out front of his bar while I presumptuously filled my tank from a pump that only looked nonfunctional, never inquiring who I might pay.

We spent some time inside the bar; it had not taken us long to confirm to each other that we were all monsters—aimless beasts without direction or purpose. I was offered some "work" with the boys, and before long I was in the pack. The allure was powerful, and I was easily drawn into the circle. For a number of months, Curry was a mysterious figure, forever hidden in the back rooms, sending orders through Seth and his other boys. We ran errands with mysterious packages, intimidated a number of people, and raised hell, generally, when needed. Nothing that required serious thought and nothing too clear; no one seemed to have a handle on what was going on, exactly. No one in the pack died until much later. It *was* a good time while it lasted. Until I met Curry personally, or more to the point, I met Constantina.

Shortly after meeting Tina, I had a purpose.

I'd seen her before, sure, passing through the bar. I was usually caught up in some raucous conversation or conflict while waiting for Curry's orders. Stupidly, like everyone else, spending the money we'd earned from Curry in his own damn bar. She moved quickly, smoothly, a well-honed glide that took her in and out of places unnoticed. I never looked at her until the last moment, when she'd pass the threshold to the back of the place and I'd catch a glimpse of her smooth profile and shiny black hair. She smelled good, I knew for sure, all-natural product clean—always clean. I tried to be smart and never pay her any particular mind, as I was too busy reliving my teens with a pack of supernatural adolescents. When I finally, properly, met her with Curry, my aimlessness dissipated.

She had been dressed down, wearing jeans and a formfitting white T-shirt. Barefoot, I remember, with slim, expressive feet, skin the color of fresh milk with a splash of coffee in it. Nails untouched. She'd had a body that was built to carry lean muscle, not fat, so she was forever bereft of the kind of curves that some women are voluptuously blessed with. Curry usually got her to smile, but the smile never reached her eyes—I knew this in hindsight. When she really smiled, her eyes sparkled and collapsed into comic slits and her ears rose slightly.

Regarding her supernatural side, she seemed to be sitting on her power. It was curled tight somewhere inside her, or—I don't know—Curry somehow managed to dampen it. Despite that, she never seemed weak or vulnerable unless she was around Curry. I don't know what in particular about her that I found so compellingly sexy. Despite those circumstances, she'd somehow been erased from my mind over the years and now she was figuratively back. Perhaps she'd always been a little too deep in my head.

I could reminisce later—a bitter and currently not-so-fruitless thought, so I decided, rather than fool around with the Internet searching for scraps, to poke around in periodicals first. Just five years ago, these archives would've existed on microfiche. I would soon run down the list that Majispin had given me. It was nearing midmorning—what better time to visit someone possibly using vampires as muscle? Regardless, I wanted to be done with the piece of paper Majispin had given me. I had the impression I was carrying a live hand grenade in my pocket. The page felt as if it were pulsing with untapped power, waiting for a trigger.

Nowadays, an entire newspaper could be compiled as a PDF, or whole pages character-scanned into the computer and converted to Web pages. Obtaining a workstation was far simpler at this time of the morning, but locating the proper information was another matter entirely. I had to engage the help of the attending librarian.

There were two at the desk as I approached. The obviously younger of them glanced in my direction and quickly looked away. Her face pinched and she hugged herself, eyes scrunched. When she opened them, she stood up stiffly, made a quick apology to the older librarian and scurried away, shoulders hunched, obviously crying.

I felt a surge of elation and buried the urge to follow her. Instead, I approached the remaining librarian, remaining focused on the task at hand.

"Excuse me."

She paled, swallowing hard, obviously and detrimentally affected by my presence. I did what I could to pull back—now was simply not the time for this.

She finally answered, "Oh, yes, how can I help you?"

"I need a list of newspaper periodicals from Philadelphia, Trenton, New York, and Washington, D.C. from the past year." My attempt at a smile caused her to shrivel. She shrugged, shook it off, and gave me a weak smile in return. Normally I'd guiltily enjoy something like this, but right now it began to annoy me.

"Okay. Yes, hold on a moment." She turned away and moved to a workstation farther behind the big desk. After tapping a few keys and taking a few deep breaths, she began jotting items down on a scratch pad. "Do you just want the major papers, all newspapers, or all newspapers and magazines?"

The information I'd need wouldn't turn up in a magazine. "Just the newspapers. All of them."

"Okay," she whispered.

Shortly, she handed the over the list, and I asked, "Does this include Philadelphia as well?"

She looked quizzically at me, double-checking the list before replying. "It was the first item you asked for. Philadelphia. Are you...are you joking with me?" She smiled nervously.

"Why would I be joking with you? I just need to find the newspapers for Philadelphia as well."

Her demeanor shifted from skittish to wary in an instant. She slowly reached out and took back the list she'd given me. Then she handed it back.

"Here you go. Will you be needing any additional help?"

"Uh, no. Thank you." I moved quickly away from her, embarrassed. I could sense her eyes boring into my back after the ridiculous, senile moment I'd dragged her into.

Settling into a walled workstation for privacy, I flipped through the records of newspapers in Philadelphia, determined to keep my brain clicking. The top two were the *Inquirer* and the *Daily News*. Neither paper held any items of interest. I frowned and assumed that the victims had been chosen for their public invisibility. Looking at the list the librarian had given me, I needed to narrow my immediate choices down.

I did a quick Internet search and turned up the African-American newspaper called the *Tribune*, whose primary target market was urban. Referring to the list, I found it in the library's archives, and it had the coverage I was looking for. Two children had been murdered under unusual circumstances in a public-housing facility, but the incidents had been filed away under gang-related intimidation and violence. The housing had been torn down recently.

Searching local papers in Trenton, New York, Philadelphia, and D.C. yielded similar results between two weeks and a month apart in occurrence. In all, little or no coverage was available from the major newspapers. Someone had been carving out a four-hundred-mile swath of the East Coast beneath everyone's noses.

Turning back to the Internet, I found an interesting bit of information from D.C. There'd been a series of news segments recorded that involved the history and the downfall of a block of projects scheduled for remodeling. On one of the segments, a reporter gave an on-the-spot account of an unusual pair of murders that'd occurred "only a few weeks ago," tipping the scales on the decision to remove the buildings sooner rather than later. I ran the clip over and over, not hearing a word the vapid reporter said. Instead, I focused on an area just over her shoulder where an occluded view of the feces-rendered symbol was visible. Freezing the video only produced a grainy, motion-blurred image. During playback, however, the mark was clear.

My quarry had been at it for some time now, and we were near the end of something big. Each pair of murders had occurred in the week before the full moon. Once done, it was on to the next location. It'd be next to impossible for individual investigators in each city to piece this together. A task force, maybe, but that kind of attention wasn't going to be brought to bear on murders in the projects.

Roberts would have access to police files and details that public sources wouldn't. I didn't have an easy way of perusing such secure files, so I'd have to wait until I spoke with Roberts to compare notes. Perhaps gaining access to police files could be a new project one day. Regardless, it was time to turn to other matters.

The first name on the list Majispin had given me was only a fifteen-minute walk away and didn't have a surname. It simply said "Pat," with the address. It was on one of the side streets between Tremont and Washington near Downtown Crossing. Obviously old, the sidewalk was cobbled and irregular. The number led me to an old bookstore. Windows made of the same thick, brick-like glass used in P.O. buildings obscured the foyer. With no way to see in, I moved slowly into the doorway. The door was a heavy, mixed wood affair—oak, cherry and…bubinga? I hadn't smelled that particular hardwood in a long while; its origins are South African. *Useless fact*, I cursed to myself.

A tiny bell on a primitive spring announced my entrance. The now-familiar jolt of electricity that signified an active spell tingled along my spine as I crossed the threshold. The second thing I noticed was the strong scent of starch and sweet oil in the air.

Hundreds, possibly thousands of books lined shelves that stretched from floor to ceiling, all the way to the back of the place. There was a long counter in front and no obvious access to the rear. In front of each bookcase were a rail system and ladder. Slowly, a head appeared from behind the counter.

The figure's cranium was rather large and malformed—shaped not unlike a marshmallow. A full head of grey hair cascaded around all four corners of the oddly shaped skull. It looked as if a mop had lost its handle and settled there. His—or her—face was both androgynous and ugly, smooth but soft features, rather flat, with a round and short nose, wide thin lips, and broad cheeks. Small, gleaming eyes watched me unblinkingly from underneath manicured eyebrows.

Other than the strange head peeking over the counter, of more concern were the cavernous dual barrels of the shotgun. The sweet smell was gun oil—I should've known.

The individual couldn't have been much more than head and shoulders taller than the counter—five feet at best. I could smell the gunpowder in the shotgun shells as well as the scent of the creature. This collection of scents and sights was no human being. It was wielding, however, an all-too-human weapon.

"Oi," it said, "whaddya want wit' me, monster?"

The "R" in monster fired off its tongue with the burr of a Scotsman, but its opening syllables sounded British. Come to think of it, some of the accent came across as Irish as well. What was I dealing with here?

The next sound I heard was the *click* of the hammers being locked back into place on the cannon that the creature shouldered. I could barely make out the collar of an immaculate white shirt between its chin and shoulder, heavily starched.

I slowly raised my hands, palms forward, and said, "No trouble. Only visiting to talk. I got your name from Majispin."

"Talk, ay?" One of its eyes twitched before it spoke again, "I'll do the talkin', sir, aye? An' if Majispin sent ye, perhaps ye've murdered him, aye, stole me name from him?"

"Uh, no, I just needed some help with information."

"Mmm, really, can ye prove it?"

I nodded and pointed at the list in my hand.

"I'm bettin' ye're here regardin' the Thrall Alivara mentioned?"

I nodded again. Majispin had called ahead as promised, so what was Pat's game?

"I'm tellin' ye now, I've done no such thing."

"Okay. Can I put my hands down?"

"No, ye may not! Ye'll back out of here and be done with or I'll splatter yer—"

Pat's eyes spasmed, fluttering and clenching shut, its entire body rippling slightly. This was a moment I could capitalize on. I brought my left hand down while simultaneously twisting to the right, moving myself out of the line of fire. I wasn't sure if the dwarf were capable of not pulling the trigger while spasming. If it wanted to fire now, the front door would be blown out. With a twist, I wrenched the weapon out of Pat's hands.

"Aaaaah, damn it!" It clawed at its face with short, articulated fingers. "Ah, you there. I'll have nothin' to do with this, aye? Nothin'! I told Alivara I didn't want nae callers, an' I meant it!"

I slowly let the hammers of the shotgun drop back home, unlocked the hinge, and split the weapon in half, exposing the shells. Pulling them out, I saw that they were slugs, not buckshot. Clicking the hinged halves back together again, I held the weapon loosely in my hand, juggling the shells in my other. I didn't doubt Pat could've killed me with it. I was obviously faster than it was, but the rounds would've blown me to hell. Even if it were a glancing shot.

I placed the gun on the counter with both of my hands on the weapon and sighed. "I'm not here to hurt you. I just need some information."

Pat's only response was a laconic middle finger.

The small being watched me as I took several deep breaths through my nose, maintaining as much calm as possible, taking in as much as I could. I hopped lightly over the counter and slowly walked to the back of the place, breathing deeply. I still carried the shotgun loosely in one hand. The proprietor stood by the counter, impeccably dressed and waiting. There was nothing about the small being that I could identify as human.

There was not a trace of any familiar scent from the murder scenes here. The entire time, Pat watched and followed me with spastic eyes. I came back to the front and hopped back over the counter. I turned the weapon so that I held it by the barrel and presented it to Pat, placing the shells, business end up, on the counter.

It snatched the gun and shoved it under the counter, swatting the shells to the floor. Then it leveled a small finger at me and said, "I'd never create something as abominable as a Thrall. Never!"

"Do you have books here that would detail the process?"

Pat looked thoughtful for a moment and answered, "Yes, o' course. The books are kept locked away and, to the casual eye, they'd appear blank anyhow. The things're, eh, encrypted"—when Pat said the word, it performed a sarcastic wave of its hands—"to use some o' that modern parlance. Only a precious few practitioners could penetrate me cellar undetected. An' then, the theft would not go undetected but for 'n hour or two. I check 'em every day, sunup to sundown, an' I know every top-notch sorcerer 'n' sorceress in the area." Pat tapped its misshapen noggin sagely.

"And if someone were to kill you?"

"Tsk. Please. Then all this would be lost to *everyone*. This place is as much a part o' me as I am a part o' it. Inextricable."

"Are there other ways to learn?"

"'Course there are, ya daft—oh, the uneducated masses, how I weep for ye! Someone else could tell someone else. No, aye? Ever cross that beastly walnut of a noggin there?"

Pat had a point. I curiously inquired about the shop—or what I thought was a shop.

"It's a bookstore, lad; ye truly are soft, aren't ya? We all make a living now, don't we?"

"I suppose so. Are books about magic the only thing you carry?"

"You're serious, aren't ye? Gods above and below." Pat's eyes rolled, twitching in their sockets, and it continued, exasperated, "I got sci-fi, romance, mysteries, a comprehensive selection of used books—that includes recent textbooks, if you're interested in gettin' some education, dummy—history, pure fiction, and more. Lemme guess; ye're probably quite the Harlequin man, nay? Nah, betcha like the torrid histories, aye? Youngish gentlemoron such as yourself? Got a real steamer right here, and I'll give it to ye for ten even."

"Ten seems a bit steep for a mass-market paperback."

"In my store, dullard, ye pay for content, not construction, an' this stuff, me furry trespasser, is *important*."

Pat waited, book in hand and extended in my direction for an uncomfortable amount of time. I relented, handed over the ten dollars, and tucked the paperback into my pocket without looking at it.

"Thanks." I said and couldn't resist a final question. "Where are you from, Pat?"

The small, warped being exploded with anger. "If ye canna tell on your own, then it's none of your damn business—get the hell out of me store!" That last bit came out amongst a spray of spittle that might have been pure venom for all I knew.

Dodging the stream of incoherent invective coming from Pat's ugly head, I backed out as quickly and quietly as I could, satisfied that the shopkeeper wasn't involved in this.

Once outside and several steps down the block, I produced the list Majispin had given me. Sure enough, Pat's name and address blew off the page, tiny particles of charged ink, and I felt a small pop of electricity at my fingertips. The writing left no trace.

My next stop was in the South End. Oddly enough, the "South" End was not located in the southernmost part of Boston. What was once primarily a black neighborhood was now largely white, gay-friendly, and affluent but for the Hispanic pockets in the area. I stood on the corner, wondering how I could remember those immaterial facts about the South End, but not how to get there quickly. I concentrated for a moment, trying to imagine the streets and major landmarks, gave up, and pulled one of the maps out.

The fastest way there from where I was, on foot, was straight down Tremont Street. The closer I got to the South End, the more beautiful the brownstones' façades and verandas became. The change was gradual as I progressed through Chinatown and the sundry limbo between New England Medical and the South End proper. I thought more about Boston's recent history, working to retain information rather than lose it.

One of the city's major newspaper's headquarters was nearby—what was the name? The elevated train used to run straight past it. Since the last time I'd been here, Boston had removed the rails and sent the elevated transport partially underground and parallel to Tremont Street in what is now known as the…as the… as the Southwest Corridor.

The resulting move cut off nearly one-third of Boston's residents from rapid transit. That third lived along a condensed section of the Washington Street corridor and was primarily nonwhite. Racism? Always difficult to prove. On the other hand, it was obvious that a major mode of transportation had been removed from inner-city residents. Since then, intermittent development was improving Washington Street commercially and bringing the slow, exclusive pall of gentrification. Where it had already occurred, Washington Street in Roxbury mysteriously became Washington Street in the South End. These thoughts stirred undeniably awful and authentic racist memories of my own. None of this was useful information to unravel the plot, but it felt damn fine to recall it all. I knew they were self-satisfying facts reinforcing stereotypes, but they were satisfying nonetheless. Then it just made me wonder again, how long had I been in Boston, and what had brought me here?

Across the street, in the crowd, I could see the little blond boy again. What in my thoughts could have dragged him into view? He flickered as pedestrians streamed past, oblivious to his presence. Pale, bluish skin stretched tightly around his neck and shoulders as he pumped his thin arms in frustration. I could clearly see the puncture wounds around his torso bleeding freely down his legs. Puncture wounds that matched my teeth. I still couldn't remember his name. I'm not sure that I ever knew it, but I could clearly recall the taste of his flesh, and I shuddered. Not with grief or sorrow, but with pleasures long past and desperately ignored.

Emotion and logic dictated guilt; my appetite only craved. In a brief moment, when he was completely obscured from my vision, he disappeared. I stood, jaw clenched, a cold feeling between my shoulder blades. He'd never appeared this often before, only occasionally at murder scenes or at times of my near-death. What was different now?

Shaking the moment off, I realized that I wasn't too far from Maria's place; she was closer to Roxbury and in a Spanish enclave. She could be following me right now. Or not. Since Majispin knew exactly where I'd be going, I didn't think it mattered anymore. I was certain he hadn't worked any tracking magic on me, so he'd have to use Maria or one of his henchmen to follow me. More likely, he could divine the list's location.

Majispin was only being cooperative insofar as he was likely to gather more information. He seemed reluctant to grasp the size of the situation, so sure of what he already knew. The magician didn't strike me as a coward, but we were all cruising into unexplored territory. Was he being cautious or dissembling?

As for Maria, I didn't have a real clue regarding her whereabouts, and I realized I hadn't seen her for nearly twenty-four hours. My thoughts turned briefly to Tina, and to Seth's unrequited love for her. She, too, had disappeared, and no one had noticed for twenty-four hours. Could Mark have done something to Maria? Possibly. Her reactions to Mark were decidedly passive-aggressive. That, on the surface, seemed odd to me, since Maria appeared so independent and openly defiant. Whatever it was that I was getting myself into, it kept my mind racing. That was good. I, at least, understood my own motivations. I blandly hoped that my attraction to Maria wouldn't motivate me any more than it already had.

The next address on the list brought me to a very upscale brownstone on a bisected, tree-lined street. A water fountain bubbled in the center of the green strip—coincidentally, in front of my target's address. According to the mailbox, there was only one occupant here. So the inhabitant used all three floors. It was a very luxe address.

I rang the bell and waited. A tinny, clipped voice came through the small speaker beneath the buzzer.

"Yes?"

"This is Alexander Smith. Alivara Majispin gave me your name; you must be expecting me."

"Ah. Mr. Smith. Come in." The door buzzed and unlocked.

I stepped into the small foyer and through to the reception hall where a glowing, ornate chandelier dominated the ceiling. The floor had been laid with impossibly tiny tiles. Everything was impeccably clean, but I couldn't detect much more than a hint of disinfectant, or what must have been the building's sole occupant. Lacquered original hardwood had been intricately inlaid into the floors and beadboards, not a lick of pine. It seemed that the entire interior was composed of expensive, natural materials. There was a gigantic, bulbous pot on the floor near the corner of the reception area. A plant with a stalk as thick around as my thigh stood stock-straight to the ceiling. It reached towards the sunshine pouring down the open stairway from the roof, where, apparently, a skylight was set. Velvety red petals clung seductively around the head of the segmented topmost portion of the plant. I took a curious step forward and the plant moved slightly in my direction.

I took a cautious step backward.

With my eyes closed, I took several deep breaths through my nose. I was trying to determine if anything at all was familiar in the scent profile of this house—anything that I might've picked up from the case. Nothing struck me, but that didn't mean something wasn't hidden at the very top or bottom of this structure.

Shoefalls sounded on wood before I saw him. He carefully walked down the stairs with precise, confident steps.

Like your murderer. Kill him before he gets to you, too, reverberated somewhere in my mind.

Not now, damn it, be still.

His scent washed ahead of him, indicating that he was swathed in a light sweat, and confirmed that he was alone in the building. I also smelled blood.

A slender, pale man with long, dark hair combed backwards to his shoulders came into view. Beneath a thick rubber smock, he wore a suit that mirrored the slate color of his eyes perfectly. In his hands, he loosely held a pair of gloves that matched the smock, and a pair of goggles with clear glass lenses hung around his neck.

At the bottom of the stairs, the alchemist extended his hand and said, "Pleased to make your acquaintance, Mr. Smith. I am Dr. Quentin Bismark." Bismark had the cultured affectations of a classic Bond villain, and he looked the part.

"Please, call me Alexander, Doctor." I shook his hand. It was a firm shake, and when he withdrew, I could feel a frictionless powder on my fingers. I rubbed the tips together, looked down, then up at him. It was talcum, probably from the gloves. I hoped it was from the gloves.

He smiled briefly and said, "Shapeshifter, hm? An old one, at that."

I must've looked a bit surprised and started to worry if it really was talcum on my fingers.

"This way, please." Dr. Bismark indicated a sitting room with a graceful gesture. As we moved in and sat, he added, "I didn't use anything on you, Mr. Smith; it's in your eyes. They're unusually clean. I've only seen clearer blue sclera on babies. And...the movement of the body. You're radiating some kind of power, though, being human, I can't really sense it; to do what I do requires observation, you understand."

"And my age?" I asked.

"Simple deduction. Knowing that you're a shapeshifter and seeing such a strong ethnic mix of African and Native American, I felt it reasonable to assume you've been around since the mid-1800s or so."

The doctor was keenly observant. I could be as well, when I managed to put my mind to it. His immaculate suit had a stretch crease around the shoulders, and there was a tiny spot of blood on his tie-crumpled collar. I wasn't a shark with miles of ocean connecting us, so that small amount wouldn't tweak my nose and raise an alarm, but a wound in his hairline might do it.

"Bump your head, doctor?"

Bismark glanced back over his shoulder; a nervous look flashed across his features before he smiled and replied, "Lab accident, Mr. Smith; careless of me. Tell me, should I be concerned that you're here?"

I was puzzled by that question. "What do you mean?"

"Like vampires, your kin have only the potential for immortality. It is a long life with a price, in my experience."

Clearly he was referring to our propensity for time-induced insanity, the instability that I had, so far, been able to keep at bay. "My time may come, Doctor, but it won't be today, I can assure you." An easy lie, honed by several years of covering up memory loss. I couldn't honestly assure him; my mind had taken too many unbidden turns lately. That, at least, I *could* remember.

"Tea?" He raised his eyebrows and reached for a silver tray set on the coffee table.

The thought that it was probably a bad idea to drink anything in an alchemist's home crossed my mind, but a cup of tea sounded very good at the moment.

"Yes, thank you. Black, please."

The doctor made a show of preparing the tea, carefully measuring out the leaves into the strainer and setting the tray.

"Have you ever had tea with an alchemist, Mr. Smith?"

"I can't say that I have. You're not going to call me 'Alexander,' are you?"

Dr. Bismark simply smiled. "Hm. This particular brand, like all others, stems from the singular tea plant, *Camellia sinensis*. It is the preparation of such that makes the tea unique. Blowing air across its leaves, such as the variety we're having here, withers the tea, so that the leaves can then be oxidized, a process also known as fermentation—a misnomer—in the tea industry. This is whole-leaf, which affords us the most expansive and flavorful experience. The best teas, as this one, are produced and sorted by hand, not the barbaric methods of cutting and grinding and stuffing into insulting little bags."

Bismarck finished his explanation rather bitterly as he rolled the last bits of tea from his fingers into the basket, retaining a few leaves in his palm.

"Tea is also used in divination—I'm sure you know—to determine the course of one's destiny."

"I've...heard that." I was trying to divine Bismark's motivation. This rant, from someone I'd just met, someone whose appearance seemed so very controlled, but whose demeanor skewed erratically, confused me.

"Certainly you have, but did you know that tea has many other fabulous properties as well? I mean, just imagine. A few leaves left in the bottom of a cup say ever so much about the individual who drank the tea— if one knows how to read such things. Such a small thing, but it indicates so much potential in other uses."

Bismark held a small portion of leaves in his palm, scattering them with an index finger, then he brushed them into the pot as well, with a brief, but sad smile.

"And do you know how to use them, Dr. Bismark?"

"Of course, of course; it's quite simple, really. I mention this to you out of respect, Mr. Smith; I can see the look of confusion about your eyes. I would not wish you to leave such things lying casually about. One with a long life behind him has many things he would wish to remain private, I'm certain."

The teapot heated and steamed without an apparent heat source, and Bismark dropped the strainer into the top of the pot. "It will be a few minutes. What specifically brings you to me, Mr. Smith?"

I didn't hesitate to answer. "Thralls."

He sputtered, hands shaking, and said, "What? Where?"

"I came across one yesterday. It's been killing children. I'm here to find out who could've made it and where they might be. Naturally, you're a suspect."

He settled back thoughtfully, fiddling with his black tie and loosening the crooked knot to smooth out his deformed collar before saying, "Perhaps I should've taken some *time* to speak with Mr. Majispin earlier and considered the *possibilities* before you arrived." Bismark spoke through a clenched jaw. "Naturally, I'd never create such a thing."

"It seems that no one would ever confess to it."

"No, they wouldn't. It's an abominable practice, very cruel. I doubt there are many individual sorcerers alive today who might do it."

The teapot rattled; Dr. Bismark carefully poured the hot liquid into silver-laced glass cups and handed one over. Once we'd each taken a sip, I asked, "Then who else?"

"Perhaps a group. Druids. A coven." He shrugged. "I wouldn't know unless I had the Thrall to examine carefully."

I still didn't like the idea of considering a group of people. It was a rare thing for serial killers to operate in tandem, and just as rare for vampires to hunt that way. They didn't have any clear reasons to share in such things. There simply was no need, and any quarry taken would disappear, not be ritualistically bled and discarded. Too messy. Then again, my quarry wasn't exactly in this for the thrill of killing. Perhaps they were being controlled or manipulated? I was again reminded that I was in new territory and had better catch up quick.

"Why a group?"

Bismark took another sip of his tea and seemed to settle on some course of action. He sighed, set his cup down, and took a deep breath before speaking. "The creation of a Thrall is an abhorrent practice and generally frowned upon, but—you've heard of 'wilding,' or perhaps seen a riot, I assume?"

I nodded and waited for him to explain.

"Well, in a group—any group—atrocities that are generally discouraged become easier somehow, more accessible. Stoning in the Middle East, lynching in the old American South, the Nazis and their Holocaust—there are many examples. Not that a Thrall would be created in the heat of the moment, but it would be easier on the conscience to 'share' the evil, as it were." He took a sip of his tea and added, more to himself than me, "A group like that would need to operate in the utmost secrecy; discovery would only hamper their efforts. Creating a Thrall is a practice for those whose beliefs and behaviors are not necessarily in the best interests of society at large. Perhaps a group of creatures that didn't require a conscience, a group that would violently resist any efforts to stop them." The doctor made to run his hand through his hair, but stopped himself and clenched at nothing before dropping his hand into his lap and sucking his teeth.

I saw his point. It fit, but I couldn't discern where his emotional connection to this was coming from. There was a lot going on here, and all indications thus far were that a group or network of some sort was behind the murders. No one had yet admitted having any real idea of who it might be. I didn't think Bismark was involved; he had been the most forthcoming amongst anyone I'd yet spoken to about this. I considered the man sitting resignedly across from me; his entire bearing continued to shift from when we'd first met. He seemed to be flowing between a tightly controlled anger and a weary disgust.

Whatever was bothering him wasn't my concern, however; I needed to stay on target. Keep moving. If this were a group of some sort, the trick, eventually, was going to be cutting off the serpent's head and hoping that it wasn't a hydra—if I could find the serpent. It was possible that all of these men were covering for each other, that I was being manipulated, stumbling from one co-conspirator to another. How thorough could they be in concealing clues from my senses? I dismissed the idea. No normal human being could be that thorough. We all had something in common on this plane of existence—human foibles were hard to shake.

"How would you propose finding the culprits, then?"

He shrugged and answered, "Luck?"

This wasn't getting me anything but tea and more friends. All of this information was helpful mostly as insight into the magicians' culture. I could only hope that it might help me bag the perpetrator—or perpetrators. I started to wonder why Dr. Bismark was being so forthcoming and asked him as much.

"The sooner I get you out of here, Mr. Smith, the sooner I can finish what I'm working on. Besides, it must be important, or Mr. Majispin wouldn't have given you my address. Sending you here is not the kind of personal capital that is spent lightly."

"What are you working on—if you don't mind my asking, Doctor?" I had thoughts of cauldrons of lead bubbling over into gold.

He smiled and I was reminded of a ferret. He set his tea down, leaned forward, splayed his hands on either side of his face, and said, "The distillation of pure good and evil." He seemed, faced with considering his work, to have immediately forgotten whatever was bothering him.

I blinked twice, unsure I'd heard him correctly. I wasn't sure how to comment so I asked, "How?"

"Like most conundrums, Mr. Smith, the immediate problem is likely not the one that needs to be solved. I have deduced, for instance, that the distilled essence of evil would need to be housed in, perhaps, the hollowed bone of an innocent child. The same for the inversion, I suspect—storage in the hollowed bone of a guilty man. I am not sure I can ethically acquire such things, Mr. Smith. Of course, this also raises more questions. When is a child considered no longer innocent, and when is a man truly guilty?"

Some kind of understanding came to Bismark just then; his face cleared and his eyes met mine. "Immediate issues cloaked within larger conundrums, the distance between guilt and innocence, problems within problems, you see?"

I was starting to understand why Ana and Maria described men like Bismark and Majispin as mad scientists.

I stood up and thanked the doctor. He shook my hand again and hesitated when I handed him the tea cup. There was a small puddle with several leaves floating in the bottom of the cup. Oh, yes, bottoms up. I downed the last bit and handed the empty cup to Bismark. He escorted me to the door. As I was stepping out of the building, he called to me.

"Don't sell luck short, Mr. Smith. Luck's just another word for random occurrences and information colliding to give new insight. The prepared mind, you see."

The words, true as they might be, triggered literary memories for me. Currently useless memories, but how could a monster losing his mind pass up an opportunity to appear present? "Paraphrasing Jefferson and Pasteur in one breath, Doctor?"

He smiled sadly with a soft snort and closed the door with an antique *click*.

A wisp of particles wound its way up and out of my pocket as I reached for the list. Only one name and address remained, near the expressway, on the other side of the Financial District.

Blood for the Sun

"Problems within problems." I knew there was more here than met the eye, but I had nothing else to go on. Or did I? Maybe I'd forgotten some crucial detail or missed something. I might be tackling this problem entirely from the wrong angle. All the same, until something else occurred to me, I had no choice but to forge ahead.

The sun would be setting within the next hour. I could probably run there in five minutes or less, but speeding through the gridlocked streets of Boston on foot isn't the way to avoid drawing attention. Besides, I was burning with hunger. I dipped into a sub shop and picked up two of the biggest steak sandwiches they had. It took me the better part of a half hour to arrive by cab and less than ten minutes of the ride to devour the sandwiches. I nibbled the basket of French fries thoughtfully. Despite Boston's relatively humble size, it can take an interminable amount of time to get from one part of downtown to the other.

I had the cab drop me off at the corner, not feeling patient enough to wait for the block-long crawl through traffic. This part of town was especially noisy during rush hour; thousands of commuters were busy stuffing their cars onto the so-called expressway. The reek of exhaust was acutely irritating to my sensitive nose.

Maria trotted up to me and matched my brisk pace.

"Maria."

"Alexander." She matched my tone mockingly.

I handed her the fries. "Majispin already knows what I'm doing and where I'm at; why are you here?" My question was tinged with a genuine curiosity, not malice.

"Couldn't think of anything better to do." She smiled. "Kidding. Majispin said you might need my help with something here."

Okay, she was still on my good side, and I swear she didn't remind me of Tina. They were nothing alike—

177

well, except for the inexplicable-lust part. It wouldn't hurt to have an extra pair of hands with me for this last stop. It was a sort of gentleman's club for practitioners of magic. Not the sort of place that was part of the safe-house network, it was an entirely unknown quantity to me. The man I was supposed to see, Dochevsky Popov, was the proprietor, so I hoped that I had a good chance of getting to him at the door without having to go in.

I abruptly stopped walking. Maria took two steps and looked back.

"I'm hating it when you do that. What's wrong?"

I looked around and glanced at the list again, feeling lost. This was the right place. My patience was already close to an end—how could Maria stand this concentrated pollution? There are some things I've never been able to get used to, and the rank smell of concentrated exhaust was one of them.

Without looking at Maria, I said, "This is the right address, but there's no club here."

"Really? Lemme see." She held out her hand.

This annoyed me a bit more. I don't know what it is, but most men can't stand it when a woman double-checks on them during travel. I handed the paper over without complaint, however. She looked it over, handed it back and said:

"It's blank."

"What is?"

"The list you just gave me! Good God, what's your problem?"

What the hell? Then I remembered that Majispin had cursed the list for my eyes only. I explained Majispin's trick and read the address out loud to her.

"Oh, no problem."

She pulled a tiny leather sack out of her pocket and kissed it. There wasn't a flash of light or puff of smoke. No sound. The only indication that power had been invoked was the uncomfortable trill up my spine.

Maria shivered like an ice cube had slid down her back. The entrance was simply *there*. Small magic. I looked at Maria and raised an eyebrow.

"The boss gave us all one of these sacks for errands like this. The entrances of places like this are hide-y. Keeps the riff-raff out."

I was starting to feel very grateful that Maria had turned up. I was also grateful that she hadn't asked for the list to verify that I was an illiterate idiot. Asking to look at the list was easier than playing twenty questions with me regarding this place.

The entrance was set six steps below street level. A small purple awning on slim brass posts framed the simple affair. At the bottom of the stairs, a brass plaque set in a brass-studded, leather-bound door read: VIRTUS EST QUAM APPLICATIO SCIENTIAE.

I pointed at the plaque and asked Maria, "Can you read that?"

She scrunched up her face and stared at me.

I translated, to the best of my poor Latin, "'Power is the application of knowledge.'"

She rolled her eyes and said, "Whatever." When she pushed on the door—it had no apparent doorknob or push plate—it didn't budge.

We stole a glance at each other and waited a beat before I reached towards the barrier. A doorknob appeared and I was able to open the door. A dry heat crept out of the establishment. Most of the seats were full, and all the attendees spoke in hushed tones. I stopped just inside the doorway and looked back. The entrance had closed behind me and there was no sign of Maria. I started to head back when a hand touched my arm.

"No ladies allowed, sir, sorry." A squat, hairy man smoking a long ivory pipe had stopped me.

I simply nodded and turned back to the room. It was similar to The Sweaty Magus in that the front was a

Errick A. Nunnally

combination of foyer and lounge bar. Plush Edwardian chairs and couches were scattered about, encircling small tables made of dark-hued woods. A large, copper-plated door at the back of the room was under guard by a burly man with a grey complexion and a symbol etched into his forehead; it looked like Arabic.

The bar wasn't crowded, so I stepped right up to it. The bartender, a nondescript man with dark hair, white shirt, and black pants, wandered over. I couldn't exactly place his accent. Maybe Central European or thereabouts.

"How can I help you, sir?"

"Can you ring Mr. Popov, the manager?" I asked, "He's expecting me."

The barkeep nodded and picked up an antique phone behind the bar. I took a seat. "The manager will be out in a moment; he'll be coming from the copper door," said the man, hanging up the house phone and lackadaisically going about other business.

It was odd that he'd told me where Popov would be coming from, but moments later, the copper door opened and I understood why. The manager sported a long salt-and-pepper beard that mingled with the black of his suit. I couldn't tell if he wore a tie or not, but his white shirt seemed to glow in the weak lighting of the place. As he got closer, I could see that his eyes were very small, compared to the size of his head, and his pupils were pinpointed so that the irises overwhelmed. They gave his eyes a fiery blue center. He was blind, or something very like it.

Dochevsky Popov walked carefully down the aisle between the bar and the lower seating, stopped one pace in front of me, turned, and extended his hand.

As we shook hands, he inclined his head in a polite bow. "Mr. Smith, I've been expecting you. Drink?"

"Call me Alexander, and no, thank you."

"Nonsense, you will drink vodka with me." Popov slid into the seat next to me, raised one hand, middle, index finger, and thumb extended, and remained that way until the bartender poured two shots of vodka from a tall bottle with rounded corners and placed a small bowl of pickled gherkins and tiny forks between us. Popov expertly speared one of the pickles and placed it under his nose before raising the vodka in appreciation.

"*Za vas*, my friend! Ivan Kalita to warm your soul."

The drink was indeed warming, but I doubted my soul benefited in any way. I took a deep breath, sorting scents out in the bar, testing the air as discreetly as I could. Popov had chosen an unusually public meeting place for our conversation.

The Russian spoke around his gherkin as he crunched. "Alivara sketched out, in general, the problem you are having. There are very few people here who could—" Popov stopped abruptly and held one finger up: *wait*. He reached into his jacket and placed a coin on the counter. When he traced his finger around the edges of the coin, I felt a pulse of air, the *zing* of supernatural energy, and the room went dead silent.

I looked around us, the patrons' mouths were still moving, but no sound reached us.

"I can only imagine what your face looks like, Alexander." Popov leaned in close—too close—and, grinning, added, "It's simply for a measure of privacy. One does not discuss these matters for the general public to hear." He shifted back in his seat, to my relief.

He began again, "Where was I? Oh, yes. There are precious few individuals in this town, that I'm aware of, who could create a Thrall, let alone would care to do it."

"I'm beginning to understand that."

"Yes, well, I'm not sure how I can help you."

"I'm sure you understand that you're a suspect."

"Of course."

In this enclosed space, I wasn't getting any kind of body language that hinted at guilt or any kind of evidentiary scent related to the case. I recalled that none of the men I questioned gave any indication that what they were being asked was unusual. Liars, even good ones, uncontrollably alter their scent, their physical mannerisms change, and the timing of their answers is delayed or rushed. How often did one of these practitioners go rogue and perform some forbidden act? Any number would be uncomfortable to me. Popov, unlike Majispin, wasn't bothering to mask his scent markers; I had full access and what I smelled was a normal human being.

Most humans immediately deny or lie when even remotely accused of any wrongdoing. The last two men I'd met simply admitted that they could've done it without any of the telltale signs of dissembling. It struck me as odd that so few women were involved in these sorcerous circles, as far as I could tell. I'd have to remember to ask Ana about that. Well, I'd have to try to remember.

I asked Popov, "Do you know of any groups— covens, druids, and such—that might practice this kind of thing?"

"You suspect that a group is behind this?"

"I believe that only a group could orchestrate the amount of activity I've become aware of."

"I see, I see." Popov became reflective and sipped another shot of vodka, placed with sly skill by the nonchalant bartender.

I waited and assessed the room again. One man watched us. When I had come in, he had taken notice but had been mid-conversation. Now, he was alone. There was nothing immediately familiar about him. He was restless and watchful. Could he be a spy, a coconspirator? Maybe both. Maybe I was being jumpy, maybe not.

I turned in my chair and excused myself to Popov, begging for a moment of patience. I looked directly at the gentleman across the room and waited. He only glanced at me, but now he knew I was watching him. If he wanted to leave, he'd have to go past me. I didn't get the impression that passing through the copper door was a simple or readily available process.

The subject was average height, about five foot ten. He had short black hair and an athletic build. He wore grey pants and a black, silken shirt; leather shoes, black socks—very casually chic. His nose was slightly crooked, as if it had been broken at least once, long ago; prominent eyebrows and full lips above a pointed, cleft-less chin. Not exactly Caucasian—his skin was an unusual tone—I couldn't place his ethnicity, perhaps southern European.

Studiously keeping his eyes off me, he twirled an empty glass between his hands and bobbed one leg impatiently.

"Something caught your eye, Alexander?" My name, coming from Popov's lips, sounded magical in a Russian accent.

"Not something, some*one*. He was watching us."

"Well, my friend, that is interesting."

Abruptly, the fellow stood up, grabbed his jacket, and breezed past me. For a moment, something about him seemed familiar—the walk, clutch of the hand, or his scent, perhaps. Definitely the scent, but I'd never met this man. I was distracted, though, by the makeup he was wearing. Foundation. Plenty of the clay-like smell trailed him. Something else tugged at my mind, and I realized he'd popped out of his seat almost exactly when the sun went below the horizon. I could thank many years of being a part of the circadian cycle for that sense of time.

Popov broke me from my reverie. "Eh, that reminds me, I only know of one person who may be a member of a coven—can't remember his name. Male witches, hm. Odd fellow, wears enough makeup that I can smell it occasionally. Perhaps he just walked by?"

It seemed that this discussion was going to have to wait.

TWELVE

I was neither polite nor gentle about it; I blasted off my stool as if I'd been set on fire. Popov gasped as I popped through the invisible bubble around us. His entourage—the grey-complexioned giant—lunged at me. I hadn't realized how close he was. His hand closed about my bicep and I swung around at the surprising strength of that clasp. He'd been able to close so easily because he had no human scent to speak of and his grip was like steel, so as I spun I turned out of his grip, exploiting the weak points of a grasping hand, seized him at the wrist, and twisted his arm in turn. I had no quarrel with Popov or his guard, so I wanted to get out without any real violence. I went completely around the man, knocking over chairs, breaking his grip, and continued straight down the length of the bar to get out. I shouted a brief apology to Popov over my shoulder.

The door took a moment to open, though, and when I got outside, Maria stood there with a basket of fries and a disgusted look on her face. I'd been wondering where I'd put those fries—and what the hell was she doing here and where the hell was I going? *Goddamnit.*

"Are those my French fries?" I asked her.

"What?"

"The fries, are they mine?"

185

"Well, yeah." Her face scrunched up and one corner of her mouth quirked as she squinted at me. "What the hell is wrong with you? You gave me these damn things; you want 'em back? Take 'em!" She shoved the basket in my direction.

Movement caught the corner of my eye, and I saw a man moving quickly down the street, shrugging into his jacket. Oh, yes, I'd been right in the middle of that. My quarry couldn't have been twenty feet away from her.

With no time to explain or mince words, I pointed and shouted, "Stop him!"

Maria had begun to step toward me but didn't hesitate when I shouted; French fries scattered across the sidewalk. The foundation-wearing man didn't even turn around. He broke into a flat-out run. If Maria hadn't taken off when she did, he'd have outpaced her shortly. As it was, we'd all nearly reached the end of the block when the man suddenly whirled.

There was a flash of light and a burst of smoke, and the acrid scent of sulfur and ammonia twisted up my nose with jagged purpose. My eyes felt like they were melting; there was a sensation that I can only describe as a hot poker being shoved into my head. I gagged once and pressed on through the dark-grey cloud, clenching against the pain. I almost tripped over Maria; she was on the ground with her face pressed into her hands, screaming between sobbing and choking. She'd gotten the worst of it.

On the other side of the dissipating mist, there was no sign of my suspect. This man was definitely not a human being—he'd exploded down the street with the immediate speed of a supernatural creature. My eyes continued to water and my throat itched. It would be a good while before my sense of smell healed itself, so I helped Maria to her feet, ignoring the futile chase.

She had been affected much more seriously than I had. It wouldn't do to have to answer any questions on this busy street. I led her to a more secluded area, where she leaned over a mailbox to get her breathing back to normal.

"What the hell was that?" she said around coughing fits.

"The smoke or the guy we were chasing?"

She managed to shoot me a dirty look despite the acidic smog's effects.

We'd be operable soon; our systems would filter out the chemicals quickly enough. But the sudden blast had served its purpose. "It was a mix of sulfur and ammonia. Confounds scents and burns the nasal passages."

She coughed again. "That last part I knew."

"I think we can consider this confirmation that he's involved."

She straightened angrily and said, "What the hell is going on, anyway? Majispin won't say a thing about it, and he's twitchier than usual. No one at the club has really spoken for days. I get the impression that there's more going on than a zombie in the sewers. What gives?" Then she sniffed and her eyes watered further.

I couldn't tell if she was going to cry in earnest, or if the chemicals were still causing her eyes to burn. I was suddenly reminded of Tina again. There had been a great deal of crying near the end, and tremendous heartache—the last heartache I could honestly admit to owning. Tina had been fragile, more delicate than I was willing to admit at the time. As far as I had been concerned, Curry was dead and she should've been happy about it.

On a whim, I pulled out a blank scrap of paper and wrote Tina's full name on it. Unimaginable, that I could be so immature in thought and behavior at that age. I had been a relatively young shapeshifter and it had shown, but I had already spent over forty years as a human being. And I was powerful, thankfully, just strong enough at the time to take down Curry, though he'd nearly killed me instead.

Maria swore under her breath, sniffed, and said, "Never mind, I don't wanna know." Dragging the heels of her hands across her eyes, she started walking away. "You comin'?"

"Where are you going?"

"This guy used magic, right? Well, we've got our own magician."

Back to Majispin's, of course; she was right. Seeing Maria walking next to me tickled my memory. My subconscious was trying to put some pieces together, but it was a jumbled mess. There was a connection between her and the character we'd briefly chased. I stopped angrily, and she took two extra steps.

"Aw, c'mon, cut that out, Jesus."

"I remember... that man from before."

"You've met him before?"

I started to walk again, and she took two quick steps to catch up. I told her, "Not exactly. The fight in the tunnel, remember?" She nodded. "That man's scent was on the Thrall, the foundation he was wearing. He's had some kind of direct contact with the thing."

"One of those vamps got away. Fat lot of good that does us now." She plucked at her red nose.

"Are you serious? I thought you'd killed the third one!" When I said it, she just looked at me. I cursed long and hard; the bastards had probably been foiling everything I'd been doing since that fight. Even if they didn't know me, anyone dealing in magical shit this big would know of Majispin and his connections. If they spent any time at the club, then they knew Maria. I was being played from all sides by a group of magic-practicing vampires, and I growled as much.

"That's ridiculous," she said. "Vampires don't practice magic." She snorted. "You've felt the pain just being near a large spell, I'm sure."

I left it at that; there was no need to have this argument with Maria or anyone else. They could believe what they liked. I knew that pain could be managed; that much was true for anyone. For proof, one had to look no further than the growing industry of body modification sweeping the world—and those were just the humans.

It didn't take long to get back to Majispin's. His response was virtually the same as Maria's.

Incredulous, he said, "What? That's unheard of." Then he sat down, fidgeted a bit, stood up, and walked away. Majispin stopped short and waved irritatedly for Maria and me to follow him. He went through a side door that led to a steep set of steps. It was dark, but no one seemed to care. Majispin started talking when we were out of the main room.

"This is something that's…"—Majispin searched for the words—"it's just not done. Vampires don't dabble in serious magic. It's not done." He waved his hand dismissively.

"Why not?" I asked.

Majispin stopped on the stairs and turned around. "Look, how do you feel when magic's active and afoot?"

I didn't like to discuss my weaknesses any more than the next person. I waffled and couched my answer. "Uncomfortable."

Majispin made a dismissive sound and waved his hand rudely. "I know it intrudes aggressively into your person, like a sonic wave on your bones. Your very spine quakes. You ever been hit with the click of a sperm whale? Who has, hm? *I have*, just to get a sense of the equivalent effect, to learn what it's like to have your bones vibrate in your body, to taste the possibility of being liquefied from the inside out. Magnify *that* discomfort exponentially and you'll get a sense of what it'd mean for one of your kind to personally practice magic." He started up the stairs again. "Vampires are already infused with power, like yourself. It's not natural for them to fool around with the magic forces. There's no need, and I don't think that they really could. Not with much success, anyway."

"Pain can be managed, and we're the most unnatural fucking things on this planet." I told him exactly what I was thinking, although I was sure that he'd considered it. He was being dismissive, egotistical, and not honestly examining the information right under his nose. For someone so keen on learning more, his operative thought process regarding shapeshifters and vampires seemed dogmatic. In my own experience, vampires were far more resilient than 'shifters. If either of our kind could successfully practice magic, it'd be them.

He stopped again. "Yes, yes, I know that. What exactly do you know of the origins of shapeshifters and vampires?"

"I know we've been around since as long as human recollection. I know that vampires are parasitic in nature, more viral in transmission of the condition, as it were. I think that whatever powers us probably isn't from this reality."

"Astute enough." Majispin continued up the stairs and rounded a landing that I guessed was on the third floor. "There are humans and there are other things. Vampires and shapeshifters are somewhere between the two," he said.

We are a *mixture* of human and other—I already knew that.

The magician took on the tone of the scholar lecturing his class. "Some believe that vampires and shapeshifters are the remnants of two opposing armies, their spirits cast adrift in the ether, occasionally finding their way here to some human host, waiting for their respective leaders. Others think that the energy that powers one or the other has been deliberately cast into this dimension as a portent of invasion by opposing forces—something to soften us up, if you will, to tenderize human society. Yet more dismiss it all to a legend that the two groups are the souls of the cursed dead, forever doomed to repeat an ignominious end."

Majispin stopped in front of an inconspicuous wooden door and faced me. "The point is this—the common thread is that vampires and shapeshifters are *always* depicted as opposing forces and pawns in a larger game, beings of lesser value in the grand scheme of things, expendable. I know, I know." He raised his hands. "The idea probably irks you."

Majispin was not mistaken; I was insulted. I would never willingly follow some interdimensional despot, no matter what the cause. *Or the promise*, I reassured myself. I couldn't even come close to imagining what could turn me against Ana. She'd certainly suffered enough to simply exist, but it did point to a bigger picture—powerful beings dabbling here in our world.

It was, I had to admit, an intriguing idea that my distaste for magic had more to do with my power source's place in an interdimensional hierarchy than my personality, or perhaps, the personality of my source? Problems within problems; Bismark was right. I ground my teeth in frustration that I'd never really thought about this before. Perhaps that was by design?

"Now, listen." He went on in front of the door. "You're not supposed to be here. This breaks with my usual protocol, but now that you're a part of this house—"

I raised my hands, palms outward, and said, "Understand this, Majispin. I am not a part of this house, this pack, or any other organization. I'll walk out of here if I have to and deal on my own. It might take longer, but I don't give a damn."

Majispin took a deep breath, glanced at Maria, and said, "Fine. Control your temper. I just want you to understand that I've sworn my employees to reveal no details from my lab, study, or any other private area or my behavior in this building. I don't have the time to ensure that matter with you, so some assurances would go a long way."

I thought about it—the safe houses were a long-standing tradition. The people who ran them were not only honor-bound but watched over by the others in the coalition. When the chips were down, it was the only place in the preternatural world that any of us could have some kind of sanctuary or privacy to gather for meetings, negotiations, and discussion. I didn't necessarily trust anyone, but I'd have to trust Majispin for now. It occurred to me that he was probably banking on Maria to keep me in some kind of orbit.

I raised my arm to my mouth and bit through the skin. I held the wound out for Majispin to see and said, "I swear it."

As the blood dripped from my forearm, the drops burst into tiny flames before they touched the floor. The small wound healed quickly, and there were only a few drops before my skin closed. I'd only intended to spill some blood per an oath, but this reaction to the air was wholly unexpected. At most, the blood should have reached the floor and sizzled away to its untraceable elements.

Majispin nodded curtly in response. He seemed very interested in the volatile results, and somewhat surprised. Maria stood silently, thick eyebrows knit and eyes wide at the entire scene.

I had barely contained my shock. I'd never seen my blood do that before. My thoughts raced back to the Dragon and our deal. She'd referred to my legacy.

I ran the definition of the word down in my thoughts; the modern meaning was "something handed down from an ancestor." The classic meaning of the word was the "office of a deputy." What exactly was I destined to become? What were all of us once-humans, in the end?

Why the fucking hell could I remember the definition of "legacy" and not what had happened to Tina?

THIRTEEN

Inside what I assumed was an antechamber, a set of four claw-footed chairs nestled on a blood-red carpet. The carpet, woven with a chaotic pattern I couldn't discern, seemed vaguely Middle Eastern and featured metallic highlights reminiscent of the brass studs on the chairs. I could easily imagine Sherlock Holmes enjoying a respite with his pipe and needle. The warmly done walls featured rich wood paneling, and the lighting from a pair of waist-high Victorian lamps glowed, subtle and inviting. Set in one wall, a small open nook held a decanter set arranged on a silver tray. The back of the nook was mirrored. I noted that the wood paneling gave the impression that there were several doors in this cozy space. In an unoccupied moment, I wondered why Majispin wanted secrecy for this area. It occurred to me that the framed panels truly were doors leading to additional rooms.

Majispin gestured for us to sit. All the chairs were tall wing-backs. I didn't like this kind of seating because it limited my field of vision and sense of what was behind me. I chose one farthest from the flat of any walls, in the corner, facing the door we had entered through. The book I'd bought from Pat dug into my side, reminding me that it was still in my jacket pocket.

He asked if we wanted anything to drink. Both Maria and I refused, but he poured himself what looked and smelled like port. Getting to know Majispin, though, made me think that the liquid might be anything but. After taking one sip and having a seat, he began to talk.

"I've gotten word back from the other safe houses."

"And?" I prompted.

Majispin took a longer pull on his drink. "The long and short of it is that they are frightened."

"Of what, specifically?"

"A scholar in Trenton—of all places—thinks this is tied into some kind of prophecy that foretells an uprising of vampires. Our friend Pat disagrees and so do I. However, they're afraid of the same situation I told you about earlier, Alexander—the size of an organized group of vampires and what they might be up to. The idea that they have organized or formed an alliance with a coven is unthinkable. We need to find the witches responsible."

"One and the same." I reiterated. Majispin was being arrogant, assuming that only people like him could practice magic, falling back on superior behavior.

"Nonsense," he retorted without a thought.

"You have to admit, at the very least, that it's possible. Don't discount what you haven't yet experienced or what someone else can imagine."

"It's still highly unlikely, but that's not the point. *Whoever* is doing this must be found. Whether it's the vampires themselves"—he nodded to me—"or someone working with vampires."

I could imagine what would be possible. Vampires are difficult to stop under normal conditions; their bones are pliant and only a severe trauma to the head or spine can kill them outright. Or direct sunlight. If they were organizing and using magic to strengthen their position or themselves directly, they'd be nearly unstoppable. The real question was, to what purpose? If vamps did organize and rise up, they'd ultimately be forced to eliminate their food base. Humans would fight in a consistently escalating manner—as history has shown—and Americans, at least, would never flourish under dictatorial conditions.

The uprising would have to be immense, devastating, and tightly organized simply to take any form of control. The amount of industrial science and magic it would take to subjugate humanity—not to mention rival supernaturals—would need to be unimaginably involved. Just the public knowledge that monsters like us existed would be enough to cause mass hysteria and suspicion. Logic dictated a shadow society, quietly taking control behind the scenes. To date, none of us have been able to organize that well for very long.

How deep did the roots run in this organization? Would killing the leaders destabilize the movement, if there were one? One safe bet was that all the dead men leading this effort must be eliminated first.

The magician downed the last of the port and grimaced. "The other safe houses sent operatives to check the locations that you gave me. Two of them have found the symbol so far, same as you did—and they were unable to erase the taint left behind. The spell is charged; it's waiting to be tapped. The others will most likely turn up the same evidence. This has to be the last stop for the spell to work. It has to end here, one way or another."

"And the date?" I asked.

"Well," Majispin began, "according to the lunar cycle, it's a full moon."

"That I knew; so what?"

"We aren't sure. However, I can reasonably guess that it has more to do with some kind of cosmic alignment—not simply the full moon. There are various methods of using calendar systems and mathematics to make projections about the future—divination, astrology, whatever. The Maya divided time into hierarchical units and figured out how to manipulate reality within those blocks, reportedly. But there's no telling what this date means without an intimate knowledge of those techniques. Working backwards without knowing the why would, ironically, take too much time."

Still, either way, this had to be stopped. Right now. But first, I—we—had to find the culprits. Judging by the methods used by the suspect Maria and I had pursued, I thought Dr. Bismark might be able to help us. "Perhaps, considering what just happened to me and Maria, Dr. Bismark could provide some more assistance." I choked on the last word of my sentence. It isn't typical for me to gag. I swallowed hard and settled myself.

Majispin wasn't enthusiastic about the idea. "He's probably long gone. When anyone uses his contact information, it'd better be good because he relocates soon after. It'll be some time before I hear from him again. Your field trip cost me dearly on that front.

"Alexander, I'd appreciate it if you and the pack worked together to track this man you pursued earlier." He jumped into the space of my hesitation and added, "You could cover much more ground. You both know where you lost him. I *could* just have Maria and the rest try to do it on their own."

Unfortunately, he was right. It might be cliché for me to work alone, but the truth was that most people got in my way.

My throat constricted suddenly and I coughed hard.

"That might be a problem," I said, sounding strangled.

Both Maria and Majispin stared at me with blatant suspicion on their faces. I cleared my throat.

Maria spoke for the first time since we'd entered the room, "If you mean Mark, he'll behave. I'll talk to him."

"Fine." I relented, and Majispin smiled. The rough feeling in my throat resurged; I choked and coughed again. Maria stood up and put one hand on my shoulder.

"Are you all right?"

Majispin was happy to ignore my escalating respiratory ailment. "Excellent! Maria, corral Mark and have him organize the outing. Stress the importance of working together. Tell him there will be consequences."

"Fine, I'm fine. Excuse me; I'll be back." I left without looking back.

Outside, I made a call to Detective Roberts on another battered pay phone. I was starting to consider them my personal property. It was a sure thing he'd be on shift this late in the day. He answered on the first ring. When I identified myself, he tersely put me on hold to move to a private line.

He exploded back onto the phone. "What the fuck is going on? A friend of mine is dead!"

Calmly, I replied, "Did you look into the information I asked about?"

"What? Fuck that! I need some straight answers from you, Alexander, or whoever you are, or I'm going to track your ass down and bring you in!"

"Detective, listen. We've already covered this. I will disappear entirely if you try to do that." My throat rasped and my voice dropped an octave to an irritated growl.

"You son of a bitch, didn't you hear me? A *good friend of mine* is dead, and the harder I look at this case, the more fucked up it gets! *You* are becoming my problem."

"I know that. I'm sorry." I didn't know what else to say. I was falling back on convention, spitting out "I'm sorry" and hoping platitudes would smooth things over. I wasn't sorry—not really—and that worried me a little. I should have felt more empathy—something beyond what my own survival required. I knew Terrell had been a decent man. I hadn't known him long at all, but Roberts had. The truth was that I could probably have saved Terrell's life, and some sympathy would be appropriate, but what could I say? There was no way I could muddle through my dampened emotions in time for this conversation, so I settled on some truth.

"Lieutenant Brown died dealing with a similar situation. He didn't listen to me either, not when it really mattered. Near the end, he ignored my warnings and followed his instincts. He was unprepared for where they led him."

"Don't throw that at me," he growled back. "I can take care of myself."

"I know that. It's true, to an extent. Listen, if you want to stop Terrell's killers, you'll help me now." I suppressed a coughing fit, focusing on the conversation, resisting the need to gag.

An electric silence bristled on the line for several beats before Roberts spoke again with steel in his voice. "You said 'killers.' I need to know what you know. What do the other cities have to do with this?"

"They've been moving from city to city, visiting projects just like the one Rhonda Lloyd was murdered in. I don't know how many, and I don't know where they are. Right now, you have no suspects, no real evidence, and no theories that anyone will believe. You have to trust me, Detective. Tell me what you found out—or shall I tell you?" I was beginning to let Roberts annoy me, and my throat threatened to rebel entirely. I had other things to do than coddle the man. For instance, I could at least find a drink of water.

"I'm willing to bet that you found those identical murders in the cities that I named. You found that little interdepartmental effort has been made to solve those murders, due to locations and statistics. You found that no one put these murders together. Until now, by me."

His breathing caught; the line went dead. He'd hung up. I had my confirmation, but it would've been helpful to know if the police had turned up any details that I hadn't. I went ahead and allowed myself to cough freely, trying to clear my throat of whatever irritation was there.

My hand on the phone, I stood confused, desperately trying to remember what to do. There was a gap, a lost moment, that perfect little piece of time when you've decided what your options are and when to pull the trigger on them. I rifled through my pockets for a clue and found nothing but the usual lint, money, and crumpled paper. I had to think, to jog my memory; I knew I had a contingency plan if I felt someone was getting too close to me. I started spreading sheets of paper out on the ledge in front of the pay phone. *This isn't working*, I thought acidly, shoving the ephemera back into my pockets.

I felt the lump of the book Pat had sold to me in my jacket, and I abruptly remembered something. Shrugging out of the jacket, I turned it inside out and found two hidden pockets just underneath the arms. Inside I found multiple sets of instructions in my handwriting, tucked into a Ziploc baggie. The one titled "Apartment Contingencies, dumbass" caught my attention.

I made one more call, this one to the property manager of my apartment building. We had a simple arrangement—if I gave the word, he would clean out the rooms and mail a package of my stuff to a P.O. box, no questions asked. Subsequently, the prepaid rent for the remainder of the lease was his to do with as he pleased. Good conduct ensured a bonus. It would only be a matter of time before Detective Roberts managed to trace the phone line to the apartment and the package to the post office box. The less the officer knew, the better off he was. If he did find the apartment before it was cleared out, I'd only lose what few materials I kept there, anyway. For Detective Roberts, the mystery would become a quagmire.

All I needed to do was figure out the P.O. box and location. *Damn it to hell.* I wrote a note to look that up and shoved it into the bag, hoping I'd find it later.

I made a mental note to look into prepaid cell phones, then thought better of it and wrote the reminder down before I forgot it completely. The tickle resurged within my throat. It felt like I was getting clogged with sawdust. Against the warning, I decided to head to Dr. Bismark's regardless of Majispin's advice.

It was well past midnight, but I hoped the alchemist would still be experimenting, too busy to pack up and leave with much urgency. Desperation tugged at the corners of his eyes when it came time to learn something. Majispin bore the same look when we had discussed the involvement of vampires in this. It was a bizarre hunger that drove these men to quest for information about forces that drove the hidden universe.

After two steps, I doubled over in a coughing fit that threatened to collapse a lung. My diaphragm lurched, and I felt an urgent need to expel whatever was inside of me, but nothing came except a creeping dryness up my throat. I coughed for what seemed like an eternity, and when I stopped, I was on my knees, breathing raggedly and blinking spots out of my eyes. I relaxed, raised my head and promptly hacked up a neatly rolled piece of paper. Now, when the hell had I eaten that?

I gingerly lifted the paper from the sidewalk and unfurled its tea-stained edges. *Oh, no.* I had eaten that or, more specifically, drunk it, when I was with Bismark. It was a simple note:

Mr. Smith, I apologize for the inconvenience, but as you read this, I am most likely dead. It was vigorously requested that I mislead you; however, I could not abide the consequences of such an action. I was pressed for time when I formulated what I did; please forgive me for what happens next. I wish you Godspeed. Perhaps we'll see each other again someday. Sincerely, Dr. Quentin Bismark.

The note dissolved into a powder, swirling around my fingers and up my arm. A blast shot up my nose, burning the passages and causing a sharp burst of pain to skate across my forehead. I dropped to the sidewalk, forgetting where I was, and I pressed my palms to my face. No air would pass my nose or lips, not a cough or a sneeze. For a moment, I thought I might suffocate. Death wouldn't claim me, but it'd cause severe coronary damage that'd take serious time to heal before I could breathe again.

Just as suddenly as it began, it was over. There wasn't a trace of powder anywhere on my hands or face. I only had a moment to ponder what Bismark had done to me when the scent of the man I'd pursued earlier swarmed over me. The scent rushed in, a tide of particles to drown me. It was all around and so powerful that I thought I might be able to see it. I stumbled to my feet and down the sidewalk. The scent only grew stronger. Every sense was competing for control. I was going to be able to track him, my one lead; I could find him with relative ease. I didn't need Majispin's shapeshifters to finish this.

A fresh jolt of the man's scent rammed into the olfactory membrane at the front of my brain. I pressed on alone, confident and fueled by my rising elation at the loss of control. I was losing myself to this drug, swimming in the possibilities, inhibitions sagging. I wanted to eat children, I wanted to fuck the Dragon again, I wanted to tear loose on the streets of this city and dare anyone to stop me.

If this was Bismark's idea of helping me, I could've made another suggestion or two. I would be sure to discuss this with him if I ever did see him again.

My brain was on fire, processing the amount of sensory information bombarding my system. I was dizzy with the onslaught as I made my way, following the scent, driven by the need to find the owner. Fortunate for me that Boston went to sleep so early; it wouldn't do for hordes of people to see me rumbling down the street, possessed. The scent pulled me past downtown and the financial district, back to where I'd first seen him. I did my best to make a straight line.

My path took me along the waterfront, near the Leather District and into the remaining portion of the incomplete, massive construction project called the Big Dig. Pheromones and other scent markers pelted my nose. The syrupy mixture hung in the air, suspended like a stream of water at a loss for gravity.

A menagerie of design firms and startups had moved into the industrial buildings in this area during the Internet boom. Since the bubble had burst, a little more than half were either partially occupied or empty, waiting for the next economic boom that Boston's perpetual construction promised. I tried to stop and get my head together, but the scent was so powerful it seemed to be displacing the air in my lungs—my breath was coming in rasping heaves, processing the viscid trail.

It was all I could do to keep my hearing and eyesight focused enough not to stumble into the street. This powerful new nose of mine had begun to supersede my other senses. I felt like I was listening through a mattress and seeing through a cloudy glass.

I could tell by the intensity of the particulates thudding against the membranes of my nose that I was close to the source. Thrumming in waves, the malefactor's odor beat a steady rhythm on my brain.

The ground beneath me was composed entirely of broken asphalt and dirt. I moved through a tight collection of brick buildings with large, dusty panes of glass. It was clear to me that the vampire was close, and he was not alone. *Good, that would simplify the solution, if complicating the situation.*

I willed myself to remove my clothing as quickly as I could and stashed the pistols as well. I was driven and had a strong hunch that there was only one way I was going to get this out of my nose. Confrontation. When they saw me, there would inevitably be a fight. I relished the idea and abandoned my humanity effortlessly, adopting my more powerful form.

With a running start, I rebounded off the opposite wall and plunged through a second-story window into the building where my quarry should be. The glass and framework made a tremendous noise as I burst through; sharp slivers and metal scattered everywhere, crunching under my feet, leaving tiny cuts.

There was no doubt that anyone in the building must have heard it. I was making snorting and growling sounds that must've sounded like a bear in the high-ceilinged hallway. The powder's strength seemed to be weakening, but with the relative intensity it was difficult to tell. I'd come through the second-floor window to determine whether my target was above or below. He was beneath me, so I plunged headlong down the stairs.

At the bottom of the stairwell, near the far end of the hall, I saw four figures, two of whom carried a large, metal cube between them. One of them was my dead man. The object was too big for only one of the vampires to handle—about five feet square—despite their preternatural strength. My senses were abruptly my own again, and I charged at them, literally roaring down the hall. In tight quarters, roaring at the top of my lungs can take anyone aback. This occasion was no different; they hesitated.

I wasn't ten feet away when more vampires began pouring out of the doors on the sides of the hallway. I didn't slow down but barreled into the crowd. The powder had led me here; I didn't need the backup from Majispin's pack, I told myself. We all selfishly reserve our best lies for ourselves.

I tore into the mass of them, going completely berserk. Rather than trying to kill the vamps, I pushed the crowd into the four shuffling monsters trying to exit the hallway. They stumbled and dropped the box with a crash. I was outnumbered, but I exceeded any one of them in bulk. As they lost footing around me, they clawed at me, drawing blood, but had no purchase for bites.

Plunging forward, I stepped on toppled bodies and crushed any individual I could. My main goal was to reach the four vampires. The group handling the cube was all neatly dressed, pale, and doing nothing to conceal their true selves. Their slightly elongated arms and legs undulated as if they inhabited bodies composed of rubber and gelatin.

One of the vampires proved to be wiser than his brethren. He first announced this by swinging an errant piece of rebar into the back of my head. A muted *ping* sounded in my ears and a dull ache crept into my molars. Two more seized steel and went to work. Each way I turned, I was met by claws or ridged, reinforced steel.

The familiar tingle that meant the sun was rising washed over me. With all of these vampires around me, the sun was going to be my only chance.

The battle intensified as I forced the fight into an adjacent room, nearest the outer wall. I was surprised to catch a glimpse of the Thrall standing in the center of the room. Tears streamed down its face. One of the vampires rushed over to it and started whispering in its good ear. The cursed man began to cry harder.

I managed to snag one of the small army in my jaws and toss him through a window just as a jagged bar of steel pierced my side and burst through my skin on the opposite side. The underling screamed and burst into flames as he cleared the glass. Sunlight streamed into the room; vamps dissolved into greasy puddles around me as others scrambled back against the walls to avoid the encroaching sunlight. I roared and reacted, spinning and swiping the vampire who'd stabbed me off his feet. He skittered into a puddle of sunlight and writhed into a puddle of ichor.

Though a vampire could be my equal in strength, I was the big kid at the table. Thrashing wildly, I was unconcerned by the makeshift weapon I'd been pierced with, as if it were merely a sewing needle.

Their dying flames sparked my fur and I attempted to roll in some of the resultant muck to keep from becoming a ball of fire myself. The rebar served as a potent reminder that rolling was not in the cards, and I instead slapped at my smoldering fur. All the vamps in the room were either scrambling deeper into the building or melting away, except for the four nearest the wall, out of the direct sunlight. They'd hesitated again, wanting to collect the box, but my stunt had thrown the group into complete disarray. I looked up, clutching the bar in my side, propped up on one hand.

One of the fleeing vampires paused in the doorway and shouted, "You promised, Estoban, you gave your fucking word!"

I assumed it was the leader who shouted in return, "Leave him; we've no time for this!" He bolted from the room, directly through rays of sunlight. With no apparent effect, not even a singe!

The sun's light hadn't affected him. The action was fundamentally wrong. The Thrall rushed me, whimpering and slashing with its long, curved knife. I was prepared for the relatively slow thing and made short work of it, biting off the arm that wielded the knife and breaking its legs.

The other three vampires made a break for it through the sunlight, as well. I lunged for the last one, biting off a trailing hand. He gasped, spun, and slashed his fingernails across my eyes. The cut was the final blow for me. I lost my balance and rammed into the concrete wall nearest the door. Bright spots swam in my eyes as I stumbled backwards. When I'd blinked the blood out of my vision, they were gone.

I was left panting, burnt, and sticky with decomposing blood clotting my fur; standing in a hazy room full of ichorous smoldering puddles. The Thrall lay in pieces, still sobbing, near the metal box. A piece of steel protruded from my side. Pushing on one end and pulling on the other, I dragged the bar out of my flesh, letting it rattle to the floor, and sat still, just trying to breathe normally for a moment. The bar crackled in front of me as my blood boiled off its surface. I thought the bar reminiscent of my life—a straight but ragged line, pitted and suffering decay.

This close to the box, I was able to notice that it had a series of tiny holes—the size you'd find in three-ring-binder paper—along the top of each face. Then I realized that when the leader had shouted about leaving "him," he'd meant whatever was in the box, not me or the pissed-off vampire whose hand I'd ingested.

FOURTEEN

A slithering sound caught my attention. The Thrall was dragging itself toward me by its one good arm. It clawed its way slowly across the floor, seeking to complete whatever instructions its creator had left for it. I tiredly stomped on the arm and broke it at the elbow. The wretch flopped and undulated, still trying to move, its body incapable of providing locomotion, entirely wracked with sorrow, and tears streaming down its face.

The transformation washed over me, the monstrous form retreating into my skin, spinning down to coil at the core of my being, wound according to my will. Welts, bruises, cuts, and more showed on my skin. My vision swam and I swayed, dropping to a knee so that I wouldn't tumble to the floor. Without realizing it, my hand had remained pressed into my side over one of the ragged punctures. Blood made my fingers tacky, but the bleeding was beginning to stem, and my vision clarified as it returned to normal.

Pulling some of the plastic off the walls and windows, I wrapped the sobbing, broken Thrall and its severed arm into a tight package and tossed him over my shoulder. It wouldn't do to leave a thing like that lying about, and I wasn't sure how many pieces I'd have to cut it into before it died. Some of the smoldering vamps had ignited the old building and a slow, smoky fire was spreading. I awkwardly pushed the box outside, not taking the time to peek through the holes, if that were even possible. By the sound and uneven weight of the thing, it was clear there was a body of some sort in there.

Once outside, I had to make a decision quickly—sirens sounded in the distance. The transformation back to human form had brought aches and pains all over my body. Most of the remnants of vampire death sloughed off when my fur disappeared, but I still had clotted cuts and sticky patches on my skin, as well as open wounds and bruises where the steel bars had struck.

Collecting my clothing and weapons, I got dressed, pulling jeans and shirt over sweaty skin and rapidly healing wounds, shrugging sloppily into my rig and jacket. I was a mess and run down, exhausted from the wild fight, I hadn't truly eaten, and I'd been awake for twenty-four hours or more. If not for the sun, I most likely would have been dragged down. I checked again to see if I wanted to die. No, not yet, but I couldn't justify what I'd just done as any kind of a survival technique.

My thoughts meandered around to how I'd transport the box—my enemies thought it was important but had been willing to abandon it—when I heard an engine rumbling closer. It sounded like an SUV, which could be emergency personnel. I would hate to have to leave the box, but it was too awkward for me to carry on my own. There were no apparent seams or openings other than the quarter-sized holes. I'd have to go on without it.

Then a familiar voice called out from above: "Dad, stay there. The pack's on their way; they've got a truck!"

I looked up at Ana through a window in the adjacent building. She grimaced down at me and pointed in the direction the engine sound was coming from. Standing inside the building, safe in deep shadow; she must've used the subway and sewers to get here— not her favorite mode of travel. I've suspected that her uncanny ability to locate me was a result of weaning her on my own blood for months at a time. Ana never questioned it.

"Tell your new playmates not to ever call me again; this is a one-time deal. Ugh, it stinks here." She finished, annoyed. I knew she was cranky, being awake at this time. One of the pack must've contacted her just before dawn, wondering where I was. Majispin, I bet or, gods forbid, Maria.

She held out a mobile phone and disappeared from my view, saying, "Don't be so analog, Dad; join the twenty-first century."

A black SUV whipped around the corner and came barreling down the alley. As it skidded to a stop, all four of the pack jumped out. Barros went directly to the back of the vehicle while the other three faced me.

"You couldn't wait?" Maria was irritated, but added in a curious tone, "What's in the box?"

Mark glanced at her, then back to me, scowling. Barros came from behind the truck with edged weapons about a meter and a half in length. One half was a straight blade, the other half a leather-wrapped handle with a weighty bulge at its base. They were stunted long weapons that I'd always known as *pudao*, perfect for dispatching things like vampires if wielded by powerful hands. Getting the general feeling that the pack's fighting style was crude, I reckoned they used them like lumberjacks, to swing and hack. Automatic weapons would be more efficient but noisy—far noisier than a blade.

Mark was still scowling at me when he noticed the smoke coming from the windows of the building behind me. He cocked his head and listened, I assumed, to the approaching sirens. Seth looked around and scented the air. I'm sure they all smelled the vampire death inside; it would be apparent even to a normal human for a few more minutes, at least.

Mark spoke up first. "Everyone in the car. Seth, help Alexander with that box."

Seth hesitated for the briefest of moments before moving to the other side of the box.

He then looked back at me and asked, "Care to tell us what's going on?"

"I'll explain once we get back to Majispin's."

"This isn't going to work, Alexander. We can't work together if you snub us, and you won't have anywhere safe to be in this city."

It was a mild threat and the thought was so absurd to me, I almost missed it. I'd only be barred from the safe house in the most extreme of decisions. There was the remote possibility that I could be barred from the entire system, depending on how elaborate a yarn Mark could spin to Majispin. It'd be more of a pain in the ass than a serious problem, but it wouldn't help the situation if I nudged things along.

So I told Mark, "I didn't snub you, I was…coerced. It was the wrong thing to do. Majispin should have more answers than me; I'll explain everything that happened when we're all together." Heat crept into my face, and I was thankful for my dark skin. I wasn't sure if I could fight anyone off at the moment. Apologetic truth was the only defense I could offer, and it wasn't my normal *modus operandi*. I bitterly spat a congealed glob of blood onto the pavement and stepped over the sizzling glop to climb into the truck.

After packing the weapons into the Jeep and piling in with the box and the Thrall, I could smell the faint scent of whatever was inside. It was very old and dry. Natural wood oils, some stone, and a few other miscellaneous aromas that were fleeting and elusive.

My head throbbed in the cramped space; I needed food. Contrary to popular marketing, most SUVs aren't all that roomy. This one was a Grand Cherokee, and with the box and the plastic-wrapped, sobbing Thrall in the back, the five of us were packed in good. Maria sat to my left, Seth to my right, and the larger Barros sat up front. Mark drove. We rode in smelly silence for a few minutes until Mark broke our reverie. Maria's head remained cocked and turned three-quarters in my direction as her eyes passed up and down my battered and filthy body.

"Feel free to pull him into your lap and coo over him, Maria." This from Mark, who'd been peering into the rearview mirror. We passed a contingent of fire trucks as they roared down the side street, headed for the fire we'd left behind.

I felt Maria tense next to me, and I continued to mind my business when Barros broke in.

"Too bad you pulled a fast one, Alexander; I was looking forward to making a mess together." The big Mexican craned his neck and grinned at me.

I got the distinct impression that Barros enjoyed carnage. He was the biggest 'shifter in the car, but not necessarily the strongest. He probably wanted to see up close what I was capable of. Though, at this point, I was fast reassessing what I was capable of. The fight had taken way more out of me than I expected. It was a humbling experience, and I realized that I'd never met that many vampires in combat. They were cooperating in an unprecedented manner, and I'd been behaving in an epically foolish way. Traveling alone for so many years hadn't seemed to hone my abilities into anything a group might find useful.

"Maybe next time, *asesino*," I said, mimicking the twang of the barrio that Barros's speech indicated.

Maria said, *"¿Hombre, crees que eres del barrio?"*

Seth, who'd been looking out the window the whole time, grinned mirthlessly and Barros chuckled.

Mark perked up and said, "What?"

The three of them continued to smile, and Barros said, "*Nuestro jefe no habla espanol.*"

Mark perked up. "Okay, I got that. So what?"

"*¿Seth, entiendes?*" I asked.

Seth never looked into the car from the window, but replied, "*Sí,* but you fucking knew that already."

Hell, I probably did.

"All right, enough!" Mark was a little red in the neck.

"It's not like you don't have the time to learn, Mark; everyone around you speaks Spanish. *¿Sabes lo que digo, gringo?*"

The other three started giggling, and Maria said, "*Apestas como el muerto!*"

The three of them started snorting and stifling cruel smirks at my disposition. Not that my "stinking like the dead" was all that humorous, but the banter annoyed Mark, and he was reacting like an insecure little boy. I hazarded a guess that Seth was enjoying this because, I recalled, the last time I'd seen him, he'd been the butt of most of the gringo jokes.

Mark hunched his shoulders, scowling the rest of the way. It was the perfect opportunity to ask him to pull over so I could grab a sandwich or three. Why was I always hungry? These three never seemed to eat.

My belly temporarily full after wolfing down the sandwiches, we pulled into The Sweaty Magus through a back street and down the service alley. There was a small loading dock where we unloaded the box and other sundry items. Inside, Majispin met us in the foyer and directed us upstairs to his study. On the way up, I succinctly explained how I'd come to find the vampires, the box, and the Thrall. Majispin only clucked under his breath, nodding. They all froze incredulously when

I told them of the four vampires cutting through the sunlight without harm.

"That's impossible," Mark said.

"I have to agree, Alexander. That would run counter to everything we know and have known for centuries. There's something timeless about the sun and vampires; various legends put Apollo, Ra, or some other sun god at the head of one of the opposing legions. There's no magic that I'm aware of that would make even contemplating such a thing possible."

"I know what I saw, and this thing has something to do with it." I pointed at the box as we moved on up the stairs. "They were desperately trying to get it out with them. Obviously they were willing to abandon it to escape."

I found out why Majispin wanted some sort of guarantee on secrecy upstairs. Beyond the study, there were two rooms—a library and a laboratory. We went directly into the laboratory. From the glimpse I had of the library, it was mostly full of leather-bound texts and had a warm atmosphere, not unlike the study. A large countertop constructed of stainless steel and hydraulic legs crouched in the center of the lab. On this we placed the box. Majispin immediately used a hidden crank to lower the table so he could more easily fiddle with the find. The Thrall was dumped in the corner, crying and heaving.

"Oh, this *is* interesting," Majispin said, eyeing the box. He looked at me and pointed to the short hallway. "There's a small bathroom adjacent to the library, Alexander, if you want to clean up."

"Wait, there's more."

"Oh? What now?" Majispin was visibly irritated, champing at the bit to get to the cube. He rubbed his hands in front of him, impatiently waiting.

"Bismark is dead; they got to him."

"You can't be serious!" Majispin, momentarily distracted from the prize of the cube, gave me his full attention. "Dr. Quentin Bismark is the most meticulous and knowledgeable man I've ever met; you may think he's dead, but the man has a backup plan for his backup plans!"

"Regardless, he's likely dead; his note heavily implied that. He'd given me misleading information, but he also gave me a dose of something in my drink. It's what led me to the vampires—*drove* me to them, actually."

"You drank something in an alchemist's home?" Maria was incredulous and Barros laughed openly.

Seth just shook his head; he didn't think I was capable of much other than fucking things up, so I was simply reinforcing his opinion of me.

Barros guffawed again and said, "Not too smart, m'man."

I made no reply to any of them. In hindsight, it was obviously not the smartest thing to do, but if I hadn't, we wouldn't be here now. Bismark had helped, and he'd paid for it. He must've known they were going to kill him and came up with his plan on the spot. All of that exposition about tea simply masked what he was doing to the leaves. I should've guessed something was up. The rabid scientist had been wound far too tight.

"Bismark was a hellion for research," Majispin said finally. "His work pushed boundaries the rest of us only dream of."

It was my turn to shake my head. "I bet. The point is, who else may have been compromised, who can we trust, who can't we?"

The pack shuffled their feet, waiting for Majispin to respond. He was having trouble imagining this scenario. According to his worldview, this sort of thing was simply not done.

"I…we can't trust anyone, I suppose." Majispin was somewhat crestfallen, but he was correct; anyone not in this room could've been or could still be coerced by the coven. Considering that they'd been operating up and down the coast, there truly was no one for us to turn to. We were alone on this problem.

Seth spoke up. "Surely Benjamin would see something like that coming, or one of the other powerful sorcerers might be of use?"

Majispin stuttered, so I answered in his stead, "No, no one. Bismark was the smartest among them, and Benjamin is only human. If they went at him, he'd be gone, no matter how much of a threat he saw coming. Any one of Majispin's employees might be involved; any one of the vampires who frequent this place could be involved. If the coven has figured out how to make themselves immune to the sun, that's an awfully fine offer to promote loyalty."

I went to the bathroom, leaving the pack standing around aimlessly while Majispin switched gears and began to cluck over the box. In the small bathroom, I grabbed a face towel. The gooey remnants of the vampire's hand I'd swallowed still stuck under my chin, black and oily. I wiped a copious amount onto the towel and placed it in the sink under hot water, then stripped off my shirt. Using the hot water, I scrubbed most of the decomposed gore off my face, chest, and hands. I didn't want to spend too much more time in here, since I didn't want to miss—what didn't I want to miss? Whose bathroom was this? *Crap.*

I turned, cracked the door slowly, and, not seeing anyone in the adjacent room, tiptoed out to where I heard voices. Majispin and his crew. They had a box on a shortened steel table, and the Thrall sobbed in the corner. That's right; I didn't want to miss whatever Majispin was doing with the box. I slid back into the bathroom.

Getting dressed again and leaving the bathroom for a second time, I paused in front of the library.

Then I stepped in and took a quick look at some of the books on the shelf. A few titles jumped out at me: *Real Magic* by Isaac Bonewitts, *The Malleus Maleficarum* by Kramer & Sprenger, *The Tragicall Hiftorie of the Life and Death of Doctor Fauftus* by Christopher Marlowe, and *Mephistopheles in His Own Words,* which I could only assume was penned by Mephisto himself. Just standing in this room was causing my spine to buzz as badly as usual around active magic. I hastily stepped out and joined the others in the lab.

When I entered, Majispin had an ear-to-ear grin on his face. Pointing at the box, he said, "Quite simple, really, as most clever things are in the end. Opening this box to various degrees is a matter of tracing the appropriate gestures on the surface one would wish to open. Like so." He moved to place a finger on the box.

I crossed the room and clasped Majispin's wrist in one motion. Seth and Barros, nearest to him at the time, moved to grab my arms. I didn't know who or what was in the box, and I didn't want to find out at the pace Majispin was moving.

There was a moment of silence as I looked into Majispin's surprised eyes. All that could be heard in the room was the crying of the Thrall.

"Do we want to open the box *before* we have any idea what's in it?" I asked, and released Majispin.

He rubbed his wrist and jerked his head to the left. Seth and Barros let me go and moved off. "Good point," he said apologetically. "I let my curiosity get the best of me. Seth, grab a scalpel and cut the Thrall's stitches; that'll release him—but only the stitches! If you cut the poor bastard in the process, his soul won't be able to escape his inert body until given a proper burial. *Tsk*, an awful practice." Looking back at me, he asked, "Any suggestions, then?"

I tried to peek in through some of the holes but still couldn't make out exactly what or who was inside the box. In the corner, Seth had already cut through the stitches over one eye and moved to the other. I spoke to the room as a whole. "They referred to it as 'him,' so it's safe to assume it's male. Judging by the scent, he's very old, but completely inert. What could possibly be ancient and seemingly dead, but humanoid?"

"A vampire." Maria's voice, clear and sure, cut across the abruptly silent room. The lightest wave of warmth passed through us all. Seth had finished cutting the Thrall's stitches, and it was finally dead for good. Its soul had departed. I seemed to be the only one who'd noticed.

Majispin put his fist to his mouth and rolled his eyes. "Of course, of course, of course."

Mark said, "I don't get it."

Maria snorted derisively under her breath. Her sassing Mark was probably going to get in the way later. "Save that for private time."

Majispin hummed in agreement and approached the box. "I think I know who—or what—our friend here is. Tell me, what do you smell in there?"

I explained as best as I could. "Old flesh, dried plants that I can't place, bones, bird feathers, some minerals."

He turned and rummaged through a drawer and produced a squat carving bound in vine. He unscrewed the head and said, "Take a whiff."

"It's some of the same, much stronger."

He screwed the head back on, saying, "Yes, yes, yes." Then he asked, "And the stone, can you place it?"

"Uhmm, I think... Maybe limestone, but there's something else."

"Close enough. The plant is *Protium heptaphyllum*. Its resin is used for incense, and I believe the limestone you smell is from the chert, deposits of which are found embedded in limestone and used for tools. Jade, limestone, feathers—these are all products that were routinely used by the Maya."

Grasping what he was saying, I replied, "That would make this vampire ridiculously old. He'd have to be totally insane by now, extremely dangerous."

"Ah"—Majispin pointed his index finger straight up—"not too dangerous if he's kept inert and fed only minute amounts of blood. Besides, the box binds him. Maria, go downstairs and see if one of the Faithful are about. I want a willing volunteer."

"You're not seriously thinking about feeding this thing?" I couldn't imagine the kind of damage a vampire this old might wreak.

"It's the only way to find out what they were doing with him."

"Hardly. It's the only way *you'll* find out. That's assuming he's coherent." I squared off on Majispin. The rest of the pack tensed and faced me. "Don't let freakish curiosity make a disaster out of this. It's too dangerous."

"You don't have to be here, Alexander."

He had a point there. I didn't. I looked around the room and what I saw were two relatively young shapeshifters in Mark and Barros; Seth, whose power hadn't grown much since I'd last seen him; and a dangerously inquisitive, yet experienced, sorcerer. Just then, Maria came back into the room.

She stopped in the doorway, sensing the tension, surely, but not knowing what to do about it. "I've brought someone, Mr. Majispin."

I raised my hands in surrender and stepped back. The rest of the pack relaxed, and Majispin waved Maria in. The Faithful was a young woman in her early twenties with long, dark-brown hair. She wore tight, faded jeans, black boots, a formfitting blue knit top, and a black choker. Only a slight bulge beneath the choker indicated the arterial valve. Everything about her person screamed vulnerability and weakness.

"Majispin, she's too young. This is a bad idea," I said.

Majispin ignored me and addressed the young woman, "You understand what we're about to do here?"

She nodded with a little embarrassed smile.

This was going too far. "I don't think *any* of you understand what might happen here."

Seth spoke up with the usual heat he employed when speaking to me. "Why don't you enlighten us, Alexander?"

I was dead certain that none of them had met an insane vampire in person. I had. Twice. One monster had brought Ana into my life, and the other had taken Lieutenant Brown out of it.

"All right, fine. You all know what awaits when you get old enough. It's not a perfect system and it isn't pretty, but it weeds out the less stable *potential* immortals—which is most of them.

"In the past, either the locals or preternatural creatures would band together to eliminate the wild vampire or shapeshifter. We know that some rare vampire lines have paranormal abilities beyond the average vamp. Those powers only intensify with age. What do you think happens if the berserker gets away or maybe gets trapped somewhere and goes dormant for lack of sustenance?

"Their uncontrollable nature is only going to get worse over time, and with it, the 'shifter or vamp's strength grows. Who knows what the thing in the box is capable of? It might start spitting fire or telekinetically breaking bones—we have no idea what its reaction will be when you give it blood. You don't even know how much will revive it, or to what degree."

Seth and Barros knitted their brows and stared at me; Mark eyed me with open contempt. Maria, however, eyed the box suspiciously.

"How old are *you*? Why aren't *you* trying to kill us all?" Seth asked.

"My age is irrelevant right now, but I'm a hell of a lot younger than what's in that box. Whatever I'm doing won't be nearly as dangerous as reviving that thing."

"If you're all finished?" Majispin stepped to the box, pointed three of his fingers, and traced a square at the very center of the top. Then he tapped the center three times with each finger, and a three-inch square hole appeared.

I shifted my weight, nervous, prepared to fight.

Majispin beckoned the Faithful over and whispered in her ear. I don't know how he did it, but I couldn't hear what he was saying. She giggled nervously, lowered her choker and placed her tiny spigot to the valve at her jugular. After a careful twist, she placed one hand at the base of the spigot to steady the valve and the other on the small faucet. Leaning over the box, she gave it a tiny turn and the barest drop of her blood slipped out.

It fell like a globule in zero gravity, dropping dramatically through the air, past the opening in the box. Everything in my perception moved slowly; I was experiencing the clarity of action that a tense moment creates. I could hear the wet *smack* it made as it hit, not unlike a drop of wine on leather. Majispin nodded and she issued another drop. The same sound followed. He nodded again and she leaned over.

The box shifted violently, scraping across the table. A long, dry, and cracked pink tendril whipped out of the opening and lashed itself around the Faithful's throat before she could jerk away. The strength and force of the tongue slammed her face into the top of the box. She grunted with pain but didn't begin screaming until the vampire's teeth gouged her throat and we could hear wet gulping sounds. The monster was drinking her by pints. Seth and Mark were closest, so they grabbed the girl while Barros steadied the box. They pulled once, to no effect.

Barros grabbed a knife and, placing it on the edge of the tendril, slashed away. Another pull and she was ripped free in a spray of blood. Her skin had paled to the color of chalk, and her pupils were shrunk to pinpoints. She was shivering violently, and foamy saliva dribbled from the corners of her mouth. The ancient's tongue lashed about the outside of the box, lapping at spilled blood. The wound it had been dealt didn't even bleed; it just left a deep gash in the dry, puttylike thing.

The last arterial surges of life leaked out and left a thick trail as they pulled the Faithful away. I watched the opening intently.

The tongue quickly withdrew, and mottled grey flesh filled the small, square hole in the top. In a breadth of time too fast to count, the mound of skin had grown six inches. I could see its grey, dead eyes and the bridge of its nose over the edge of the opening. The eyes darted back and forth spasmodically, more alien than any of us in our darkest forms.

Everyone else in the room froze, stunned. They simply stared. I darted forward, raised my fist and slammed it down hard on the emerging head.

"Close it, Majispin! Shut the box!"

He rushed forward and gingerly—but quickly—made the motions to close the box. The cube shuddered once, violently, and the humanoid creature slid around inside like a giant serpent, mumbling and ranting in a dialect not commonly heard in centuries.

I didn't bother to say "I told you so." I think they all got it.

"What the fuck was that?" Mark shouted more than asked.

Seth looked at Majispin and calmly asked, "Is this what we're up against?"

Barros was grinning and muttering under his breath in Spanish, repeating the same phrase: "*Sangre hace crecer el cesped.*" *Blood makes the grass grow.* He stared at the widening pool of the girl's blood, his skin rippling as he barely maintained his human form.

Seth continued to calmly question Majispin—who ignored him—while Mark and Maria began criticizing each other in less-than-hushed tones.

Majispin had adopted an odd posture, one ear towards the box, eyes glazed. He was crouched and listening intently. The pack around him bickered while the Faithful—we never knew her name— died, shivering in Maria's lap. The smell of vital fluid permeated the room. Barros was obviously enraptured, while the others managed to ignore the thick odor. I swallowed once, letting the urge to eat pass; I was damn hungry again and tired, but now was not the time for distraction. Looking from Majispin to the room and back again, I roared, "Shut the fuck up!"

They all watched now as Majispin crept closer to the cube, listening.

FIFTEEN

The words coming out of the cube sounded like a cross between the Native American languages I knew, Spanish, and a box of Xs and Qs. I couldn't be certain of all the words, but Majispin was getting something out of it.

He'd groped for a pad and pen nearby and was now scribbling furiously. I couldn't be sure, but I think the thing started to repeat itself after nearly twenty minutes of babbling. Majispin abruptly stopped writing and stood up to stretch. He rubbed his eyes and clenched his jaw several times before he spoke.

"It's a, uh, pre-Columbian Mayan dialect. This"— he waved his hand at the grey cube—"is the source of our quarry's spells. They're definitely using ancient Mayan methods of magic to accomplish what they're doing.

"His name is Nacxit." He indicated the box again. "And he was a king and shaman for a group of the Maya known as the Kiché. He'd voluntarily had himself infected with vampirism—I guess he's *lucky* it took. It actually wove quite nicely into their existing belief system with regard to blood sacrifice.

"The name 'Nacxit' has been linked with Chichén Itzá and Kukulcán, both as a name for a god and as a royal title." Majispin started to pace; Nacxit continued to babble.

"The Kiché, he claims, ruled the highlands—according to archeological findings, about one-fifth of Mexico. This creature found a way to not only protect itself from sunlight, but also to spread the wealth, as it were. The, ah, individual spell is quite complex, but doable. Before he was entombed by a host of other vampires—probably Northern Mexicans, around the fourteenth century—he found a way to weave the spell into another significant procedure."

"The enclosure."

"Yes. Any vampire in the area would be immune to the sun. And, in accordance with other obscure Mayan rituals, children's blood is involved. You can imagine how many children were lost to secure that area so long ago."

It all came together—what they were planning, how they were able to command the loyalty of so many vampires. Why it seemed that only vampires were passionately involved. The Thrall was simply an expendable daytime operative. Until now.

Mark rubbed the stubble on his chin and said, "This vamp is over five hundred years old?"

"Very much so." Majispin waved dismissively.

"Then, April 12 is certainly a due date." I added.

Majispin continued his lecture, "We've known that the Maya experimented with the interdimensional universe—all of us have—but no one that I'm aware of has been able to successfully chart them from this dimension. No one believed they'd accomplished it, and the records that would've proved it are gone.

"As for Nacxit, before his plan could be brought to fruition, he was overthrown, as I said, by other vampires, who were, in turn, put down by the populace. All of this was very chaotic. The brief and powerful Kiché Empire was broken up into localized political spheres. Another ruler bearing the same name ascended the throne, and history continued normally. There are no direct records of this and, of course, no physical evidence, since vampires, like shapeshifters, leave nothing other than water and carbon traces behind.

"The former Nacxit, our friend in the box, was forgotten but for legend." Majispin wandered into his library and returned with a thick book. He flipped through the pages a few times, then recited:

"And when they arrived
Before the lord,
Nacxit was the name of the great lord,
The sole judge
Of a huge jurisdiction.
And it was he who gave out the signs of authority,
All the insignia.
Then came the sign of the [ah pop, "Ruler"]
And [ah pop q'am haa, the "Assistant Chief"]
And then came the sign of the power
And authority
Of [ah pop]
And [ah pop q'am ha]
In the end Nacxit gave out
The insignia of lordship.
These are the names of them…"

"It goes on, but I've read the significant part. This must refer to the first Nacxit, not the second. These signs of 'power' and 'authority' and the 'insignia of lordship' must refer to his blessings, the spell." He closed the book, looking lost, and his eyes roamed aimlessly around the room.

Mark shook his head and asked, "But what was the plan? Sounds like he just wanted to be able to wander around in the daylight, maybe bless a few of his cronies."

"The plan was for a vampire ruling class to control the area. By day or night," I said. We all stood silent for a moment, letting it sink in. Majispin certainly had put more thought into this than just in the last hour or so. What had he been up to and for how long? I didn't think I'd ever be able to let go of the notion that men like Majispin were endangering everyone and everything on Earth.

"These vampires are more dangerous than any before. They've been using magic for years, and we don't know how long they've been up to this, questing for more power." I shook my head. This was unheard of in my time. We tried to maintain a certain level of secrecy, but these fools wanted to step it up. Inevitable, I suppose, this mad ego, this uprising and desire for the power to control others. How very human of them.

"Seth, have maintenance dispose of these bodies and clean up the blood. The rest of you, relax in the study or library; have a drink if you want." Majispin moved to leave the room.

"Wait a minute," Maria said. "Is this girl going to become a vampire?"

We all looked at each other. No one else said anything, so I chimed in. "No. The process is more involved, more purposeful, like ours, and not always successful. Vampires would have you believe otherwise, as futile as that is. I'm sure you remember what it was like to become a shapeshifter."

She clenched and unclenched her jaw. We'd all cannibalized our progenitors to complete the process. For every shapeshifter, only time dulls the experience of that first uncontrollable urge to kill and eat. For some, their messenger was a well-known relative.

I hadn't known my great-great-grandfather, only heard tales of his exploits and mysterious disappearance. He was rumored to have become part man and beast, one with the forest. I'd only considered the stories part of our family myth until he'd burst through my window and attacked me. When I awoke, ravenous and psychotic, the only memories I had of his face were a contented relief and then contorted pain as I did what I was driven to do by the curse.

There was still one more item that needed to be checked off. "Nacxit needs to be put to bed," I said to everyone.

Mark sneered at me and said, "How do you propose we do that? Open the box and cut its head off? It'll have us for lunch. Expose it to sunlight? He's probably protected, right? So, what, we can't open the box and we can't let a little sunlight in either. What?"

"There's always burning," I replied.

Majispin said, "We can't set fire to the cube; it won't burn. We can't open it, either."

I was getting a little frustrated with this circular train of conversation. "Give me a can of accelerant, a funnel, and a match. I'll kill him."

Barros shot me an appreciative wink; everyone else raised his or her eyebrows.

"See to it, Mark," said Majispin. "And give Alexander a hand when the time comes."

Mark grunted and the others shuffled from the room. Majispin had turned his back to me in thought. I broke his reverie. "Can you track them?"

"Eh?"

"Can you track them? The vampires. Is there some way to track them?"

"Pfft. Only with some physical remnant—which is impossible, since when you remove something from creatures such as yourselves, it dissolves, becomes nothing worth mentioning."

I thought as much. "But if you did have something?"

Majispin turned and faced me, more than a little exasperated. "What are you getting at?"

"I bit off one of the vampires' hands."

"So?"

"I swallowed it not much more than two hours ago."

Understanding bloomed across Majispin's face. A devious grin tickled the corners of his mouth and he said, "Let me get a few things first."

When he returned, he had a large glass bowl, a candle, a silver spoon, and a small pouch. He placed the bowl on a table in front of me and then moved to the other side. He lit the candle. The room filled with the expanding scent of a curious mixture of frankincense, hemp, and sulfur. We could see Nacxit's gleaming eyes watching through the holes of the cube.

"Excuse me," I said to Majispin. I walked over to the cube and kicked it off the table with a crash. Then I kicked it into a corner out of our line of sight. The monster inside laughed; I ignored it, content that I had a permanent solution in mind for Nacxit.

The door flung open and Maria stood in the doorway, followed closely by Barros.

Majispin shooed them away, and Maria closed the door gently, peering at me with intense curiosity.

I came back over to the bowl and asked, "What now?"

"Now you regurgitate the hand and I very quickly perform a ritual," he said matter-of-factly as he pushed his sleeves up and grinned over the bowl.

Vomiting isn't something I do frequently, or at all. I had been hoping that Majispin had some way to spell the vampire's hand out of my stomach or…something. I'd been willing to withstand the pain of magic, but this would take some real effort. Whatever I ate, no matter how dreadful, stayed down; I couldn't ever remember regurgitating anything since my introduction to being a monster. Despite any distaste I might have for whatever I consumed, I was designed for eating. Vampires were literally distasteful, though. I thought about the flavor of a vampire's flesh long and hard before I put my finger to the back of my throat.

I gagged hard, but nothing came. Again, I leaned over, tickled the back of my throat and tried to relax. A horrific noise traveled up my throat, but nothing came up. On the third try, I managed to heave up the hand. Thankfully, it'd been partially dissolved by my uncanny gastric acids. Otherwise I might've choked on the damn thing. Now it floated in a pool of rank bile at the bottom of the bowl. I wanted nothing more than an entire bottle of whiskey at that very moment to cleanse my palate and numb my sore throat.

Majispin immediately began the ritual. The hand was beginning to dissolve very quickly on its own, now that it was outside of my sphere of influence. He recited a few guttural phrases, passing his hand over the bowl. Then he picked up and tipped the burning candle into the basin, letting a few drops of hot wax descend into the vomitous mixture. There was a dull flash and a theatrical puff of smoke. An electric shock straightened my spine, and I sucked air through my teeth.

"Sorry." Majispin falsely sympathized.

Where once there were smoldering liquids now lay a pile of caked ash. Majispin scooped enough into the pouch to give the sack weight. The rest of the powder slowly dissolved away, leaving just short of nothing.

We left the lab and entered the library. Mark and Barros were having a heated discussion that stopped as soon as we were within sight.

Majispin tossed the bag to Mark and said, "You know how it works."

On the floor near Mark was a can of kerosene. I scooped it up and handed it to Maria, then asked Seth to help me with the cube. To his credit, he didn't hesitate.

Barros asked, grinning, "¿Vamos a matar?"

"Sí," I replied. "We're going killing."

He chuckled, and it sounded like he was gargling blood.

It was midday when we got the box out onto the loading dock. Nacxit had cursed and spat at us the entire trip down. We callously dumped the box at the far end of the concrete dock, and Maria handed me the kerosene. Mark pulled a small metal funnel out of the back of his pants.

I kicked the cube on its relative side to make it easier to pour the liquid through the holes. As I poured the stuff in, Nacxit started to sputter and writhe about. I steadied the box with an elbow on it and kept pouring.

Barros handed me a book of matches, I struck one and moved to light the book when Nacxit spoke. "*No puedo ser matado.*" *I can't be killed.*

"You died a long time ago." I tossed the burning book onto the cube. Flames immediately engulfed two sides of the container. The inside caught with a muffled burst and fire shot out of the holes. Nacxit was screaming and thundering around inside the cube. There was a blast of thick, black smoke, and the flames died down. The cube suddenly shrank to the size of a gambling die. We left it there, with the kerosene fire smoldering around it on the concrete.

As we headed to the SUV, Barros was having a furious round of nasty looks with Mark. I glanced at Seth with one eyebrow raised. He shrugged casually and said, "It's the usual shit with you, apparently."

Stopping, I said to them, "All right, what?" I suspected, however, what was going on.

Barros grunted one more time and Mark shot him a sideways glare.

Mark pointed at me. "You're not in charge here," he said.

"What?"

"You heard me."

"Yeah, I heard you, and you're right, I'm not in charge here. I'm not challenging you at all, Mark, so let it go."

Stepping up to me, he said, "Damn right." At the same time, he poked his finger into me. The. Last. Straw. Every bit of frustration I'd held for the last several decades roared up from within me.

I reached across my body with my right and elbowed him hard in the face while grabbing his index finger. As he stumbled to his right, I twisted to my right, snapped the finger, and let go.

"No!" Maria shouted and grabbed my arm.

I flung her hand off of my arm and squared on Mark. He lunged at me, snarling through bloodied teeth, and swung a wild left hook at me. I skipped backwards a bare inch, allowing his fist to whiz past my nose, and punched him square in the face with my right as hard as I could, straight through, nothing wild about it. His head rocketed backward and his feet lost hold as he stumbled backwards onto his ass and skidded to a halt.

Blood poured down his face as he stopped short of a Dumpster. I stole a glance at the rest of the pack, and they were jaw-drop shocked. I *had* been holding back. No more. This tension was going to break right now, damn the past; to hell with Seth and whatever else I could remember. For once, I was going to let the pack instinct drive me, do what felt right.

Mark's face was crushed inward. He sucked air through the center of that mass and bled out of it. A few teeth trailed from the hole of his mouth, and he struggled to roll over and sit up. No one moved to help him.

I addressed them all, "You suck as a pack."

I walked over to Mark's still-struggling form and grabbed him by the lower half of what was left of his face; he warbled sickly in the back of his throat. My hand was slick with blood in an instant. I pointed at him.

"Is this the man you accepted as your leader?"

Seth's face was impassive, Maria looked concerned, but Barros was grinning.

"Is it?" I yelled directly at the hulking Barros. He stopped smiling and chewed the inside of his mouth.

"Are you with him, Maria?"

She surprised me after a heartbeat by answering quietly, "No."

I pushed that news out of the way. I had a point to make, and if Mark had to suffer for it, so be it. There was no way I could face this many powerful vampires alone. I needed the pack's help. I was forced to admit they were all I had; shapeshifters were the group I belonged to. For better or worse, these were *my* monsters. The loose coalition of safe houses was just that—loose. So we couldn't expect them to organize any kind of a strike force efficiently. This was it, the five of us. Majispin had brought them together, but I was going to fuse them into something worthwhile. I hoped.

My thoughts raced. Majispin had put them together, so they'd never really coalesced, didn't come together naturally. This group wasn't the result of a natural process, more like a collection of employees. Pack dynamics just don't work that way.

I hauled the barely conscious Mark all the way to his feet. In severe pain, he desperately grabbed my wrist with both hands, his broken finger pointing out at an awkward angle. There was no need to pry him loose; I needed him close, anyway. I could feel that this was right; I needed to share blood with Mark, to bind his energy to mine, we needed to be *we* where it mattered, at the core of our power.

With one clawed finger, I cut the back of his hand open, then pressed my nails into my own palm. I held my fresh wound over the cut I'd made on his hand. His eyes rolled backwards into his head as he convulsed twice and relaxed. I willed the power of my blood into his, releasing his face and clasping his hands, supporting rather than punishing. For one sublime moment, Mark and I existed in the same space. In that moment, I could see everything that made him who he was—the insecurity, the mask of muscle and swagger, his need to be accepted—all of it. Mentally, the entirety of Mark read like a wickedly sloped sine wave. I wrapped my thoughts around that distorted line and pulled on both ends, smoothing it out as much as I could, pushing and pulling the mountains and gorges into gentler hills and valleys.

The rest of the pack was too confused to comment or move. I could feel his bones knitting, his teeth realigning and growing back in, his nose re-forming. I shared what power I could with Mark, and what I could share was apparently formidable. I briefly felt the heat of the Dragon, warmth that fleetingly floated through both of us. Letting us know she was pleased? More likely, letting *me* know she was watching.

When the power subsided, I had made Mark my blood brother purely by instinct. We were now bound by ties that neither of us truly understood.

SIXTEEN

When I released Mark, he stood easily on his own. I hadn't been sure I'd be able to do what I did, but it had felt natural and jibed closely with tales and beliefs held by natives the world over. The metaphysical idea of such things was supposed to be a two-way street, and Mark hadn't asked for this.

The feeling of success sparked melancholy in me for Tina and how we'd parted distastefully over my failures. My false sense of availability at the time had been our ruin. When I'd tried it then, it had been by instinct as well, but I had ignored that and gone with my thoughts, my inhibitions. It had ruined everything. I wondered peripherally if I'd ever see her again. The path I'd chosen for my next life was an uncharted one, not even a path at all. Some of what the Dragon had told me was starting to make some sense—my "inheritance" and my "legacy." As far as I knew, I was one of the oldest shapeshifters on the planet. The faerie had referred to me as a "king." I was willing to deny what I saw as the full truth of it because ultimately it wouldn't wash. The legacy she had referred to implied much more than I thought I was capable of or willing to do.

I couldn't come to terms with the suggestion that I was some natural-born leader of shapeshifters. The way my blood had behaved inside Majispin's lair cut through my thoughts. The theory of shapeshifters' and vampires' origins followed closely. What were the origins of the power we were bound to? There was a bigger picture remaining to be seen. We were all, quite possibly, pawns in some greater scheme. Whatever the truth might turn out to be, I was unwilling to be a pawn. For anyone or anything. *Ever*.

Mark took two slow steps backwards, eyes unfocused, hands raised. He licked his lips, and emotions flowed across his face without restraint. He ran both hands through his hair and pulled his head back to take a deep breath that filled and expanded his torso. When he breathed out, the relief was nearly palpable; he looked controlled for the first time since I'd met him.

"What did you do to me?" There was no malice in his voice; it was a straight question, but one I was incapable of fully answering.

The whisper that had been so quiet for the past day or so surged back, echoing inside my head between my ears, just out of comprehension, but the feeling was clear: *take what is yours, damn the rest*. It all felt wrong and right at the same time; I didn't know what to do next. So I did what I've always done: barrel forward.

"I don't know, but I know it helped; it felt right." There was more to be given.

Mark's blood was all over my hands. I closed my eyes and smeared a haphazard line across my face. I remembered the red ochre my mother's people—*my* people—had used to ritually darken their faces. It was why the white men called the Kainai the Blood Tribe, or simply the Bloods. It felt right to me, so I continued with what I was feeling.

"This is what I am. We don't control our destiny; we face it, we mount it. This is what I offer you." I held my bloody palms out. "I ask you to be my *tuka*, my war partners. Will you?" As I said it, I approached the other three 'shifters, palms up. In front of each of them, I ran a thumb along their foreheads, leaving a thick red trail of Mark's sizzling blood. When my finger crossed Maria's skin, her golden-brown eyes reflected eerily like a cat's and she slightly swooned. Before I could paint Seth's forehead, he grabbed my wrist.

I looked deeply into his dark eyes and he returned the stare with cool steel. He was mulling something over, and I was willing to let him. The rest of the pack tensed, and Seth broke the moment first by speaking.

"I don't know what's changed with you, but something has. Not much, but something. I'll never forgive you, but this I'll do." He released my wrist, and I drew the red line across his forehead.

I had never expected nor wanted Seth to forgive me, but this gesture I could accept without guilt or judgment. I only had one question, and now seemed like as good a time as I was going to get to ask it of Seth.

"Do you know where she is?"

Maria's forehead creased with curiosity briefly before Seth answered, "Yes."

I was surprised; it was a long shot. There would be time enough to pursue the matter later. *A foolish thought.*

Punctuating each word as I spoke with a jab of my finger, I addressed the pack. "This is not my pack— it is his." I moved next to Mark, placing my palm on his chest. "My brother's. You are my siblings." I let the center of me bleed out, the magic that powered shapeshifters, the hot strength of our core. "I need your help in war." I let that power follow the course of blood, from mine to Mark's, from his to the pack's by his own blood on them. Whatever comprised the ball of power at my core, the shared energy in all of us, it was hungry for something violent. It liked the idea of a messy fight and encouraged the coming conflict.

There was a deep rumbling coming from the back of Barros's throat, and he nodded vigorously. Maria, eyes unreadable, gave one slow nod, and Seth simply bowed his head once.

I pulled Mark close and whispered fiercely in his ear.

"There are two things I will tell you now. First, Isna-la-wica said that 'in any great undertaking, it is not enough for a man to depend simply upon himself.' Second, and remember this proverb, Mark, 'The spirits warn you twice. The third time, you stand alone.' As long as you know me, you can live your life by these words."

"Alexander!"

Majispin's angry voice cut across the loading dock. I didn't care; there was more happening here amongst us, and by "us," I meant us shapeshifters. The sorcerer just didn't matter at the moment.

Majispin stormed down the concrete stairs and came right up to my face.

"This pack is under my employ; don't even think you're assuming control of it," he hissed.

When would my arrival leave a positive impression on someone—anyone? I assumed he was using the same trick he'd used with the Faithful to keep eavesdropping to a minimum. I put all of my presence into my reply. Leaning over him, stepping close, and looking him in the eye, I snarled, "Go back to your test tubes and books." I pushed past him callously and added, "This isn't *my* pack and it's not *yours*."

I could feel his eyes stabbing my back. In fact, I could feel his power swelling. Undoubtedly everyone did, but we stormed quietly to the truck, a barrier of amorphous heat and energy building around the pack. There was no darker cloud than us on the horizon, and the sorcerer's magic sluiced off of that storm without a spark. I didn't believe Majispin could stop us—no one did. It didn't matter if he wanted to or even if he tried.

This was the kind of energy I expected to find when meeting a pack; it was dangerous and enticing to equal degrees. It's what had been missing from this one. The grouped power of shapeshifters is tempting, and I understood the allure and the danger of it. I would always feel that pull. There was a delicate balance, however, where a pack became more dangerous for those within than those without.

In the end, I didn't think my temperament would allow such a deep level of belonging to thrive for long, but I craved it like anyone else. It was an entirely new experience for the young shapeshifters around me. They privately reveled in it, peaking early with unrestrained, wild power. Only Seth seemed relieved; he'd been in a pack before, and I guessed he'd missed it as well.

Majispin had become resigned when he realized what was happening. Now the observer, he held his hands out, standing on the dock, as if warming his fingers near a fire. A thought creased his brow, and he abruptly closed his hands.

I was the first to the vehicle, and I set the tone by piling into the back seat. Since it was Mark's SUV, it was obvious he was going to drive, but I was letting him decide who'd be up front with him tracking the vampires.

"Maria, up front. Seth, Barros, in the rear." Mark sounded more assured than I'd heard him in the few days that I'd known him. Everyone moved without complaint. It was tight in the back seat, but none of us cared.

Majispin closed his eyes, seemingly reverent, and pursed his lips thoughtfully. He turned stiffly and marched back into the club.

Inside the car, Mark hung the pouch from the mirror and drove to the end of the alley. The pouch swung forward and to the left. It hung there, suspended by invisible forces.

Little black girl, your head a-twirl, I know where to find your blood.

SEVENTEEN

They had experience following the fetish. We found ourselves careening down Commonwealth Avenue following the taut sack. I thought we were driving too fast and might draw the attention of the police, but I kept my mouth shut. Let Mark make that decision. After twenty minutes of following the charm and swerving in and out of busy traffic, it was clear that we were heading back to the P.O. projects. They had to go there to finish the job tonight. We all knew that the sun would be low enough on the horizon within an hour, and the situation would become more volatile than ever.

The four vamps would be dangerous enough with their immunity to the sun. Once the burning disc set, the vampire foot soldiers I'd encountered at the warehouse could be brought to bear. As we approached P.O., I made the conscious effort not to make any suggestions to Mark as to our approach. I waited for him to make a decision. Instead of entering the projects, he turned onto one of the abutting main streets and followed it around. The charm strained on its cord, consistently pointing towards our destination as we circled. When we rounded the northernmost edge of the development, we had an unobstructed view of P.O. From this side, there were no trees or structures other than the blighted industrial area surrounding the complex.

Mark pulled over while Maria leaned towards the mirror and sighted down the length of the charm. "There," she said, and pointed.

I struggled to recall the image of the map from the tunnels. I could barely remember the pursuit and the man who'd been killed—Terrell was his name. *Terrell.*

David, however, was another matter. The image of his convulsing body still shone bright in my mind whenever the thought of him crossed my mind. Instead, I tried to focus on Terrell and Rhonda, exhausting whatever mnemonic constructs I had and giving up on the rest.

I recalled that I'd copied the map on a scrap of paper. A quick rummage through my pockets produced the crumpled sheet. I consulted the crude map and verified that where the fetish pointed was, indeed, one of the alternate locations. My thoughts were suddenly sharper and clearer than they'd been in days. The hunt was on.

Mark looked back over his shoulder and into my eyes. I nodded once, and we all exited the vehicle. It was fast becoming that delicate balance of day and night when human eyes have the most difficulty seeing. For us, though, we could see as clearly as if it were midday.

At the rear hatch, Mark handed out the weapons. Both Maria and I refused them, but Seth and Barros eagerly took one each. They had stripped themselves to bare skin; we'd have to move fast before someone noticed us. Seth's skin glowed coolly in the deep blue haze of light, a strong contrast to Barros's dusky appearance.

Mark spoke to Seth and Barros as I tossed jacket, shoes, and guns into the truck. "You two are point. Fan out and approach the building from either side. Alexander?" The pair shifted in a wash of heat and loped off into the growing shadows at a speed that would be difficult for a human to track.

Mark slipped the vehicle's key into a magnetic box under the rear wheel-well before looking me up and down. "Maria and I will flank you, follow your lead."

"Fine."

Just then, I heard Detective Roberts's voice; he was calling out to me. I spotted him in the distance; he was coming our way as quickly as he could without breaking into an embarrassing run.

"You two, go! I'll catch up."

They disappeared in the opposite direction from where Seth and Barros had gone, avoiding Roberts's approach.

I stepped up and met him halfway before he could close the distance between us. I didn't want him to pay too much attention to Mark's vehicle.

"What are you doing here? Who were those people?" Roberts demanded. His tone changed and he added with bewilderment, "Why are you barefoot in the goddamn projects?"

"I could ask the same of you."

With the briefest of glances, Roberts looked to his feet as if to be sure he had his shoes on. The absurd moment passed as quickly as it came, and he brought himself back to his full breadth and height. "Yeah, but you won't. You know why? I'm a cop and you're not. You don't have any authority in this matter. You're involved at my discretion, remember?"

I just stared at him. I knew I was making him nervous, but he was too angry to listen to reason. His career was inextricably tied to me by the murders of Rhonda Lloyd and Terrell, not to mention all the victims taken to make hunting blinds out of their apartments. He was well within the field of power we tended to generate, and though he suffered it better than most, I knew it was affecting him. Deep down, Roberts was no coward. We all have our fears, and courage is what allows us to face them. I hoped he would go somewhere else, but seeing me here would only cement any suspicions he had about tonight.

"Quite a disappearing act you pulled on me; I knew you'd get back here sooner or later."

"I'm glad you're paying attention." Then I walked past him and spoke over my shoulder, "I have to ask you to stay back for a minute, Detective."

"What? Are you gonna give me another 'Lieutenant Brown' warning? Please. I've had enou—"

There was a scream and several shots. I left Roberts's side in a blur of motion, clearing the distance to the building in question quickly enough that I couldn't hear Roberts's inevitable dash to keep up.

The steel door to the building was ajar, and I slammed it open with malice. One of the hinges ripped free of the concrete wall, adding a puff of mortar dust to the gloomy hallway, but the other hinge held, and the door hung like a broken tooth in the old building's façade.

I craved a fight as badly as the rest; the beast in me reveled in the idea. I wasn't prepared, however, for what I saw in the stairwell.

Barros's markings in monster form were distinct—warm red fur with dark grey accents. The size of the 'shifter was also a dead giveaway. He was up to his chest in vampires, swinging his blade wildly, lopping off a limb or colliding with three heads at a time, until the blade was suddenly caught. I could barely make out Seth's dark brown fur, as he was on his back, buried beneath several vampires. All the creatures in the hallway were growling and screeching, pouring in from underneath the stairwell.

Neither Mark nor Maria was to be seen. Farther down the hallway behind the stairwell, there were three bodies on the floor—two men and a woman. No children. Upstairs then, but first I had to help Barros.

I hadn't shifted yet, partly due to Detective Roberts's proximity and partly arrogance—I wanted these leeches to understand how dangerous I could be. I tackled the mass in front of Barros and pushed the bulk of them off of his flank. Reaching behind me, I bellowed for him to give me the blade and for him to help Seth. The weapon wouldn't aid in pulling the vamps off Seth, anyway.

He handed me the odd weapon I'd seen earlier at the waterfront, and for the first time, I appreciated the balanced weight of the thing. In Barros's crude and powerful hands, it was used like a scythe. I was stronger than Barros and more skilled. I plunged into the mass in front of me, hacking them to pieces.

Nearly half of the modified *pudao* was hilt, the other half single-edged, straight blade. At the end of the long leather-wrapped handle was a ball of steel for counterweight and bludgeoning power. It was an art to use a long, bladed weapon. Slashing and stepping forward, I cut a crude path through the bulk of them. They screamed and hissed as I chopped legs and arms, disabling them in one pass and killing them in the next. In the close quarters of the hallway, I fell into a pattern that made the passage impassable. In the interim, Barros was able to make short work of the pile on Seth. They never saw him coming.

Once, during my attack, one of the apartment doors opened and closed quickly. I caught a glimpse of eyes aghast—they might never sleep comfortably again. The hall was becoming slick with the simmering, viscous deaths of vampires. My blood dripped and hissed into that mess as my own scratches and tears bled and began healing in short order.

There was a sudden burst of warmth behind me. A glance confirmed that Seth had just died, overwhelmed by another wave of vampires. I'd known and not known him for many years, and in many insidious ways I could read this as a personal blessing, but his death bothered me anyway. There was some kind of unfinished business between us, and I never seemed to be able to correct any of my wrongs before someone died. I always felt I was the one who should have gone before them.

While vampires fizzle and burn down to a sloppy black ichor, 'shifters burn hot and fast, leaving little trace but a charred spot and a pile of carbon. His death was followed by the invisible wave that is the definitive shift from day to night.

From the rear door, more vampires piled into the hallway on cue. I tossed the blade to Barros and yelled, "Hold them!" His eyes burned red, but no tears flowed from them, only wrath.

I jumped straight up the center of the stairwell and vaulted onto the stairs over the railing. A few vampires followed me. I was going up, to find and stop the ritual. Our only chance was to disrupt that ritual; we were horribly outnumbered, and one of us had died already. I hoped no more sacrifices needed to be made, no more miscalculations on my part that might cause someone else's death.

There were more shots upstairs, a strangled cry, and then nothing. On the second landing, the unconscious Pepperman skidded down the hallway, his spent pistol clattering across the concrete. He groaned—no bites on him—but blood splattered his face where he'd been struck. He was just a minor obstacle, a hurdle to be vaulted. The vampires who'd disabled the detective were to be met, and I had a group on my heels. If Pepperman was going to survive and not become a meal, I needed to distract all of them quickly.

A straight kick to the chest sent one of the three sprawling backward; the two flanking him spared a glance over their shoulders at their hurtling compatriot. I thrust my clawed hands into the throats of the two. I could feel their spines as they gargled in shock and scratched at my arms. I pulled hard backward, snapping their connection to this reality. My elbows smashed into the vampires bearing down on me from behind with fangs bared. They stumbled backwards as I spun and kicked hard at the leg of the one nearest me, becoming the aggressor and controlling the flow of the fight. None of these monsters were skilled, simply reacting like animals using whatever their instincts told them.

The impact would've broken the bones of any other creature, but the vamp's leg simply flexed, and he tumbled to the ground. I stomped on his head, exploding it like a grape around my foot. One of the two remaining recovered fast enough to take a swing at me. I leaned back, driving the top of my foot into his crotch as hard as I could. He gagged and doubled over, allowing me to toss him into his partner. They tumbled to the floor in a heap. I whirled away from them, determined to get upstairs quickly.

The first one I'd kicked away made an effort to turn tail ahead of me. I suppose the promise of protection from the sun wasn't motivation enough. I caught him by the belt of his pants as he hit the next flight of stairs, and hurled him over my shoulder. His skull slammed into the wall, but the pliant nature of vampires prevents crushing death in this manner. I followed the motion and drove my fist as hard as I could into his face. My knuckles brushed concrete as the top of his head burst around the blow. The body skidded to the floor, dissolving into a smelly puddle.

I could hear a scuffle on the next flight up, and I could barely contain my human form any longer. Half-shifted, straining my shirt and pants, I cleared the next landing and saw Mark going toe-to-toe with the vampire I'd mutilated earlier this morning. The dead man's hand hadn't quite grown back yet.

Mark's fur was an impressive golden brown, not unlike his human hair, and he fought with passion. He was trying to get a grip on the vampire with his jaws, but the vamp was successfully keeping that deadly mouth at bay. They clawed at each other maniacally as another vampire appeared, waved one hand enigmatically in the air, and struck Mark with that palm.

There was a flash of light, and Mark gave a high-pitched howl as he shot backwards down the hall and through the glass-brick window. In the same instant, I closed the distance and tore the throat out of the vamp that had tossed Mark, but missed his spine. Desperation was beginning to cloud my thoughts and actions. We needed to settle the source of this quickly.

He stumbled backwards, eyes wide with shock, when the one-handed vamp pushed him out of the way and threw some kind of powder in my eyes. I lunged forward through the sharp, burning sensation, but missed the two of them as they scrambled up the last flight of stairs.

I blinked hard, my eyes clearing and healing quickly. There were more shots downstairs, and I could hear Roberts cursing in the stairwell. For me, there was only one more flight to go.

EIGHTEEN

On the fourth floor, the fighting on the roof could be heard through the concrete ceiling; a steady scrabbling of claws, growls, and sharp hissing accentuated what was happening inside. Maria was on the roof, most likely, cutting off our quarry's only other avenue of escape. Exposed like that, she must be in a desperate situation. There was no way she could successfully engage a gang of vampires out there for long; we outmatched this ragtag force in skill, but we were outnumbered by what looked like five to one or more. Near the end of the hall, next to the narrow stairwell leading to the roof, the true coven stood together.

The one-handed vamp supported his gurgling, throat-less conspirator, and behind them I could see the third monster, holding a black male child by the chin. He pressed the boy to his chest and raised a long, curved blade for the first stroke. I recognized the knife-wielder from the incident at the gentlemen's club.

Without hesitation, I elbowed the wounded vamp aside and grabbed the remaining one-handed bloodsucker on either side of his jaw. With only one hand, he couldn't do much to stop me as I planted one foot on his chest and pulled. There was a splash of blood, which turned to unctuous, black fluids on me and the walls. The gap-throated vampire scratched both hands down my side, sinking teeth into my upraised forearm. I stuck my fingers through his eyes and into his brain for a firm grip on his skull. His body convulsed—the mind and body connection only interrupted—and I was prepared to yank his head off as well when the third vampire spoke up.

"Stop! I'm sure that's excruciating, so why don't you let Timothy go?" He smiled and emphasized his point by pressing the blade into the child's throat.

"All right," I said, and let Timothy slide off of my hand with a sucking slurp. His inert body slammed to the floor and wobbled slightly as he began to heal and regain control. The vampire wiggled slowly backwards but didn't get far, as I stepped on his chest and leaned my weight into him. I continued in my native language. "I will release him."

I was slowly letting my human form go. It was an attempt at intimidation, growing larger, filling the hall, and becoming one of the monsters in full form as well, but I couldn't have predicted what came next.

The vampire holding the child responded in my native tongue. "You don't stand a chance, you inferior beast; I will kill this child before you can act." He smiled briefly, literally from ear to ear, full of teeth and vinegar. "Now let Timothy up. Bad enough you took his throat, but his eyes as well?"

I eased the pressure of my foot off of Timothy. He writhed beneath me, incoherent and smearing a puddle of blackening blood as he rolled over to crawl out of my reach. I stomped on his back, holding him in place.

I continued in Kainai. "Have we met?"

"Blackfoot is only one of the languages I speak, you stupid animal."

These vampires had been hunting for ancient and obscure methods; it only made sense that they'd have investigated native aboriginal cultures as well. It didn't matter, however, how well you knew the language;

natives still hold that grudge and are still stubborn to share with non-natives. I was certain they'd learned nothing from Native Americans.

"Kill the boy!" The gargled plea came from Timothy, who was recovering nicely under the pressure of my foot. He struggled to keep my full weight from bearing down on him.

The lead vampire responded in English. "In due time, Timothy. Patience. We are in control."

Each word from Timothy heralded a bloody gob from his throat. "He killed Mikel, Estoban; kill the boy! We can finish him together! You can hear the fighting; there are others!" With great effort, Timothy slithered out from under me and raised himself up on one arm, facing me with eyeless sockets.

I kept my eyes on Estoban as I said, "If you kill the boy, there'll be nothing between you and me." I was doing my best to allow my aura to flood the corridor, to gain some leverage against them with the power I wielded. Estoban's only reaction was to twitch as the power washed over him.

"You are powerful, but together we are *more* than you'll ever be."

Was he bluffing? I could see that the boy was still very much alive, and my nose told me that he'd defecated himself. A glance confirmed that they'd already drawn the symbol nearby. The hall was becoming glutted with conflicting, untapped energies, and Estoban's knife-arm tensed. The telltale bucket squatted below the boy's limp form, its filthy mouth agape and waiting. My only chance was to disrupt the spell by interfering in the ritual. I didn't think I'd be able to save the child.

Scuffling continued below us; footsteps pounded up the stairs. Detective Roberts, bleeding into his eyes from a gash on his forehead, a ragged cut on his arm slicking his shooting hand, had the look of a deranged and desperate man.

NINETEEN

Roberts took in the scene; he held his weapon in both hands, shaking but at the ready, with a wild look in his eyes. I couldn't imagine what his opinion might be, but it was obvious what he was seeing. A larger, deformed me; a pale, blind, throatless freak on the floor, writhing away; another pale man with a misshapen mouth, holding a child, and a curved knife poised to kill.

Roberts unfroze and pointed his weapon.

"Shut the fuck up; nobody fucking moves! You hear me? Not a goddamn move!"

Timothy became more frantic. "Is that a policeman? We'll be overrun by humans and beasts alike, Estoban; do it now!"

Roberts became even more agitated, trying to cover all three of us with his weapon. He repeated, "Shut up!" He was shaking violently and slowly let his eyes focus on me.

Estoban muttered to Timothy in Latin, "*Cum præscinderem iugulum pueri, succendam eam pariter.*"

"What?" Roberts whispered more to himself than anyone else.

"*Conventione,*" Timothy responded.

They'd agreed to act in accordance. In one breath, I pulled the monster back inside. Bits of loosened mortar fluttered to the floor, the concrete structure shaking with the altercation on the roof, as I took in the space and its occupants. Inhuman noises reverberated all around us, and I didn't see any other choice than taking advantage of Roberts's presence.

"We want the same thing here, Detective, to save the boy."

I continued repeating "save the boy" over and over, trying to get through to Roberts. Everything depended on his actions in the next few seconds. It also depended on Estoban not realizing my half-baked plan.

The hallway started to heat up. I glanced at Timothy, who was weaving an intricate pattern in the air in front of him. He was reciting something under his breath, over and over, his voice returning as he healed on the floor. There wasn't any time left; I made my repetitions to Roberts more urgent as Timothy's recitations climbed to a zenith.

Roberts continued to swing, indecisive, from me to Estoban. I heard more struggling on the stairs. Barros and several vampires appeared behind Roberts, whose panicked shaking managed to increase, completely unsure of where the most serious threat was coming from.

"Barros," I hissed, "keep them down!" The hulking form spun and tumbled down the stairs, growling and twisting with the pile of vampires. The noise was unnerving and chaotic.

I turned my attention to Roberts again. From the corner of my eye, I could see a glow near Timothy. The hallway was filling with the dry heat of a sauna. Sweat rolled freely down Roberts's brow, and the building trembled slightly with all the activity. I could hear someone crying behind one of the doors in the hallway, another praying loudly.

"Put that boy down; drop the knife!" shouted Roberts.

He leveled his weapon, sighting on Estoban and the boy. His breathing became deeper, more relaxed, and Timothy's palm, facing us, smoldered, then burned white-hot. Sweat beaded and ran down my body. Estoban tensed to pull the knife across the child's throat.

The single shot echoed in the hall, louder than the other amorphous organic sounds. I had tensed to spring when Roberts's finger pulled the trigger and the bullet exploded from the barrel. I was halfway to Estoban and trampling Timothy when the sound of the weapon smacked into my ears. The vampire's head snapped back, stunned, as he dropped the boy. Thick glass chunks from the window behind him exploded inward. Mark surprised us all as he shoved Estoban and grabbed the unconscious child. Estoban's eyes fluttered; he managed to recover enough to see Roberts, myself, and the angry, consuming heat behind us. The head wound wouldn't kill him, but it would keep him out of play long enough for us to get out of this building.

Scooping Roberts under my arm, ignoring his protests, I made for the window. The disrupted spell Timothy hadn't completed ran wild. Flames leapt from the writhing form behind me, a blast of heat singeing my feet and back. Timothy completely lost control of the spell; whatever my crushing footsteps had caused him to utter, it manifested an inferno in the hallway. Fire shot out like water from a burst dam and engulfed the stairwell, consuming the vampire who'd originated it, flowing from him and covering the walls, floors, and ceiling. Timothy lay screaming in a fireball, and the flames continued to fill any open space as if they were fluid. It was suddenly very difficult to breathe; we were caught in a tunnel of flame that was voraciously eating all the air in the hallway.

Mark, carrying the boy, leapt from the window first. I followed while gouts of flame stung the back of my head and lapped at Roberts's feet. I protected him as best I could as we tumbled the four stories. In midair, I felt a jolt of Mark's energy twist and claw at mine, then desperately scatter in all directions, grasping at whatever it could. Instinctually, I reached out and I held it together as I contorted to avoid a misshapen, dead tree in the yard. Dry branches cracked and scratched deep, gouging my flesh with stinging abandon. The landing was rough in my human form—especially carrying the detective. We rolled hard into the dirt; Roberts sprawled out of my arms, coughing, gasping from the impact.

When I looked up, flames spit out of the broken front door, and I covered my head. The entire hallway, top to bottom, convulsed in a fit of fire and wild heat, killing anyone in the hall and consuming any evidence that we'd been there. The thick glass windows glowed orange, and the building's hallway breathed the fire like an angry god. As suddenly as the flames had begun, they disappeared with a loud, sucking *thump*, leaving only heat-scorched metal and smoldering ruin.

Maria and Barros were unaccounted for, as was Pepperman.

TWENTY

When the seemingly insatiable flames abruptly vanished, I could make out the fuzzy figure of Barros rolling around in the dirt to put his coat out. He'd made it out alive. I heard a crash and looked up to see Maria, scorched but also alive and angry, on the hood of an abandoned car. She'd jumped from the roof as the blaze spilled from the doorway, spreading across the roof and flashing into the night. A few shadowy figures plunged into the darkness around us, vampires who'd survived the conflagration as well.

As my blurry gaze came back to where I'd landed, I saw Roberts batting at his legs and trying to hold his weapon on me at the same time. I was tired, and my feet and knees hurt badly from the fall.

I looked around again, trying to find where Mark had landed. For a moment, I couldn't understand why I didn't see him on the ground since he'd left the building in front of me. Looking up, I did find him, impaled on one of the broken lower branches, gulping for air in small spasms like a fish on a dock. He let the boy in his arms slide gently to the ground. I stumbled to my feet and went to him. I could feel his life ebbing away; the branch had cut across his spine, and his death was inevitable. The only thing that had held him here was me; my instinctual grab at the power we shared had held him together this long. He looked at me when I touched him, sadness clouding his face and eyes.

"Mark," I simply said.

He made to speak, but nothing came out. Angrily, I tried to piece his aura back together, closing my eyes and mentally reaching out for all the fragments of energy flitting about. It all slid away like mercury on glass.

With a heart-wrenching effort, he grinned and finally said, "I'm fine." Then he slumped and his body began to burn hot, setting the dry tree on fire—a funeral pyre for my new, dead blood brother.

I decided then that Mark didn't represent anything from my past. This was all coincidental; I'd made the right choices for once—I had to have, to keep going, to move forward. But I knew I hadn't. I shouldn't have interfered with Mark's relationship with Maria. I shouldn't have done whatever I'd done to this pack. Now two of them were dead, and I had no idea where I stood with Majispin or the safe-house network. I could only hope that this was worth the carnage I'd managed to strew across so many lives. Lives that had had nothing to do with my own until the past few days.

There will be more sacrifices; you'll see. My power burned hot inside me. *Embrace me, taste the spoils you've wrought. Take the boy, take all you wish; it's what you are.*

I picked up the boy and moved away from the growing fire before the tree toppled. His warmth and helplessness in my arms piqued the awful truth inside me. I could smell the sweet succulence that lay limp in my hands, taste the possibilities. There had to be something more than this, something worth considering rather than simple craving.

I struggled to find reasons to maintain control until a distracting thought from my recent memory bubbled up. The child in my arms reminded me of the kid from Terrell's story. If he grew up making decisions like that one had, was this all worth the effort and sacrifice that some of us had just made?

I still believed that the public would find out about us soon enough. It was inevitable that our existence would come to a boil. Time has allowed plenty of other hated or misunderstood groups to integrate into society, but this was a completely different matter. Most of us preyed on humanity, and I didn't think they would take kindly to us. Damn it, I shouldn't have a hard time justifying restraint.

Then don't. The voice was getting louder, coarser, and more commanding.

Over my shoulder, I could see Maria hunched over on the crumpled car, shifted back to her human form, cradling her ribs, blood overflowing her fingers, a purple bruise blooming on the side of her neck. She was wracked with emotion, grinding her teeth against a deep and guttural scream. She was only partially successful; the sound that came out of her was a mix of pain that was both physical and raw energy. I could feel the heat coming off of her, but we were out of time for mourning at this moment.

"Maria, Barros, get to the car; we have to leave!"

Sirens whined in the distance, just beyond the perception of human ears. The entire battle had lasted barely ten minutes, and a crowd was inevitably going to gather now that the fighting had died down and the fire burned down to something passing for normal. People continued to stumble out of the building, choking and crying out to each other. This was a chaos they could understand; it was relatable. Fires, disasters, accidents, and more appeared on the news every night.

Still watching Roberts, I checked the boy's vital signs as the detective leveled his weapon at me. There was only the bloody welling of a nick where the blade had been pressed to his throat. I spoke to Roberts. "The boy is fine, thanks to you."

"You're a fucking monster!" The detective's eyes blinked rapidly and his voice lowered to a whisper. "I don't know…what I saw. You're all…monsters."

In an oddly tender moment, uncharacteristic for the area, one of the building's initial stragglers, an old woman, spread a blanket over Maria's bare shoulders, whispering blessings in Spanish. Maria pulled herself off of the vehicle, thanked the woman, and limped into the night. Barros hadn't passed me yet, so I assumed he was behind me still. Although I was nearly nude, I didn't feel threatened at all. Unless Roberts got very lucky, there was no way he could put a bullet through my spine and kill me. What difference would one more sharp pain have meant?

"You can put that gun away, Detective; it won't do you any good against me. I'm going to leave now. I need you to think this through."

"'Think.' *Right.* I think you're responsible for the death of my partner—both of them!" Roberts suddenly tensed, looking over my shoulder.

I could smell Barros approaching from behind me, and I started to raise my hand to let him know everything was okay. Instead, the hulking Mexican addressed Roberts. With him shifted, his voice sounded like a gravel crusher, forcing words through a mouth that was not designed for subtle vocalization.

"You talkin' 'bout this idiot?" He summarily dumped Pepperman's unconscious body to the ground next to me and rumbled past us, ignoring Roberts's pointed weapon, limping for the car, looking like a gigantic, shaggy mastiff with oversized teeth as he shuffled on all fours. He must've scooped up Pepperman on his way out.

"I trust this is something we can keep between us," I asked Roberts.

"Are you threatening me?"

"No. I'm not; I'm leaving." I walked around Roberts and added, "Take care of your partner and this boy. We stopped what we needed to stop. I'll be in touch."

"Did you kill Brownie—Lieutenant Brown—to protect this?" Roberts's eyes pleaded; he had nothing available to deal with this, no context to put this in. A goodly portion of his world was cracking, and I hoped—I really did—that he was strong enough mentally to deal with the truths in front of him.

"No." I answered truthfully, walking away. Brown could handle the truth, but he couldn't resist what he saw as his duty. He was a good cop to the end, a good person. I was still alive, however, and not Brown.

Humans occasionally found out about us or became involved with monsters, as evidenced by the Faithful and other fetishistic individuals at the club. So far, discretion and lack of proof held our existence to nothing more than conflicting myths. Anyone determined enough to try to prove our existence tended to disappear. If humanity at large knew there were monsters like us among them, they'd waste no time going to war. They'd lose if we put up a concentrated effort—which "we" could never make happen.

We would be wiped from the face of the Earth. For the time being, a bit of anonymity was best. It was imperative, if we were to continue to exist, for us to nurture our relative invisibility in the fallible balance that we tried to maintain.

Once we were inside the vehicle and speeding off, what was left of the pack started to relax. No one said anything during the ride. Barros had gone back to human form and stared out the window like Seth had been prone to do. He was covered with bite welts and seriously charred on his back and shoulders. He'd go into a paralytic state soon; a significant amount of vampire venom coursed through his veins. He'd most likely survive, but this kind of damage would leave scars.

Maria sat quietly, looking straight ahead. She was bruised all over, with scratches on her arms and a chunk torn out of her side, bleeding freely despite holding her shirt to the wound, and I was sure most of her ribs were broken. The tear would close up soon, but she'd be woozy for the next few hours or so and tender for a few days. Fortunately, she seemed to have suffered no bites, and she'd likely heal clean. Mark and Seth, of course, had not been so fortunate.

I was the only one who hadn't suffered any debilitating injuries, so I was driving. They'd done well, but the pack was out of commission for a few days, quite possibly forever.

Before we arrived at the safe house, I felt something bumping against my foot. When I reached down, I realized it was the fetish that Majispin had given us to track the vampire whose hand I'd swallowed. Useless now. I stuffed it into the ashtray. My fingers lingered on the rough cowhide; a thought nagged at me. An important bit of information, I thought, simply because I couldn't remember what it was.

I was tired, but not that tired, so I concentrated. Then I gave it up. I couldn't dredge the information out. My head was a mess now that we had accomplished our goal. In the heat of action, everything is clearer; afterward, not so much. Then the recollection ran through my brain like an ice cube across the kitchen floor—the vampire coven. There had been four *de facto* members at the building; we had only managed to kill three. One was still at large. I'd naively assumed that Estoban was the leader.

Yes, I'd seen four in the Leather District. Three of the dead men had been dealt with, and I couldn't shake the feeling that the last vampire was going to be more difficult than the first three.

TWENTY-ONE

I maneuvered Mark's SUV into the loading dock. We clambered out, and I wrestled the unconscious Barros up the stairs while Maria limped behind. She had called ahead on her mobile phone, and Majispin was supposed to be waiting. No one had said anything about Seth or Mark yet. I certainly didn't want to think about it. Now that Seth was dead, I couldn't seem to forget him or what he represented from my past. He'd admitted knowing where Tina was.

I was still trying to figure out what Mark's death meant to me.

We made our way to the small two-bed infirmary off Majispin's lab. It had been dark in the lower hallway, but that didn't mean anything to us. I laid Barros down as gently as I was able, carrying the big man had been awkward. Maria sat on the other bed with a first aid kit popped open next to her. She was awkwardly trying to dress her own wounds. Without a word, I walked over and took charge of the job, wrapping gauze around her torso to hold her ribs and the clean dressing in place. She winced more than a few times while I did this, but the most unusual moment happened when I placed my hand over the dressing of her open wound. It needed to be adjusted, but there was a sudden surge of power that made us both jump, which she immediately regretted.

We stared at each other for what seemed like several minutes until Maria pushed me away and averted her eyes. I retreated to the study, leaving Maria to her thoughts and wounds. She would make sure Barros was stable.

I cleaned up in the small washroom off the study and tried to collect my thoughts. The fourth vampire would certainly be the most cunning of the group. Since I'd crashed their party once, it seemed that he'd smartly excused himself from this final mission. I didn't have a clue how to find him, since I'd never gotten a scent or anything else to track him with. I needed to speak with Majispin, despite the heat of our last exchange.

Perception of my surroundings came crashing back to the present, a jarring transition where I found myself standing in a bathroom, staring into a mirror. For the barest of seconds, I wondered what I was doing and where I was. Something had swelled inside me, washing my consciousness away for a moment. I "listened" for the internal whisper, sought to feel the power inside me, but to no avail.

The Sweaty Magus, a club and safe house in Boston, I thought to myself. I was in Boston, Massachusetts, but what had originally brought me to this city eluded me. I had no recollection of coming here, or why. Why had I come here to Boston? The first thing I could recall was getting the phone call from Detective Roberts and the blood, the little girl's blood—what was her name?

Soon. I heard the internal voice at last, one chilling word dragging itself like a raptor's claws across the back of my head.

The door opened and I startled. Maria stood in the way, holding a pair of jeans and a T-shirt. Her face was smudged with blood and dirt, thin, wet lines running from her eyes to her chin. By the scent of the clothes, they were from Mark's wardrobe. We were about the same height, but he'd carried more weight in his upper body. Despite this, our waist size was exactly alike. I nodded and took the clothing, I was unwilling to speak first, and I didn't know where I stood with her after this.

Once I got dressed, I headed downstairs to find Majispin on my own. Nearly deserted, the club was gloomy. Emergency lights glowed red, and what precious few patrons remained seemed to be heading out at a leisurely pace. Adrenaline pumped and my skin began to prickle; the scent of natural gas came and went with the air currents. Something was wrong.

Benjamin was closing up shop when I bumped into him.

"Hey, Benjamin, what's going on?"

The bartender looked up from his bag and nodded. "There's some kind of electrical problem; power's gone wiggy. We found a small flood in the basement, so Mr. Majispin is closing for the rest of the evening until he gets it fixed. He turned off the power to the lower floors." He eyed me warily and added, "What happened to you?"

My scratches and bruises showed. "Business. Where's Majispin now?"

Benjamin snorted before answering. "Last I saw him, he was with Ms. Ducat. Make of that what you will."

"Where's access to the basement?"

"Next to the bar, first door on the left." Then he left, still keeping true to his habit of not revealing his boss' location.

Well, the flood in the basement meant that was the first place I was going to check. I headed for the exit sign nearest the bar. Beyond the doorway, there was a short hall with two doors at the end. One emergency doorway with a crash bar led outside, and the other to the basement.

Just as I crossed the threshold under the exit sign, a familiar feeling passed over me. I stopped, turned around, and looked up. Ana was crouched above the doorjamb, wedged in the corner.

She grinned and said, "You'd be surprised at how few people look up." She then hopped down and added, "Now that you're here, I can quit hiding. Alivara's staff was trying to get everyone to leave, but, you know, I'm not just *everyone*."

"Of course." It was good to see her, as usual, even though her wardrobe lacked anything I'd approve of. She wore thick-soled boots, torn fishnets, a brutally dyed pleated skirt, a couple of studded belts, fingerless gloves, and a worn scoop-necked shirt. All of it was black and a stark contrast with her pale skin. She looked like an anti-Catholic schoolgirl.

I moved to hug her, just a touch, to be present and grounded, but she stepped back a pace, seeing the state I was in.

Then she smiled again and asked, "Did you get your ass kicked?"

I snorted and answered the sarcastic question with one of my own. "Did you use a rat to comb your hair today?"

She mussed her hair further and said, "You're lookin' for Alivara too, huh? Last I saw him, he was with Mizz Doo-cat. I don't trust that smelly, nosy woman. Speaking of smells, do you know why it stinks like gas down here?"

"Ana, you should know what's happened. Both Seth and Mark are dead."

She didn't bother to contain her surprise and blurted out, "Did you kill them?"

"Of course not! Why would you even think that?"

"I dunno; seemed like where things were going."

"Why?"

"Because you used to know Seth and couldn't remember him, and y'all had bad blood between you."

"You knew Seth too; you met him before, same as me, didn't you?" I couldn't believe that this had slipped my mind as well. Ana was around when I ran with Curry, but not often. She had certainly been old enough and independent enough that she came and went as she pleased.

She squirmed a bit before she spoke. "It was obvious that you couldn't remember him and just as obvious that he already resented you even before he found out you didn't recall him at all. I thought it best to keep my mouth shut."

Ana had probably met Tina, as well. I almost asked about her but thought better of it. Ana had never been fond of any women I'd kept time with.

Then she added quietly, without prompting, "I remember Constantina, too."

I shook my head, sighed, and moved on, picking up on what she'd said of Ms. Ducat. "What does Ducat smell like to you?" My interest was piqued in several ways, but only one mattered at this moment.

"Too much perfume, lots of flower smells. Yuck."

Seemed like all the monsters thought she smelled like a flower shop gone awry. Vampires have a decent sense of smell—not nearly as acute as a shapeshifter's, but good enough. I was glad I wasn't the only one who found her scent disturbing.

"To the basement, then." Before getting to the door, I could hear the rush of water, and the brain-killing scent of gas grew stronger. I quickened my pace and snatched the door open. Water rushed along the floor at the bottom of the stairs, and an invisible cloud of gas wafted up and out of the basement.

"Whoa," Ana said, "that doesn't look like a small flood to me. Ugh, I'm done breathing tonight."

We darted downstairs, and I saw a familiar, white-suited form with his face resting on a concrete block just above a foot of water. Ana turned him over and started lugging him up the stairs while I found the drains. They were plugged with rags. I pulled them all out one by one and started looking for the gas leak. The water was coming from somewhere beneath the waterline.

Once the flood receded some, I could shut it off, but the priority right now was the gas. My head was starting to ache; a sharp pain slid down the center of my forehead, and it was becoming difficult to breathe. Perhaps Ana should've done this; she didn't have to breathe if she didn't want to.

I spotted a clutch of wires hanging from the fuse box—which explained the lack of power. The wires dangled precariously close to the water level. I shifted priorities and quickly found the main breaker next, as it was still live. If the water had reached the wiring, I don't think many of us would've survived.

I quickly pulled the heavy lever down to cut the power running through the exposed lines and found the gas leak next. Someone had removed the incoming line from the meter. It took a minute, but I was able to fit the pipe back on and screw the nut down enough to stop the flow. I started to feel like I weighed ten times more than I normally did. Rectangles of wan light were obvious here and there around the basement. Thick bricks of glass filled the tiny windows. As spots started to swim in front of my eyes, I stumbled from window to window, busting out bricks with my bare hands. It would take a while for the gas to dissipate; fortunately, the club was empty, and it wouldn't be a problem. Blood flowed freely from my knuckles, but a light breeze swam through the space, taking the gas away.

Now that the water was draining and the gas had been stopped, I took a slow look around and saw one thing of note—a small metal sign for the local gas company. The plaque was secured to a metal door leading towards the street; it read "AUTHORIZED

PERSONNEL ONLY." The lock was intact. I slogged through the water and ran upstairs.

Ana had been performing CPR on Majispin, taking in unneeded air and blowing it into his lungs. Ironically, vampires were ideal candidates to perform resuscitation, as their lungs didn't steal any oxygen. He coughed once and took a deep, ragged breath before his breathing settled into a comfortable rhythm. Ana sat back and looked at me.

"I found bite marks on his legs. They paralyzed him and left him in the water. Whoever did this didn't want that little fact to come out too soon," she said.

"Isn't the club warded against this sort of thing? Shouldn't Majispin be able to defend himself here, or at the very least repel invaders? He seemed quick about it when it came to me." The question was rhetorical; in my mind, I was working out how this might have been accomplished. The who was as obvious as the nose on my face.

"Yeah," she replied, running her fingers through her mussed hair, "I don't get how anyone could get him completely off guard here."

"Unless they didn't just enter Majispin's property. Perhaps they were already here."

"Ducat?"

"Anything's possible. There's an access door in the basement for the gas company."

"An easement," she said knowingly, and I nodded.

That was the loophole in the building's security system; it was the one place where any spell Majispin might cast could be bypassed, since the city's gas companies needed access at all hours.

I didn't know Majispin well enough to consider who else might want to kill him. The safe-house system usually put the owners and operators above contention or controversy. Why wreck one of the few places you might be safe in? However, he *was* directly backing the effort to shut the coven down, so it made sense that the fourth vampire had tried to kill him. With Ducat's help maybe, or she was under the fourth vampire's control somehow.

I picked Majispin up and tossed him over my shoulder. We headed for the club's infirmary; the place was completely empty now. On the first flight of stairs, Majispin stirred and spoke very weakly.

"They've taken Ms. Ducat."

I stopped and half-turned to Ana. "Did you hear that?"

"Yup."

"Why would they take Ms. Ducat?"

Ana shrugged in that offensive teenage manner that says *how the hell should I know?*

TWENTY-TWO

Maria was utterly shocked when we carried Majispin in. She shakily exclaimed, "What the hell's going on?" Then she rolled off the second bed, took Majispin from me, and laid him down. Every move she made caused her to clench her jaw audibly; I doubted all of her ribs had set enough for her to haul her own worn body around, never mind Majispin's weight.

Maria began getting Majispin comfortable while she grimaced and spoke. "What happened to him, and what's with the power? And you're both wet."

Before Ana could make a wiseass comment, I held up my hand to her. "There's a flood in the basement. Someone plugged the drains and opened the gas line. If the water had reached the wires, this place would be a hole in the ground."

Maria just crossed her arms and shook her head slowly.

"Do you know who it was?" Maria asked. "Couldn't be the coven we just broke."

"We only got three of them there. There are four that I'm aware of."

"God *damn* it," Maria swore. "What now? They're way off the board now; they've challenged the safe-house system. Majispin's out, this pack is busted for now, and we're…down two sets of hands."

She was correct. Maria sighed heavily and winced.

Ana rolled her eyes. I think sometimes she forgets how the other half has to live with bones that aren't pliable.

Maria asked, "How'd they get in?"

"I think they got around any wards placed on the grounds by coming through a utility access in the basement, but the locks on that are intact. So I think someone already inside helped pull it off."

Ana tossed a question to the room. "What's all this got to do with the smelly lady? Why take her?"

"Maybe it was you, freak," Maria said, indicating Ana. "You've been spending a lot of time with Mr. Majispin—when was the last time you saw the sun?"

Ana crossed her arms and squinted at Maria. "Maybe you're right; maybe I should leave now. Or maybe you should make me." Maria had no idea that Ana had no recollection of ever being in the sun. She'd been a vampire since she was a baby, and talk of seeing the sun tended to be a sore spot for her.

"Quiet," I interjected, then I asked, "What do you smell on Majispin?"

She shrugged, regretted the motion, took a deep, ragged breath, and knitted her brows before answering. "Same as usual, only wet this time."

"Ana?"

"Yeah. The same."

"He was with Ms. Ducat last. He regained consciousness long enough to tell us 'they've taken her.'"

Maria scrunched up her nose.

"So, what's wrong with this picture?" I questioned the room.

Both of them lit up, but only Maria said, "I never put much thought into it, but her stink should be all over Majispin. It never is. But so what? Maybe she uses some alchemist's potion as her perfume."

"It's just…"—I wasn't sure what to say—"…odd. Look, I'm going to follow the gas company access out to the street. Maybe I can track Ducat to the coven. Find her, find them."

Ana grinned and said, "Dead or alive?"

"Dead or alive," I agreed.

Maria got back to her feet and wobbled.

She wasn't going to be able to help at all. "You're staying. You're not going to be much use to anyone in the field right now, and if something happens here, you need to watch over those two." I indicated Majispin and Barros.

Ana followed me out. I knew she would. When we'd gotten far enough down the stairs, I asked her why she was always so snippy with Maria.

"Well," she started to say, while stomping petulantly on the stairs in her boots, "she hit on you, right?"

"I suppose."

"She was with Mark, right?"

"Yeah."

"She's not exactly a bimbo, but her behavior is too…" She couldn't find the words.

"I never realized you were a feminist."

"Yeah, whatever. She's too clingy with men that might help her."

We rounded the bottom of the stairs and entered the main bar. I stopped and asked, "What is it that she needs help with?"

Ana rolled her eyes, looked up, and shifted her weight to one foot. She continued to look at the ceiling when she said, "You'll have to ask *her*."

Knowing that I'd gotten as much out of her as I could, I said, "Look, I want you to make sure the club is secure before you follow me."

"What makes you think I'm going to follow you?"

"Yeah, whatever," I mocked. She scrunched her face up and grinned as I walked away into the basement.

There was still a significant amount of water on the basement floor. I slogged back through to the small metal door. It was locked, of course, and still marked "AUTHORIZED PERSONNEL ONLY." I broke open the door, stepped up out of the water, and entered the tunnel.

The passage was short and clean. Not much to speak of, just a method of entrance and exit. I took a deep breath and miraculously picked up hints of Ms. Ducat's flowery scent. This was getting stranger by the minute. Unless she'd intentionally left it, hoping that one of the pack would pick it up. Until now, her scent had come and gone as she did. Time to follow the trail of breadcrumbs.

My nose took me to the alley between the buildings, which emptied out to the side street. From there, the scent trail tracked along the rear and sides of buildings until it hit the Common. It took several minutes, but I was able to pick it up again by skirting the edge of the Public Garden downtown. Darkness had fallen, and several more hours needed to pass before the sun came up. I hurried along the edge, not staying still long enough to catch the attention of anyone passing through.

The air was cooling rapidly; it was going to rain soon. If the rain were heavy enough, it would make this already-difficult tracking harder. By the time I reached the apex of Beacon Hill, tiny drops were starting to fall.

The trail led up through Beacon Hill and down the other side until it crossed Washington Street further downtown. Through the Financial District, and on the other side of South Station, the downtown area became more industrial. Compound that with the construction, and it became a challenge to navigate by car and virtually impossible by foot.

Irregular traces of Ducat's scent took me down the underside of Summer Street, farther into Boston's gigantic highway project. Regular traffic and inhabited buildings were becoming scarce, as hardhats and heavy equipment appeared more frequently.

There was nothing but dirt and gravel underfoot when I came to the fence of a secure construction site. Inside one of the huge tunnel boxes, there were fifty or so men milling about, performing various tasks to drain the state's budget in as efficient a manner as possible. The site was bathed in high-wattage halogen lights and the high beams of various dump trucks and tractors. The noise in the pit was a huge distraction, a cacophony of metal scraping against metal, rocks being dumped, and diesel-powered engines roaring. As long as I stayed outside the circle of light, I wouldn't be seen. Within the light, you could see the rain falling harder now, and I could feel the cold, pelting droplets through my hair.

Everything was clear now. I could think freely, and I remembered everything I needed to know to accomplish the task at hand. Most of it, anyway. The chase, a hunt, the killing—I never seemed to have any problem remembering the killing. At the highest moments like this, it was as if all were well in my world, like a good friend accompanied me, making sure I was comfortable and encouraging me to continue—*insisting* that I continue. But good friends aren't most interested in blood and mayhem.

Not like I am, my innermost voice whispered. *Let me help. If you don't, you'll die for sure, and where will that leave us? Let me out.*

The trail led straight up to a deserted section of chain-link fence and stopped cold.

TWENTY-THREE

Dogs might come unhinged at this point, but I was at least smart enough to realize that they'd leapt over the fence. Taking two steps back, I easily vaulted the twelve-foot barrier without touching it, but winced on the landing. I was still battered but coming back together quickly. And damn hungry, as usual. On the other side, I ran along the perimeter of the lights, being careful not to trip over any of the thick wiring, concentrating on my footsteps.

I was headed for the only logical place they could be, inside the nearest construction, a monolithic ventilation structure jutting up from the ground. It appeared that the thing had burst straight up from the earth. Eventually, these vents would channel exhaust from the underground highway into the open atmosphere. I needed to get out of the city for a while; it was driving me mad. *Everything* was driving me mad these days. Ana thrived on urban conditions such as these, a consequence of her maturing over the second half of the Industrial Revolution, I suppose.

I gained access to the building the most likely way the vampires had, by scaling the outer wall to one of the unfinished windows higher up. The inside of the building was warm, the machinery humming and lively, although no traffic passed through the tunnel as yet. A test run must have been in progress.

Keeping Ana's comment about "how few people look up" in mind, I stuck to the girders and crossbeams inside the building. Making my way up to the top level, I found massive turbines that ran the length of the concrete structure, as well as car-sized ducts sticking out of the floor. On the walls, massive caged fans turned lazily, venting nothing but air at the moment. It was in this cavernous room that I found Ms. Ducat chained to a piece of machinery, her head lolling and her Victorian outfit disheveled.

I could neither see nor smell any blood from this vantage point. Ozone spiced the air, and a heady mix of concrete and dirt followed that. As I crept closer, I could smell the powerful field of electricity being generated, as well as wet concrete and well-oiled machinery. Above all this wafted only her flowery scent. At the far end of the hall, I could see two figures lurking about. They paced back and forth.

Timing their patrol, I quietly jumped down to the concrete floor, squeezing my aching knees; the machines' humming masked any incidental sounds. Moving over to Ms. Ducat, I checked for a pulse. I couldn't detect one, or it was very weak. Hard to tell, but she was probably dying. Her skin was soft and her body pliant as I tested the chain links holding her up and to the machinery. This still didn't make sense; why take her? Of what value was Ms. Ducat? Perhaps she was to be used as a source of information to replace Nacxit? Worse yet, she was probably bait. Shit.

This close, her scent masked my surroundings and made me uncomfortable. I had no idea how many vampires were playing follow-the-leader. With Ms. Ducat so close, I couldn't discern how many of them were near us now. When I pulled away from her and was able to stick my head up, I smelled more than a few vampires nearby. They were closer than I was comfortable with, and I was sure they knew I was here. I needed to get out. Now.

I whipped my head to the side and saw a couple of platoons' worth of vampires scuttling in our direction—on the floor, across the walls, and above the two of us. We were surrounded by oversized, grinning faces in seconds, and Ms. Ducat was still swooning. What had they done to her?

The surrounding horde bared their fangs, enjoying the moment. They weren't making the attempt to maintain a human posture. Various inhuman contortions dotted the group surrounding me, lending a brazen, otherworldly, and serpentine quality to the horde. In amongst the crowd, a little blond head peeked through—my constant companion, come to see me die.

The vamps ignored the ghost that was pointing at me with a bloody stump. After all, I was the only one who could see the dead boy. My basest, most craven moment, wrapped up in a recurring, supernatural nightmare. A stupid, careless, and racist decision, come to haunt me to my dying day. *Today*, I reckoned. Maybe this was it, the end—an eye for an eye for an eye. The father, who had given the order to kill so many sons and daughters of the Kainai, had lost his son to my teeth and claws. And now, that boy's spirit was patiently waiting to bear witness to my demise.

One of our greatest moments, my power sighed. *Now look where ending that glorious behavior got us.*

I crouched, waiting for their attack as they moved into position. I couldn't afford to make any mistakes here, or both Ms. Ducat and I would most certainly die horribly. I'd never faced this many vampires before. The boy simply stared, stone-faced; he was certainly prepared to watch me die.

Where was Ana? She always bragged about being able to find me; she should have been following not far behind. I reconsidered the thought, because she'd likely be killed as well. Better that she wasn't here now.

One of the vampires strode forward on the floor. He raised a clawed hand in my direction and said, "You've killed many of us these last few days. Tonight, it's your turn."

Itching to buy some time, I replied, "So, you're in charge? You've tried twice already; you think the third time's the charm?"

The jingle of chains behind me sounded a split second before I felt the knife pierce my back. I shifted my position to skew the full thrust. The edge of the weapon grazed my spine and passed through a lung, collapsing it with a wheeze. The tip of the blade protruded from between my ribs in front of me.

Behind me, Ms. Ducat answered, "Apparently so."

With a sudden movement that brought a gasp to my lips and me to my knees, she twisted the blade, wedging it between my ribs.

Then she added, "And he's not in charge here."

In my head, completely beyond my control and sounding stronger every minute, my power whispered to me. *Told you so.*

TWENTY-FOUR

I looked back at Ms. Ducat. The blade was buried up to the hilt in my back, and blood had gushed over the pommel. She no longer held it, as I had fallen to the floor and she had let the blood-slick grip slide from her palm.

"You have been an incredible pain to me, Alexander," Ms. Ducat said. She raised a bloody hand to her lips, licked, and sharply spat, her fake teeth tumbling out with the spittle. "And in such a short fucking time."

My breathing was labored and I coughed blood. The blade was dangerously close to my spine, but I considered myself fortunate that our proximity to the wall had prevented her from simply cutting my head off.

Her face started to elongate and her features sharpened. Her voice became deeper and she pulled the wig off of her—well, *his*— head. Black veins stood out on his dull, white pate. He became slightly taller and passed one hand in front of his face as he whispered, "Away." The flowered scent dissipated and he tore the ankle-length dress from around his waist.

"It is a distinct pleasure to finally meet you under the proper circumstances," he said. "My name is Damon."

The vampire wore a close-fitting, black Mao. Rather than offering his hand to me, as I absurdly hoped, he slowly drew another blade from a sheath on his back and held it casually. I couldn't move—I could barely breathe. I couldn't do anything with the other blade in my back, the edge scraping against my spine. One wrong move and I'd kill myself. Estoban, Timothy, Marsan, and Damon. How filthy—Eurotrash vampires. *Screw this.* I started to crawl; I'd be damned if I was going to just lie here and die. Damon was going to have to expend some effort, even if it were only to casually walk across the floor.

"Do you have any idea how long it takes to plan something like this? How long it took to locate Nacxit? And you just *burn* a treasure like that? It took years to set up and move, over and over and over again. It's not every properly industrialized country that has a prime, self-segregated class that would not be missed! Then you walk into the picture." His last words cut off with a hiss, and then he continued in a calm voice. "By the way, the alchemist's blood is on your hands. I don't know what he did, but he failed to put you off the scent. Died squealing, didn't really put up a fight. Feckless human." Damon sighed. "What kind of black serendipity brought you to my doorstep, I'll never know, but enough's enough."

Damon continued to follow me as I crawled and gasped for air, dribbling blood from my mouth. It was impossible to move with any freedom; the wedged blade limited my movement and brought fresh, wet pain with every weak breath. While I was crawling, if I allowed my torso to touch the floor, the point of the blade would drag and pull against my ribs.

He went on in a hissing speech. "I didn't think Majispin would be stupid enough to let you burn the old vampire to death. Nacxit was an incredible repository of information! Do you have any idea? Any?"

"Some," I managed to respond.

The first slash brought a fresh gasp to my lips and a shallow cut across the side of my midsection; I couldn't move. All I could do was tumble to my side, desperately trying not to twist my torso. The second slash forced me to grit my teeth as he took a powerful swing at the back of my thigh, opening a sickening gash and allowing wet warmth to coat the inside of my leg to my knees. The third blow laid me out flat in a puddle of my own smoldering blood and spittle with a gash in my shoulder. I distractedly watched the edges of my puddle crackle as the hot fluid dissolved. Damon knew the situation he had me in and was taking full advantage of it. He was slowly cutting me to pieces while I was forced to hold as still as the pain would allow. If I jerked violently, the blade in my back would surely sever my spine, ending the game for good. Maybe that was for the better?

My existence, I realized, to date, had been a largely selfish one. My only redemptive action in the last two hundred years had been saving Ana. Everything else—and I do mean *everything*—had been calculated behavior to benefit me. To what purpose? None. I still couldn't recall everything I wanted, and I'd been hearing voices in my head. My random amnesiac acts of schizophrenia and mayhem had cost more than one person a normal life. Again, for what? This moment? Was this my destiny? Perhaps the Dragon had overestimated my value. In a few moments, she wouldn't be able to collect on my promise at all. My pointless existence was about to end, and I'd not made one real sacrifice for anyone in my second life. Nothing I'd done amounted to any real meaning, I realized, not even raising Ana. What had that cost me? Nothing. She was a benefit to me; I'd sacrificed nothing to save and raise her.

"Fortunately"—Damon straightened and eyed the bloody blade in his hand—"there's still time. With you securely out of the way, we will complete the ritual and overrun the Eastern Seaboard. And don't worry, we'll do it quietly; they'll be none the wiser. We'll be good masters, not that you'll be around to witness it." With that, he knelt down and caressed the back of my neck. Pulling back the edge of my shirt, he blew a breath across my exposed skin and slowly sank his fangs into my neck, releasing a torrent of venom. It entered my bloodstream like acid, beating a flaming path to my heart and spreading throughout my body. Then he bit me again, further down on my shoulder, just to spite me. *Fucking bastard.*

I struggled with self-destructive thoughts and my inherently defiant nature. Perhaps my refusal to die for such a long time was born of a need to resist, to run contrary to whatever was being asked of me. Not that much had been asked. Occasionally, some victim or another had begged for survival, and I had not granted it.

"What do you think, Alex? Should I wistfully mourn the loss of my three partners? Hm, you know better, I'm sure. Monsters like us don't have friends, do we?" He chuckled in my ear. "We have plans, though, and you're in the way of my plans. A loose thread. So I've decided to take some time to pluck you out and cut you loose. Your fault, you know. I hadn't been paying enough attention to you, but lately…" Damon shook his head and waggled a pale finger. "I suppose I should thank you. Despite the time it's taken, the journey has been largely uneventful until now. Active learning, you know, keeps the mind keen."

"I'm nothing like you," I choked out.

"Nonsense! I've spent some time looking into your past, Alex; you're as much a murderous psychopath as you *think* I am! Just remember, I have a fucking *plan*; there's a reason for my existence, but there's none for yours. Heh, 'fucking plan.' I really am going to fuck over plenty of people tomorrow."

Damon wasn't entirely wrong about me; I couldn't argue the salient points. My history was a patchwork of murderous applications, a life I'd believed a monster should live. A life I'd thought a monster deserved. At this point, I didn't deserve to live, but it was my decision, ultimately, whether I would allow Damon to kill me outright, or whether I would die resisting.

Smiling, Damon pushed me aside as he stood up straight. "Tomorrow brings the new moon, Alex. The Maya knew more than anyone ever surmised! *This* new moon is in alignment with more than the rocks in our solar system. The power of another galaxy—another dimension—will be channeled here, and we'll be ready to harness it." He turned to the clambering faithful around us and raised the blade high. "We will rule the day as the night!"

They cheered, they clapped, and they whooped. Their leader looked back down at me and said quietly, "This is so much better than killing you with an exhaustive spell. The pain is just so"—he shivered—"uncomfortable when it comes to the big, instant-gratification magic. Yes, this is much better, more natural." He grinned and considered his next slash.

We all heard the scraping click that ran counter to the smooth humming of the turbines and the sudden deathly stillness of the surrounding vampires. It was followed by a sharp hiss. Both were sounds I hadn't heard since 1915, during World War I.

Ana's voice sang out. "Cheese!" All the vampires turned to look.

I could only see her by peeking through the legs of the surrounding vamps. She had a pair of tanks strapped to her back and held a long, black nozzle attached to them by a worn hose.

My little girl had brought a *kleinflammenwerfer* to the party, a goddamn German flamethrower.

TWENTY-FIVE

The nozzle blazed to life.

I covered my head as residual spray from the burning fuel splattered around me, bits of flame marking the backs of my hands. When I looked up, burning vampires were screaming and scattering everywhere. Damon, with a stunned look, abruptly turned his attention back to me and raised the blade.

Another blast of the flamethrower drove him away from me as Ana shuffled in my direction, and I struggled to put some distance between my neck and Damon's blade, hot gelatin splashing on the floor between us. My daughter was laying down a swath of hell as vampires dissolved into smoldering, oily puddles all around us. I weakly batted at little flame-ups on my legs, desperately holding my back rigid, avoiding any twists. The pain never stopped, never got easier to bear, and it certainly kept me awake and aware.

She had to stop firing as she put one hand on the pommel of the blade and her small foot squarely on my back. The weapon had to be removed in one straight pull. With a sucking sound, it came free. One of the vampires rushed at her now that the flamethrower seemed to be out of play, and she neatly removed his head before dropping the blade with a clatter. She then opted to generate more chaos with the flamethrower.

Another blast of fire drove others backwards. I came to my feet very angry—angry at being deceived, angry at letting my guard down. Just plain pissed off at Damon. I ignored the rest of the horde—as Ana was happily killing them in groups of two or three— and drew the gleaming pistols from under my jacket. I emptied them at Damon's scrambling form, keeping him from escaping. He dove behind steel-reinforced bracing as several shots slammed into his torso. They wouldn't kill him, but they would damn sure hurt.

"That thing'll probably explode if you keep using it," I shouted, out of breath, over the din, and holstered the guns. I concentrated on forcing my wounds to close and counteracting the venom coursing through my veins. My vision swam once and calmed; air flowed into both lungs.

"You're welcome!" she shouted. "This thing is so cool! I had to beg to get it; sorry it took me so long." Then, whooping crazily, she charged after a pack of vampires, blazing away. I was relatively certain she'd heard my warning.

I faced Damon, who was still tucked behind steel, out of the reach of Ana's belching torch. He stared at me, hatred boiling in his eyes, as he slowly stood up. Blood smeared the backs of his hands and neck. I knew that all he wanted to do was get out and finish his plan, but I was still standing in his way. He was no coward; running was simply a path to victory for him.

I used my sleeve to wipe the blood off my chin as I watched him. He crept towards me with the long blade in his hand. I reached down and picked up the one that had been wedged in my back and drew a finger down the flat edge.

As he approached, I ran my bloody finger from cheek to cheek leaving a line of my own blood across the bridge of my nose; it sizzled hot as it wavered between decomposition and resolution in such proximity to my body. Then I pointed at Damon, holding the knife in my right hand, and slid my left foot back. I kept my left hand loose in front of me and waited for him.

He didn't disappoint, charging madly with death in his eyes. At the last moment, I tucked my free arm in and used a slashing defense with the knife, whipping the blade in a tight circle. We closed, and our blades rebounded off of each other, pinging loudly each time. He renewed the attack, and it was clear that the sloppy-looking charge was a ruse. Damon was skilled with a sharp edge; he was using the same techniques that I was. Just as fast, just as deadly.

So few of our kind bother to train in any kind of martial art, preferring to rely on their strength and speed to get by. It's born of a human weakness that most of us carry into our secondary lives, the weakness of arrogance.

He whirled and feinted. Thrusting and renewing, never pausing, he attacked. I parried and blocked as best I could and determined that I couldn't afford to wait for an opening. I'd need to make one. Blades ringing brightly with each tight and circular slash, I looked for any weakness I could exploit. Damon had pure murder in his eyes. I stepped into his attack, locking our knife arms together, and slammed my palm into his chest, grabbing a fistful of shirt. Spinning him around, I tried to knock him off-balance, when he performed an unexpected—but perfectly sensible—move for an experienced vampire.

His arm suddenly bent at an unnatural angle, and I barely avoided having my skull impaled from jaw to pate. The tip of the blade sliced up the side of my face, missing my ear and coming off at my hairline as I jerked away. Damon didn't let up and slashed, backhanded, at my head.

I ducked underneath, bending at the knees and springing up to cut him across his mouth, cheek to cheek. He stumbled backwards with a muffled scream and stopped with one hand to his mouth, swearing profusely through the blackening blood.

"You should watch your mouth, Damon," I said sarcastically.

He replied, words thick with blood and hate, "You are not leaving here alive!"

At that moment, we felt the heat and concussion of an indoor explosion and saw Ana climbing over every available surface to avoid the last group of loyal vampires. My wounds were still serious, and I could feel the venom that Damon had so carefully delivered starting to slow me down; a hazy darkness crept in at the corners of my eyes. I tried not to let it show, but I could feel my face tightening uncontrollably as my jaw clenched and unclenched, bereft of my control.

Damon rushed me, and in a surprise move I met him halfway. The collision caused us both to drop our weapons. He managed to strike me first with a painful left hook to the first wound he'd dealt me. I drove my left forearm into the next swing from his right and grabbed his wrist and bicep. With an elbow smashed into his face, I twisted his arm back, stepping forward at the same time. I could tell he was confident since I couldn't break the arm, but I surprised him again by twisting backwards and yanking down hard. His whole body jerked, and he stumbled to the ground away from me.

Ana landed next to me. Vampires were scattered around the room in a loose circle. Despite the damage she'd done, we were still overwhelmed. Damon, especially, was a considerable, underestimated threat, and I'd been weakened beyond hope. There were small fires burning all around us, adding a warm but foreboding glow to the room. Men would be coming soon, and they'd be in danger, too. There was no more time.

I'd had enough time in my life. Stolen enough time. I was being forced to accept that my life might end today, but I'd never accepted that my life might have some meaning. There had to be more to who I was than a cage for a rabid monster in a near-perpetual state of undisciplined weakness. I had to choose to be more, to allow others to live in lieu of me, to make a decision that didn't begin and end with what I wanted or what I thought I needed.

"Get out of here, Ana." I growled at her, my breath coming in shorter and shorter turns.

"That is *so* Hollywood. No!"

There were a hundred things going through my mind, a swirling mass of memories and thoughts, all of them coalescing into a hodgepodge of an idea. Theories I'd come across, comments that Majispin had made about shapeshifters and vampires, some of the words that the Queen of Dragons had shared. My eyes were losing focus, the edges of the world began to blur, and my thoughts became feverish. Bits and pieces of intentions and wishes lay in my mind like so much shattered crystal, with no apparent form. All the information I needed lay scattered about, shimmering and attractive, with no indication as to its original configuration. I was losing it altogether, and I didn't want my daughter to be there when I did.

"I'm serious, Little Crow," I muttered in our native language, "I'm going to do something stupid and impossibly unselfish." Damon was on his feet and smiling again. He untwisted his arm with a snap like an uncoiling rubber band and nodded to the vampires around him. They all began to converge on us.

Ana spared me a serious look, a look of absolute maturity at that moment. Old as her years were, her face, her mannerisms, everything about her was disarmingly young. It was always hard to keep in mind that she was over one hundred years old. I knew she wouldn't falter, wouldn't cry.

Without another glance, she jumped straight up and, in a huge, uncanny arc, straight through and out one of the ventilation shafts—thank the great spirits she'd been practicing.

Damon watched and whispered to himself, "A telekinetic. And a powerful one, at that. Amazing."

Now was the time, while he was distracted. All of these madmen interested in the intricacies of magic were always trying to gather new information. It was their one shared weakness.

He gave an order to the surrounding vampires who'd previously tensed. "Leave her; the main problem is right in front of us."

They all turned back to me. I straightened up proudly and stripped my gun rig off. Then I pulled my shirt off, swaying dizzily as it passed over my head, and laid it aside as well. They all watched quizzically.

Damon commented, "Shifting won't help you now. You're too weakened to do anything to save yourself."

I ignored him and stared straight ahead. I could tell that some of that morbid curiosity kept him from ordering the final attack right at that moment. Now was the time for my daughter's survival, for the lives of every innocent person who would fall under the bootheels of this psychotic vampire. I did not wish to die. I didn't want my life to end, not like this, not on Damon's terms or even my own. This decision I had to make with more than myself in mind. I would never be a hero—I had too much blood on my hands for that— but it was certainly possible for me to make a choice that might benefit others. At the very least, I could gamble.

In my native tongue, thick with poison and failing strength, I intoned by rote, pleased to have the clear recollection, "'Everything on the earth has a purpose, every disease an herb to cure it, and every person a mission. This is the theory of existence.'"

All the vampires around me glanced at each other, some shrugged, and Damon cocked his head, grinned, and said, "Sitting Bull."

I met his eyes and corrected him. "Humishuma, asshole." I relaxed and untwisted the knot at my core, and I let the change flow over me, take me as never before. I blew the dam and waited for the flood.

TWENTY-SIX

For the first time in my second life, I completely released that invisible muscle inside of me. I unwound whatever it was that had been holding the growing power inside, and I breathed it out. The experience was fulfilling and calming as I finally and entirely uncoiled the kink of energy in the center of my being, allowing it to spin out and gain momentum. There was no pain, only relief. Rapturous relief washed over me. The feelings were not mine, and I became helpless upon the wave. *Weakling*, it hissed, shoving me aside, surging with newfound drunken freedom.

Until now, I could always feel it—whatever it is that powers shapeshifters—on the edge of my awareness. I'd never tapped into it fully, and it blasted awake with the realization that it would have the opportunity to revisit this plane of reality. Revisit? It had been here before? *It has been so long—to be free again! Fool.* The words shivered over my skin.

We exchanged places, the two of us, and I gasped with shock and awe as it stepped forth from me, folding me within, swapping space with my body. I felt my entire physical self dissipate in a fountain of pleasure-wracked pain and become amorphous, as if I'd closed my eyes on my entire being, turning inside out as I was dismissed and thrust back. When I was able to open my eyes, they were greeted by a murky darkness; a cloud of ink enveloped me in a sea of filth. Through the haze, my perspective was twice as tall as ever before and stretched up and away. Full of pleasure and *hunger*. Its center was not hollow, as I was trapped there, but the belly of this thing was empty and longing to be full. Anything would do to sate this centuries-old hunger.

Millennia, it growled. *Pay attention.*

I could see Damon through the dark cloud as he watched wide-eyed. Somewhere in the back of his mind, he was probably cataloging the experience for future evaluation. I was certain he'd never get the chance. My monster shifted its weight forward, and vampires scattered in all directions. Reaching out, it knocked several off their feet and consumed them, in greedy bites. Their entire bodies disappeared into it with ravenous gulps of its nightmarish maw of pure midnight, of gleaming black teeth in an ebony snout.

I'd released the All-Eater inside me, and it was gorging itself. It had been waiting for so long to be free, to eat unbound. I had unknowingly discovered a way of holding it back with my lifestyle. I couldn't understand how I'd managed to keep *this* at bay for so long—how any of us could. Its misshapen body gave the appearance of a dark and deadly storm trapped in a bottle, like a whirlpool of living smoke granted form. Jagged edges of pure black outlined the monster, though its general shape matched my own when I shapeshifted.

Anything would do as a meal at the moment. Great chunks of concrete disappeared as massive, black, swirling arms gouged wildly. The turbine abruptly shut down, a chunk of machinery torn away by my beast. When a blast of electricity issued forth, it swallowed that, too. I was merely a spectator and fading fast. A slow look at my person confirmed my suspicion—I was being digested as well. Bits and pieces of my body were floating away like embers from the fire. Glowing ashes whorled up, around, and down. Perhaps

I'd miscalculated. There was still time to find out. I wasn't dead yet, and I still had some of my cherished memories.

I remembered my father. His back had been carved with the hard experience of slavery and a life on the run for months into the northwest wilderness trails that led to Canada, hard-won freedom. He was tall, with shoulders that cut across the vertical plane of his body like a cross made of oak beams; skin the color of the coal he mined; close-cropped hair, tight curls hugging his oval head; a broad, flat nose atop which balanced deep-set, almond-shaped eyes; corded muscle spun the length of arms that ended in hands that could crush stone.

I remembered my mother. Her forehead was broad and punctuated only by delicately curved eyes; thick, silken black hair indicative of her lineage with the Kainai of Saskatchewan; a stout torso which rightly reflected the raw strength she could bring to bear when chopping wood or handling horses; small, rough-hewn hands, callused across palms where many a rope had been woven or leather been cured; round, undefined thighs and knees which belied the speed with which she could run; all wrapped in sun-kissed skin and a warm smile.

I remembered my sisters up to the day they had married back into the tribe. I remembered the small home, built on land and wood that my parents had carved out of the wilderness for themselves; the rifle with which my father taught me to shoot during one long summer; and the hunting knife whose sheath my mother had fashioned.

These were my favored memories. The thought cut through me that I didn't want to die like this, helpless, floating in the dark. I was trying to hold myself together, and all I had to remember were the fragments of my life. The experience was tattered and full of holes, but patched here and there to keep it from coming completely apart. *Like I am now. Like I do not wish to be.* When one gambles, one must be prepared to fail. Even now, despite my initial certainty, I faltered, wondering if I'd placed the bet on information that was too thin.

Meanwhile it scanned the room and spotted Damon as it scooped up the last of the loyalists available and absorbed them into its dark core; body parts tumbled past me and dissipated with a fading hiss. It was still hungry and roared its impatience. It was the most alien sound I'd ever been privy to, and the building shook from top to bottom. Piles of unused materials clattered to the floor, and I saw Damon stumbling for the exit, holding his ears.

It reached out and plucked him from his feet. Damon let himself go limp in its grasp. The sight was not unlike watching a worm struggle; he twisted his body inhumanly as it sank obsidian claws into his torso. Damon squirmed and gurgled, impaled on hooked claws, twisting like a dirt-grubbing worm. He tried to scream and managed to incant something that burst along the deep-black, undulating fur on the monster's body, burning a good amount of shimmering hair. The blast of magic had tasted foul and caused some damage to both the All-Eater and Damon—it had cost him more to toss that spell than the results bore. The source of my power was a maelstrom of hunger and need that did not belong in this dimension, and it hated vampires.

No shit, it whispered. *Pay attention, Alexander; what I do, I do to thank you for releasing me. I do this, as well, as you are dealt with, my warden.*

It bit an arm off, and then a leg, enjoying Damon's agony. Then it popped him, damaged, into its mouth. As Damon's near-corpse passed me on the way to oblivion, his eyes focused briefly on me as I hung, suspended in the dark matter. His face was passive, thoughtful, as he twisted away into nothing.

It was still unquenched. Unsatisfied and irritable, it turned to the wall and, howling the entire time, plunged through it. I felt as if nothing could stop this monster, and I could do nothing but wait for the end. At least the blond boy wasn't here, a small comfort in my final death. Masonry collapsed around the All-Eater, and it swallowed chunks of rock.

I will feast on your world now. A matter-of-fact statement from the invader; it was fast embracing a wilder side, ready to move further out into my reality and cut it into little bits that it could chew on without thought.

Self-pity isn't one of my strong personality traits. Of course, I wallowed like everyone else on occasion, but it always led to contempt and anger. I had been feeling sorry for myself the entire time that I'd been swallowed by the power that had ridden inside me for years. Enough. We were still metaphysically bonded, the power and I, and as hard as it had been trying to dissolve me within, I still remained. I seized on that bit of reality and psychically dragged myself up the shaft of darkness.

I remembered my humanity.

Foolish human, it intoned. *You are a weak thing.*

I didn't bother to remind it that it'd been stuck inside me for nearly two hundred years. I pulled my humanity around me as a shield, the part of me that had been dissolving, that I had been allowing to dissolve, for years now. I grasped at all that was left of me from this nightmarish journey of a second life I'd been leading and wielded it in my defense, holding the existence of me in place. I couldn't win this fight on my own, it was clear, but I would not die as if I deserved to be erased at the whim of this thing. It would not have the satisfaction of simply discarding me as a used vessel. I fought with every psychic trick I'd ever learned while controlling this power, imagining nets and lashes, chains and walls, pushing, prodding, and pulling.

Summer Street had been elevated to the side of the ventilation building, and my unconfined monster stumbled out onto the roadway, into a driving rain. Dark clouds rumbled overhead, and chaotic water droplets tore at the air. Where water hit the powerful body, it dissipated with a hiss. Thankfully, there were no cars on the street as its expanding presence shorted out street lamps far up and down the byway. The area was plunged into spotty darkness as a rain of sparks dropped down from the exploded hoods of the lamps onto the wet asphalt. The All-Eater tore into the surface of the road, fighting me, fighting my world. There was an explosion as the turbine behind the monster finally fell off its moorings and ignited. The beast absorbed the heat of the electrical blast and sucked up any flying debris. Was there anything it couldn't eat?

It was still hungry, and it roared to the heavens, ending in a coughing fit as I tore at its control. Still, it was a deafening cry that had people scrambling on the gravel below, clutching their heads in agony. Windows burst all around it.

I felt more than saw the presence below me, swimming up. It grasped at the liquid darkness, clawing its way into reality. Is this what we were at heart, shells for other beings, mere victims of possession? The darkness began to close in around me, a thick, inky blanket that suffocated. I twisted and struggled physically with the amorphous mass of being, succumbing faster and faster as it focused more of its attention on the nuisance it had tried to digest offhandedly.

As the last vestige of consciousness slid away from me, a velvet-laced voice whispered in my ear, "Not yet, naughty, naughty boy. Soon, I'll see you soon." The words caressed our shared form with heat.

A cloud of flame enveloped us, separating our two energies. The fireball swept me up and pushed hard against my new prison from all directions. I could feel the power of the Queen of Dragons compacting the surly intelligence, forcing it back down and into my core, wrapping discipline around it, reversing the transformation, punishing it, coaxing dormancy. I didn't think there was anything left of the human form I'd worn all these years, but I could feel the familiar tingle of the mortal plane coming back, reality as I'd known it for the last two-hundred-odd years as I was turned outside in.

My body tumbled under the overpass, dumped from the street into the gravel, and came to rest amongst a clutch of weeds. The air was bracing against my skin as I hugged my knees tightly to my chest and tried to breathe. The last brilliant vestiges of the Dragon's presence dissipated in the rain. I could hear the echo of my prisoner screaming in my ears, pure rage melting to a coarse pleading. Raw with passion and emotion, it did not go quietly back to my core, buried behind new and desperate walls of my own making stretched over the Dragon's constraints.

My teeth began to chatter, and I cried hard for the first time in a hundred years, screaming with emotion. I wanted to die; I didn't want to die, I was caught between two perfect extremes. My daughter was all grown up; she didn't need me, not really. I didn't need me, the world didn't *need* me, I deserved to be obliterated for the crimes I'd committed. I screwed my eyes tighter and embraced the self-pity wholeheartedly. When I looked up from my despair, my tiny victim stood there. Still incomplete, blood dribbling from his head and truncated arm, the boy accused as always. Ethereal tears slid from his ghostly eyes and malice creased his brow. He turned and faded away.

Fuck this. I ground my teeth and swallowed the despondency. Anger and depression run hand in hand, and I reckoned I had no choice in how I felt. But if that were the case, I was not going to embrace depression,

297

and I was certainly going to be responsible for my own actions. I could *choose* to be more than a monster.

Pain caressed every nerve and bone as I began to gradually uncurl myself on the rough gravel. It was, again, a sharp reminder that a shapeshifter's existence is firmly rooted in reality.

Ana eventually came to me. She carried a bundle and placed it on the ground. Then, she knelt down and hugged me around my own self-hug. I was still shivering and very nearly incoherent.

"I thought I told you to go," I managed to stutter through spastic lips.

"I didn't."

"That's my girl." I smiled weakly.

She helped me to my feet and pulled my jacket around my waist. Then she slid my holsters and guns over one of her own shoulders. She must have watched the entire affair, ducking back in before the transformer blew. Somehow, she had found the time to scoop up Damon's long knives as well. Sure, I could use those one day. Why not?

"What was that?" she asked me quietly.

"What?" I barely heard her over the rush of my own brain coming back online.

"That thing. And the flames…"

I was slow to respond, but I remembered the voice, the presence I harbored, and the Dragon. "It was what I am inside. A force that doesn't belong here, a kind of demon, I don't know. Something we all are, something you might be someday."

"A ball of fire?" There wasn't a hint of sarcasm in her voice, only confusion.

"A war leader, a soldier from some endless conflict, or something other. I don't really know; I'm just guessing. I'm not sure what we're mixed up in."

"Oh." Her voice was small.

"Where the hell did you get a working flame-thrower?"

She smiled. "A friend who, uh, collects things. He's going to flip when I don't return it to him. That's what took me so long—I had to persuade him to lend it to me, and he had to show me how to work it."

I left it at that. I was lousy at prying into Ana's personal life. We waited for an opportunity to cut through the swarm of emergency personnel and make our getaway. The book I'd bought from Pat slapped against my leg, tucked into a pocket of my jacket, reminding me that it still wanted to be read.

This was going to become known as one of the worst accidents in Big Dig history—with not a single human fatality, but something *had* died here today. I had learned more, though, than I ever anticipated, more than I should know. I wasn't sure what to do with this information, but I was probably going to treat it like I had when I was presented with Rhonda Lloyd's death—keep moving forward.

Ah, yes, that was the little girl's name: Rhonda. *Little black girl, your head a-twirl, I know where your blood went.*

TWENTY-SEVEN

Ana helped set me up in a new apartment. A relatively quiet neighborhood in Boston proper, near the Fenway. It took over a week for me to fully recover, and when I was moving confidently on my own, she disappeared. Just as well. Everything was getting back to what passes for normal around me.

I learned some new things about myself, and as I got healthier, more of the world was holding a kind of clarity that I'd never known. I still couldn't remember everything I wanted or needed to. My mind continued to be a bit of a mess, but I was onto something new, and I was rewarded with clarity. I also became a little concerned about the future and what it might hold. My promise to the Dragon to do her a "favor" when she called was surely going to haunt me, and she'd certainly found a way to remind me of that. She'd also found a way to shut my power up. I hadn't heard a peep from my possessor since the monstrous altercation at the construction site. I knew it was there—it couldn't escape—and we were bound, but it was quiet, biding its time. I was fully in the driver's seat. *For now*, I reckoned. It was, in the end, good to know that I hadn't been schizophrenic all along.

I was positive that I wouldn't be able to find the Dragon again, so that was a dead end. I planned on going to visit Pat, though, to do a little research into the history of shapeshifters and vampires. Now that I had more insight of my own, maybe I could isolate some facts. Of course, I'd have to calm the little bastard down long enough to have a civilized conversation. Maybe I could convince him—her—it that I had some intelligence. The book Pat had sold me was a treatise on the origins of vampires and shapeshifters. It contained an extensive history, attempting to make sense of our origins and purpose. It's as plausible an explanation as any other, and I was curious why Majispin didn't seem to be aware of it. What other information might Pat be sitting on?

Maria has been getting along just fine without Mark, and I can see what Ana meant when she described what it was that she didn't like about Maria. It's just as well; my depth of feelings for her was physical at best—*is* physical. I still don't know what, if anything, Majispin has on Maria. I'm sure it's something, because I doubt that a woman of her demeanor would behave as she did without cause. She'll tell me if she wants me to know. We've been spending a little more time together, for better or for worse.

Majispin's on his feet again as well. He came out of his coma just after Barros and is now getting around on a cane. He suffered some kind of irreparable nerve damage in his leg. I'm not sure how he survived the vampire venom, though. When I asked, he touched the side of his nose, smiled, and swallowed the last of a glass of absinthe. The man's probably got more poison running through his veins than any vampire could match. He's become very interested in me after the episode at the ventilation building. Neither I nor Ana— I'm sure of that—told him exactly what happened there, but he's still deadly curious. He's hinted that there are some rumors going around that he's been able to pin to my past.

Now that I've gotten used to him and his tactics, I mildly enjoy playing out the slack of our relationship, then plucking the string tight. At least he lets me poke around in his library on occasion. Although I bet it's because he knows the number of magic-infused tomes in there makes me rather uncomfortable. I'd rather suffer that than try to bring one of those books back to my place and let it spend the night.

Majispin didn't know what he was getting into when he put his little pack together. He politely asked if I wanted to be within the circle, and I politely told him no. Barros went right back to his brooding, intimidating self, but I think Seth's death affected him more than he wants to let on. When I asked if he would head back to his home state for a spell, his response was simply "No, homes." "Hell no" could be read in his voice from a mile away. He's taking some time off while Majispin looks for new employees.

I got the impression that the magician wasn't trying to put a pack of shapeshifters together again. Who or what he might gather makes me a little nervous. At the very least, he's considering his employment problem a little more carefully. He needs some new employees of particular talents, and he's willing to pay for them— whether they're fully human or not.

Detective Roberts is still a loose end, in my estimation. I've been keeping an eye on him, and he's kept everything he knows to himself—so far. The whole incident has taken its toll on him, and he has no one to talk to about it. I'd hate for something to have to happen to him. He's a good cop who cares about his duties. So few people understand the responsibility of the badge, including a number of folks carrying them. We haven't spoken since I last saw him at the Peter O'Neil projects. When all was said and done, I called and left him a message that our business was concluded and that Rhonda Lloyd, as well as Terrell, had been avenged. Pepperman seems to think he'd found himself in the middle of a gang war and gotten himself knocked out. It's all for the best.

Maybe I'll give Roberts my new number one of these days.

To be honest with myself, I've decided to stay in town for a little while. I have to sort a few things out, and this is as good a place as any to do it. It's not like I have to work nine to five. One of the few benefits of long life is being able to save money or acquire it when in need. The human criminal class is quite wealthy from time to time—and quite vulnerable as well. My expenses are taken care of and I do what I do to keep myself sane. Though a great deal of things seem to have changed on that front.

Perhaps I can learn a bit more about magic and myself for the first time, something I should've done a long time ago. I can also try to find out exactly what it is that shapeshifters and vampires are containers for— not theories or myths. Maybe even solve a murder or prevent one, at the very least, in my copious spare time. I still have stacks of missing-person bulletins that come in the mail disguised as coupons.

I also don't know if I'll be able to find Tina, but I've had some new ideas since the end of this current mess. Ana's mind is still clear, however; I'll start with her and hope she gives me straight answers. I feel like I owe Tina an explanation at the least and a full apology at the most. I'll get the chance, hopefully, one day soon.

The oddest thing that's happened since the confrontation at the construction site is a letter I got in the mail. It was smudged with clay and dirt inside and out, but carefully written and stamped with a wildly ornate crest. Dr. Quentin Bismark's letter— absent a return address. He is back from the dead. The note contained just a few words of apology and encouragement from the good doctor, explaining that, obviously, he was "back amongst the living of a sort" but had "no plans to make an appearance anytime soon." Just as well; he'd wanted to focus on his work anyway. He did, however, write a series of numbers at the bottom separated by periods. Ana thinks it's an IP address, but there are too many numbers. I checked. I have no idea how he survived or how he got my new street address. I'm not sure I want to know.

What I'd really like to know, what's been troubling me since this all began is, what the hell brought me to Boston in the first place? "The Hub of the Universe," they called it many years ago. The nickname that stuck for the colonials: the Hub. Most tourists called it "Beantown." Beans. Boston baked beans. That couldn't possibly be the reason, could it? I tried to recall the first time I'd had the dish. It wasn't in Boston, and I thought the effort was unimpressive. Of all the things I've been able to recall, what I was doing before I came to Boston isn't one of them, which troubles me. Had someone contacted me? Had I contacted them first? If so, who and why?

Home crossed my mind. I haven't thought of my birthplace for some time now. Perhaps I should go there, back to the Saskatchewan province where my ethnicity would make me neither Kainai nor African-Canadian. I wish I could return to the early 1800s when I still knew of my sisters and my mother was still alive. I wish I could make new decisions and unmake old ones, bathe in the Saskatchewan River, and hunt for my food—not mine coal as my father had done and suffer a slow, agonizing death. The death I'd already suffered had been bad enough. I wish I'd never met my great-great-great-ancestor, who'd passed his burden on to me. I absently wonder if I should have properly died when I was supposed to. The transmission of the curse isn't guaranteed, even with a blood relative, but it had worked with me.

I wander into my small kitchen, pull a glass from the cabinet and pour a tall drink of water. Sitting down in the living room, next to the biggest window in the apartment, I start to think about how this all began and who I was *before*.

Acknowledgements

To Javed Jahangir, Bracken MacLeod, Chris Irvin and the other Mad Dogs (TJ May and KL Pereira) in my writing group who have helped to make me a better author—look up their formidable work; you won't be sorry. To CJ Lyons, the teacher who put my story over the top and to my father, William, whose relentless advice on being an adult got me this far (thanks, Dad). To the Marine Corps who tested previous lessons learned in rigorous manner, and to my Krav Maga instructors who continue to do so. To my editors Vikki Ciaffone and Richard Shealy: the work you did was invaluable, I'll not soon forget. To Lisa Amowitz, instrumental in designing the rugged cover of this book. To anyone who felt that my work was worthy of publication: let us continue those relationships! To my wife, Erica, the other fifty percent of my life, and to my two children, the other other fifty percent: your love keeps life full of pleasure.

To everyone who read this book in its many stages over the years and offered solid advice, experience, and translations (Vanessa Sanchez, in the kitchen, with a script), I can not thank you enough. And finally, to you, the reader, for giving me a chance to invade your mind.

D C F A R M E R

the 400lb gorilla

SOMETIMES YOU HAVE TO MAKE YOUR OWN LUCK,
OR DIE TRYING

About the Author

Born and raised in Boston, Massachusetts, Errick A. Nunnally served one tour in the Marine Corps before deciding art school would be a safer—and more natural—pursuit. He strives to develop his strengths in storytelling and remains permanently distracted by art, comics, science fiction, history, and horror. Trained as a graphic designer, he studies Krav Maga and Muay Thai kickboxing after dark. Errick's successes include: the novel, *Blood For The Sun*; a comic strip collection, *Lost in Transition; Who Bears The Lathe?* in eFiction's inaugural SciFi issue; and first prize in one hamburger contest. The following are short stories and their respective anthologies: Lycanthrobastards (*Wicked Seasons*); Harold At The Halfcourt (*Inner Demons Out*); Legion (*Doorways to Extra Time*); The Last Apology (*A Dark World of Spirits and The Fey*); You Call This An Apocalypse? (*After The Fall*); Recovery (*Winter Animals: stories to benefit PROTECT.ORG*); The Ghosts of Franklin Park (*Dreadworks Journal*) and We Should Meet (*In Vein: stories to benefit St. Jude Children's Research Hospital*). He also has two lovely children and one beautiful wife.